Clandestiny

a BALEY NOAL novel

Also by

Grit City

THE STARSTRUCK DUOLOGY:
Starstruck

Starstruck: The Trials

Cover by Baley Noal & ElfElm Publishing
Book design, interior and ebook formatting by ElfElm Publishing
www.elfelmpublishing.com | Tacoma, WA

The text is set in Adobe Caslon Pro

ISBN (paperback): 979-8-9914667-6-9

10 9 8 7 6 5 4 3 2 1

First Edition 2026

01

Jett grabbed his ball cap, harshly rubbing it against his chocolate-colored hair, trying to maintain a controlled demeanor.

"Miss, I'm telling you right now, she had no right." He took a breath, not wanting to give the shelter staff any more reason to deny him information that would reunite him with his dog. "Please." He set his palms on the reception counter in front of him. Jett wasn't an outrageously muscular man, he was proportionately built. His six foot presence always commanded a certain level of respect and at times fear. His outward manner was that of a man who spent his career and most of his life in the military—right down to the buzzed haircut and a several-days old, managed scruff on his face. He wore a short-sleeved shirt which showcased part of the patriotic tattooed masterpiece he had on the right side of his body. In most situations he'd have no interest in softening himself for anyone, but at this moment he considered it because all he wanted was to be reunited with his beloved canine.

"I can pull *years* of pictures, vet records, her license number, she's microchipped and that's all linked to me—literally anything you'd want to prove Mags is my dog, I can provide it." His hazel eyes begged. "I'll pay whatever you want, I just need my dog back."

Vera felt for the guy, but wasn't going to give him any personal information regarding their volunteers; especially since Moxie, her best friend, was the one who'd adopted the German Shepherd.

Vera was a tall, thick-boned, and pleasantly curvy Samoan woman in her late twenties. She sat down to seem less combative, flipping her onyx-black hair with the most gorgeous natural wave to it behind her shoulder.

"Sir, I *truly* am sorry. I can't say I've been through what you have, but I do know what it is to lose a dog." Her voice was calm and steady, examining the handsome man in front of her. She wasn't trying to give the guy a hard time, he looked *and sounded* like he was currently going through it without her piling on.

"Look"—she took a deep breath, her palms pressing together—"you seem like a nice guy, and this sounds like a fucked-up situation." She glanced around to be sure none of the other employees were within earshot. "I know who adopted Magnolia. I can assure you, she's been very well taken care of."

Visible relief blew over Jett at hearing Mags wasn't sitting in a crowded shelter—or worse. It was great that this lady deemed her new home as a seemingly suitable one, but he wanted her back with him—not settling into some new lifestyle.

"I appreciate that, Miss, but is there *any* way you can reunite me with my Mags?"

"Give me a day or two." Vera watched disappointment consume the man in front of her. "It's just that this is completely inappropriate for me to be doing in the first place, not to mention it's not ideal timing—"

"Not ideal timing? Is Mags okay?"

Vera quickly nodded. "Yes, sorry—yeah, no, she's fine," she assured him and placed her hand on the desk. "Look, just leave your number and I'll call you when I have an answer from her new home whether you guys can meet up, okay?" Her fingertips slid a neon-pink sticky pad Jett's way.

Jett didn't have a choice, he reached for a pen and scribbled his name, number, and 'Mags' down on the brightly-colored note.

"I'll meet anyone at any time. *Please*, Miss, anything you can do to make that meeting happen I would really appreciate it. I'm staying not too far from here. I just miss my dog—I miss Mags."

She stuffed the sticky note in her pocket. "I'll try, I really will. She's in a good home and I know I can talk to her adopter. I just can't make any promises beyond that."

"Thank you." Jett looked around and offered the woman a flat smile before he reluctantly walked towards the exit.

Once he stepped outside he took a gulp of the city air. *How did life get so completely fucked so quickly?*

Jett angrily parked a borrowed car in front of his cousin's house. He took a deep breath, giving his face a harsh wipe from the crown of his head to his chin. His homecoming wasn't supposed to go like this at all. *Ten years*, he thought. *Together for ten years and that's how she treats our marriage? Un-fucking-believable.*

The two weeks he had off upon his return from a six-month training program wasn't starting out like he planned. As if the lying and cheating wasn't enough, of all the things she could've done to make the situation a million times worse, his *very* soon-to-be *EX*-wife took his dog to a shelter. That was the most unforgivable act. Even beyond the cheating and the resultant pregnancy, taking Mags to the shelter was a new fucking low. Jett didn't know if he'd ever see his dog again.

It was probably a sign he was more concerned about getting Mags back than considering anything at all about mending his marriage. She could've done him a favor and started the divorce papers since it was clear she knew things would be changing. He'd focus on finding Mags this weekend, and the second any law office opened Monday morning, that's where he'd be.

He looked at his cousin's house, taking a deep, controlled breath before getting out of the car. This situation wasn't ideal either. Of course his cousin agreed to let him crash for a couple days, but the little shit had to have known what was going on while Jett was away. His cousin's damn wife was best friends with Jett's. He figured he'd sleep it off for a bit and then put a good game plan together for the rest of the weekend. Right now he just wanted a shower, a bed, and sleep to take over the fuckery he'd come home to.

"Hey, Jett." His cousin, Trevor, scurried to the door when Jett walked in the house.

Jett handed him his car keys without looking at him. Trevor resembled Jett in their brunette hair and height, but that's where the similarities stopped. His cousin hadn't lifted a weight in his life and his skin tone was much lighter from years spent indoors versus Jett's more exposed lifestyle. Trevor had curly hair that looked like his mom's perm, and dressed in khakis and a polo more days than not.

"No Mags?" Trevor looked around.

"No." Jett shook his head, flooded with disappointment. "I left my number, but all I can do is pray that gal will be able to talk the adopter into at least meeting with me."

"I'm sorry, I—"

Jett put up his hand, palm facing his cousin. "I don't really want to talk about it right now. I'm pissed, Trev."

"Sure, of course, I…" His voice trailed off while checking Jett's expression.

"Look, I just kinda want to get cleaned up and hit the sack. I appreciate you letting me stay."

"Of course. No problem." Trevor's hands were clammy and his breath irregular as he walked with Jett towards the living room.

They heard Trevor's wife, Julia, on the phone and Jett picked up on Trevor's hesitation.

"Just say it." Jett shrugged, never a fan of anything other than shooting it straight.

Trevor grabbed the back of his neck. "So, I didn't realize they had plans today… Uh, Hallie's gonna be over here soon. They're planning a gender reveal so the girls are gonna—"

Jett firmly put up his tattooed hand to stop him again. "It's all good, don't worry about me, I can manage," Jett assured his cousin.

As if he hadn't been hit with enough upon his return, he watched *his* family side with his cheating wife—his very soon-to-be *ex*-wife.

He couldn't grab his bags and leave his cousin's house quick enough when he found out she was on her way over there to finalize plans for her gender reveal party.

"Jett, you can still stay, you don't have to pack up." Trevor watched Jett walk to the door with the two duffle bags he'd brought over.

"Thanks for letting me borrow the car," he said over his shoulder, marching out of the house. He already had his phone in his hand looking for a decent hotel to stay at for the foreseeable future.

02

Moxie was no stranger to horrific days, unfortunately. After the terrifying text she'd received that morning, she wasn't sure if she'd need to move again. She lived very simply because, while she was strong, she didn't have much to her stature; she kept everything in her life as manageable as possible. The task of a manageable life had been a difficult one for her to accomplish the last couple of years. Moxie spent the entire day frantically packing her apartment back into the large rubber totes she kept on hand to prepare for yet another sudden and unplanned move.

She set out a few bags of essentials in case she needed to make a mad dash. In her rush packing all day, she realized she hadn't taken her dog, Nolie—short for Magnolia—on a walk yet.

The dog had been a blessing the last couple of months. While Moxie spent a lot of time volunteering at the local Humane Society, she'd never adopted a dog until she stumbled on Nolie. The universe had screamed at Moxie to take the nervous, but beautiful canine. Since that day, her life had been better—until this morning.

"I know, pretty girl, I'm so sorry." Moxie knelt down and slipped a collar around the long-haired German Shepherd's neck. Nolie was a model representation of the breed. Her hair was lush and gorgeous with show-quality black-and-tan markings. The dog patiently waited for Moxie to put her shoes on and then they headed out.

Moxie loaded her loyal companion into the car to go to the park. Her petite hand touched the driver's door when she realized she didn't have her phone. She gave Nolie a quick smile and a signal through the window to wait before heading to the apartment to retrieve her cell. Just as she spun around, terror struck.

03

Moxie and Nolie cautiously made their third trip from the car to bring overnight essentials to a hotel room. She couldn't bring herself to stay at her apartment after what had happened.

Her badly injured body was in no condition to hold more than one bag at a time, and even that small task proved to be a struggle. They made multiple trips to transport everything they needed to the room, attempting to get as comfortable as possible for the night. Moxie had a petite build. She kept a healthy lifestyle and a routine weight training regimen, but nothing could curb the pain she felt from the injuries she'd sustained that evening.

She hated walking through the lobby because the man working the counter already had it out for both her and her dog. Poor Nolie was on alert and Moxie couldn't blame her. She stood, closing her eyes and taking as deep of a breath as she could manage just outside the main lobby door. It automatically parted upon their approach, and as they stepped through the threshold she hoped no one was in the lobby. The second they touched down on the other side of the door Moxie lost all control.

"Nolie!" Moxie tried but her injured body was no match for her powerful and determined dog when she uncharacteristically yanked on the leash. Nolie pulled so hard she managed to rip the bandage

Moxie had not so securely thrown on her palm before they walked into the hotel that night. A rush of tears flooded her eyes as she watched Nolie sprint toward a man standing at the check-in counter. It'd already been a stressful day for both of them, and now her dog charged some guy to release the aggression she'd built up after watching one of Moxie's worst episodes just a couple hours prior.

To her surprise, the man turned around with open arms and caught the dog mid-air as he belted out her name like they were long lost friends.

"Mags!"

Moxie, with obstructed vision due to the swelling and tears, watched them just before receiving another scolding.

"Ma'am! We're going to have to ask you and your canine to vacate the premises *immediately*!" The short statured man had a red face and a sharp tone as he marched towards Moxie, shaking a pointed finger.

He'd already put Moxie on notice when Nolie growled at another male patron walking through the lobby as they checked in; and again when the dog had her hackles up on their second trip bringing a bag to their room. This was, apparently, their third strike.

"You've already been warned! We *cannot* have an aggressive dog like that in our establishment!" His stubby finger angrily gestured toward Moxie's dog, still in the stranger's arms. "You have precisely ten minutes to remove your items from your room and leave. I *will* be calling animal control and the authorities if you're still here in eleven minutes. And you will *not* be granted a refund for your room." He turned on his heels and headed towards the man who held Nolie, straining to listen to the conversation.

"My deepest apologies, sir." He offered a small, awkward bow. "The dog will be leaving the hotel and we can finish getting you checked in."

Jett held tight to Magnolia as she licked his face and swung her tail in every direction possible. He examined the dainty woman who'd come in with his dog—this woman was *tiny*. Most of her face and the light brunette hair she had twisted in a low bun covering a portion of her neck were hidden under a ball cap that had a single embroidered magnolia flower on it. He watched her timid body language as she slowly made her way towards them. His focus then turned to the grumpy man who continued apologizing to him. This was Jett's opportunity to show a little good faith in hopes it would pay off and he could eventually get his dog back.

"Excuse me, did you say the dog needs to leave the hotel?" Jett asked.

"Yes, sir. The dog is out of control and this isn't the first incident they've had this evening." He glared at Moxie who struggled to make her way to them while wiping her tears.

"Granted, this is the first time the dog *hasn't* growled, but it's still unacceptable that this woman doesn't have control over the animal."

"I'm so sorry." Moxie finally reached them, and looked at the ground to hide her face, her voice shaking. "It's not her fault at all, we've had a… difficult evening. She's just anxious, I—"

"There you are!" Jett smiled widely before realizing this woman had markings of a violent incident on her neck and face. "Darlin', are you okay? What happened to you? I didn't know you girls checked in already." He gave Magnolia a final ruffle of her extra neck skin and then kissed the side of her head before putting her down and commanding her with a quick snap of his fingers to take a seat next to him.

"Come here, sweetie pie." Jett quickly closed the gap between himself and the small stranger. He carefully put his arms around her so he could help mask the shocked look on her face to continue playing out his act.

"Sir, I don't know who raised you, but this isn't any kind of way to treat a damsel in distress. My wife's obviously had a rough night and our dog's been protecting her if she's been growling at anyone. As you can see, our Mags isn't aggressive." Jett gestured to his pridefully obedient dog who sat attentively by his side. "But we'll go ahead and leave if that's what you see fit to do. You'll be giving me longer than ten minutes to gather their things." He glared at the hotel employee, challenging him to object.

The hotel worker looked back and forth between the two guests in front of him, completely confused with the new turn of events. "Sir, my apologies, I—"

"To her." Jett pointed at Moxie before gently moving her from his chest and putting her under his arm so the man could face her. "You owe my wife and my dog an apology."

"Miss." He offered a quick bow. "I do apologize, I didn't reali—"

"We *will* in fact be taking a full refund for the room as well, because we won't be staying here tonight. I'm gonna get my girls settled in the car, I expect you to be ready to help me with their bags and that refund when I get back in this lobby. If you're incapable of making that happen, then I suggest you have your boss out here when I return."

Jett didn't say another word before he escorted Moxie and Magnolia out the lobby doors. When they got outside Jett still had Moxie under his arm and Magnolia twirled uncontrollably around them, letting out a shrieking howl. Once they were far enough away from the doors, Jett kneeled down and gave Magnolia another greeting—the dog absolutely lost it seeing him.

Moxie watched and wasn't sure if she'd hit her head too hard or what happened, because she had no recollection of this man who just saved her from an even more uncomfortable scene. Her dog never reacted like this to anyone—not even her.

After Moxie had stared for what she thought was an eternity, the man finally looked up at her.

"I'm sorry, Miss." Jett stood and extended his tattooed hand to her. "My name's Jett."

Moxie gently put her hand in his and angled her head down to try and avoid him seeing her eyes; the darkness of the night and the bill of her ball cap helped. "Nice to meet you. I'm Moxie."

"Moxie"—Jett tried to get a better look at her face—"are you okay?" He maintained a comforting hold of her hand. "I know we're strangers, but do you need anything I can help with?"

She shook her head but couldn't stop the tears streaming down her face.

Magnolia took a break from hopping around Jett and sat next to Moxie. The loving and protective dog leaned her body into Moxie's leg as she looked up at her and Jett knew things were about to get complicated.

Jett watched Moxie reach down and stroke the top of the German Shepherd's head. He didn't have a speech prepared, but he went for it.

"I know you don't know me, or owe me anything at all—and I understand what I just said and did in there seems crazy—but will you allow me a chance to explain some things? Please?" He hoped the desperation wasn't seeping through his voice. His shock was still fresh that Mags literally ran into him after he thought he may have lost her for good.

Moxie didn't really know how her night could get any worse. Why not trust the complete stranger? Her dog wasn't one to go around getting excited about just anyone and she appeared to love this man. It was more than obvious he knew her.

"Okay," she agreed in a soft voice, with a nod to match.

Jett's chest jumped in excitement and relief. "Thank you, Moxie. Can I take you and Mags to your car to wait while I go get your stuff from the hotel room?"

"You don't have to do all that—" Moxie tried to decline, but Jett was already assuring her this was more than fine.

"I'm not about to subject you to that asshole again. I promise I'll be right back with your things, you don't have to worry about going back in there."

Moxie slowly tipped her chin up but stopped before he could see her eyes and replied in a hushed voice, "Thank you, Jett. We're parked on the other end of the lot."

"It's not a problem at all. I'll walk you ladies over there before I head back in," Jett said.

Moxie realized her friend Vera's text to her earlier that day telling her she had some 'news' about Nolie might actually have something to do with her new friend. Nolie's demeanor and fondness of

Jett helped put Moxie's mind at ease about trusting the stranger. Not to mention he'd been unnecessarily kind since Nolie rushed him in the lobby.

He assured Moxie he'd be right back and now she watched him make confident strides toward the hotel to retrieve her things. She knew he'd be back soon enough to explain whatever it was he wanted to tell her. In the meantime, she'd try to get what she could from Vera to confirm whatever story Jett would spin for her. *Trust but verify*, she thought.

Moxie looked down at her phone and was immediately overcome with shaking. Twenty-six missed calls and four texts that made her stomach crawl.

Unknown

So good to see you again Mox.

You sure turned my shitty day around.

Looks like you've been a good girl but don't go far.

You know I'll find you again.

She wiped her tears, blocked the unknown number, and deleted his texts before opening her chat with Vera.

Hey V, sorry I couldn't talk earlier, work stuff. Can you give me a CliffsNotes-text version of the Nolie girl issue?

Moxie wasn't surprised when she watched the text bubbles pulsing seconds after she sent her text; Vera's phone was essentially glued to her hand night and day.

V

Well ……

Moxie waited, that intro text always paved the way for times Vera planned to send a novel.

V 🐰

The HOTTEST GI Joe I ever did see came into the shelter today. 😜 🔥 Idk if I'm inclined to believe him because he's hot AF or if he's legit telling the truth, but he claims Nolie girl is his dog. More specifically sounds like he's going through an ugly divorce and his biatch wife sent her to the shelter while GI Joe was away on assignment. He came home to find that she got rid of our Nolie girl and he was begging us for info today on where she went. Mox, I'm sorry babe - he does want her back. I got his number and told him I'd see what I could find out about a possible meeting with her new home. BUT I did inform him she's healthy and happy. I didn't say who she went home with, he knows nothing about you. I only told him I'd check to see if the new home was okay to meet with him.

Also I figured if nothing else perhaps my girl could meet a guy since you like living under a rock. I mean as if he isn't HOT enough, he legit came home and the first thing he's worried about is chasing down his dog. BE STILL MY DAMN HEART!!!! He had an entire photo album on his phone of puppy Nolie pics, it was so sweet!!!!!!!!!!!!!

So, if you want my two cents, I think you should at least meet him here at the shelter and see for yourself if you want him to see Nolie at all. He seems like he's worthy of a chance at the very least.

0 - 10 where was he on the creeper scale? And what did he look like? With your spectrum of 'hot af' he could look like anyone.

V

He's NEGATIVE ∞ on the creeper scale. ZERO
heebie jeebies while I was talking to him. Not
usually a fan of the buzz cuts, but this man owns
that shit. He's a lean kinda buff. He was giving
Southpaw Jake Gyllenhaal vibes FOR SURE!!
Just looks though, he's not all punchdrunk or
whatever the hell. He may be a bit older than
us, but I'm telling you babe the man is ripped,
tatted, military—HOT AS FUUUUHHHHHHHHK!!
And obviously single or headed for it after that
twaty wife of his sent poor Nolie girl to the shelter
while he was away. So again, I think you should
consider at least meeting with him.

From what Moxie could make out through her blurred vision,
Vera's description seemed to fit the guy she'd just met.

What's his name?

V

Jett Sharpe

Well, that all but confirms it, Moxie thought. *But how in the world
did we end up running into each other if V didn't tell him anything? V
didn't even know where we were tonight.*

Thanks V. I need to sleep on all that.
But I'll let you know tomorrow.

V

Of course babe. I hope work wasn't too
crazy! Let's get together this weekend.

Sounds good, I'll text you.

V

Goodnight babe!

Moxie put her phone in her lap and reached to scratch Nolie's head that rested on her chair from the backseat. She scanned the dimly lit parking lot, anxiously searching for signs of anyone watching her. She looked down to check the time because it felt like Jett had been gone longer than what she'd expected for him to simply be grabbing the two bags she'd managed to get in her room. She'd barely been able to handle Nolie's leash and the gym bag on her first trip.

It was likely she had at least one broken rib, her hand throbbed from having scraped it on the ground, her throat was sore and was sure to bruise by morning, and she also felt the outside of her left eye as it was swollen and very likely already black and blue. She wasn't a stranger to these injuries, sadly; this was the first time she'd been that scared though.

As she thought about how she could've possibly put herself in that situation again, she noticed Nolie lift her head and stand at the back window. Her tail flew around in the air watching Jett approach the car. He politely waved to Moxie upon his arrival.

She unrolled both her and Nolie's windows and noticed he didn't have either of her bags.

"Well"—Jett took a deep breath—"Moxie, my stunt in there may have set us up for more than we bargained for. I'll apologize for that." He reached out, rubbing the side of the dog's head when she begged for his attention. "I'll leave it up to you on what you're comfortable with, but uh… The manager actually came to talk to me. He apologized on behalf of his employee. For the disrespect you received they're offering us the Presidential Suite—at no charge—for the evening."

Moxie looked up at him, expressionless. She didn't know what to say.

"They've got a separate bedroom in the suite that has a lock on the door, and a couch in the common area. I'm happy to take the couch or even the floor if I have to. Long story short, I don't have another place to stay tonight—it's either the Presidential Suite here, or I'm gonna have to find another hotel. Like I said though, I'd like a chance to explain a few things to you and I'd really love to spend some time with Mags. But I also understand I'm a stranger and I don't want you to be uncomfortable. I can always go back in and decline their offer, leave you my number, and we can connect if and when you're more comfortable." Jett continued to rub the jubilant shepherd, waiting for Moxie's decision.

Moxie watched Nolie completely melt around Jett. She couldn't deny her gut felt settled around this new seemingly respectful guy, despite his intimidating appearance. He'd received the Vera stamp of approval as well—she couldn't doubt both Nolie *and* Vera's opinions.

In spite of what had happened to her earlier that evening, Moxie agreed. "Please just promise me you won't ax-murder me in my sleep," she said in a soft voice without meeting his gaze.

Jett belted out a laugh. "The ax didn't make its way into my bags for tonight, because it doesn't go with this outfit." He gently smoothed out the black hoodie he wore. "So, no worries there."

"Okay." She tried to take a deep breath despite the aching throughout her torso.

Jett didn't like the pain he saw all over her. It hit him like a bullet in the gut, and surprisingly to him, his heart. He noticed other bags in her car. "Can I help you bring anything else up to the room?"

Moxie let out a grateful sigh before she finally looked into his eyes. "I just need two more of these and that would be so helpful if you can please carry them for me. Thank you, Jett."

"It's not a problem at all, Moxie. Come on, roll these windows up and I'll help you girls up there," he encouraged.

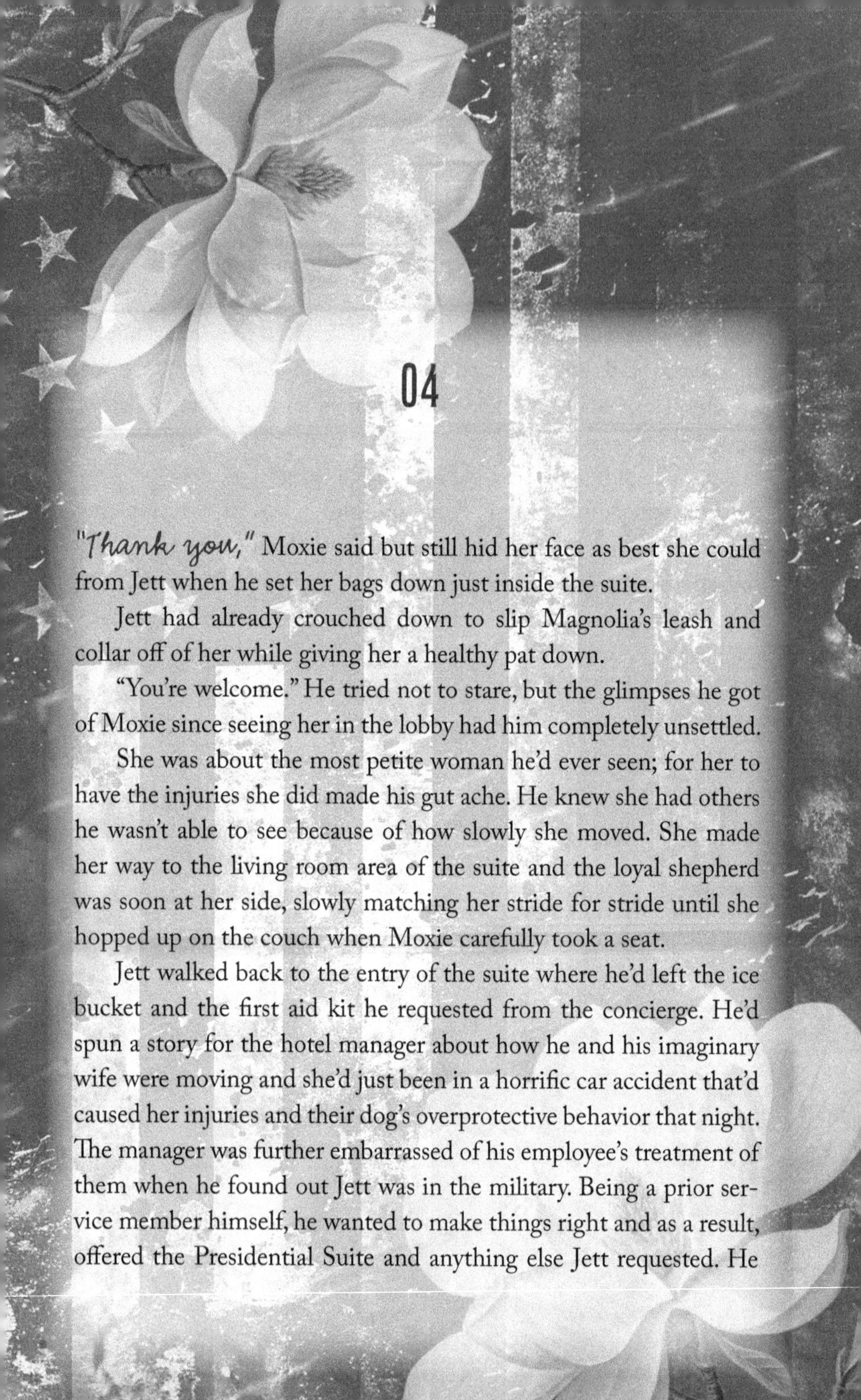

04

"Thank you," Moxie said but still hid her face as best she could from Jett when he set her bags down just inside the suite.

Jett had already crouched down to slip Magnolia's leash and collar off of her while giving her a healthy pat down.

"You're welcome." He tried not to stare, but the glimpses he got of Moxie since seeing her in the lobby had him completely unsettled.

She was about the most petite woman he'd ever seen; for her to have the injuries she did made his gut ache. He knew she had others he wasn't able to see because of how slowly she moved. She made her way to the living room area of the suite and the loyal shepherd was soon at her side, slowly matching her stride for stride until she hopped up on the couch when Moxie carefully took a seat.

Jett walked back to the entry of the suite where he'd left the ice bucket and the first aid kit he requested from the concierge. He'd spun a story for the hotel manager about how he and his imaginary wife were moving and she'd just been in a horrific car accident that'd caused her injuries and their dog's overprotective behavior that night. The manager was further embarrassed of his employee's treatment of them when he found out Jett was in the military. Being a prior ser-vice member himself, he wanted to make things right and as a result, offered the Presidential Suite and anything else Jett requested. He approached Moxie, now sitting on the couch and Mags at her side, with the medical supplies in hand.

"Before I can try and relax at all, can you please tell me how you know her?" Moxie lovingly stroked the dog's fluffy head.

"How 'bout I tell you that story while I help you out with some of those injuries?" He pulled the coffee table closer to the couch before taking a seat on the sturdy glass piece.

"I'm okay," she tried to decline. "It's not that bad. You don't have to do that."

"I'm certainly not going to sit here and do nothing." He opened the bucket where he'd already packed a few smaller bags with ice. Before placing any ice packs on her, Jett got up and made his way to the oversized bathroom to find a few hand towels.

Magnolia crawled on the couch until her front paws rested securely across Moxie's lap. She smiled warmly down at her dog and placed her uninjured hand between the pretty girl's shoulder blades to pet her.

Jett walked back into the living room and cracked a grin when he saw the scene in front of him. "Mags really seems to love you. She's never been one to really leave my side." He wrapped one of the ice packs in a hand towel. "Here, let's get this on your eye there." He cautiously reached towards Moxie.

"Thank you." She took the ice from him and winced when it touched her face.

Jett didn't ask when he carefully took her hand and put it palm up on his knee to assess the injury under the tattered bandage that barely hung on at this point.

"I don't mean to be rude, but it seems like you're anything but okay." He tried to gently clean the scrape on Moxie's hand. "Is your head feeling alright?"

She nodded, watching him work on her scraped-up palm. "I'll manage."

Moxie studied the artwork on the back of Jett's right hand. She concluded it was simply a piece of something much larger that was hidden under the hoodie he still wore. The ink she could see looked like striped fabric and it touched almost all four of the knuckles on the back of his hand.

The worried dog stretched to lick Jett. "Hey, Mags." He leaned into her and let her lick his cheek.

"Mags makes more sense than Nolie," Moxie admitted in a quiet voice.

"I was wondering what you called her earlier." He smirked, eyes maintaining focus on her injured hand. "I wasn't sure if she had a name change since I saw her last. I know Magnolia's a mouthfull," he acknowledged. "For the record, I like Nolie too." His gaze lifted momentarily, trying to gauge Moxie's demeanor but the petite woman mindfully watched Jett tending to her hand.

"When did you see her last? Were you the one who took her to the shelter?" Moxie knew the answer but wanted to see if this new friend was genuine.

"Hell no," he emphatically responded but finished cleaning her palm. "Mags has been my girl since she was eight weeks old. My fuc—" Jett took a deep breath. "Not to unpack my fucked-up life on you when you've already had a rough time, but I wasn't home for several months because of work. My soon-to-be ex-wife took it upon herself to drop Mags off at the shelter because the cheating she was doing wasn't enough for her. She wanted to go for the damn jugular." He tried to be conscious of his hands working too rough on Moxie from the irritation thinking about everything he'd found out since being home.

"When did you adopt her from the shelter?" he asked.

"Tomorrow will be four months since I officially adopted her and got to bring her home. They wouldn't let me take her initially."

"Can I ask why?"

Moxie tried to take a full breath. "I volunteer at the Humane Society multiple times a week. I walk the dogs and basically give them breaks from the cages in there. I remember the day Nol—Mags came in. She was terrified and lashed out at some of the staff." She set the ice pack in her lap so she could stroke the side of Mags' head and continue the story. "I can't explain it, but I felt like she and I were just meant to cross paths—I knew I had to take her. She wasn't going to last long in there, they would've put her down."

She shook her head as her lips curled down and tears started again. "I begged them to let me do an emergency foster that night because she was so miserable. My best friend Vera works there and pulled some strings to at least put her in a quieter area of the shelter, but they made her stay anyway. They never wanted to allow me to adopt from there because I live in an apartment… They were even less inclined to let me take Mags because of her size and the behaviors she'd shown in her short time there." Moxie considered not adding to Jett's anger about the situation, but felt he deserved the full story. "I looked at the owner's surrender paperwork too… whoever dropped her off said the reason was she'd been increasingly aggressive."

Jett blew out an irritated breath but held his tongue. That couldn't be further from the truth. Sure, his dog knew how to be a watchdog and a protector, but she was never aggressive without provocation.

"How long did she stay in the shelter?" He wanted the horrible details all at once and then hopefully would find a way to make it up to his dog.

"She was there for a week before I was able to bring her home." Moxie shook her head. "They required us to clear the adoption with a behaviorist—her aggression towards the rest of the staff in com-bination with my size and ability to handle her worried them. I did make it a point to go in there—multiple times—every single one of those days though." Moxie rubbed Mags' neck and looked fondly at the dog. "It made me sick every single day I had to leave her there."

Jett rested Moxie's hand on his knee now that it was properly cleaned and bandaged. He reached for Mags and scratched under her chin. "I'm so sorry, girl. You know I'd never abandon you."

Moxie realized her touch lingered on his leg so she pulled her hand back to rest in her own lap. "I know I just live in an apartment, but, Jett, I promise I've done my very best to take care of her. She—"

Jett put up his hands, palms facing Moxie, chuckling. "You don't have to justify *anything* like that. Like I said, she's not usually like this with anyone but me. I'm still fucking pissed my wife—*ex*-wife— did this, but you have no idea the relief that's been settling since seeing her down in the lobby. I can tell you've been taking really good care of her. She looks great, and she obviously loves and trusts you. Thank you, Moxie."

"She's a really good dog," Moxie cried. "I know you want her back… My friend at the shelter texted me and—"

"Moxie, I…" Jett blew out an uncertain breath after interrupting her. He genuinely didn't know what to do in this situation. Ultimately he did want his dog back, but somehow it felt very wrong. He'd faced life and death situations multiple times in his job, but nothing compared to how his gut and his heart were wrenching at him in this moment. Realization set in that dealing with a divorce was going to be the least of his worries.

"Moxie, please don't worry about anything like that tonight. You're right, I went into the shelter today with every intention of getting my dog back—I won't deny that in the least bit. But I promise you, I won't sneak off in the middle of the night with her. You can rest easy that we're all just gonna stay here tonight and catch our breath, okay?"

She nodded, trying to suppress her tears. A long moment passed before she asked, "How did you know we'd be here tonight?"

A chortle shot out of Jett's nose. "Pure coincidence, I promise you. I wasn't exactly supposed to be at a damn hotel tonight." He shook his head. "I haven't even been home for twenty-four hours— trust me—the Presidential Suite with a complete stranger wasn't exactly on my homecoming BINGO card. In fact, up until about two hours ago I assumed I'd be staying with my cousin for a couple nights."

"I'm sorry," Moxie offered.

"Are you kidding me?" He laughed. "You are the *last* person who owes anyone an apology." Jett watched her carefully put the ice back on her swollen eye. "Look, I know we just met, and it's obvious we're both in shitty spots right now, but let's try to make the most of this. I for one want food and a shower. How about I go grab something to eat for both of us? It'll give you some private time here if that's what you need. I promise I won't take Mags, you girls stay here. I'll leave you my number in case you need anything while I'm out." He looked at her for any kind of response. "I just ask that you please don't leave while I'm gone. I truly have missed Mags. Like I said, I just want to catch my breath tonight."

"I promise, I wouldn't do anything like that to you." Moxie finally met his gaze. "You don't have to pick up anything for me. I appreciate the gesture, but I'll manage."

"The first thing you'll learn about me is that I'm not a complete asshole. I know how to treat a lady. I promise, you'll be safe around me, Moxie; *and* I'm also getting you something to eat." Jett stood. "I'll probably be a while too, so you'll have the place to yourself for a bit—I need to get an Uber or hoof it to something."

"You're welcome to use my car," she offered.

"You don't have to do that," Jett declined.

Moxie slowly pulled her keys from her pocket. "I'm not a complete asshole either, let this gesture be my first act to prove that to you."

Jett gave her a flat grin and accepted her offer.

05

Jett set a few bags down on the coffee table when he got back to the hotel room. He wasn't sure if it was his business but he asked anyway because it would be very out of character for his dog. "Did Mags tear up the interior of your car?"

A tear slowly made its way down Moxie's cheek as she solemnly nodded. "That happened tonight…"

Jett waited to see if she wanted to share anything else. She'd showered while he was gone and he could see the full impact of the injuries on her face and neck now that her hat was off and her hair was up in a wet twist held together by a claw clip.

"We, uh… I—I'd just loaded her in the car. I didn't even realize my ex had been in the parking lot… I wouldn't have run back into the apartment if I knew he was out there, or I would've at least had N—Mags with me. I'm not mad at her, I think she was just trying to get out to help."

"Is this the first time he's done this?" Anger flooded his body upon her confession that a man had done this to her.

Moxie shook her head. "No… But it's not what you think."

Jett waited for the whole 'he's not usually like this' or 'he's getting help' excuse that sometimes a battered woman would settle with because she felt trapped.

"I admit, I didn't leave after the first incident." She swallowed hard. "The first time he ever hit me it was a single punch. I thought about it for days on end as if I made it up in my head because otherwise he'd been such a great guy. And after that first time you couldn't find a more devoted boyfriend."

She wiped the steady stream of tears that flowed freely. "I'm sure you don't want to hear about my problems. I can manage. You—"

"Moxie." Jett sat on the coffee table directly in front of her. "I want to hear everything you're willing to share with me."

She looked at him for a long moment. He seemed sincere and gave her all of his attention which encouraged her to continue.

"I *did* leave after the second time." Her voice shook as she tried to choke down any more tears. "That was a different fit of rage than the first time and at that point I'd never been so scared in my entire life."

"Do you have a restraining order?" He couldn't break the stare he had on her horrific injuries. They gave him phantom pains just thinking about the severity.

"I did." She shook her head. "I tried, but I haven't bothered since that initial report because to file that I have to provide my address and I just didn't want him finding me anymore. I've moved seven times in the last year because he keeps resurfacing."

Jett felt the blood rush up his chest. He didn't know this woman, but he wasn't heartless either, and Mags was an excellent judge of character. Nothing about Moxie's situation seemed anywhere close to right.

"I sincerely don't know how he keeps finding me. I've tried to keep a very low profile, and I work for myself so I don't have a normal schedule or papertrail in that sense. And honestly I don't know why he *wants* to keep finding me. We hadn't even dated for six full months before I left. I haven't dated at all since, so it's not like he does it just to chase anyone away. He keeps calling and sending texts from different phone numbers too—he knows I can't hide from him."

Her eyes glazed over and she stared across the room. "I've gotten comfortable the last couple of months because I hadn't heard from him. I didn't even see him tonight before he grabbed me. He sent me a text this morning so I'd spent the better part of the day packing and gathering essentials from home to just stay somewhere else for a couple of days until I could find a new place. I was only a few steps from the car when Mags started barking and all of the sudden his hands were around my neck."

She covered her face to gather herself.

"I've uh… I knew from the first time that there's absolutely nothing I can do while it's happening. Honestly, it gets even worse if I try to fight back or resist at all. So I just have to let him get it out of his system and hope I can make it through each one."

"*No.*" Jett shook his head. "That's not the final answer. You give me his name and I can assure you he will have touched you for the very last time."

Moxie watched as his hazel eyes turned dark and he shot harsh breaths through his nose. She didn't know him at all and certainly didn't expect him to risk anything on her behalf.

"I'm in a very specialized line of work. Nothing will ever lead back to you and I promise you, I can find him on a name alone."

"Jett, you don't even know me," she murmured, barely audible. "You don't have to add my problems to your plate. I appreciate it, but I'll manage."

"That's not how I operate." He inadvertently looked at the handprint bruise around her neck. "How many times has he done this?"

"This has been one of the worst… But he's done something like this eight times now."

Eight fucking times. Jett's mind was rabid thinking about the kind of sick, poor excuse for a man that was capable of doing something like that to a woman even once—let alone eight times. And this dainty woman had taken it, and survived, each and every time.

"Have you reported all of this to the police?"

She shook her head. "Having to do that report was awful. I…" Moxie didn't want to share the details of that event so she tabled it and addressed his question more directly instead. "I reported him and filed the restraining order after that second incident. He'd only given me a busted lip and bruises on my arms and legs, so they basically didn't do a ton to punish him in addition to the RO. The third time, right after the break-up and the RO, I really thought I was going to die. He told me if I said anything to anyone, he'd be back to finish. I left virtually everything I owned behind that night and found a new place. Two nights later he came by my new place to let me know I'd never be able to hide from him—just in case I got any ideas about going back to the cops."

Mags felt Moxie's discomfort and laid her furry face on her lap.

"I *know* this isn't right—but I don't want to die." Moxie swallowed down the lump in her throat. "So, I just keep moving and hoping that one day he gives up the search."

Jett was at a loss on what he could possibly say to her that would make anything better. As if his heart hadn't been through enough the last several hours, now he felt it squeeze tighter with every detail of Moxie's story. The rage brewing inside of him for a man he'd never met made his chest pound uncontrollably. He couldn't even place a mission in his entire career that made him feel so much fury—and he'd seen his fair share of shady shit.

"Mox, I'm so sorry you've had to endure that—you should've *never* been touched like that. Feeling like you have to live in fear isn't right either." He tried to be gentle while his insides screamed. "I swear to you, on Mags, you are *safe* tonight. Not only that, but I'd love nothing more than to take care of that piece of shit—you just need to give me a name."

Moxie's tears steadily flowed. She wasn't crying per say, but her eyes were certainly watering at the disclosure and Jett's response. He was a perfect stranger and seemed eager and willing to end her misery. She was grateful and terrified at the same time. Maybe this was the exchange Jett planned to offer so Moxie felt like she needed to hand Mags over without a fight. If she was being honest with herself, she didn't have any fight left in her. She loved Mags and didn't want to lose her, but she was pretty well spent on the energy she had in general—for anything at this point—she was quite broken after today.

"Uhm, I-I can't—" she stuttered. "Jett, you have no idea how comforting you've been—thank you for that. I'm grateful for your offer, but I think it's probably best if I sleep on things because I don't want to make anything worse for you. I don't want you to have to worry about this."

"Mox, I'm gonna worry. I know we aren't really familiar with one another, but I know right from wrong—this is wrong."

Moxie hesitantly reached for the inked hand on his knee and gently covered it with hers. She didn't look up at him, but she spoke softly, "Thank you."

"Moxie, you're welcome. Like I said, this isn't right. Just know I'm ready and willing if you feel comfortable sharing that name." He rubbed her hand.

They sat in silence until Mags decided to lie down next to Moxie on the couch instead of sitting on the floor next to her. Both Jett and Moxie reached out to pet her once she settled.

"Are you tired? Why don't you go take the bed? I'm sure a good night's sleep will help. I promise, nothing's going to happen to you tonight—you're safe here."

"I appreciate it—really I do—but you can take the bed."

"I'm not leaving you out here alone all night." He shook his head. "And I can sleep quite literally anywhere. The couch will be a luxury for me compared to where I've been sleeping the last few months— trust me." He chuckled, recalling the random beds he'd made do with during training—and his career in general.

"I don't think I can sleep lying down tonight." She didn't want to look at him when she disclosed the extent of her injuries. "I think at least one of my ribs is severely fractured, if not broken. I need to stay sitting up."

Jett let out a worried exhale. "I'm gonna go grab extra pillows and blankets for you then; you're not resorting to couch cushions to keep you comfortable."

He walked back into the living room with an armful of bedding. He studied Moxie's face for the first time since meeting her. He only got a profile view while she stared at the television. The side nearest him was relatively untouched, and he noted she had a pretty face. If Jett had to guess he'd put her at about 5'3". If she was lucky—with sopping wet hair—she'd be around a hundred and twenty pounds, maybe a little more given she had lean muscle versus just being skinny. Her tiny stature, Disney-esque large blue eyes, and button nose made him even more upset to know a grown man had beaten her the way he did. He didn't care what the reason was, there wasn't a possible valid excuse for it—it was wrong. He thought about his own laundry list of personal problems and suddenly they seemed to completely pale in comparison to what Moxie had been going through.

"I think if we wedge a couple of these on either side of you it'll help keep you comfortable. I also saw an upholstered bench in the bedroom. I'll bring that out here for you to prop your feet on." Jett set one of the pillows next to her on the couch.

"Thank you so much, really—this is just so nice of you. I think I need to get up though. I can't expect Mags to hold it all night, she needs out again before I try to fall asleep."

"You don't need to worry about that either. I can take her." He snapped his fingers to get the protective dog off the couch so he could place another pillow on Moxie's other side. "I promise you, Mox, we're *all* staying here tonight. I'm not leaving with her."

Moxie nodded, surprised at how confident she felt that this stranger would be true to his word.

"Do you feel safe up here alone for a minute?"

"I'll manage," she assured him.

Jett shook his head smiling. "I would never doubt that you can manage, but that doesn't answer my question."

"You said I'm safe tonight. I'll try to focus on that instead of being scared."

"Here"—he grabbed her phone from the coffee table—"why don't you give me a call? We'll talk while Mags takes care of business. It'll hopefully keep your mind off things, you can keep tabs on us, and I'll come flying up here if you say the word, okay?" He grinned.

Moxie looked down at her hands, very unsure of her next

question. "I don't want to seem ungrateful—because you've been so kind—but why are you doing all this for me?"

He smirked at her. "I'm not a complete asshole, remember?" Jett stood close, waiting for Moxie's gaze that never came. "Plus, Mags adores you. If nothing else, I'd like to repay you for being so good to her."

She couldn't bring herself to say anything else at that moment so she simply offered a careful nod.

"Call me." Jett still tried to catch her eyes. "Okay?"

For the first time that night, Moxie cracked a smile. It was only a partial one, but he'd take it. She dialed her phone and Jett immediately picked up.

"Mags' answering service, how can I direct your call?" Jett answered, winking at Moxie as he made his way through the door.

Jett was right, the phone call helped ease Moxie's feelings about being alone. He didn't sit on the phone and coddle her, instead he kept the conversation going, finding out all the most important surface-level information one would need to start a friendship—or build trust enough to share a hotel room with a complete stranger. They discovered several things about one another: Moxie was a freshly twenty-six-year-old Leo and Jett was a thirty-four-year-old Libra; Moxie's favorite color was pink and season was autumn, while Jett loved green and summer; and arguably the most important facts they learned they had in common were that pineapples undoubtedly belong on pizza and *Die Hard* is in fact a Christmas movie.

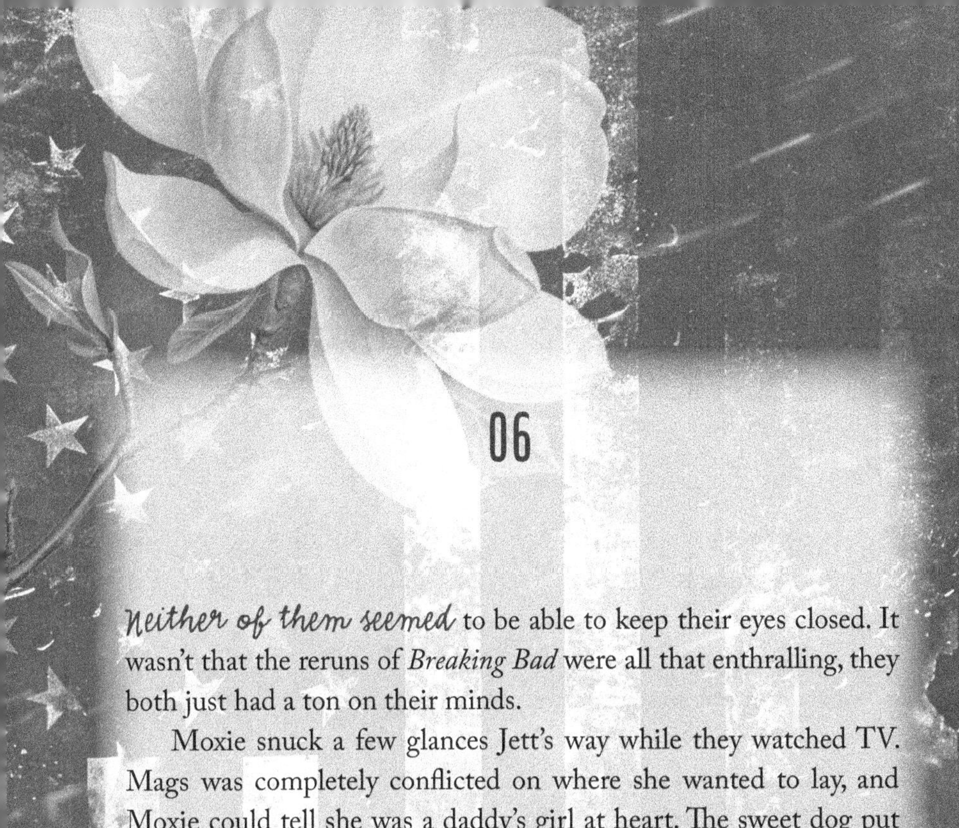

06

neither of them seemed to be able to keep their eyes closed. It wasn't that the reruns of *Breaking Bad* were all that enthralling, they both just had a ton on their minds.

Moxie snuck a few glances Jett's way while they watched TV. Mags was completely conflicted on where she wanted to lay, and Moxie could tell she was a daddy's girl at heart. The sweet dog put herself on a timer essentially, getting up every so often to change the direction of her head. When they got back from their walk she had curled up next to Moxie with her head on the pillow Moxie leaned on. About fifteen minutes after Jett sat on the chaise portion of the couch Mags got up and spun in circles until she laid her head on his chest. She had just made her way back to Moxie when Jett spoke up.

"I figured I'd pay for having left her for so long in the first place." He chuckled but was happy to see his dog again either way.

Moxie stroked the side of Mags' head a few times before she responded, "Can I ask what you do in the military?"

Jett had always been proud of his career, so he happily answered her question with a quick resume overview. "I did the whole military route straight out of high school—I'd always known I wanted to be a soldier. For the majority of my career I've served in the Marine Corps. It was all pretty basic for a couple of years, but then in my early twenties I got into the MRR, which is a special operations force. I did that for several years, but I'd had my eye on something even bigger for a while. That opportunity presented itself about two years ago so I transferred to the Army. I joined a clandestine unit within the Ghost Shadow Elite. You may've heard the term GSE?" He watched Moxie nod to confirm. "That's why I was gone recently— the training's unlike any other and was a six-month commitment. Having been in the military since I was eighteen, six-months didn't seem like much."

"I don't really know anything about the military," she admitted. "I've *heard* of GSE, but what does GSE do?"

"It's what they call a tier one special mission unit—some may consider it similar to Navy SEALs, MRR, or Delta Force. Technically speaking, my squad is in that unit, but we're a bit different. We basically do covert jobs *no one* should ever hear about."

"So, secret missions that nightmares are made of?"

Jett had to chuckle at her assessment—she wasn't too far off. "Depending on who you ask, I suppose. I actually enjoy it—to the extent one can enjoy it anyway. I'm not unhinged, just running around with some psychotic thirst for blood or anything like that. I like the satisfaction of a job well done and I don't need fame and glory to motivate me. I like that it's quiet, as far as the general population knows, and I've got my brothers around me."

"Are you just on-call all the time or something?"

"It's definitely not your average nine-to-five," he confirmed with a grin tugging on the corner of his mouth. "There's less than twenty of us in this squad and only six on my team. I haven't officially been on any missions since we just completed our training as a team, but unofficially we're on-call rotationally and the other days it's continuous training or filling in on other teams if we have to. It's similar to previous special ops I've been in, this one's just basically the pinnacle of what the military has as far as clandestine units. I never get much of a heads up on when and where I'm headed—or for how long."

Moxie thought about how funny it was that Vera referred to him as GI Joe—he was exactly that. She lived a very simple and quiet life. To think this man sitting next to her trotted all over the globe carrying out likely terrifying missions but also sat here like the most carefree gentleman she'd ever met made her smirk.

"I've never met anyone with that type of job."

"Not to sound like a conceited asshole, but we're pretty exclusive." Jett sat up and leaned his back on the couch so he could fully face Moxie. "You've got over a ninety percent chance of having your application denied outright, and if you're lucky enough to be accepted, the training process has a ninety-eight percent failure rate. They don't let just any old schmuck in."

Now that Moxie felt more comfortable with Jett, and didn't feel the need to hide her face anymore, she found herself watching him more than the TV. She tried not to stare too hard at him when he spread his arms across the back of the couch. Vera, again, was pretty spot-on when she'd said he gave *Southpaw* Jake Gyllenhaal vibes—Jett was a very handsome man. He wasn't a beefy meathead, he was genuinely ripped for his height though. One of his arms and the top of his hand were completely covered in what looked like a single tattoo. She imagined he likely had them on other areas of his body as well.

"What do you do for work, Mox?" Jett propped his feet up on the coffee table, crossing his ankles.

"Certainly nothing like saving the world." She fondly shook her head, catching Jett's amusement at her comment. "I'm a CPA"—she grinned—"and the C doesn't stand for clandestine."

She enjoyed watching Jett's smile, but looked away as she continued, "I started with like two clients that were just friends of my mom and now it's just developed into my own business. I started my company a couple years ago. It's just me, but I like the flexibility."

"Being your own boss seems like a great gig."

"It's been treating me well so far. I'm a numbers nerd—I could probably take on double the clients, but for some reason V insists I should also have a life outside of work."

Jett chuckled at her confession. He was happy to know that she had a flexible enough schedule to where she'd likely been spending every waking moment with Mags. His dog wasn't subjected to a kennel all day and was probably showered with more love these last couple of months than she'd seen since he left her.

"So Mags has been spoiled with your mostly undivided attention, huh?"

Moxie looked down at the sleeping dog whose head rested on her leg. "She's been training me well on taking breaks from work and getting out to new places. The only times this poor girl gets any kind of break from me is when I have certain client meetings and when I go to the shelter to walk the dogs. Initially, I thought bringing her would be nice since she's such a calming presence, it might help some of the anxious dogs. But I felt like—this might be stupid—but I just felt like she might have some kind of PTSD or something if I brought her back there… And I didn't want that for her."

"I can't properly explain to you how grateful I am that it was *you* who saved her. It seems like you've bonded with her and taken better care of her in the few months you've known her than my wife ever did in four-plus years."

Moxie's face deflated, knowing they'd need to have a serious discussion about Mags soon. "Jett, I—"

"We're not worrying about that conversation tonight, Mox." He quickly and gently interrupted, not wanting her to be upset. "Remember, we're just catching our breath. Mags and I will both be here when you wake up in the morning and we don't have to worry about anything beyond that right now. Thank you for loving her like you do."

"Forever," she confirmed before diverting her attention to the television. She realized they came from two completely different worlds, but their mutual love for Mags bonded them. Moxie had no idea if that bond would move forward—she tried not to think about the likely separation from her pretty girl.

"Good morning." Jett waved when he noticed Moxie's eyes open the next day. "Sorry, I didn't want to wake you. I left a note on the coffee table there, but we're gonna go for a quick walk and then I'll order some breakfast to be sent up for us."

"Thank you." She held her breath, wincing as she sat up taller. "I think I'm going to attempt a shower to get presentable for the day since I'll probably need to leave this room at some point." She took a deep, bothered inhale and felt her ribs stab at the slightest movement.

"I'll see if they have any ibuprofen while I'm down there too."

"It's okay," she declined while scooting to the edge of the couch to stand. "I have some I was planning to take."

"Do you need some help, Mox?" He noticed her pause and instinctively took a step in her direction.

Moxie swallowed as the next piercing pang rattled throughout her torso. "I can manage, I just need a minute."

Jett didn't believe her. If he knew her better he would've insisted and plucked her up from the couch himself to avoid having her utilize any additional strength. The urge to help her grew when Mags trotted to the couch to sit next to Moxie. He watched the petite woman's face brighten as she reached for the dog who gently set her head in Moxie's lap. After Mags checked in she dutifully returned to Jett's side. He ruffled the top of her head and looked across the room at Moxie. "We'll be back in a bit, but call me if you need anything, okay?"

"Thank you, Jett."

"You're welcome." He offered a flat, conflicted smile before opening the door.

Tears flowed freely when Moxie finally stood after Jett and Mags were gone. This incident ranked among the top two based solely on how bad her body felt. She was convinced her ribs were broken, not bruised.

The walk to the bathroom felt like it was ten miles long. Looking in the mirror she could tell the ice had helped a bit. Her eye was still swollen on the outside, but she decided it could've been worse. She'd be able to cover most of the discoloration with makeup, but she wanted to freshen up in the shower before masking the bruising on her face and neck. YouTube had been a dear friend since these incidents started. She hadn't been one to wear much makeup before, but she was grateful to have picked up the skill set as a way to erase these markings to the rest of the world.

Once she was finally able to remove her shirt, the mirror showcased the dark spots along her torso—they were scattered on her front and her back. She looked away from her reflection in shame and cautiously stepped into the shower.

Mags led Jett down the sidewalk as her nose looked for the perfect spot to perform her duties. Jett's demeanor had lightened since being reunited with her, if only this feeling could last. His phone brought him back to reality.

TREV

Just checking in today. You in town?

Jett rolled his eyes. He didn't need a babysitter, least of all from his cousin who'd clearly made his choice on who he'd be supporting publicly through this divorce.

> Yeah.

TREV
I can meet up in a bit if you want.

> You get clearance from your
> wife and Hallie on that?

Jett realized how rude that was after he hit send, but he didn't care.

TREV
Come on man. They're best friends, I can't expect
Jules to just drop her. This pregnancy has been
hard on Hallie and I'm just trying to do what I
can. It doesn't mean I don't care about you.

> Like I said, I'll manage.

Where are you staying?

> Around.

Jett shoved his phone in his pocket to focus his attention back on Mags.

He'd only been gone six months and in that time his life completely changed. Since being reunited with Mags he was able to keep the fury at bay for what his wife had done. Of all the damn things she managed while he was away, taking Mags to a shelter was the most unforgivable. He assumed friends and family would've intervened on his behalf knowing what Mags meant to him, but no one did—not even his cousin, Trevor, who seemed to be fully aware of everything that had been going on in Jett's absence.

He knew taking this new position put pressure on his marriage, but he didn't do it without discussing it first. The length of the training wasn't ideal, but he was playing the long game with his career. This move—he'd thought—helped his work-life balance more than it would hurt it. Looking at how things had unfolded, he didn't regret the decision at all. Hallie clearly wasn't the one he was meant to spend his life with. She took full advantage of Jett's job taking him away for an extended period to cheat.

They were married while he was on active duty—she knew the lifestyle since the day they'd met—and to his knowledge, she'd been faithful all those years. He had to question that now, seeing as how quickly she brought a co-worker into their home. That guy was damn lucky Jett had his mind fixated on finding Mags when just the day before he watched the little schmuck pull into their driveway in *his* truck. Jett didn't want anything more from his marriage when he saw that—he just wanted out.

He assumed the worst of it would be the fact that his wife was four months pregnant with her co-worker's damn kid. Jett knew his wife wanted kids—hell, they both had—and it wasn't as though they hadn't tried. He'd gotten Hallie pregnant twice and she'd had two miscarriages. They'd talked about taking a break from trying while he settled into his new job and *both* of them had agreed that was for the best. He'd given her ample time and space to vocalize if she felt differently, but she never did. She allowed him to believe she was happy with their lives and the direction they were headed.

He looked up and realized they were about a mile from the hotel now. *Shit.* He didn't mean to go that far, especially knowing how uncomfortable Moxie already was with the thought of being left alone. Jett turned around, and he and Mags headed back toward the hotel while he pulled out his phone.

> Hey Mox, you doing alright? I'm sorry, our walk's been a little longer than I intended.

Mox

> It's okay, I'm sure Mags needs it.

Jett shook his head, smiling. In the short time he'd known her, she'd rarely considered herself and it was clear she wasn't accustomed to anyone worrying about her.

How are you feeling?

Mox
I'll manage better when the ibuprofen kicks in.

I'm sorry. Are you craving something
in particular for breakfast?

Mox
Not especially Do you want me to
call down and order it so breakfast is
ready when you guys come back?

If you do that tell them I'll be by to pick
it up. I don't want you having to open the
door for anyone when we're not there.

Mox
Thank you for that. Are you craving
something in particular?

He chuckled as his fingers slid across the screen to reply.

I could crush some pancakes.

And bacon!

Mox
Done and done.

Thank you. We'll see you soon.

Jett looked down at the sound his phone made, Moxie had 'hearted' his text.

"Well, you've done a number on throwing me a good ol' curve-ball, girl." Jett looked down at Mags. "You like this one, huh?"

Mags continued trotting along the sidewalk towards the hotel, her fluffy tail swishing behind her with each step.

"We'll figure somethin' out," he promised her. He had no clue what that solution would be, but it was clear he couldn't simply take Mags from Moxie.

"Good morning, Nolie Lollie." Moxie leaned down as best she could to give Mags a proper greeting. The German Shepherd sat next to her and nestled her head against her hip so she could continue to get pets. Mags reached up and licked the side of Moxie's face.

Jett noticed how different her face looked. During her morning preparations she had completely concealed any traces of the abuse she'd received the day before. Given how bad it looked once she'd taken her hat off last night, he expected to see even more severe bruising today. By all accounts, she just looked like a lady who enjoyed a full face of makeup.

"Oh, thank you pretty girl, I love you too." She smiled.

Jett was momentarily stunned by the smile, it was the first full one he'd seen from her and it was beautiful.

Moxie glanced up and saw Jett watching them, her smile faded and she looked down at Mags. "I'm sorry, I—"

He immediately shook his head, interrupting her. "You don't ever have to apologize for loving Mags," he assured her as he held up their breakfast. "Ready to crush some pancakes with me?" He pumped his eyebrows, grinning and ready for food himself.

Moxie's eyes softened while the corners of her mouth raced for her ears and Jett loved it.

"So," Jett started as he set everything on the dining room table. "The manager stopped us when I picked this up and he said they've set us up for a late check-out today as a final apology for the rudeness we experienced."

"I'm still surprised at their sudden change. I thought for sure the guy was going to call the police on us last night—he'd already warned me twice about Mags growling at their guests."

Jett shook his head. "That prick's the type who gets off on feeling big when in reality he's probably living in his mom's basement and his side gig is some self-appointed block patrol captain." Jett set Moxie's coffee in front of her. "I'm not one to allow that shit to happen in front of me, and I think his manager knew that."

"Jett…" Moxie swirled the straw in her iced coffee, unable to look him in the eyes while she delivered her next line. "Thank you for everything you've done. I truly appreciate it."

"You're welcome." He confidently smiled at her. "And for the record, you're helping me too—so by all accounts, we're even." He winked, popping open the biodegradable container his breakfast came in.

"I can't imagine what I've possibly done—besides randomly showing up with Mags that is."

"That's a huge part of it, I'll admit that." He dove into the pancakes after smothering them in butter and syrup. "But, you've also helped me avoid the brooding piss-fest I would've been throwing all night if I was alone."

"I know it's none of my business, but I'm a good listener if you want to vent about anything," she offered.

Jett considered it for a long minute before he swallowed his bite. He took a deep breath before starting on a streamlined version of the events that had taken place the day before.

"Well, my life was a damn country song the second I got home yesterday." He tossed Mags a piece of bacon and took another healthy inhale. "The soon-to-be ex-wife didn't show face to pick me up like we'd planned after I'd been gone for six months. I ended up taking an Uber home to find the code on the door had changed, so I had to knock to get into my own damn house." He put another piece of pancake in his mouth, swallowing before he got to the juicer parts of his previous day. "And what do I have to greet me at the door but a pregnant wife—who *undoubtedly* wasn't pregnant when I left.

It took me all of five seconds to figure out my dog was gone. We argued about that for a minute until she gave me the name of the shelter where she dropped Mags." He dumped more syrup on his pancakes and firmly set the dispenser on the table. "I was obviously overrun with joy when I went to the garage to take my truck to go get her only to have the bay door open when her baby daddy came rolling in like he owned the place in *my* fucking truck." Jett shook his head in disbelief. "I grabbed a couple bags of clothes as quickly as I could and then walked about five miles to my cousin's to borrow a car to get Mags."

Moxie put her hand over her mouth. "I'm *so* sorry."

"Yeah, it hasn't exactly been the homecoming I had planned." He looked at her, his face brewing. "It's obviously not your fault though—you don't have to be sorry." He gave Mags another piece of bacon. "I thought I'd had my fill of good news and was expecting things to take a turn, but I was devastated to find out Mags was gone when I got to the Humane Society. So, with that gut punch of defeat, I went back to my cousin's to drop his car off. I fully planned to stay there for a couple nights—since he offered—but then he informed me they were hosting a gender reveal party for Hallie and she was headed that way to bring a few things over and do some planning. I couldn't get out of there quick enough."

Moxie sipped her coffee and offered silence in case he wanted to continue. When he took another bite she decided to speak up.

"I'm really glad we ran into each other last night," she admitted and played with the straw in her iced coffee. "You needed to reunite with Mags… And, Jett, I haven't felt as safe as I did last night in a very long time—you have no idea what that meant to me. I'll be forever grateful for that night of peace, especially when I needed it most." She finally peered up at him, balancing tears on her eyelids. "I'm truly sorry others haven't been showing you lately, but please know if no one else appreciates you right now, Mags and I certainly do."

Jett felt her sentiment hit him right in his chest, and he didn't think twice about his response. "Since running into the two of you, I'd have to admit, my mood's shifted for the better." He reached out and lightly rubbed her wrist for a split second before he pulled his hand back. "So, what are your plans today?"

She shook her head, looking down again. "I need to look for a new place to live."

Jett felt his heart constrict and before he could stop himself the words were already coming out of his mouth. "Do you want company for that?"

"You don't have to do that," she tried to decline.

"What if I said it's something I'd like to do today?"

"With everything on your plate, you'd like to help a perfect stranger find a new place to live?" She bit down on the smile tugging on her lip.

"Come on, Mox, we're not strangers anymore." He smirked. "Plus, I likely won't be able to find a divorce attorney on a weekend, I'm still trying to spend as much time with Mags as you'll allow, and getting to know you has been a pleasant damn surprise." He gave her an encouraging smile. "So yeah, I'll happily spend some time making sure you feel safe again."

Moxie reached for her phone, her fingers flying over the screen for a bit before she set it down.

Seconds later, Jett heard a text notification from his cell. When he glanced down he saw it was a contact card from Moxie.

"He's a client. Mr. Roman is an assassin in the divorce realm. If you'd like to aim for her jugular, this is who you need to contact. Tell him I sent you."

"Now I *really* owe you." His smirk graduated to a full-blown smile.

"I do have one embarrassing request if you feel you have a debt to pay."

"Anything." Jett was still overjoyed to have found Mags *and* now an attorney after less than twenty-four hours of the homecoming fuckery.

"I'm not sure if you can tell, but I struggled with my hair because it doesn't feel great to lift my arms. Do you have any experience with ponytails, buns, or something that'll get my hair up?"

"I don't." He laughed but got up to stand behind her. "I will say though, I *am* quite resourceful and an elite problem solver, I think I can come up with something to help. What tools are we working with—rubber band, scrunchie, clips…?"

Moxie's lips curled up. "I'm not picky, I just want it off my neck please."

Jett plucked a rubber band that was sitting on the table and started to gather her hair. He was surprised to hear a soft giggle from Moxie shortly after he started.

"Is he not doing it right?" she asked Mags, who was in an obedient sit next to her, cocking her head to the side while watching Jett twist the rubberband around.

"Mags, that's pretty fucked, girl," Jett pretended to scold her. "I think for my first time this is turning out better than expected."

His smile faded when he looked down at Moxie's neck and noticed that while she had used plenty of make up on her face and neck from a frontal view, there was a deep bruise in the shape of a thumb on the back of her neck. She likely hadn't seen that one but he was sure she felt it. He'd work on getting that name from her because this wouldn't go unpunished. As he got to know her more he knew he couldn't allow anything like this to ever happen to her again—that guy wouldn't lay another finger on her. Once he decided the ponytail he created would hold, he backed away with his palms raised in the air.

"I think I nailed it," he decided.

"Thank you," Moxie said as Jett sat back down in his chair.

"You're welcome. I'll be updating my resume with that new skill. Never know when I'll need it in the field."

Moxie sipped her coffee again but he could tell she was smiling.

"I think I'll go shower so we can head out soon. Do you need anything from the bathroom before I get in there?"

"No, I packed all my stuff already."

Jett grabbed his bag and headed to get himself all cleaned up.

08

"*I know it's your car*, but how about you let me drive?" Jett insisted.

"If you don't mind, that would actually be really nice. Thank you, Jett."

"It's not a problem," he assured her. "I can also put a call in to a buddy if you want to see about fixing up the inside of this driver's door." He pointed at the clawing and chewing damage Mags had done in her frenzy. Moxie had a newer model Jeep Cherokee that was otherwise in pristine condition.

"Thank you."

Jett opened the back door for Mags to hop in when an unsettling idea ran across his mind. He knelt down and began inspecting the wheel wells. "How long have you had this car?"

"Almost two years."

He felt along the undercarriage and was soon lying on the ground in the parking lot continuing his inspection.

"What are you doing?" she asked in a curious tone.

"I'm checking to see if you have any kind of tracking device on your car." He slid back out from under the rear of the vehicle. "I hate to say it, but I have to imagine if that degenerate keeps finding you, there's a reason for it." Jett made his way around the passenger side of the vehicle. Once he laid under the front passenger door near the wheel he caught sight of an AirTag. His eyes narrowed and he felt his chest beating harder. He yanked it from the Jeep and came back out from under the car holding it out for Moxie to see. Tears immediately fell from her eyes, which widened in horror.

Jett only paused for a split second before he closed the gap between them and carefully put his arms around her. He wasn't sure how bruised her body was so he didn't want to hurt her, but she needed to be held, and he needed to hold her. He allowed her to sob silently into his chest as he stood steady.

When it seemed like her cries were slowing down Jett leaned his head towards hers and spoke softly. "Mox, is it okay if I keep this on me for a while?"

She nodded but didn't look at him, she knew he was referring to the AirTag.

They both turned towards the Cherokee when Mags let out a quick, sharp yelp.

Jett slowly backed up and gently squeezed Moxie's shoulders. "Things are gonna be okay. Let's get out of here." He opened the passenger door for her, watching with worry while she slowly eased into the seat.

As Jett walked around the car, he took note of the serial and phone number for the AirTag, knowing he'd need both to track down the degenerate who put it there. He turned off the device and popped out the battery before shoving everything into his pocket.

"Is there somewhere I can take you to catch your breath for a bit?" Jett asked as he started the Cherokee, watching Moxie swallow down more tears.

She reached for her purse, shakily pulling out tissue and concealer to fix her eye. "I'll put it in the GPS." She went to her recent destinations on the car's navigation screen and landed on Golden Ridge, it was only a twenty minute drive.

Jett didn't ask any questions, he followed the directions and waited to see if Moxie had anything else she wanted to share. Besides Moxie's phone automatically connecting through Bluetooth to project a classic rock playlist, the ride was silent.

They arrived in front of what looked like an old manor. The grounds were meticulously maintained around the large white building and there was an elegant wooden sign in the front lawn that read Golden Ridge Memory Care Community.

Moxie's tears had dried up by the time they arrived. Jett parked the car but wasn't really sure what role he needed to play in this scenario.

"My mom lives here." Moxie met Jett's curious eyes. "I don't want you to feel obligated, so I'll leave it up to you, but you can just drop me off for a while, or you're welcome to come in." Her focus fell down to her hands in her lap as she continued, "She only remembers me a handful of times anyway, so she won't mind another visitor."

Mags made her presence known in the back seat, barking at the familiar building.

"I've been bringing Mags in to see her too, she's an approved pet visitor in the facility."

"Are you okay with an additional visitor?"

"I'm more than okay with you joining us, Jett."

"Let's go then." He offered a soft smile that left his mouth crooked.

Despite never having visited the facility, Jett led them from the parking lot to the building.

"Hey, Mox!" A round Indian man seated behind a small desk greeted them. "And you brought our favorite girl again today!" He smacked his lips at Mags and opened a drawer. "Are you gonna sit pretty today, or are you shaking for a treat?" He waited and then accepted the long-haired beauty's paw when she reached it out to him.

Moxie let them have their customary exchange while she signed the three of them into the visitor's log.

"Hi, Amir. Thank you for giving her a treat."

"Always for the prettiest Nolie girl." He smiled and then took a quick glance at Jett.

"This is Jett." Moxie gestured and watched Jett reach out his hand.

"Nice to meet you, Jett. Lucky guy you are walking in here with our two most popular ladies."

Jett dipped his chin with a charmed smile on his face. "It's nice to meet you as well, Amir."

Amir turned his attention back to Moxie. "Mama's in a good mood today. She even had breakfast with Harry again this morning—that's *two* days in a row," he gushed.

"Please be sure Harry stays in *his* room at night." Moxie shook her head but smiled as she led Mags and Jett towards her mom's room.

Jett thought about how comfortable Mags was; Moxie had truly incorporated her into her life. Mags trotted alongside Moxie like they'd been here a million times, and she'd clearly made an impression on the place from Amir's reaction and comments surrounding his dog. Or what used to be his dog—he still didn't know what the solution with Mags would be. The more time he spent with Moxie the more conflicted he became.

They walked down a long, carpeted hallway past several doors on either side before they reached the end. Moxie's mom appeared to have a corner room and the door was open. It was laid out like a hospital room but the decor was much more homey versus the sterile, uniform look of a hospital. While it had large tiled floors, they were covered in tasteful area rugs. Her bed was very neatly made and just under her window was a plush loveseat. They didn't see anyone, so Moxie poked her head into the bathroom.

While Moxie scanned the room, picking up a calendar from her mom's nightstand, Jett walked over to the dresser and looked at her mom's framed pictures. There were only a handful, but he took note of the decorative frame that held a picture of Moxie and Mags, making his heart warm. Moxie had her arms around Mags who looked like she had a smile on her face as the sun shone down. Given the scenery around them, they appeared to be on a hike of some sort. Moxie had made sure Mags was living her best life after being scooped out of that shelter, and he'd never know how to repay her for that.

"She must be out back," Moxie guessed and walked to the window to peer into the courtyard. She quickly noticed her mom occupying a park bench with her on-again, off-again special friend, Harry, as they watched a game of bocce ball.

On their way towards the exterior doors Moxie prepared Jett, "Mags has about ten different names when we visit because some of the residents believe she's theirs. My mom has three rotating names for her besides Nolie—none of which have any likeness to Magnolia. Since Amir said she's in a good mood today, my guess is she'll likely remember her and she's going to call her Luna. I just roll with it."

Jett chuckled.

"My mom doesn't always remember me—even on her good days—so I just talk about whatever she's in the mood for when I visit. You're welcome to share with her whatever you'd like, but please know she's on the later end of the spectrum for moderate stage Alzheimer's so sometimes she'll get a bit frustrated or snap. She doesn't mean anything by it."

"Mox, I'll be respectful, I promise."

"I wasn't worried about that." Moxie shook her head. Jett had been the poster boy for respect since the second they'd met. His behavior was the last of her worries. "I just wanted to prepare you with where she's at."

"Ryder!" an older man called out the second they stepped onto the patio. He hastily shuffled over with his walker. "There ya are, boy. I've been wondering where you ran off to."

Moxie flashed a smirk at Jett before she greeted the elderly man. He wore freshly pressed khaki pants, a long-sleeve button up under a knitted vest, and his signature fedora. He always kept himself nicely dressed, despite the house slippers he insisted on wearing.

"Hi, Mr. Thompson."

"Oh, thank you for bringing him home. He gave me such a scare after that thunderstorm, I know he doesn't like those." Mr. Thompson turned his walker around so he could take a seat and pet Mags. "Hey, you wanna go fishing later, buddy?" He shook the sides of Mags' face as she wagged her tail at the old man.

"Ryder has his grooming appointment in a bit—I've gotta take him to that first," Moxie told him.

"Oh, oh! That's right." The man waved his hands around like he remembered the fabricated grooming appointment. "Thank you for doing that, I'll be sure my wife has his bandana all washed up for him when he gets back."

"That would be great. What color are you going to put on him today?" Moxie indulged in his story.

"Orange today, we're going duck hunting later!"

Moxie smiled. "That sounds like so much fun, I'll be sure to bring Ryder back in time for that."

"Okay, good to see you guys—you take care."

They were a few steps away when Moxie felt the corner of her lip tug into a smile so she turned and looked up at Jett.

"That would be Mr. Thompson, and *Ryder* here has been his for over ten years. I'll have you know, Ryder has also sired several litters of puppies, all AKC quality who many have gone on to win Best in Show. And despite what his comments would have you believe, Mr. Thompson has never been hunting a day in his life."

Jett laughed before quickly covering his mouth. "I'm sorry, it's probably overly inappropriate to be laughing at his condition."

"It actually puts me in a good mood to be around them a lot of times. At first it was really hard with my mom because I've nearly lost the woman I knew my whole life. But the last year or so, things have gotten better for me with my acceptance journey or whatever you want to call it." She gently shook her head and continued walking, not wanting to dive too deep into that conversation. "But now coming here is like walking into a library full of interactive audiobooks or something. You never know what stories you're going to hear and you can be anyone you want—free of worries." She ruffled the back of Mags' tailbone. "And honestly, I talked to Mr. Thompson's grandson one day and the poor old guy did have a German Shepherd named Ryder. He told me the dementia got significantly worse after Ryder passed."

"That's actually really sad." Jett didn't think about it before he put his hand on Moxie's shoulder to give her a few comforting rubs. "Mox, you're one of the kindest people I've ever met."

Moxie didn't respond because her mom spotted them and was practically jumping out of her skin to greet Jett.

"Oh, honey, come here! Brody, I missed you so much, son!" Her arms flew open as she rushed to Moxie's new friend.

Moxie froze, she had no idea where this was coming from. Sure, her mom had remembered Vera a handful of times and greeted her similarly, but she'd never even met Jett. She'd never heard the name Brody from her mom either, and was shocked she gave such a warm welcome to a male stranger of all people. Her confusion settled into a wave of relief and gratefulness when she looked up at Jett, who wrapped his arms around her mom and matched her greeting.

"Hi, Mom. Sorry it's been so long." When he caught Moxie's gaze he had an ear-to-ear grin crawling across his face.

"That's okay, son. I'm so glad you brought Luna." Her mom reached down and kissed a very patient Mags who tried to suppress the hopping motion in her front legs.

Moxie's mom kept herself attached to Jett's side with her hand around his midsection while she looked at her daughter like she was a complete, but welcome, stranger.

"I'm Alison, Brody's mom." She held out her hand to Moxie.

Moxie smiled. Her mom remembered her own name, but forgot the part where 'Brody' wasn't her son at all.

"Hi, Alison, I'm Moxie."

"Oh, I *love* that name! How unique! If I had a daughter, I think I'd pick that name." She gave Jett a few more healthy squeezes. "Honey, do you guys want to sit with us? Your father's trying to explain this game to me." She pointed towards the lawn of bocce ball players. "Harry, aren't you going to say hi to your son?"

Harry looked over at Jett, staring for a long moment with furrowed brows. "I don't even know who the hell that is!" he exclaimed.

Jett's face turned red, and Moxie knew he was trying his best not to laugh at the terse old man.

"That's awful, Harry. Apologize to your son."

Moxie took a seat on the park bench across from them and waited for Jett to join her once her mom let him go.

"And who the hell is that?!" Harry seemed even more agitated when he saw Moxie.

Alison reached over and softly put her hand on top of Harry's but it was Jett who responded.

"Dad, you don't remember Moxie?"

"Honey, be nice. That's Moxie, Brody's wife," Alison assured him.

Moxie winced at the word *wife* in front of Jett—probably not what he wanted to hear given his situation.

Harry looked at both of them with a scrutinizing glare until Mags greeted him, tail whooshing back and forth.

"Luna! Hi, sweetie." The man immediately lightened up and gave the dog a few firm scratches along her sides. "Dear, where did I put that tennis ball? You know Luna loves chasing it."

"I don't know." Alison happily shrugged before she leaned her head on Harry's shoulder and reached for his hand. She had a blissful smile on her face and it made Moxie happy to see her mom like that.

Jett couldn't help but notice how young Alison looked in comparison to the other residents. She had a small frame, just like her daughter, and similar facial features. The woman did have wrinkles, but her hair wasn't completely white; in fact, she still had quite a bit of pepper in the sea of gray. She was also very nicely dressed. He didn't know why but when he thought of any assisted living facility he assumed everyone would be walking around in pajamas and nightgowns. Not Alison, who was ready to hit Sunday service with her tasteful and age-appropriate sundress, cardigan, and sandals.

"Brody, son, how's the practice going?"

Jett smiled, nodding slowly to buy himself some time to think about what kind of practice she assumed he had. He didn't have to consider it long before Alison helped him out.

"I've been meaning to call and schedule a cleaning for both your father and I, but things have just been so busy for us."

Jett caught on that she thought he was a dentist, so he played the part. "That's okay, just get in there soon so I can make sure you don't have any cavities."

Alison wiggled around in her seat. "Cavities!" She swished her hand at him with a smile. "You're such a rascal."

Moxie couldn't help but giggle and she shared a genuinely grateful smile with Jett.

"What the hell did you do to your hand?" Harry leaned from his bench seat towards Jett, pointing at the inked hand he had resting on his leg.

Jett lifted the artwork, smiling as he flashed the back of it towards Harry for a closer look. He wore another hoodie which concealed the fact that the tattoo actually covered his entire arm as well. The portion visible on his hand was only a remnant of the bottom, tattered edge of the American flag that was draped over his entire shoulder.

"C'mon, Dad, you forgot about my tattoo?" Jett smirked.

Harry shook his head. "You kids and your impulsive choices. That's permanent, you know." He watched as Jett nodded, unable to put his smirk away.

"I think it looks great." Alison shrugged and Harry rolled his eyes.

"You can't even tell what the hell it is. Looks like a damn ripped-up pair of prison pajamas." Harry's gruff voice was thoroughly unimpressed with the inked artwork that met his imaginary son's knuckles.

Moxie couldn't help but giggle along with Jett at the old man's grumpiness. She reached over to briefly and softly touch the top of Jett's hand, thanking him for being such a good sport.

They spent a portion of the early afternoon updating Alison as best as they could about 'Brody's' new dental practice and Moxie's successful coffee stand, when Jett felt his phone buzzing. He looked down and saw it was his wife. *Fuck her*, he thought and ignored the call. He looked at the screen again when a text came through seconds later.

> BABE
>
> Jett I need a favor. Can we talk?

He rolled his eyes and shoved his phone in his pocket, taking a mental note of the fact that he needed to change her contact to something more appropriate to what she was to him now.

Moxie noticed the slight change in Jett's demeanor when he harshly shoved his phone back in his pocket.

"Are you okay?" she asked in a soft voice.

"I'll manage." He winked at her, his stare lingering until Alison broke them up.

"Brody, honey, when are you guys going to give us some grandbabies?" Her voice was full of excitement.

Moxie's eyes widened and her face blushed. Surely Jett regretted his decision to join her in visiting her mom now. To her surprise he answered Alison with a friendly and welcoming voice.

"We've given you a beautiful granddaughter already." Jett gestured towards Mags with a grin on his face.

Alison laughed and held her hand to her heart. "Of course I love Luna! She'll always be our first grandbaby, but she better not be the last!" she warned with a shaking finger towards Jett. "Moxie"—her gaze shifted—"I was about your age when I had Brody. I think you guys are ready."

Moxie smiled at her mom, avoiding all eye contact with Jett. "Brody's had a lot on his plate with opening his own practice; plus, we don't want Luna to have to share us with anyone else yet. Our pretty girl deserves all the attention."

"We're also going to need a bigger house if you want a herd of grandchildren, Mom." Jett briefly rubbed Moxie's hand. "Now that the practice is up and running, we're going to be looking again. In fact, that was on the agenda today."

"I guess I can wait." Alison playfully rolled her eyes before leaning her head back on Harry's shoulder.

Harry's face brightened and he reached for Alison's hand to pick it up and give it a light peck. While Moxie was still skeptical of Harry getting too close to her mom, it helped to watch how Harry's gentle touch seemed to bring her such comfort and joy. She never thought she'd see anything like that.

"Well"—Alison took a large breath and patted her lap with both hands—"I hate to have to say goodbye, but your father has an appointment with the eye doctor soon, he—"

"I'm not going to that," Harry interrupted.

"*Yes*, you are." Alison caressed the side of his face as Harry mocked her with his mouth.

"That's okay, Mom." Jett stood. "We need to head out anyway. We have a few errands to run to get the coffee stand stocked." He turned around and held out his hand to help Moxie up, knowing full well sitting on the hard park bench didn't do her injured ribs any favors.

Moxie took his hand and gave him an appreciative look.

Alison hugged Jett first, giving him a few friendly rubs up and down his back as she told him how much she loved him. She turned to Moxie to hug her as well and when she did she swayed side to side pulling Moxie's body along with her. Jett watched as pain shot through Moxie, initiating a couple of silent tears.

"Come on, Mom," Jett interrupted them. "You're making me jealous." He gave her shoulder a few squeezes to encourage her to let go of Moxie, or at the very least to stop rocking with her.

"Oh, honey! You're such a rascal!" She laughed and waved them off, watching as the three of them headed out.

They were just steps away from Moxie's Cherokee when Jett turned to her. "You were right, that place does set up a pretty great mood." He smiled. "Thank you for letting me tag along."

Moxie smirked without looking at him. "I'm glad you had a nice time, *Brody*."

Jett threw his head back, laughing. He walked Moxie to her side of the car and opened the door for her. "That's *Dr*. Brody, *DDS*, to you—thank you very much."

Moxie's smile was temporarily halted when she slid into the seat and felt her ribs screaming at her again.

"Mox, we should get ibuprofen and some ice going for you," Jett suggested. "Do you want me to adjust this seat for you at all?"

"I know." She tried to take a deep breath, but it was cut short. "The seat's okay, but thank you—I do appreciate it."

Jett rubbed her shoulder a couple of times before closing her door and then helping Mags into the back.

"Please don't feel any pressure—this is just an idea…" Jett looked into Moxie's eyes when he got behind the wheel. He waited for her to nod. "I get the feeling that neither of us have a real urge to be alone right now, and we obviously both want to be with Mags. Do you want to keep hanging out together, or are you ready for some space?"

"Honestly?" she asked in a delicate voice, hesitating to look him in the eyes.

"The only response I'll accept." Jett nodded.

Moxie glanced down at her lap, staring at the bandage Jett had reapplied for her that morning. "While my body feels pretty terrible and my mind's a bit lost, I've really enjoyed having you around, Jett." She found the courage to look at him. "I think I'd be sad if we parted ways right now."

"We don't have to part ways, Mox," he assured her and offered a comforting smile.

They held each other's stare for a long moment before Moxie broke it. "So, what do we do now?"

"Well, I'd invite you to come stay with me"—he forced a chuckle—"but I don't particularly want to be in my house… Well, I don't want to be around the people who are likely staying there and wouldn't subject you or Mags to that either. There's always the Presidential Suite, we can check in to a different hotel, or I know you wanted to look for a new place. I don't think we'd find something in the next couple of hours, but we can start the search."

Moxie considered all of it as they sat in front of her mom's facility. She just wanted to rest, she didn't really feel like running all around town. She considered Vera's house at one point, but didn't think that would be the best place for Mags and Jett too.

"Are we all planning to spend the night together again?" she asked hoping that would help her decide on a viable option for them.

"That's your call. I was happy with that arrangement last night and won't mind it at all tonight. You're not a snorer, which was a fear of mine." He smirked to lighten her mood.

"I don't really love the idea of staying at my apartment alone… But if you're with us it would be okay for tonight and then I can try to find a good route for searching for other places tomorrow after getting some sleep."

"You want me to take you home then?"

"Are you okay with staying at my apartment?"

"I'm okay with whatever's gonna be most comfortable for you, Mox. I do have one, non-negotiable, condition if we're staying at your place though."

Moxie lifted her chin, peering up at him, waiting for his condition.

"I'll absolutely make sure you're safe tonight, but if that piece-of-shit ex surfaces I can't make any promises about his safety, *or* his life for that matter." Jett tried not to scare her with his tone, he knew how intimidating he could be.

"I have to make a counter condition to that," she hesitantly stated. Realization settled in that Jett would make good on his statement—he wasn't just saying it to make himself feel better. "You can't do anything that would jeopardize your life or your career." She looked at him with pleading eyes.

A sly grin tugged at the corner of Jett's mouth, consuming his handsome face. "Mox, I'm a professional in the field of covert operations. I wholeheartedly accept your counter condition because *stealthily* ridding the world of degenerates is exactly what I do for a living."

She knew the pride exuding from Jett after making that disclosure should've set off a fight-or-flight warning, but she felt completely settled by him. Fear was the emotion she'd become all too familiar with over the last year, but she wasn't afraid around Jett. That lingering terror that'd consumed her life waned with each passing moment she spent with him.

09

"It's not exactly the presidential suite… And I did do quite a bit of packing yesterday, so it's not going to really look like a home," Moxie warned Jett as they approached her door.

"You don't have to be embarrassed at all. If you've changed your mind about me being here, I can find a hotel. You don't have to feel any pressure from me, Mox."

"No, that's not it. I just… I move a lot so I don't keep a lot at my place." She pushed the key into the door and flicked on the lights.

Jett assumed she lived in a small apartment based on her comments about doing her best with Mags despite their dwelling. When they pulled up, however, he found it was an upscale complex set near the waterfront. He looked at the entry that led straight to a living room with a great view of the sound beyond the second floor balcony.

The apartment was spotless; in fact, aside from the totes, it looked like a model unit. He immediately saw the stack of Rubbermaid containers when he walked into the living room—she had about a dozen and her couch was closer to the size of a loveseat versus the sectional they'd shared the night before. She didn't appear to have a dining room table, but there were a couple of stools at the breakfast bar going into her kitchen that didn't have any walls obstructing it from the living room or the breathtaking view through her slider.

Her balcony was perfectly decorated with a tasteful rug, an oversized wicker rocking egg chair and a plush dog bed, large enough for Mags to share with a friend. The hallway beyond the kitchen looked like it had a few doors so he made the assumption it wasn't a one-bedroom unit.

"I packed a lot of bedding and everything yesterday, but I can get it out." She picked up a bowl from what looked to be Mags' feeding area to fill it with water. "I've got my bed, there's a futon in the office, and then my couch here. You're welcome to take the bed if that's not awkward. I'll likely be more comfortable out here or on the futon."

"You're not sleeping out here by the front door alone," Jett decided. "But if the living room's really your plan then I'll drag the futon out here to sleep with you."

"This is the only TV I still have plugged in." She gestured towards the flat screen that hung above the electric fireplace in the living room. "So, if you want to have a slumber party out here, I'm okay with that."

"I'm sure neither of us enjoyed the things in life that caused that slumber party last night, but I've had a genuinely good time with you, Mox." He offered a comforting smile. "I'd love to keep our new tradition going. So, how 'bout you show me where the futon is and I'll get things set up."

Moxie shook her head and let out a short breath of relief. "Jett, you have no idea how much I appreciate you and everything you've already done. Thank you—truly."

She didn't want to make things awkward when she felt her throat tighten and tears threaten so she turned towards the short hallway and continued over her shoulder, "The futon is in the first room on the left down the hall here. I'm just going to put some comfier clothes on, please make yourself at home."

Jett watched her until she walked into what he assumed was her bedroom. Mags took a few steps after her before the loveable dog sat in the hall looking back at Jett. He didn't lie to Moxie, he'd thoroughly enjoyed his time with her, but their situation was completely unconventional and undoubtedly complicated.

They'd ordered pizza and wings for dinner and were in the middle of a Christopher Nolan directed Batman binge when Jett's phone blew up. He tried to ignore it because his evening had been pretty fantastic despite the current state of his life. Since arriving at the apartment the conversations with Moxie were all enjoyable and flowed without effort, he'd spent quality time with Mags after thinking he'd lost her for good, and the pizza place Moxie introduced him to had, hands down, the best lemon pepper wings he'd ever tasted.

The first in the stream of phone calls was another attempt by Hallie, his wife; immediately followed by his cousin's wife, Julia. Both times Jett looked at the screen and ignored them, letting them go to voicemail. The third call was from his cousin, which he also ignored.

Moxie sat on the couch with Mags but could see the glow of his phone as he reclined on the futon.

TREV

Jett are you okay? I know you're in a mood
but will you call me back please?

Jett stared at the screen. His whipped-ass cousin was clearly doing this on his wife's behalf. He and Trevor had been close at one point—he wasn't sure when that life-long cousin bond broke—but from his point of view, he couldn't trust Trevor anymore. Without trust, Jett had very little interest in even being friends or communicating with him.

It was bad enough he'd have no choice but to deal with his wife's new lover until his divorce was finalized, but he had zero interest in also dealing with Trevor and Julia sticking their noses in his business. He couldn't wait to talk to Moxie's lawyer friend on Monday. A couple minutes went by before his cousin tried again.

Jett shook his head and took a deep breath, this was definitely kicking him into the brooding piss-fest he'd been trying to avoid. Funny Trevor'd care about Jett being alive or not. He'd ignored half of Jett's texts the last few months, when his life was undoubtedly more in danger versus being home on a two-week vacation from his perilous career.

Jett didn't even have a second to finish rolling his eyes when his phone rang—*again*. It was Trevor. With a huff he got up and headed for the balcony. "I'll be right back," he told Moxie as he opened the slider. "What the hell do you want, Trevor?" He shut the door behind him.

"Wow, what a greeting," Trevor's wife, Julia answered.

Jett let out an acidic laugh. "Of course it's you. What the hell do you want, Julia?"

"Where are you?" she asked.

"None of your damn business."

"Your *wife* is looking for you. She needs your help."

"My *wife*?!" Jett choked on his laugh this time. "Yeah, you've got the wrong fuckin' number. If she's looking for help you'll want to call her boyfriend. Actually, I think the more appropriate term is baby daddy."

"Come on, Jett. You guys have been married for *eight* years, you can't just turn your back on her like this."

"Fuck you for even having the audacity to say something like that to me." He put his free hand on the railing of the balcony and looked out onto the water. "Actually, you know what, I'd love to hear what it is she thinks I'm gonna fucking help her with. You know, since we've been married for eight years and all."

"This isn't easy for her either, you know," Julia spat back into the phone. "So you can quit acting like you're the only one hurting in this situation."

Jett grabbed his head and ran his hand from his forehead to the base of his neck. "Yeah, I can't imagine how hard it would be to get knocked up by some wet noodle of an office boy and have to call your *husband* for help… This truly must be tearing her apart right now. And for the record, I'm not hurting. I'm fucking pissed I have to deal with all this shit. I can assure you, my give-a-fuck meter surrounding my marriage ended the second I saw her pregnant stomach."

"You know better than anyone how tough pregnancies have been on her." Julia wanted to fire shots now.

Of course Jett knew. It wasn't like a miscarriage was anything people planned for or easily navigated when they happened. Those losses ate at *both* of them. He was in a hateful mood now though, so he wouldn't allow any kind of sympathy to ring through his voice. He thought about all the ways his wife had tried to ruin him for no apparent reason so he'd take the opportunity to return the favor of putting a metaphoric bullet in her heart.

"Yeah, well, congratulations to her little noodle boy for doing such a stellar job impregnating her. She looked like she's made it further along than those other two times now hasn't she?"

"I can't believe you just fucking said that!" Julia growled. "How heartless can you be?!"

"Not heartless at all." He shook his head. "I'm happy she got what she's been yearning for with the partner she replaced me with. I won't stand in their way of living happily ever after."

"So you'll help her out then?"

"I'll help her out in a way that I feel best suits the situation, yeah."

"I don't know what that means."

"Tell me the problem and I'll let you know." He put his hand on his hip. "And why don't you go ahead and put me on speakerphone if I'm not already. I'm sure she and Trevor are both there; let's have everyone weigh in on what a heartless asshole I am."

The line was quiet for a long moment before it was clear the entire room had now entered the chat.

"Hey, babe," Hallie's voice was hesitant.

"I'm guessing baby daddy isn't around if you're going with *babe*. What do you want? And make it quick."

The line was quiet again.

"Jett," her voice trembled, "I'm sorry."

He didn't respond. He let silence take over for an uncomfortable amount of time.

"Jett, you there?" Trevor asked.

"Yeah," he answered immediately. All Jett could hear was whispering on the other end—he had to assume it was the girls. "Will you just say whatever it is you want? I'm busy right now."

"I know I hurt you, and I'm sorry," Hallie started again with more confidence in her voice. "It just happened, Jett."

"We can go ahead and skip the 'sorry' speech because at this point I don't give a shit. What do you want?" he asked again, increased irritation pouring through his tone.

"I know I'm not in a position to ask for a favor, but I need one."

"Can't wait to hear about it," he sharply replied.

"Jett, I know you have a way of finding things—finding out about people anyway. I need your help."

"You're barking up the wrong damn tree because I'm clearly lacking when it comes to finding shit out. Not only do I not want to help you, but I can't help you."

"Please," she pleaded before Julia stepped in again.

"Look, this isn't an easy ask, Jett. We need you to see if you can find out about Billy."

Jett barked out a laugh. "The baby daddy?! This is *fucking* rich! I honestly can't believe this." He shook his head in disbelief.

"This is serious," Julia urged. "We think he's into something shady."

"None of this is sounding like my problem." He shrugged, slapping a hand on the railing.

"She's still your wife, Jett," Julia pointed out.

"Not for long if I can help it."

"Jett, please don't be like this!" Hallie cried. "I wouldn't ask if I wasn't desperate."

"Again, not my problem. You don't get to turn to me for help anymore. You have a new partner you need to lean on for support. You're gonna want to sort out your shit as a couple before you two bring a child into the world."

"I can get Mags back for you if you help me with this," Hallie offered, knowing Mags would always be the one thing Jett would sacrifice anything and everything for.

Jett's heart stuttered in response to this new tactic. She knew exactly how to get under his skin, but he couldn't figure out why she'd make such a bold claim that she'd clearly be unable to deliver on. He played along.

"Yeah?"

"Yes, I'll get her back for you in exchange for your help."

Jett opened the slider and put his phone on speaker so he could use the camera function.

"You told me she was at a shelter. Was that just another lie we can add to the on-going pile?" he asked, walking to the couch with heavy steps. "And you'll want to be sure you've got your lies straight because I'm sure Trevor already told you I went there yesterday and she was gone."

"She is—well, she *was* at the shelter," Hallie admitted.

Jett snapped a picture of Mags lying comfortably next to Moxie. He didn't get Moxie in the frame because he wasn't trying to drag her into the drama.

"Which is it? She's either at the shelter or she's not. It's pretty fuckin' simple. How do you plan to get her for me if you don't even know where the hell she is?" He stared at his phone, brows furrowed as controlled breaths steadily rolled from his nostrils.

"I called them today and the man I talked to said if I come in tomorrow around one I can talk to her adopter. He assured me I can get Mags back. It didn't sound like her new home is working out— she's living in an *apartment*, Jett. You know Mags deserves better."

Moxie's worried eyes peered up at Jett. He could see the heartbreak in her expression which only pissed him off even more that his wife would be such a conniving piece of shit. Jett hit send to his cousin's phone and was met with silence on the line.

He let the stillness sit in the thick air before laying into her, "I'm guessing you got the fucking picture I *just* took." Jett slammed his finger into the screen, taking the call off speaker before putting the phone to his ear. "Don't *ever* try to use my dog as a pawn again." He walked around the corner into the kitchen.

"Please, Jett, can we just talk about this?"

"I told you yesterday, there's nothing to talk about. You didn't send flirty texts to some guy—you're fucking *pregnant*, Hallie. I'm *done* and I'm sure as shit not helping you find out whatever your baby daddy's into."

"Is that why her credit card doesn't work?" Julia chimed in.

Jett snorted out a laugh. "I couldn't tell you why her credit card isn't working, but if you'd like to know why *my* card isn't working for her I've got a few ideas."

"So, you're just cutting her off?!" Julia was fuming. "She's got a kid on the way, Jett."

"Not my kid, not my problem." He now paced in the kitchen but Moxie could still hear his half of the conversation.

"You better tell loverboy that utilities and every other goddamn bill I've been carrying ends in about four days too. You both are gonna need to start stepping up financially because I cancelled everything yesterday."

"Jett, you know I can't pay for all that alone!" Hallie whined.

"That's not my problem. Not sure why you'd have to pay for all that on your own—I certainly never allowed you to pay bills alone. You've got someone else living there though, he can help you pay. In fact, this is a really good exercise in teamwork since you'll be parenting together soon."

"What about the house?"

"Yeah, about the house—seeing as it's in my name I'll go ahead and take care of that too. I guess my gift to both of you to welcome that little bundle of joy, besides filing for divorce, is that you two can stay there until it sells. I'll have a realtor come by next week for pictures."

"Babe—"

"You don't get to call me that anymore," he cut her off, cold.

"This is all moving really fast, Jett, I need some time."

"Moving fast?!" He choked on another laugh. "You've clearly known for months you were gonna be starting a new life. If it's moving fast for anyone, it's me, and I can assure you I'm capable of keeping up with this pace. In fact, I'd love nothing more than to fast forward to the part where I never have to see or hear from you again."

"Jett—"

"I'll be at the house tomorrow afternoon. I'm grabbing some of my things and I'm taking my truck. Your boyfriend's too small to be driving it anyway—he about ran me over in the garage because he can't see over the damn steering wheel in there. I suggest you change the lock codes back or baby daddy will need to replace a window so I can get in my house."

"I won't be home tomorrow afternoon."

"Even better," Jett snapped.

"Jett, will you *please* just think about this? Can we just have a conversation, privately, tomorrow?"

He was pissed she'd even suggest that after ambushing him with Trevor and Julia on the phone. "I'd tell you to go get fucked, but from what I saw yesterday someone's already taken care of that." He hung up and slammed his phone on the kitchen counter.

Mags trotted into the room and sat in front of him. He let out a large, aggravated breath and then leaned down to her. "Hey, girl." He massaged her ears.

He heard the credits from *The Dark Knight* playing and decided he should go say something to Moxie. To his surprise she was off the couch and picking up their pizza and wings leftovers.

"I can help with that." He quickened his pace to take the dirty plates from her.

"I can manage," she tried to decline.

"I know you can, but you don't have to." He smiled and took the plates and the pizza box, leaving only the empty container from the wings.

Moxie followed him into the kitchen. She wasn't sure if he was the type who wanted to talk when he was mad and she had to believe he was feeling at least some kind of anger after what she caught from his phone call.

"I was going to take Mags for a walk. You're welcome to join us if you want. You don't have to, I just—I thought if you wanted—" she fumbled with words when he cut in.

"Do you want me to take her?" He set the pizza box in the refrigerator and faced her. "Not that I don't want to be around you, but are you sure you're feeling up for a walk?" He inadvertently looked at her torso.

Moxie smiled. "Dr. Brody, aren't you a little out of your swim lane right now? You're just some guy with a dental practice. I'll be able to handle a little stroll."

Jett, despite his fury a few moments ago, felt a smile tug at his cheeks. "Alright."

He couldn't take his eyes off her as she left the kitchen to put on shoes and a jacket. Her humor and angelic presence were exactly what he needed.

They got back from their walk and Jett felt a lot better about his night. Moxie didn't really talk a ton while they were out—which he appreciated. He wouldn't have been mad at her for trying to chat, but he sure enjoyed that she simply let him take in the fresh-air evening stroll with Mags leading the way.

"Do you want to finish our marathon?" Moxie asked when she slipped off her coat.

"Of course I do." Jett stood after relieving Mags from her collar and leash. "Sorry I missed the end of *The Dark Knight*."

Moxie walked to the opposite end of the living room but turned back to face him. "You can feel free to ask me to just be quiet and mind my own business, but I wanted to at least offer some things I like when life's being shitty to me."

Jett encouraged her to continue.

"I have a really nice bottle of tequila in the freezer, and I happen to be the Martha Stewart of chocolate chip cookie dough. If you're more of a cookie guy, I can bake it instead, but I always prefer rolling the dice with a little game of salmonella roulette."

He blew out an appreciative breath and shook his head. "That sounds really damn perfect, actually. Thank you."

Whatever kind of fuckery had possessed his wife to do what she'd done, karma was sure to pay him back tenfold with the apparent gift of Moxie.

"If you wouldn't mind though, I do need a bit of help getting one of my kitchen totes from the pile over there."

Jett walked to the stacks she had packed. "Just let me know which one, Martha." He grinned.

"Second one from the bottom on the far left, Dr. Brody," she quickly replied with a matching smirk.

Jett shook his head, smiling as he retrieved her tote.

The Dark Knight Rises had been over for at least an hour, not that they'd really watched it, but they were dangerously close to the bottom of the tequila bottle and had been jawing along about life.

"I gotta say"—Jett just finished another spoonful of the cookie dough—"you're not the Martha Stewart of cookie dough, you're *The* Moxie-fucking-Hall of cookie dough. Martha could *never.*"

Moxie giggled. "Thank you, I don't know if it's a good thing or a bad thing that I've basically perfected it."

"What do you mean?"

"Well, I only make it when life's shitty. So, for me to get so good at it, it's because I've made it quite a bit."

"How?" He shook his head in genuine disbelief. "How the *hell* does someone like you of all people get dealt that hand?"

"V says it's because God gives his hardest struggles to his strongest soldiers." Her tequila-buzzed eyes rolled before she continued, "I think she smokes too much because I'm a far cry from a strong soldier. *You* are a strong soldier, Dr. Brody."

Jett chuckled and then put his arm around Mags' neck who was currently snuggling on the futon with him. The dog rolled like a puppy into him so he cradled her between his arm and his torso as he laid on his back and stared at the vaulted ceiling. "I'll agree in the literal sense that I'd never want you to be on a battlefield, but you're a lot fuckin' stronger than you give yourself credit for, Mox."

"Some days," she decided.

"It still pisses me off that Mags had to be in that shelter at all, but I'm really damn grateful for her sacrifice."

Moxie didn't reply, she wasn't sure if he was finished.

Jett stroked his hand along Mags' chest as they laid on their backs. "Meeting you is like finding out I was missing a critical piece of the puzzle this whole damn time."

She didn't know how to respond to that. It was obviously very flattering, but she wasn't sure if it was the liquor talking and didn't want to feel stupid if he woke up the next morning and decided everything he said was simply out of spite from the situation with his wife.

Jett picked up on Moxie's silence. "Shit, I'm sorry. Things were going perfect and I made it uncomfortable." He put his free hand on his head, his palm partially covering his eyes and forehead. Not regretting the sentiment, but unsure of having shared it out loud already.

"No," Moxie finally spoke up. "It's not that… It's just that no one's ever said anything that nice to me."

She figured if he could bare his drunken soul, so could she, so she finished her thought, "I didn't want to wake up tomorrow and find out you regret that compliment. I was trying to soak it in for what it was tonight."

Jett's confidence soared. "At the risk of making it awkward, I'll go ahead and let you know it was sincere. I'm happy to remind you tomorrow when we wake up though."

Moxie couldn't help but smile, her face was hidden from Jett anyway. "Why don't you remind me when the cookie dough runs out so I know you're not just blinded by my culinary prowess."

Jett laughed from deep within his belly. "If that's what it takes then consider it done, Mox."

He was still laughing when Moxie got up to go to the bathroom for her nightly routine. The buzz she had going actually helped mask some of the pain throughout her body, so she moved with a little quicker pace. Mags let her out of sight for about five minutes before she got off the futon and trotted down the hall after her.

"Hey, Nolie Lollie," Moxie greeted when she came out of the bathroom with a freshly washed face and her teeth brushed. Mags' tail slapped against the wood floor at the chin scratches she was getting. "Is it bedtime?" She smiled at her.

Despite the room being dimly lit, Jett could still see Moxie's face as she sat back down on the couch. She was a magician with the makeup because ten minutes ago you couldn't tell she had a mark on her, now with everything washed away, the black and blue consumed her doll-like face and neck. He blew out a heartbroken sigh when he watched her hold an ice pack up to her eye. Just as he opened his mouth to say something, Moxie was making sure he was all set up for the night.

"Are you comfortable on that futon? Do you need another blanket or more pillows?"

"I'll be able to sleep perfectly fine, thank you though."

"Goodnight, Jett." Moxie settled into her sleeping spot with a few pillows on either side of her.

Jett tried not to be obvious when he watched her slowly getting as comfortable as she could manage. He stared up at the ceiling and spoke softly, "Moxie?"

"Mhmm?" She rested the injured side of her face on the ice pack.

"Not only will he never touch you again, but he's going to fucking pay for each and every time he made the mistake of harming you."

"Thank you." Moxie wiped a couple of tears from the conviction of his tone.

"Goodnight, Mox."

"Goodnight, Jett."

10

Moxie heard her phone vibrate on the arm of the couch the next morning, so she rolled her head to the side and reached for it.

V

Hey babe! Wanna grab a coffee before I start work today? You're coming in to walk the dogs, right?

Hey girl - I would but I don't think I can make it before you have to work. I actually might be late today.

V

Everything okay?

Yeah, just really tired and have a lot going on.

V

Have you thought any more about letting GI Joe see Nolie girl?

We can chat about that when I come in today.

🙂 Deal! TTYL babe!

Moxie set her phone down and looked over at Mags and Jett who both still slept on the futon. If she'd learned nothing else about him the last couple of days she knew he loved that dog with his whole heart.

At some point throughout the night he'd removed his shirt. Moxie had been right—he did have plenty more to his tattoo. Mags blocked part of his torso so she couldn't see all the ink he had, but his entire arm—including a majority of the back of his hand—his right pec, shoulder, and rib cage all looked to be pretty well covered. Part of her wished Mags was still on the couch with her, because she did enjoy the sight of Jett's bare chest—she had no idea patriotism could be so sexy.

There were two focal points within the artwork that permanently marked Jett's muscular body. The larger of the pieces was a very detailed monochrome American flag, tattered and weathered. The three-dimensional banner of freedom looked as though it'd been thrown over Jett's right shoulder. The greyscale stars were partially covered by a fierce American Bald Eagle with its wings splayed and head atop Jett's collarbone. The only piece she could see that wasn't a part of the military themed artwork appeared to be a small paw print over his heart. She assumed, given the detail, it may be Mags' puppy print and the mere thought of that possibility tugged through her chest.

Moxie couldn't help but think about how complicated both of their lives were at the moment, and despite it all, she was growing a healthy fondness for Jett. She didn't plan on adding anything to his plate by vocalizing that to him; he was, technically, still a married man after all. She also considered they hadn't had a deep conversation about their plans for Mags, but Moxie knew she wouldn't have the heart to ever keep her from Jett. She decided to enjoy the time that the three of them spent together for however long it lasted.

II

Jett's cab pulled up to his house that afternoon. He thanked the driver and headed up the brick paved walkway. Mags sniffed around, recognizing the house, and looked up at Jett when he stopped at the garage door. He attempted the old code to see if Hallie had changed it back and given him access like he'd told her. To his surprise, the bay door started to lift and his truck was in the garage—yet another surprise.

"Come on, girl," Jett encouraged Mags as he opened the door from the garage to the house.

Mags only trotted into the house a few steps before she did an about-face to stay by Jett's side. He looked down the hall to see his wife.

"Thought you weren't going to be here," he said flatly and opened a coat closet.

"Jett, we need to talk." Her lip quivered. "It doesn't have to be about my favor. I just want to talk to you. We haven't done that."

"You gave up any chance to talk when you got pregnant, Hallie." He yanked on a gym bag from an upper shelf. "I would've been happy to talk with you before that. Like I said last night, I'm done."

"Just like that?"

"It's not just like that. You *know* how much shit we've been through trying to start a family. I've been there every step of the way for you. *You* told me you wanted to take a break from trying, *you* told me you supported me taking this job, and now *you're* the one who chose to start a family with someone else. You and I don't have anything left to discuss."

"I still love you, Jett."

"You're gonna want to redirect those feelings because they're not mutual."

"You don't mean that."

"Oh, I've never meant anything more serious in all my life." He choked on a laugh and walked right by her on his way to the staircase.

"You can't just end this," she begged with tears in her eyes.

"I didn't. You ended this. I'm just getting out of the way now because the last fucking thing I want is to share with your beta boy baby daddy." He reached the second step when she grabbed him.

"Please, just stop!" Hallie yelled. "Stay here and talk to me! You owe me that!" she sobbed.

Jett didn't turn around. He snapped his fingers for Mags to go ahead of him on the stairs when he heard a low rumble in her chest.

"No, I don't think I do. What I owed you was upholding our vows—which I did. Given everything you've done, I'd say I don't owe you shit anymore."

He climbed a few more steps before he stopped in his tracks. "My stuff still in the bedroom or have I already been moved out? Can't imagine baby daddy's been wearing any of my clothes, he'd be swimming in them."

"Will you just stop so we can talk about this?" Hallie begged.

"Like I said, there's nothing to talk about." He continued towards the master. "You need to just go sit down somewhere—preferably away from me. You don't need to be getting so upset in your condition."

"Please, Jett, I'm scared."

"Why don't you go stay with Trevor and Julia for a few days then?" He reached the closet and began filling a bag. Mags sat obediently by him; Jett noticed Hallie try to pet her. "Don't touch my dog. You lost that privilege when you dropped her off at the shelter."

"I didn't have a choice, she got aggressive. I couldn't handle her like that."

Jett's laugh was full of doubt as he shook his head and continued to pack. "I'm guessing wet noodle Billy couldn't handle having Mags be the man of the house while I was gone. Where is he, by the way? Don't tell me the honeymoon phase is already wearing off." Jett decided he had plenty of clothes for the time being and made his way down the hall to his office.

"You can stay out here for this one." Jett glared at her before shutting and locking the door once he and Mags were inside. He planned to unpack some things from his safe and the last thing he wanted was his wife doing something stupid in there. He took a deep breath when he heard soft knocking on the office door a couple minutes later. He didn't bother to even look up from pulling one of his hand guns out of the safe. He only turned when Mags started to growl as she sniffed under the door.

"Jett, it's Trev."

Jett rolled his eyes. *What the fuck?*

"Come on, man, please let me in. I just asked Jules to take Hallie to our house—they'll be outta here in like thirty seconds."

"I don't need a babysitter, Trevor. I'm just grabbing a few of *my* things." He carefully placed his favorite shotgun in one of his tactical bags.

"I'm not babysitting, I'm genuinely trying to check in with you, man."

"You can direct all that concern towards your wife and Hallie— they need it, I don't."

Mags rumbled again with her tail straight out. Jett snapped his fingers and she immediately left the door and sat by his side.

"I shoulda reached out a few months ago. I feel like shit about that. I'm sorry."

Jett had an unfriendly smirk on his face. "Your balls have been in Julia's back pocket since the day you two met. I'm not surprised you were given a gag order. I'll be honest though, that's a new low for you considering what a good guy I've always been to you. Not even a fucking heads up before I got to the house? I guess it's a good thing I have the composure that I do, because any other man would've lost his fucking shit at how I was blindsided."

"Hallie admits it was her."

"No shit!" Jett barked out a laugh. "Are you fucking kidding me right now? I'm not the one expecting."

"No, I just meant she admits you didn't do anything wrong. She knows she fucked up."

Jett finally opened the door with a couple of now full tactical bags.

"I'm glad you got Mags back." Trevor gestured down to the dog who followed Jett's lead.

"Yeah, no thanks to any of you." He glared and marched down the hall. "You know, this is actually gonna be really great for all of you. Two beta boys who can't handle shit unless their wives approve."

"Come on, Jett. Please be serious for a minute." Trevor stopped and hoped Jett would too. When he did Trevor continued, "There's something off about Billy. You know deep down you still care about or even love Hallie. If for no other reason, please just see if you can find anything out about him for history's sake."

"You know me. You know I've always had that off switch. I don't love that woman anymore, and to hell with any history she and I had. It's over."

"I know you're not that cold, Jett." Trevor threw up his hands.

Jett shook his head but didn't turn around. "It's not cold to have self respect. You know as good as anyone I would've done anything and everything to make my wife happy. She clearly didn't want that. Her problems aren't my problems anymore. I'm doing what I can to exit her life as soon as possible so we can both move on. Given your stance on all this, sounds to me like Billy boy's *your* problem now." Jett stalked down the stairs to the garage to load his truck.

"Do you need a place to stay?" Trevor followed him.

"I don't need anything from any of you—I'm good." Jett made a sharp whistle and pointed to the truck for Mags to jump in.

"Can I ask where you're staying?"

"You can ask, but I don't plan on letting anyone know."

Trevor took a deep breath. "Look, I don't know what to do here."

"My advice?" Jett had to move the driver seat back before he could get in. "I'd encourage you to keep listening to your wife like the good little husband you're trying to be. Lucky you, you can scurry back to tell her you did your best to talk to me but I'm the predictable asshole who's still just gonna leave." He hopped in his truck and pulled out of the garage without another look at his cousin.

Moxie had just gently tossed a ball for a mixed terrier and a chocolate lab when she felt her phone buzz.

> JETT
> Hey Mox you still at the shelter?

> I am, are you doing okay?

> JETT
> I'm decent. Things are just taking longer than I
> planned today, currently hung up at Bolton Chevy.
> I didn't want you ending up at home alone.

> Thank you for the heads up, I'll stay
> out longer. Can you let me know when
> you're headed back there please?

> JETT
> Of course I will. You can come hang with us or
> just pick up Mags if you're ready to head outta
> there. It's your call. Idk why this is taking so
> long, I just want to trade this damn truck in.

> V's bugging me to catch up with her, I'll stay
> at the shelter so you can get your stuff done. I
> don't want you to feel rushed on my behalf.

Moxie wasn't sure how to respond to that. She didn't have to worry long before Jett's texting bubbles pulsed.

Moxie 'hearted' the text and put her phone back in her pocket to reach over and give the chocolate lab a good ear scratch. Just as she put the phone in her pocket, her alarm went off, it was time to get these pups back inside and end her volunteer shift. She reset it for another fifteen minutes; both she and the dogs could use the extra break.

"Hey, babe!" Vera waved when Moxie walked into the lobby after returning the dogs to their respective enclosures.

"Hey, V." Moxie took a seat next to her behind the desk.

"Not heading home right away to Ms. Nolie girl?" Vera was accustomed to her best friend acting like there was a fire anytime she left Mags at home.

Moxie took a full breath and contemplated what she'd share with Vera. She didn't want her to know about the literal run-in with the ex, she'd kept the majority of those stories hidden from her, so she came up with a version that was mostly the truth.

"Mag—Nolie girl isn't at home right now."

"What?!" Vera spun her chair towards Moxie. "Where is she? Is everything okay?!"

"Yes, she's more than fine, actually." Moxie had to admit her dog's demeanor was a constant state of elation since being reunited with Jett. "She's actually with your GI Joe—Jett has her."

"Babe"—Vera reached out and held Moxie's hand—"you gave her back?" She grimaced knowing how much Moxie had fallen in love with that perfect German Shepherd. After the initial sadness, she shook her head quickly. "Wait, how did you even know how to get a hold of him? I'm so confused right now."

Moxie rolled her head and smirked. "It's a crazy little story, and technically speaking I don't think I've given her back—it's complicated."

"And you're *obviously* gonna spill the tea."

Moxie laughed before diving into a modified story of her last couple days. She did disclose they'd ran into each other at a hotel—and ended up sharing a room. She said her excuse for being at the hotel in the first place was that there was an issue at the apartment that had to be fixed, and she didn't want to be around with maintenance in her area. Vera bought that story because she knew Moxie scared easily since her slimeball ex. Moxie also stretched the truth and told her they'd stayed at the hotel for two nights—not that Jett had a slumber party with her at her own apartment. Vera was beside herself that Moxie had been spending so much time with the 'Hot AF GI Joe' she met in the very same lobby they sat in just two days earlier.

"So, has he made any moves?" She bit her lip and pumped her brows and shoulders at her best friend.

"V, come on." Moxie laughed. "He wants to be around Nolie girl. Not to mention he *just* decided he's getting a divorce."

"Give me a break! He's a *dude!* And you're about the most adorable human I know, inside and out."

"Well, thank you for that." Moxie shook her head smiling. "But right now I think we're both just focusing on Mags and what we're going to do about our situation."

"Mags, huh? I like Nolie girl better." Vera gave her a subtle bump. "I'll always support you, babe—you know that. But that man is a bazillion shades of *YES muthafuckin' PUH-lease*, so if that opportunity presents itself just know you definitely should."

Moxie laughed and started to blush. She never denied Jett was a great looking guy. The buzzed look wasn't always her favorite, but Jett's combination of the buzzcut and his tastefully short, scruffy facial hair was perfect. She'd also caught a glimpse of his bare chest that morning and her eyes had absolutely no complaints besides the fact that they didn't see more.

On top of his desirable physical attributes, he'd treated her like she was his in the most chivalrous way imaginable. Initially, she was convinced it was only because he wanted Mags back. After getting to know him a bit more, she wasn't sure where that line was.

"He seems like he could use a bit of a break with everything he's got going on. So, I just want to roll with things how they are and worry about the actual serious conversation about Mags when he's ready. I promise, it's working out more than fine right now. Jett's actually a really great guy from what I can tell. It's been nice getting to know him."

"Shit, babe, I'm gonna start keeping a little notes page about this—you can't make this fairytale shit up. I wanna be sure I've got it all lined up in case I'm asked to be a maid of honor in the future."

Moxie laughed out loud at her. "You already know you're expected to be my maid of honor someday. But let's not hop the crazy train just yet please."

"As per ushe, no promises on the crazy train." Vera shimmied her shoulders and shook her head around while Moxie reached for her buzzing phone.

Jett
FINALLY. It's way past dinner time too. How
do you feel about Chinese tonight?

Moxie smirked, Jett was a really great freaking guy.

I could crush some Orange chicken and egg
rolls 😋 🥡 I can go pick it up before heading
home if you let me know what you'd like.

"Who you got on the textline?" Vera tried to peek over at Moxie's screen. "Please tell me it's GI Joe!"

"He's just checking in since he's got Mags." She bought herself some time and glanced down at her phone when Jett replied.

JETT

Lol, you could crush those huh? Just meet me
at home, I should be able to grab food and
be there in about a half hour. You just let me
know if you want anything else while I'm out.

Thank you, you don't always have
to get everything ya know lol.

"Sooooooo…?" Vera gushed in response to Moxie's charmed face. "Do you guys have plans tonight or something?"

"I'm gonna go meet him and Mags soon," is all Moxie offered.

JETT

Consider it payment for letting me crash at
your place. I'd pay top dollar for a Moxie Cookie
Dough filled slumber party any night lol

Lol well I can happily whip that
up for you anytime.

JETT

I might have to hold you to that.
See you soon Mox.

She 'hearted' the text and turned her attention to Vera. "Are you leaving on time tonight?"

Vera narrowed her eyes over a knowing smirk—she knew she

wasn't getting the full story from her best friend quite yet. She decided to give her a break and unpack more later. "Planning to. I might go out with Ian, I guess his friend is in some band and they're playing at a bar tonight. Maybe you and GI Joe wanna join, huh?"

Moxie shook her head. "I haven't seen Mags all day, you know I'm missing her and she can't go to the bar."

"Oh, alright, but you better keep me up to date on the *Mags* and GI Joe sitch."

Moxie stood and threw her purse around her shoulder. "I'll let you know when we decide what we're going to do with her."

"Babe, you know that's *not* what I meant." Vera laughed.

"Bye, V." Moxie didn't look back because she didn't want her best friend to see her flushed face.

"See ya!"

12

"*I'm sorry you got* the wrong chicken, Mox—I should've checked before we left." Jett shook his head. He'd already offered a dozen times to go back, but Moxie assured him it was fine.

She chuckled, mixing up her dish. "I'm not allergic, it's the same color, I *do* like sweet and sour chicken, and I promise I'll live."

"Yeah, but now you're probably just gonna eat it instead of crushing it." Jett smiled.

"I still have eggrolls to crush," she pointed out.

They continued their meal at the breakfast bar when Jett brought up something he'd been thinking about while he'd waited for hours on end at the dealership that day.

"Hey, Mox, I think I have an idea."

"Oh, yeah? Idea about what?" she asked as she slayed a piece of pineapple on her fork.

"Please don't feel any pressure about this, it was just a thought…" He put another hunk of General Tso's chicken in his mouth.

Moxie gave him her full attention.

"I know you're worried about finding a new place, and I know neither of us want to give up Mags." He prepared another bite with rice and chicken on his fork. "I've got the next two weeks off—a furlough of sorts as a treat after training—so I'll be around. How would you feel about us not parting ways quite yet?"

"Like staying here?"

"Only if you're onboard with that arrangement. If I'm here, maybe you won't feel as rushed to settle on a new place. I can also pay rent, I'm not just suggesting a freeloader situation."

Moxie shook her head with a smirk. "You don't owe me any money or anything."

Jett noticed their cookie dough was sitting on the kitchen counter within arms reach. There was only a bite left so he grabbed the container. He held the spoon out towards Moxie. "Do you want any of this before it's gone?" He grinned.

She still had a smirk as she shook her head again.

Jett took the final bite and as soon as he swallowed it he continued his pitch, "Plus, I'm still convinced there's a reason—beyond Mags—that you and I crossed paths."

Moxie's cheeks filled with color so she tilted her head down to hide her face under the ball cap from Jett. She was saved by the buzzing of her phone. Jett decided to give her a break and stood to bring the now empty cookie dough container to the dishwasher.

MR. ROMAN

Hey there Foxie Moxie, sweetie. Got a voicemail from a Jett Sharpe yesterday, says he's a friend of yours. Just wanted to confirm no one's out there pretending to know you.

Hi Mr. Roman. I sure did give Jett your name and number, he's a good one. Please take care of him for me ☺

MR. ROMAN

I'll give him a call here shortly, gonna try to meet with him tomorrow. I'll be sure to let you know if he's a good enough one. ☺

☺ You're the best!

MR. ROMAN

Take care sweetie.

Moxie still smiled at her phone when Jett returned to the barstool next to her. "You'll be getting a call from Mr. Roman this evening. He was just checking in to be sure no one was trying to falsely use my name."

"I'm gonna get a *Sunday* call?" Jett pumped his eyebrows. "You must be big time with him, huh?"

Moxie shrugged. "His daughter and I are about the same age, and I manage to keep his pockets and wallet full—so, I'm one of his faves for sure."

"I can't tell you how much I appreciate the reference—I want to get the ball rolling as soon as possible." Jett barely finished his sentence when his phone rang. He held it up for Moxie to see Mr. Roman's number before he slid it to answer.

"Hello?"

Moxie smiled that Jett seemed content despite having what sounded like a pretty shitty day. She was sure he hadn't shared all the details of his time at home that day—which was more than fine— but his ability to put up a facade was unmatched.

Moxie decided she would've been a trainwreck if she'd been subjected to what he was going through. He was able to compartmentalize everything like a professional. He'd been gentle with her, cold on the phone with his ex, and now, as she could hear part of his conversation with Mr. Roman, he was firm in his tone but in a way that sounded like he was executing a business deal.

Mags had finished her dinner and found her way to Moxie where she gently set her head on her lap.

"Hi, pretty girl." Moxie smiled at her and stroked the top of her soft, fluffy head.

"Well"—Jett strode back into the kitchen, looking even lighter than before—"gonna meet up with Mr. Roman tomorrow and he's gonna set me all up. So, I guess I'll owe you dinner tomorrow too to thank you for this hook-up." He sat down and dug back into his dish.

Moxie giggled. "We don't have to keep score around here. I like the arrangement we've established helping each other out where we can while we both catch our breath."

"Alright," Jett agreed with a charmed smile on his face. "I'll help by getting dinner tomorrow night."

Moxie couldn't avoid playfully rolling her eyes at him. For the umpteenth time that day, she decided Jett was an unbelievably great guy.

13

"So, how'd you like Mr. Roman?" Moxie beamed when Jett came back to the apartment early the next afternoon. "He texted me either during or immediately after your meeting today."

"Oh yeah? Mr. Roman telling all my secrets, or what?" Jett chuckled as he caught Mags' top half when she jumped up on him.

The amusement was still plastered on Moxie's face. "He just wanted me to know that he has a big fat crush on you now, *Cerberus.*" She giggled, disclosing Jett's newest nickname. He was going to have more than Mags if he continued to meet people in her life.

Jett laughed. Mr. Roman had made that meeting surprisingly pleasant. They obviously started on great terms since they met through Moxie and both men agreed she was pretty wonderful. Upon the first five minutes of speaking with one another, they also realized they had a second mutual connection in life. One of Jett's teammates was actually Mr. Roman's cousin. Jett immediately gained a fan when Mr. Roman found out what he did for a living, and was even more excited having met this new client when he learned he was on the *best* team.

Jett hadn't fully disclosed to Moxie all the details of his clandestine squad when they exchanged career stories their first night together. Jett's squad was technically part of Ghost Shadow Elite for all intents and purposes, but truly, his squad, Cerberus, was a black ledger group who had direct reporting straight to the Secretary of Defense. He'd reserve that in-depth explanation for now, allowing Moxie to likely assume it was simply a code name or something.

"Full disclosure, that crush goes both ways." He smirked. "We realized I actually work with Mr. Roman's cousin—he's on my team."

"Really?" Moxie's face lit up. "What a small world, I'm glad you like him. He's always been one of my favorites."

"I get why you suggested he's the type to go for the jugular." Jett held up his hands. "I gotta say though, I think Mr. Roman's got a *family*, if you know what I mean."

"Yeah, he's been married for like thirty-something years and he has two sons and a daughter," Moxie confirmed with an adoring smile, having met his family multiple times.

Jett chuckled at her innocence. "*Not* the family I was talking about."

"Mr. Roman would never run around on Ms. Stella," Moxie countered with a confused look.

"Oh, Mox." Jett shook his head with a grin, sliding both palms from his forehead to his chin. "I don't want to taint your view on Mr. Roman, because he does seem like a really decent guy. I gotta ask though, does he know about the uh…" Jett gestured towards Moxie's eye that was covered in ten pounds of makeup at the moment.

Moxie looked down with shame-filled eyes. "I haven't told anyone—well, only you and my mom know about this stuff." She shook her head, her voice even quieter now. "I mean, I told V what he did when I left him… She just doesn't know about all the other times after that."

Jett felt horrible that she'd kept everything so private—that she didn't have anyone she felt comfortable going to with this. After meeting her mom and putting the timeline together in his head, he had to believe she'd never remember any of these disclosures from her daughter, no matter how traumatic.

"The family I'm referring to wouldn't have let that go unanswered. Not that I'm backing out of my promise to you, but Mr. Roman and his family would've been safe to trust with that information. They're in a similar line of work."

Moxie finally looked up at him, eyes rounding in disbelief.

"He adores you, so you've got nothing at all to worry about—stick with Mr. Roman. I probably wouldn't go around asking him about his family, or anything like that," Jett was quick to clarify, "but like I said, he's a safe person to tell those types of secrets to." Jett reached out and held her petite hand. "And so am I. I just need a name, Mox."

"I know you're a safe person, Jett. Thank you." She didn't acknowledge his request for a name. She was still undecided on that. As long as he was staying with her, she felt safe and didn't see a reason to send Jett out on a hunting mission. She truly had no idea if he'd actually kill her ex.

They studied each other for a long moment before Jett's phone alerted him of a text. He took a deep breath before slowly letting go of her hand to check the message.

> MR. ROMAN
> We just served her with the papers. Ball's more than rolling, Cerberus. I'll let you know when I get an update. But remember to send me any dip shit texts or information if she wants to harm any of your property.

"Mr. Roman is the damn man." Jett looked like a kid on Christmas morning with his excitement.

> Thank you! You have no idea what a relief it is to have this moving like it is. I sure appreciate you.

> MR. ROMAN
> You'll be a free man very soon.

Thank you. Have a good one.

Mr. Roman
You too, Cerberus.

"I'm glad he's helping out." Moxie didn't want to prod.

"Thank you, Mox—this just took a huge weight off my shoulders," Jett admitted and then watched his phone light up and sound off with notifications. The ball was *definitely* rolling. He snickered and put it on silent before dropping it on the coffee table. He had no interest in talking to his soon-to-be ex-wife, but more importantly, he wanted to talk to Moxie about their living arrangement.

"Listen, I know we kinda made plans last night about the next couple weeks, but I stumbled on something today." He pulled a folded piece of paper out of the back pocket of his jeans and held it out to Moxie.

She accepted it from him, slowly unfolding it as he continued, "I was leaving Mr. Roman's and I saw a for rent sign at this place so I picked up that flyer." He pointed down at the paper Moxie held in her hands. "I've got a realtor lined up to get my house on the market and I'm not interested in buying right now. I know we haven't talked about Mags yet, but this place has a fenced yard, a garage, and it'll keep me close to command."

He'd been checking Moxie's expression to see if anything he'd said so far scared her or put her off. He noticed her opening her mouth so he waited for her to speak.

"Jett, I don't want to keep Mags from you—I can't and wouldn't do that to either of you. I love that pretty girl with my whole heart, but she loves you and you'll always be home to her." She felt her face flush as she tried to hold back tears. Moxie swallowed hard, forcing more words out of her mouth, "After everything you've done for me and what you're going through, the last thing I want you to worry about is whether or not you're going to get Mags back."

She blinked a few times, looking down to hide the single tear that escaped. To avoid having Jett look in her eyes she took a seat on the couch while he still stood near the coffee table. "If you want to start your life over with her there then you should rent that house. I can manage." She nodded, crestfallen, as a few more tears trickled down her cheeks. "I just ask that you *please* consider letting me take her any time you're away for work. I know I've only had her a few months, but I'd really love to at least be able to still see her… Because, Jett, I do love that pretty girl very much. I promise, you can always trust me with her."

Jett had wanted to let her finish her thoughts but couldn't take the pain he saw on her face. He sat down next to her on the couch and spoke gently, "Mox, no. I'm sorry, I wasn't showing you this to say I want to take Mags and leave you here all alone."

She wiped her eyes before looking up at him, confused.

"I need to get that damn divorce finalized, my house sold, and I'll need to report to work sooner than later. I thought this could be a really great solution for now so we can both finish catching our breath. There's no part of me that's going to leave you alone, especially here, and *especially* not before I can take care of your issue. I wasn't bluffing in the least bit when I said he's not going to touch you again. That's a promise."

Jett reached for the flyer and pointed at a few of the pictures and details.

"Mox, this place has four bedrooms; there's also two *full* bathrooms, and a garage that'll fit both of our cars. It's also only about ten minutes from the Humane Society." Jett briefly and gently squeezed the hand she had clutching the flyer. "What do you say to not parting ways quite yet?" He smiled at her.

"Are you sure?" Her face was already lightening up.

"I'm so sure that I already called and talked to the rental company. We have a four o'clock appointment today to look at it if this is something you're open to."

"Dr. Brody, you are a breath of fresh dang air," she finally said with a small smile.

Jett threw his head back and laughed. "You always have to remember rule number one—I'm not a *complete* asshole, Mox."

Moxie fondly shook her head and watched Jett scoop up his phone to walk out onto the balcony with Mags happily following him; presumably to take care of some asshole business he wasn't going to subject her to. She didn't watch him long before his face transformed to that of the one she'd seen when he was on the phone with his ex the other night. *Taking care of asshole business for sure,* she decided.

14

Over the next couple of days Jett removed nearly everything he wanted from his house and put it in a storage space not too far from the apartment. He'd rented it the same day he traded in his truck. He was making another deposit of additional items when he stumbled upon the AirTag he'd pulled from Moxie's Cherokee. Despite having disabled it, he still wanted to keep it far away from her. If her ex had been watching its movements lately, he'd surely know she didn't have it on her vehicle anymore. Especially if he'd gone back to the apartment at any point to check for her car. He was surprised she hadn't given him the bastard's name yet. Granted, he had only nudged her at this point. With everything going on, he wouldn't pressure her, but he'd make sure she knew the door was open. In the meantime, he'd keep her safe.

She was rarely out of his sight or without Mags, so he felt settled enough that the degenerate wouldn't be able to catch Moxie alone. He also hoped his own presence wouldn't scare him off completely or make him go into hiding—Jett was ready to be face to face with the fucker. Of course, he preferred the guy stay away from Moxie, but that wasn't good enough. Jett planned to make him pay for the pain he'd caused. He'd figure out how to go about getting the name, but for now, the AirTag would stay in the storage unit.

Jett brought a tote full of items from his home office into the apartment that night. Mostly sentimental items he didn't have room for in his safe.

"Did you decide to move in here instead?" Moxie asked when she noticed him add the tote to the pile she already had in the living room.

Jett chuckled. "No, I just didn't want this one at the house anymore—or at the storage unit. Lots of these things can't be replaced."

Moxie watched him, wondering if he'd share. He felt her eyes begging for more information so he smiled, popping the top off the tote.

"Here's something I know you'll love." He handed a frame to her.

Her face melted and she put a hand over her chest as she held the framed photo. Mags was just eight weeks old, a small patch of fluff with floppy ears and a cocked head sitting in lush green grass.

"Oh my gosh!" She held it up by Mags' face. "You've *always* been the prettiest girl!" Her face was covered in a giddy smile. "Jett, how did you even stand how friggin' cute she was as a baby?!" She gripped his forearm in her excitement.

He welcomed her lingering touch and loved Moxie's gorgeous face as she gushed over Mags. He couldn't take his eyes off her.

"I always wondered what the pretty girl looked like as a puppy— she was the cutest ball of fluffy fur I've ever seen! She wouldn't be obedient in any kind of way if I had her as a puppy, this furball would've walked all over me," Moxie admitted and took her hand back from Jett's forearm.

"Trust me, I struggled in those early days. The puppy breath is *deadly* for giving in." Jett rubbed the top of Mags' head and reached into the tote again. He pulled out her first collar and a few other pictures to share with Moxie. He wished he had an infinite supply of puppy items because he was practically catching a high watching Moxie's expressions.

She playfully scolded him when he had to admit he'd never put any bows in her luscious locks—apparently her puppy years were marked by more of a tom boy style since she was such a daddy's girl. Jett was beyond grateful to see Moxie had pictures of the time the groomer took it upon themselves to send her home with tiny pink bows clinging to the top of her head near each of her ears. He had to admit he'd be okay with her wearing the bows from time to time now.

"Okay," Moxie nearly sang out, hardly able to see through her eyes because her smile was so big. "Hello, baby face, huh?" She held up Jett's first official Marine Corps photo.

Jett's complexion heated up to a deep red. He'd pushed the box in front of the two of them and was letting Moxie paw through it along with him. "I was like eighteen in that photo." He reached out and grabbed his beer off the coffee table, taking a swig to hide his embarrassment behind the can.

"Like I said—baby face." Moxie caught her bottom lip with her teeth in an attempt to conceal the grin still etched on her face as she plucked another frame out of the box. "Tell me about this one." She held it between them so Jett could see what she was looking at.

"That's actually the most recent picture I have—that's my current team. This was taken about a week before we took off for training." Jett gave her a quick rundown of all the guys.

"This lanky fucker is Cappy, he's the team leader. Super nice guy, he's married, and has four kids. Fun fact about him, he's really into crocheting." He looked at Moxie who smirked at the extra information.

He pointed to himself next, standing to the right of Cappy. "That's obviously our most handsome, bravest, and most skillful member." Jett wasn't disappointed at all when Moxie playfully bumped her head into his shoulder.

Instead of physically responding to her gesture, and possibly pushing something Moxie didn't want or wasn't ready for, he offered additional commentary to let her know he enjoyed her flirtatious touch. "Fun fact about our best looking member, he's the self-appointed President of the Moxie Hall Cookie Dough Fan Club."

He enjoyed the sound of her giggling as he moved his finger

along the photo to the shortest guy in the frame who was a spitting image of a compact version of Bazooka from the GI Joe cartoons.

"This is Frank. He's also one of the new guys to Cerberus and he has a husband. His humor took me a minute, he likes to remind all of us how lucky we are to have a guy like him watching our backs."

Moxie didn't disappoint when she slapped her hand over her mouth to hide her smile.

"Honestly, he's one of the best snipers I've ever met, so he's alright in my book to have my back in *that* sense. Plus, he's actually a pretty great guy."

Mags decided she'd spent enough time lying her head and neck on Jett's leg so she got up and walked around to sit closer to Moxie, who immediately reached her hand down and started to pet her.

"Then this guy is Mr. Roman's cousin." Jett pointed at a sizable man with a deep brown complexion, a thick goatee, and a bald head. "We call him the Texican—he came to the team with that nickname. He's married and has a daughter who's gonna be fifteen soon so all he's been talking about is her Quinceañera coming up. He's a really good guy with a dirty sense of humor."

Moxie reached for her drink from the coffee table and continued to listen.

"This is Trip, I know him the least of all the guys. He and Cappy are pretty tight though, they were in basic training together way back when. He just got remarried so he's got a blended family with three kids now—he's a decent guy." Jett shrugged.

"I'm gathering you're all good guys." She smirked since he'd been sure to point that out about each of them.

"Well"—he took a healthy breath that ended in a bit of a chuckle—"then we have Hot Rod." He pointed to the final, tallest member of the team who stood at the end of the line flexing with his shirt off. His top half was quite beefy, Moxie decided, but it looked like the man skipped leg day on a regular basis.

"Hot Rod isn't married, but likely has an infinite number of offspring around the globe. He's got one of *the* foulest mouths I've ever heard—with overall questionable social skills to match, but he's also top tier when it comes to explosives. If we could add a mouth filter on him, I'd also tag him as being a nice guy." Jett laughed.

Moxie continued to inspect the picture. "So, these are your brothers, huh?"

"Yep, the Hounds of Hades," Jett proudly confirmed.

Moxie's head turned, looking up at Jett. "Hounds of Hades?"

"It's a team name," he clarified. "Each team in the Cerberus squad has a name—that's ours."

"Is this your team motto?" Moxie's fingertips slid across the wooden frame where 'GUARD THE GATE. OWN THE DARK.' had been engraved.

"One of 'em," Jett admitted with a smirk.

"Is this the motto in a different language?" Moxie pointed at the calligraphy below their motto that read 'choris iso'.

"It's a bit of a motto, I suppose—it's Greek and it means "without equal."

"Oh, so all you good guys are also *very* humble." She fought a grin, peering sideways at him.

Jett had to smile at her conclusion and grabbed another frame because he loved sharing his life with her.

They continued going through Jett's tote until they'd seen every picture and memento he'd packed. Moxie was overly grateful to have been given that look into his life. She could tell how proud he was of his career, and it restructured her entire heart to see the things he mindfully took from his house that were irreplaceable to him. She also enjoyed that it appeared to give him a carefree moment of not having to think about all the life-altering changes he'd been dealing with the last couple of days. Moxie could feel herself falling harder for him throughout the entire evening, which solidified her confidence in the decision to move in with him and Mags.

15

Jett was the first to wake up from yet another one of their living room slumber parties. There was a large part of him that would be sad when they moved into the rental house to sleep in their own separate rooms. When he fell asleep the night before, Mags was under his arm. Like she had been since they were reunited, she split her time and was now comfortably cozied up with Moxie.

Moxie was learning to cope with the more upright sleeping arrangement she'd been doing to try and let her ribs heal. Jett wished he was able to speed up that recovery for her; she was too damn innocent and sweet to have gone through anything like that. It still ate at him that she was gatekeeping the name of her abusive ex. He was confident he'd have no trouble taking care of some piece-of-shit guy who stalked and beat his ex-girlfriend on a regular basis. Despite the healing that slowly erased her injuries, Jett would never be able to forget what she'd looked like that first night. The more he got to know her, the urge to rid Moxie's life of that prick increased exponentially.

He watched as she slept peacefully with her head leaning on Mags, whose neck was stretched out to share Moxie's pillow. Mags also had her front paws across Moxie's lap. The scene made Jett smile—they truly loved one another.

Despite the couple of months Mags likely had to deal with Lord knows what with his ex, and then her short stint at the shelter, Moxie had completely put his dog back together with love. He'd only known Moxie for just a couple weeks now, but he felt like it had been so much longer.

Initially, helping the damsel in distress to grease the wheels in hopes of getting his dog back was his motivation. He figured out very quickly that it was going to be much more complicated. Moxie was not only gorgeous, but she was absolutely infectious in the best kind of way—it was hard to be in a bad mood around her. Jett's life had been a shitshow since the second he got home. By all accounts he should be a wreck, but anytime he was around Moxie it was like the rest of the world ceased to exist.

Since he was eighteen and freshly enlisted in the military, he was willing to defend and possibly die for his country. After meeting Moxie, it was only *her* he was willing to defend and die for... but what he really wanted was to *live* for her. Live *with* her. He knew his current situation didn't offer her what she deserved, so he was committed to straightening that out as soon as he could.

He also knew how bad their situation looked. An outsider could assume he was either pursuing her as a rebound so he didn't have to be the single one who'd been dumped while his wife started a family; cozying up to Moxie just to get Mags back free and clear; or simply being blinded by the abused girl that needed help. None of those things were anywhere close to being true. In the deepest depths of his soul, he felt a genuine connection.

He wouldn't say the word *love* in fear of jinxing it. He would, however, box up those feelings and stay at arms length until Moxie made it clear she wanted him to provide a closer connection. Or until he could get his divorce finalized—whatever came first. As he watched her sleep, he knew what he wanted more than anything was a future with Mags *and* Moxie.

16

It was finally move-in day at the new rental house and Moxie had invited Vera over to help her unpack. The girls went through all Moxie's clothes and organized her closet on the second floor of the new place. Jett's room was the master suite in the house; the only reason he demanded to take that option from her was because it was on the first floor and had an exterior entrance. Moxie had the entire second floor to herself—she had two bedrooms, a full bathroom, a reading nook, and a linen closet up there. She dumped another tote full of clothing on the bed next to Mags before she reached for her phone.

> V and I were gonna take a lunch break soon. Can I get you something to eat?

JETT

> We've got one more stop before we're back at the house. What are you ladies having?

> Not too sure yet lol. How many guests are coming over with you?

JETT

> Gonna be four of us guys. But you don't have to buy it all.

JETT
Don't worry about that. You still don't
need to be lifting heavy things.

It had been a couple weeks and while Moxie's face and neck were mostly clear of any remaining bruises, Jett knew her ribs were still tender. That piece-of-shit ex had no idea what was coming once Jett found him.

JETT
You're the best Mox! We're just about
to load the last safe, got one stop
then we'll see you at the house.

Moxie 'hearted' the text and then immediately caught an earful from Vera.

"Is that a standard *roomie* smile?" Vera folded a pair of jeans and side-eyed her friend.

"What?" Moxie scrolled through her phone to place their lunch order.

"You must've been talking to GI Joe, huh?"

"Yeah, I wanted to see if he and his buddies needed food too."

Vera didn't take her eyes off her friend, pleased Moxie had a lightness about her that wasn't there before she met Jett. It was like she'd stepped out of a shadow and was embracing the light around her for the first time in a couple years. Vera decided she'd go along with the whole '*we're roommates for Mags' sake*' spiel, but she didn't completely buy it. She, not so secretly, hoped for so much more to develop between them.

"Maybe I'll get lucky and one of his alpha buddies will *also* be looking for a roommate." Vera pumped her eyebrows.

Moxie only rolled her eyes and ruffled Mags' neck fur when the lovable dog rolled over on Moxie's bed to face her.

"From what I've gathered, Jett and one other guy are the only non-married ones in the squad. And technically speaking, Jett *is* still married."

"So, you're telling me there's a chance?" Vera did her best Lloyd Christmas impression. "Yeah!"

Moxie chuckled at her best friend. She always thought Vera was pretty—had a perfect face with clear skin and nice teeth. Most guys didn't have the confidence to date a tall, strong woman like Vera though. She seemed even larger when she and Moxie were together because Moxie was such a small human. At 5'10, Vera was more than six inches taller and while both women maintained an athletic physique, Vera was thicker due to her Samoan roots. Moxie wasn't sold that Jett's team had any viable options for her bestie, but she knew Vera would land the perfect man one day.

"I appreciate you guys doing all this today," Jett thanked the small group he had in his truck.

One of his teammates, Hot Rod as they called him, was the first to answer. "Are you kidding? Like I wanted to fucking go to a goddamn baby shower today. I don't give a fuck that it's for my sister. That shit's gay as hell."

Jett shot him a look since the sniper extraordinaire from their team, Frank, and his husband, Shane, were also in the truck.

"I take offense to that," Shane, sassed from the backseat. While

Frank looked like a compact-sized war hero, his husband, Shane, was lean, wore tight and fashionable clothing with his copper hair always perfectly placed, and he had a voice that rivaled any soprano. "Baby showers are a social parade brought on by *your* hetero-kind. Don't blame that tacky nonsense on our community."

Jett and Frank caught eyes in the rear view mirror. Listening to Hot Rod and Shane argue was always a treat.

Hot Rod's oversized frame took up as much space as possible in the passenger seat. He sprawled out with one of his large feet propped on Jett's brand new dashboard. Hot Rod's off-duty look could pass as a romance novel cover model. He kept his brunette hair perfectly barbered and maintained a muscular physique. He rolled his eyes at Shane's comments and turned to address him. "Oh, because it doesn't have that special fucking *Queer Eye* touch it's gotta be tacky? And you women are to blame for those whack-ass fuckin' parties anyway, not us real men."

Shane narrowed his eyes, lightly scratching a brow with a single fingernail. "It's tacky because if you're gonna have a kid, why are you expecting all your friends to pay to fill the nursery?" Shane shot back. "And don't get me started on the diaper raffles and demands to bring a book instead of a card—the actual *audacity!*"

"I'll assume you girls didn't do a wedding registry then when you fucking tied the knot?" Hot Rod smugly waited for a reply.

Shane looked at Frank, irritated to have to admit the most obnoxiously outspoken—yet somehow still tolerable—member of their squad had a valid point.

Hot Rod reached for Jett's shoulder and yanked it a few times. "Shoulda actually drug you along to that shower today. Aren't you gonna be attending a baby shower soon?"

"You are *such* a prick!" Frank sent a healthy jab to the front seat, connecting with Hot Rod's extended arm.

"What?" Hot Rod rubbed the spot of impact on the back of his bicep. "If I was in Jett's shoes I'd be crashing that fucking shower, no doubt about it."

"You're welcome to attend on my behalf." Jett shook his head, having zero interest in going and knowing full well he wouldn't be invited anyway.

Hot Rod quickly sat up tall in the passenger seat, changing the subject. "Bro, the Texican told me he saw you walking at the waterfront the other day—with your new 'roommate.'" He threw up air quotes just before slapping his buddy's chest with the back of his hand. "Besides not wanting to go to a damn baby shower, the fact that he said she's a straight dime had me wanting to come help your fuckin' ass move today. Shit, I might be making some other damn moves on top of helping you with your heavy-ass shit."

Jett turned, warning him with his eyes from under scrunched brows.

"So she's *not* just a roommate, huh?" Hot Rod whistled and smirked back at Frank. "Goddamn ink isn't even dry on those divorce papers yet and you're out here calling dibs and spelunking down into new cooch caves. Welcome to the club, brother."

"You're gonna be respectful of her or you're gonna get your ass kicked." Jett pulled into the parking lot of a furniture store. His tone was light, but he meant every word.

"Jett, my money'd be on you either way, but I'll pay extra for you to just go ahead and get that started on *everyone's* behalf—he's been needing it." Frank hopped out of the truck.

"In his *dreams* he'd come close to kicking my ass." Hot Rod rolled his eyes while unclipping his seatbelt.

"All you'd be doing *is* dreaming because your ass would be knocked the fuck out," Jett promised as he got out of the truck. "Why don't you go ahead and focus on treating her like you would a little sister so you can avoid that embarrassment."

"A little *step*-sister… via marriage," Hot Rod countered to keep the door open for his idea of panty-dropping pick-up lines if he felt the need.

They all laughed at the light-hearted argument and followed Jett into the store to pick up his new bed and a couch.

Jett backed his truck and trailer up to the garage when they got to the house.

"Mox grabbed everyone lunch, you guys wanna eat something before we get all this outta here?"

"Ooh, babygirl! I can already tell I'm gonna love her." Hot Rod rubbed his palms together. "I'll tell you what else besides lunch I might be eating from her."

"Quit being such a pig or *I'll* be kicking your ass," Shane warned.

Hot Rod pressed his shirt down and fixed his trucker hat securely on his head before they walked into the house from the garage.

"Goddamn." Hot Rod stopped dead in his tracks. "The Texican's been married too long or something, that's a fucking grizzly bear," he said under his breath.

Frank gave him a quick jab to the back of his bicep as Jett greeted the woman seated on a barstool scrolling through her phone. Hot Rod decided he'd jumped the gun on his judgement because the girl did have a beautiful face and great legs.

"Hey, V, you girls putting a dent in the unpacking up there?" Jett asked and set a few things on the kitchen counter.

"I'm sure you noticed how light she travels." Vera chuckled with a hard seltzer now in her hand. "But we've only got a couple totes left."

Jett smiled, gesturing towards his buddies. "These are a few of my guys. This is Frank, his husband, Shane, and the meathead back there is Hot Rod."

Hot Rod flipped him off.

"This is Mox's best friend, Vera." Jett rounded out the introductions.

"Nice to meet you." Shane was the first to approach her and offer his hand.

While they all exchanged pleasantries, Moxie and Mags made their way down the staircase. Moxie's tiny but strong frame was covered in athletic wear. She had on powder-blue yoga pants and a loose-fitting long-sleeve white crewneck. Her hair was spun up into a messy bun and Mags was less than a foot behind her as she reached the final step on the staircase that split the kitchen and living room.

Mags didn't waste any time, she rushed Jett the second she saw him.

"Hey, girl," Jett welcomed her when she jumped and her paws landed on his torso. "Thanks for lunch, Mox." He smiled at her as Mags still enjoyed a few scratches.

"Of course." She grinned.

"I noticed a couple big boxes in the garage, did they deliver the desk you ordered?" he asked.

"Yeah, I'll still need to assemble it."

"I'll move those upstairs after we eat. I can help put it together later too," he offered and sent Mags down so he could do more introductions. "This is—"

"Moxie, I presume," Hot Rod cut in and held out his hand. "I'm Rodney."

"Rodney?!" Jett and Frank simultaneously barked out while laughing at their obnoxious teammate.

"Since when have you *ever* gone by Rodney?!" Frank asked as Moxie politely shook Hot Rod's hand.

Hot Rod shot him a warning look.

"Rodney over here's working on his manners, but please feel free to call him Hot Rod like everyone else." Shane put out his hand next. "I'm Shane, and this is my handsome husband, Frank—he's in their little alphahole squad, not me," he informed her.

"It's really nice to meet you all. Thank you so much for helping today." Moxie finished shaking Frank's hand as well.

Hot Rod decided to test the waters. "I'm always down to help, you just call *me* if you ever need anything." He reached around Moxie's shoulders to give her a friendly hug and started to shake her.

Before Moxie was able to fully scrunch her face from the pain she felt in her still-healing ribs, Mags nudged Hot Rod away from her with a couple of light nips.

"Mags! What the hell?" Hot Rod chuckled but backed up as Mags continued to herd him another step away.

Jett looked at Moxie to see if she was okay and she tried to give him a subtle signal that it didn't need to be a big deal.

Everyone laughed at Hot Rod when he took several additional steps away from both Moxie and the bossy dog.

"Alright, alright!" Hot Rod conceded, holding both of his hands up like he was under arrest.

"Mags doesn't trust you, *Rodney*—can't imagine why not," Jett snickered and waited for the inevitable hand gesture from his buddy.

They all ate lunch and chatted before emptying Jett's truck and trailer. It didn't take long before they were joking as if all of them had been friends for years. Moxie bought more than enough so even after they'd finished moving everything in the house, they still had plenty of food. Jett and Hot Rod took off for a beer run so they could keep the party going.

Frank and Shane finally called it a night around one, but Hot Rod looked like he needed to stay because of his inebriated condition. The girls had already set up the futon in Moxie's office upstairs for Vera to stay the night.

Moxie tapped out around two and Vera agreed she was ready for bed as well. Jett encouraged Moxie to take Mags with her so they could have an all girl's slumber party upstairs. It didn't really hit her until she got to the top of the stairs how much she'd miss sleeping in the same room as Jett. They'd had living room sleepovers for weeks and tonight was the first night she wouldn't have the comfort of him just feet away from her.

"The fuck, dude?" Hot Rod was slunk into the couch but reached over and swatted Jett's chest with the back of his hand the second he heard doors shutting upstairs.

"What?" Jett finished another beer.

"What, my *ass*!?" He rolled his eyes. "I'm ashamed of you right now not tucking her in. She's fine as hell."

"Little sister," Jett firmly reminded Hot Rod he was supposed to be respectful as if Moxie was his little sister.

Hot Rod made a few jerking off motions before flashing an open hand at his buddy.

Jett flipped him off in response and suggested they go in the garage and play darts. They managed to play a few rounds before Jett was ready for bed. He set Hot Rod up on the couch, checked that all the doors to the house were locked, and then went to his room.

17

Mags perked her ears and let out a low rumbling growl startling Moxie awake. Mags paused when Moxie sat up and put her hand on the protective canine's back. Moxie heard a noise and couldn't place where it was coming from. It sounded like someone attempting to get through a door. She only hesitated for half a second, because it was almost four in the morning, before she texted Jett.

Jett's head shot up when he heard his phone. His eyes burned as he turned it over and saw Moxie's text.

Mox

Are you awake?

Are you okay?

He became more aware as he woke up, hearing a noise down the hall.

Mox

Mags is growling and I hear something.
It sounds like it's in the house.

Stay up there with Mags. Don't come
out of that room. I'm going to look.

He hastily got out of bed and pulled a pair of shorts over his
boxers before grabbing his Glock.

Mox
Please be careful.

Jett quietly opened his bedroom door with intent, the sound
immediately becoming clearer as he stealthily walked down the hall;
the rhythmic pounding came from the laundry room. Something
was slamming repeatedly into one of the machines and Jett didn't
remember anyone starting any laundry.

As he got closer, his muscles relaxed and he shook his head. Just
to confirm, he checked the living room and didn't see Hot Rod. He
had the displeasure of hearing a quick screech from what he assumed
was Vera, followed by the dirtiest invitation of where Hot Rod was
willing to stick himself next.

When he got back to his room he wasn't sure what to say to
Moxie. His face was red as he started the text several times before he
finally settled on one.

It's okay Mox, things are all good
in the house. You're safe.

Mox
Mags is still growling, was it outside?

Jett chuckled as his fingers scurried across the screen.

Uhhhhh, not really sure you
wanna know what I found.

Mox
That bad?? 😨 😨 Are you okay??

Aw shit this is embarrassing... Hot Rod
and V are doing laundry right now.

Jett watched the bubbles pop up and go away several times and he held his forehead, wondering how Moxie would react. He finally laid on his back with an arm over his head waiting for her reply.

Mox

I don't think I've ever heard that innuendo before. And I cannot express how embarrassed I am for waking you up now.

I only said that's what they're doing because that's where they are lol. I need bleach and a q-tip for my ears. I don't think you can be any more embarrassed than I am after what I heard Hot Rod saying in there.

Mox

I am SO SORRY Jett. I'll be making you a double batch of your own cookie dough tomorrow for waking you up to subject you to that.

I promise it's fine lol. I don't want you to ever feel like you can't come to me.

Honestly, I was more worried them doing laundry might be a problem. Is V too wasted for all that?

Mox

She was buzzed when she went to bed, but she's not at all going to wake up with buyer's remorse if that's what you're worried about lol - he's totally the type V would typically go for. She's also not going to be trapping your friend if you know what I mean. V is VERY outgoing in her bedroom, or I guess laundry room, offerings, but also super responsible. She's likely having a very nice time.

I just didn't want to be lying here as
a crime is being committed.

Mox

It's a crime they're in there violating the
laundry room like that lol 🙈🙉

You're telling me! I've obviously heard Hot
Rod's mouth in everyday talk but I never
imagined there was a level more shameful
than what he spews around us guys.

Mox

Oh for sure we don't have to worry about V
then. She's probably living her best life rn. Full
disclosure, she's enlightened me on a few of her
bedroom lines and I can assure you, the two of
them have met their match this evening. 🙈😷

Oh shit! LOL I'm glad I was
worried for nothing then.

Mox

I have to say I'm glad they're in there
instead of being on the couch… Or
across the hall from me rn.

I would kick his ass if he was on that
brand new couch. I don't know how or
where they started, but if they keep it in
the laundry room I'm fine with that.

Mox

I don't think I'd like to know those things either lol

Mags is still not pleased so I have to
believe they're still working on the
spin cycle or whatever the hell.

LOL! I can still faintly hear them unfortunately.

Mox

I'm even more grateful now that you sent her
up with me tonight. Your girl's growling is
protecting my ears from being assaulted too.

*Our girl 😌

Mox

OH GOD!

I just had the displeasure of hearing the end of
that load of laundry. I'll never recover from that. 😵

Mox

Noooooo I'm SO sorry 😭😭 I'm going to
TRIPLE your cookie dough batch now.

I want my own custom Moxie fuckin
Hall version of cowboy chocolate chip
cookie dough for what I just heard. That
was your friend's dirty mouth lol.

Mox

I will absolutely perfect that for you. 🤠🍪

Do you want me to send Mags down
too? Or do you prefer I get out of bed
and start on that recipe now? Lol

You girls are totally fine, I don't want
you sleeping up there alone.

Mox

Jett!! They're coming up here!!
Noooooooooooooooo!! 🙈🙈

Silver linings, we can go to therapy
together. I'll drive us lol.

Mox

Based on what I just heard from
YOUR foul mouthed friend, you'll
be picking out an apron to help
me with that cowboy cookie dough
tomorrow there, partner.

Jett's heart smiled at her text. He'd fallen hard for her and despite her only being upstairs, he missed Moxie.

You know I always have the best ideas,
wanna hear what I'm thinking now?

Mox

It surely can't be worse than what I'm currently
listening to, so of course I want to hear.

I miss our slumber parties already. You
should grab some pillows and blankets
and meet me in the living room asap.

Mox

On our way!!

Moxie scurried by the office where Vera and Hot Rod were holed up. She had a blanket wrapped around her and a pillow clutched to her chest. Mags only stopped at the office door for half a second before she followed Moxie down the stairs.

She partially covered her face when she walked into the living room and saw Jett turning on the TV. He hadn't bothered to put on a shirt and already had his spot—closest to the door, of course—claimed with a pillow and blanket.

"I figured we'd want some noise to mask your dirty friend's mouth up there."

"*My* dirty-mouthed friend?" Moxie giggled and sat down on the other end of the sectional. "You want me to repeat the care instructions I just heard from *your* foul-mouthed laundry room friend?"

Jett laughed, not the least bit interested to know what Hot Rod was spewing up there, but then his mouth curled and he called her on her offer. "Actually, yeah. I'd love to know what you just heard."

Moxie threw her head back while her face brightened to a red that would rival any strawberry. When she finally had the courage to look at Jett again she shook her head, hiding her smirk behind her blanket.

She was, thankfully, saved by Mags who decided to walk the length of the couch between Moxie and Jett to find a cozy spot next to her dad. She tried not to stare while Jett settled into his spot, welcoming Mags to share his pillow and blanket. The blanket only draped around his lower half, leaving his entire chest exposed—a sight Moxie didn't mind at all. Rather than staring, Moxie took a quiet breath and left her head resting on a pillow, avoiding any eye contact as she shared a sincere thought with her handsome roommate.

"Jett, I really appreciate you getting us all set up here... I haven't felt this safe or good about a place I've lived in a long time." She kept her eyes on the TV as she continued, "and thank you for waking up to my text tonight—even though it wasn't an actual emergency."

"You're welcome, Mox." Jett shifted his eyes to her to see if she'd look at him, but she stayed on her side watching the TV. "You'll always be safe with me."

They didn't talk anymore, they let silence take over until sleep found them both.

Jett was in the kitchen the next morning when he heard someone walking down the stairs—it was Vera. He offered a friendly wave before opening the refrigerator for some juice. Vera made her way to the living room where she found Moxie and Mags cuddled on the chaise portion of the sectional.

"I was looking for you, I didn't know you already came down. Early riser these days, huh?" Vera sat right next to her friend and pulled the blanket over to share. It didn't take her long before she put her arms around Moxie, trying to peck her cheek.

Jett walked back to his spot on the oversized couch as Moxie squirmed away from Vera.

"You better get your Scandinavian-slug exploring lips away from me *right* now!" She giggled. "You need soap for that naughty mouth of yours out on the prowl ropin'—what did you say…? Oh, whi—"

"Babe! What the hell?!" Vera covered Moxie's mouth to stop her from saying anything else and made a not so subtle gesture with her appalled eyes towards Jett.

He tried to hide behind his cup of orange juice as he propped up his feet on the coffee table, thoroughly enjoying Moxie teasing her best friend.

"I'm sure he heard you hoeing around your naughty little laundromat, no need to be embarrassed now." She tried to hide behind Mags who playfully mouthed at Vera's hands for messing with Moxie.

"Well, if it isn't the wielder of the legendary agitator, master general of the front loading spin cycle," Jett snickered when Hot Rod hit the bottom step of the staircase.

Hot Rod hadn't bothered with a shirt *or* pants and now stood in the living room donning a pair of bikini briefs.

Moxie covered her face and tried to stop giggling at the sight but was soon in a full-on belly laugh that was worth the pain. She buried her face into Mags' neck to try to stop.

"You have a nice sleep out on the couch last night?" Jett had a shit-eating grin on his face.

His buddy flipped him off and headed to the kitchen to grab a slice of cold pizza.

"Girl panties, girl panties, girl panties," Moxie quietly squealed between her giggling.

Vera pertly shoved the blanket over her best friend's head and peeled herself off the couch. "Babe, you're a bitch. I'm gonna go shower." She couldn't wipe the embarrassment from her face and refused to look back at Jett as she quickly jogged up the stairs.

Moxie finally uncovered her giddy face to peek at Jett, who shot a quick wink at her before his focus fell on the staircase again where Hot Rod hustled to follow Vera.

"Where *you* goin'?" Jett smirked.

"The fucking shower," Hot Rod proclaimed as if Jett didn't already know.

They heard the bathroom door shut upstairs, Moxie threw the blanket off her head completely and slapped her palms to her face.

"Grooossss," she sang out in disgust. "I just bought that loofa in there. I'm gonna have to scrub that shower again… and all the countertops, knowing V."

Jett set his juice on the coffee table, laughing. "You can feel free to use mine if it's that bad."

"I'm telling you right now, if he leaves those big-girl panties any-where up there I'm taking a match to this entire house."

Jett practically shouted out his laugh.

"I'm serious, I don't even know where those came from." Moxie shook her head. "That's not usually V's style, and they're *certainly* not mine."

Once Jett was able to collect enough of himself to continue, he had to enlighten Moxie on the unfortunate truth. "Oh, Mox"—he gave his face a full wipe—"I hate to inform you, but those are Hot Rod's."

"What?!" She whipped her head towards him, chuckling in dis-belief. "But they're—"

"Magenta and silk?" Jett interrupted as her amusement contin-ued. "I have, unfortunately, seen him in his mankini more times than anyone should be subjected to it."

"I'll *never* let V hear the end of this." She shook her head and gave Mags a few good rubs. "I never would've guessed. Seeing them now, it totally makes sense, but I surely wouldn't have pegged him for a granny panty kind of guy."

Jett grinned, but he didn't disagree. Lucky for her, Hot Rod didn't have the assless thong version Jett had *also* had the displeasure of witnessing.

"Believe it or not, there *is* a silver lining for me in all this. My friend, V, doesn't get to assault me with *any* of their stories since I had to see that. I'm honestly ashamed of her right now, she should've slammed on the brakes the *second* he showed those big girl panties to her." Moxie caught sight of Jett's perfect smile she'd been falling for and continued to make it last, "Those aren't Cerberus-issued, are they?"

She realized what she'd insinuated too late. Embarrassment flooding her cheeks, she leaned in to kiss Mags to hide her face.

Definitely entertained with what he considered flirting, Jett put his hands behind his head, interlocking his fingers and leaning into the couch. "*I* don't wear big-girl panties if that's what you're asking." Jett smirked.

Moxie took what she hoped to be a quick breath to try and suppress the pink in her cheeks and quickly got up to make coffee.

Jett couldn't help but watch her every step of the way, there wasn't any coming back from how hard he'd fallen for her. He physically wiped the enamored smile when Mags lifted her head and gave him a knowing look before her body wiggled off the couch to follow Moxie to the kitchen. His heart fluttered after his girls, thinking about how much he'd like to get used to mornings like this.

18

Jett drove him and Moxie to meet up with Frank and Shane at a local Mexican restaurant later that week. He'd been back at work but the squad hadn't caught an assignment yet, so they'd been reporting to command and training instead. Shane had really enjoyed Moxie when they were over helping set up the house so he urged Frank to coordinate a dinner for the four of them sooner than later. He also requested Hot Rod be left off that invite list because he'd be a distraction from 'enjoyable adult conversation.' Hot Rod had been quite occupied as of late anyway since he and Vera had started a friends-with-benefits situation.

Their first round had just been served when Shane turned his focus to Moxie and her career.

"What's the sitch on your numbers hustle, little Mox? Do you mainly work during tax season?"

Moxie grinned while swallowing a sip of her mango chamoy margarita. "Tax season is definitely my busy time of year," she disclosed. "But I work steadily all year. My clients don't all operate on the same fiscal year and they've all got different needs, so my schedule is a rollercoaster depending on what they've got going on."

"Wait, I thought you did taxes? How do people get away with filing at different times?" he asked.

Moxie wasn't a stranger to people asking about her independent CPA gig, and she also didn't mind this line of questioning. "I mean, I can and will do taxes, but that's not all I do. Lots of times when someone has just a tax person, they have an accountant. Technically speaking, I'm a certified public accountant, so I can do a bit more than just taxes. Most of what I do is financial planning and consulting for businesses, but I have a handful of clients who I consult for on a personal level too." She shrugged and reached for a tortilla chip.

Jett's eyes softened watching Moxie and he fought the corners of his mouth from rising. "I'm embarrassed to admit I thought you were like a human version of TurboTax," he disclosed with a chuckle.

The table laughed along with him while Moxie shook her head. "It's really okay, I get that all the time."

"So, damn, financial planning and consulting, huh? You must make a pretty penny," Frank commented with widened eyes.

Shane nudged his husband to let him know it was a rude statement to make. "You don't have to respond to that," Shane told her and shot Frank a disappointing look from under his perfectly maintained brows.

"It's okay," she assured him. "I'm able to make adult money to thrive now and be able to retire nicely later." Her smile was friendly and let him know that's all she'd be sharing at the table for now.

Jett leaned back on one of the bar height chairs they each sat in with his forearm casually placed on the back of the chair next to him—Moxie's chair. She sat on the edge of her seat with perfect posture, so they weren't touching one another, but the position of Jett's body was welcome and comfortable.

Frank's elbows hit the table, leaning in to divert the conversation from his rude question when an unexpected and unwanted visitor approached the table next to Jett.

"Wow, Jett—didn't expect to see all this," Julia sneered as she gestured towards Moxie before her hand landed on her hip. "Did it hurt falling off your damn high horse? Because it seems to me, perhaps you have some explaining to do. I can't believe you've been acting like Hallie's the only one who messed up."

Jett cracked a sardonic smile, nodding at his least favorite family member. "Julia. As always, what a pleasure." He didn't remove his arm from Moxie's chair and barely looked at his cousin-in-law.

"Your *wife* has been looking for you. I figured I'd let you know since all you do is ignore her these days. In fact, she just texted me about five minutes ago asking if you've even bothered talking to Trevor lately." She glared in Moxie's direction. "I'll have to let them know you've been preoccupied."

"Not sure why she's looking for me. Does she need a pen or something? My lawyer tells me she still hasn't returned signed divorce papers. He's sent her three copies now—she only needs to sign one."

"You're being completely unreasonable about all this," Julia snapped.

"Actually"—he took a sip of his beer before finally looking at Julia—"I was quite generous in the divorce settlement. She's getting a helluva lot more than she could ever dream of deserving after the shit she pulled—and that's only because I just want it done. If she's got ideas on other terms, she knows she can contact my attorney, that's what he's there for."

Julia cut him with her eyes as she seethed. She crossed her arms and snarled at Moxie. "You *do* know he's married, right? Or does that not make a difference to you?"

"Julia," Jett warned with an icy and threatening tone. He pulled his arm away from Moxie's chair as he sat up taller, challenging Julia to say another cruel word.

"Thank you for honoring girl code," Moxie politely responded but stayed seated, seemingly unphased while trying to maintain a lock on Julia's eyes. The blonde woman had a slender figure and grown-out roots on her shoulder-length hairstyle. Her nose was long and Moxie watched the hint of green in her eyes pick her apart.

Julia sized up this new lady, running her tongue along her top teeth with her lips closed. "Picking them a bit young, I see. Is this one even old enough to be in the bar?"

Jett glared. "Don't get jealous—that's just as ugly on you as every-thing else you wear."

"Fuck you, Jett." Julia held her French-tipped finger in front of his face.

"Excuse me for saying this," Moxie started in an even tone, "but this seems like a highly inappropriate conversation while you're on the clock. If you could please just put in another drink order for the table we'd really appreciate it."

Shane choked on the sip he just took and the corner of Jett's lip lifted into a smirk that he certainly wasn't going to wipe from his face.

"I don't fucking work here!" Julia spat. She shoved a menu across the table onto Jett's lap before she sneered at him. "Call your *wife* back, Jett." She stormed away from the table, returning to the dining area she came from.

Jett picked up the menu from his lap, chuckling when he looked at Moxie. "I'm sorry, Mox. That's my cousin's wife, who also happens to be Hallie's best friend. As you can tell, she's a real treat. And for the record, thank you. That was a damn delight watching her face when you suggested she works here."

Shane squealed. "Girl! That drab black button-down *did* scream hostess." He leaned across the table with his hand out.

Moxie blushed but high-fived him and looked up at Jett. She didn't vocalize anything, she just smiled with her eyes.

The server arrived and stood at the end of their table. "Looks like your food is just about ready, can I get another round of drinks for you all?"

"Yes, please," Jett answered for everyone. "We'll also take two shots of tequila, a reposado—no well options please." He looked up at Frank and Shane. "You guys in?"

They both agreed.

"Make that four shots, please."

The server nodded quickly before he left the table.

"Sure, I'll have a shot of tequila." Moxie giggled.

"I knew you'd love one." Jett's hand reached up and rubbed her between her shoulder blades for the slightest moment before he pulled his hand back and set his forearms on the table in front of him, clearing his throat.

Frank watched the exchange and respected Jett's unspoken request not to say anything. He'd watched his teammate transform since training ended. When he caught wind of what Jett had come home to, he—and the rest of the team—assumed Jett would morph into an even deadlier version of his already elite warrior status. To their surprise, Jett seemed to be a lighter version of himself. Frank felt more chemistry between Jett sitting next to his roommate in a crowded bar than he'd ever witnessed the handful of times he saw Jett with his wife. It wasn't his business to pry, but he was hopeful that something would develop between them beyond their unconventional housing situation.

19

 Mr. Roman answered the phone.

"Mr. Roman, I've got a favor to ask."

"Everything alright?"

"Look, I'm not trying to stick my nose in anyone's business, that's not what I'm doin', but I was hopin' you and your family could help me out a bit." Jett waited to see if Mr. Roman would blow a gasket for even bringing this up. When he felt enough time had gone by, Jett continued, "It's about Mox."

"Is she okay?" Mr. Roman asked with an edge of concern.

Jett blew out a terse sigh, thinking about her ex who'd be getting his. "She's had some shit go on and I'm not in a position to share the details—that needs to happen on her terms. I just got called in for a work assignment and I'm not gonna be around for a few days…"

Jett rubbed the back of his neck. It wasn't like he and Moxie were dating. Unconventionally living together? Sure. Was he attracted to her? Absolutely. But now that he had Mr. Roman on the phone, he didn't know how to appropriately explain the situation. "I've been looking out for her since we met, but I'd feel a hell of a lot more comfortable knowing she's gonna be safe while I'm away."

Mr. Roman realized Jett knew about his ties and unscrupulous activities beyond the facade of his law practice.

Jett added, "I get the feeling you've got a soft spot for her and I know she hasn't shared this particular fear of hers with you. So, I'm asking if you'll help me out by very discreetly watching out for her for a few days until I get back. I plan to take care of this issue for her, but I haven't been able to get all the information I need quite yet. I'm more than happy to pay or owe a favor."

"Mox is like a daughter to me—consider it handled."

Relief blew over Jett with that confirmation. "Thank you. I'm gonna be in and out of reach while I'm gone, but please contact me if anything comes up."

"You've got my word," Mr. Roman promised. "Do we have a name or description for this fear of hers?"

Jett loved it when he found people who were able to communicate on his wavelength. Both he and Mr. Roman had quite a few similarities.

"If I did, the fear would've been a distant memory by now. I haven't been able to track it down yet. For the record, if you find out before I do, I fully expect an invitation to that party before it ends."

"Again, you have my word."

"Thank you, Mr. Roman. I leave in about four hours and I should be back within the week, but I'll let you know when I do."

"Of course."

Jett hung up and shoved his phone in his pocket. He'd taken Mags for a walk before packing for his mission. As they rounded the block to the house he felt slightly better having Mr. Roman watching over Moxie. He tried to subtly bring up the ex topic again just that morning after she'd agreed to drop him off at command so his truck could stay parked in front of their house while he was away. Their conversation was interrupted by a work call she had to take, so he'd have to try again another time. It didn't sit well with him—he *needed* that guy gone for good.

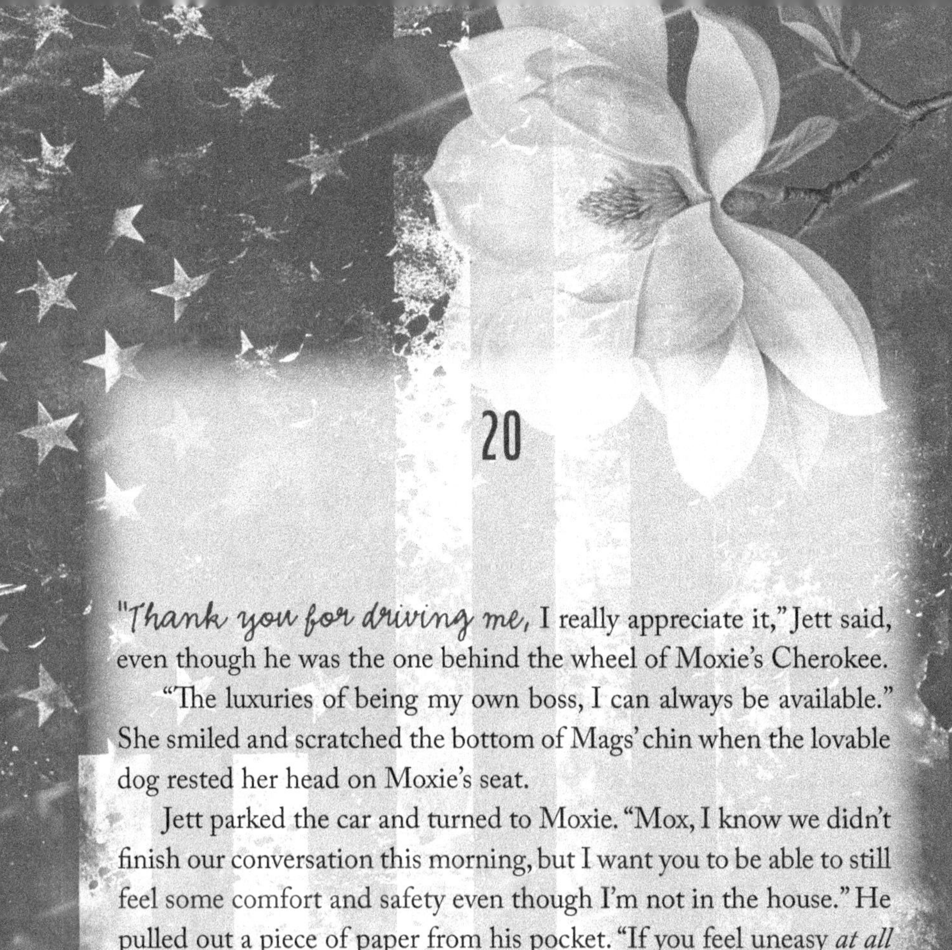

20

"*Thank you for driving me,* I really appreciate it," Jett said, even though he was the one behind the wheel of Moxie's Cherokee.

"The luxuries of being my own boss, I can always be available." She smiled and scratched the bottom of Mags' chin when the lovable dog rested her head on Moxie's seat.

Jett parked the car and turned to Moxie. "Mox, I know we didn't finish our conversation this morning, but I want you to be able to still feel some comfort and safety even though I'm not in the house." He pulled out a piece of paper from his pocket. "If you feel uneasy *at all* and need someone to get to you immediately, you call this number, okay?" He passed the phone number Mr. Roman had given him. They hadn't told Moxie about their discreet protection detail. He waited until she met his gaze. "You can call anytime and someone will be at the house within minutes, okay?"

"I really appreciate this, Jett—thank you." She accepted the paper.

"You're welcome," he replied with genuine sincerity cast upon his handsome face.

It took her a minute longer to get out of the car after Jett opened his door. He was in the cargo area grabbing his things when Moxie let Mags out of the back door. Jett had his bags and turned around to open his arms for his leaping dog.

"You be a good girl, Mags." He held the canine in his arms as she wagged her tail and licked his face. "Take care of Mox," he whispered to her before setting her down.

Mags danced around Jett's legs for a few rotations before he knelt down and gave her a few more healthy pats. He didn't love the idea of leaving her again so soon, but leaving her in Moxie's hands settled any reservations he had. "I'll be back, girl." He kissed the side of her face before standing.

Moxie held the back door open for Mags when she was done saying bye.

Jett took a couple of steps towards Moxie until he was close enough to reach her. He watched his gentle hold on her dainty wrist and spoke softly, "Mox, I'll see you in a few days, okay?"

With her eyes pointed down, she nodded. "Please be careful out there." She fought a lump in her throat, not realizing exactly how much she'd miss him now that he was leaving. She'd felt they were becoming closer, but she was hesitant given he—technically speaking—was still married.

He softly squeezed her wrist, sliding his thumb over her palm before letting go. "I always try." His adoring gaze lingered. He wanted to hug her at the very least, but he'd already promised himself to take a mindfully cautious pace with her. He took a deep breath, forcing his legs to turn away from her to head toward command.

Moxie only let him get a couple steps away before courage surged from her heart and she called out, "Jett?"

He whipped his head around and watched her large, beautiful blue eyes lift to meet his.

"I'll miss you," she said in her sweet voice, with sincerity shining from her face.

He didn't hesitate, hastily walking back towards Moxie to completely consume her within his embrace. Jett rubbed his hands up and down her back, holding firmly with each pass. His lips grazed across the top of her head as he leaned down to her ear.

"I'm gonna miss you like crazy, Doll," he confessed.

His statement made Moxie smile and she squeezed him a little tighter at the sentiment. She didn't want to let go, his embrace felt like the peace and the home she'd been waiting for.

One of Jett's hands left her back and caressed the side of her head before it slowly glided around to hold up her chin so they could gaze into each other's eyes.

He'd vowed to keep her at arm's length until she showed him clear interest or his divorce went through, but when Moxie returned his stare with the same intense surety and fondness of his own he knew they were on the same page. Jett closed his eyes as he leaned in, pressing their lips together for the very first time. It felt natural, as if their mouths had met an infinite number of times already—like coming home. He wasn't sure if she meant to, but he felt her gently tug on the fabric of his hoodie in the slightest touch; so he readjusted the placement of their lips to give her another tender kiss. They sank deeper into the exchange, feeling the uncertainty of their complicated start finally and completely melt away.

Moxie's smirk was smitten and she tried suppressing it by capturing her plump bottom lip under her teeth when their mouths finally separated. "I always thought it would feel wrong to kiss a married man." Her thumbs made short passes on Jett's lower back as her arms clung lovingly around his waist.

Jett matched her smile. "I'm only married on paper." He gently swept her hair behind her shoulder. "My heart does belong to two girls, but they're both right here with me."

Moxie blushed and her chin started to drop before Jett caught it and gave her one last parting kiss.

"Bye, Mox." Jett grinned, feeling like he just made it to the top of the world.

"Bye, Jett," she replied, unable to conceal her smile. She watched him walk into work as her mind and heart fluttered—she was in love. Moxie wouldn't deny it, Jett made her feel a way no one else had and she knew it wasn't just a crush. This was about to be the longest four days of her life.

The team had left their briefing and were now assembling all their gear in the squad room to prepare for departure. The assignment seemed straightforward enough. Why it would take four days baffled a couple of them—it was a standard rescue mission for some foreign diplomat caught up in a political dispute he had nothing to do with.

Hot Rod, as the team's self-appointed DJ, blared music and sang along to hype himself up. Today he had on a particularly rage-filled heavy metal mix that no one else enjoyed.

"You get any yet?" Hot Rod asked as he tossed extra magazines in his pack once he finished his air guitar solo.

Jett didn't respond, he was mindfully organizing his tactical bag.

"Better not be talking about your little sister he's already warned you about," Frank chimed in.

"Is that what we're going with instead of *roommate* these days?" The Texican laughed.

"You're all gonna have your asses kicked in a second," Frank delightfully informed them as Jett stayed silent with a smirk on his face.

Jett's heart still soared from the sensation of Moxie's body and lips connecting with his. It was enough for him to go completely mad having to wait four days to see her again. He had half a mind to ask her if she'd left the parking lot yet just to sneak in another parting kiss and see her gorgeous face. His enamored thoughts were interrupted when Hot Rod opened his philandering and offensive mouth.

"If she's anything like her freak of a friend, you're in for something you may not be able to handle," Hot Rod warned, bobbing his head along to the music. "She did this one thing the other night that I've nev—"

Jett put up his hand, palm facing his teammate. "I already got an earful of what you two are doing. Please don't add to that—I'm still recovering."

"Oh shit!" Hot Rod chuckled, zipping his bag while still rocking his head along. "Don't tell me your *roommate* is mad I'm givin' it to her friend? All she had to do was let me know she was jealous and wanted a ride." He held his arms out wide, shrugging. "I'm sure that little fox bounces *real* nice."

Jett gave Hot Rod a healthy jab. "I've told you not to say that shit about her."

Frank shot Hot Rod a warning look. "No one's coming to your aid when you finally piss him off."

"And no, she—not surprisingly—isn't interested in you at all. I'm damn positive you turned her all the way off when she saw you wear *big-girl* panties."

The guys all belted out laughter while Hot Rod flipped Jett off. He retracted his finger immediately to sock the Texican who'd slapped him with a hand towel.

Jett continued picking on the squad's biggest horndog. "I can't believe you pull as many women as you do. Those damn underwear and your fuckin' pillow talk?"

Hot Rod shrugged before slapping Jett's shoulder. "My style doesn't make sense to you since your unhappily married ass has been living a sexless or at the very least *vanilla* sex life for far too long."

Jett rolled his eyes. "Your style doesn't make sense to me because you refer to orifices in a way I wouldn't even know what species you were fuckin' with if I didn't know you were with V the other night."

Hot Rod howled and smugly owned every bit of his behavior, completely unashamed. "I didn't know Grizzly Bear was gonna be such a good time; that girl knows what the fuck she's doing and she's just as depraved as I am," he happily confessed.

"That's rude as shit to call her that, please don't ever say that in front of Mox." Jett zipped his bag.

"Alright, fellas," Cappy interrupted their conversation. "I know it's a change from two seconds ago, but we're actually gonna go dark on this one. No cell phones, tablets, watches or otherwise. You've got ten minutes to shore all that up with home. Satellite number's on the board as always." He looked pointedly at Hot Rod. "And it's not for sexcapades with any grizzlies." He made sure the rest of the group was paying attention. "Emergencies only."

The guys all snickered at Hot Rod before pulling out their phones to update their families.

Jett didn't love this situation, as if he wasn't already struggling with the thought of not seeing Moxie for four straight days. It was the first time he'd be leaving her on her own since they'd met, and now they wouldn't have a way to at least check in privately. Not to mention he wanted a clear line to Mr. Roman. He sucked in an irritated breath and headed out of the squad room while his fingers flew as quickly as possible across his screen to text Mr. Roman this less-than-ideal update. Mr. Roman responded immediately, confirming he had everything more than handled. Jett found a more private area and dialed Moxie.

He could hear the smile in her voice when she picked up the call. "Please tell me it's been four days and you're calling for me to come get you."

Jett leaned against a wall and let his head fall back. His heart tugged at her greeting. "I *wish*," he chuckled his response.

"Is everything okay? Did you forget something?" Moxie asked.

"Maybe I just wanted to hear your beautiful voice." Jett smirked. She giggled. "Oh, yeah?"

"Okay, I'll admit, that was just one reason—the top reason though."

"I'm gonna be in trouble not being able to see you for four days," Moxie playfully confessed.

Jett's heart squeezed, he knew the update he was about to deliver wouldn't make this first time apart any easier on either of them. "Now I'm *really* damn upset I have to let you know what we just learned in the briefing…" He took a breath, exhaling his response, "We won't have our phones or anything on us for this one. They're all getting left right here at command. This happens sometimes, but not always. I'm sorry, Mox."

"You don't have to be sorry." She didn't let her tone express her disappointment. "I understand."

"I'm gonna text you with the satellite number in case you have an emergency, okay?"

"Jett, you don't have to do that."

"But, Doll, I'm going to. I don't want you to feel like you can't get a hold of me. And you're out of your mind if you don't think I haven't already burned your number into my brain. If I have a chance to call you, bet your ass I'll be doing that."

His statement made her smile. "You call anytime, Dr. Brody."

Jett shot out a laugh. "I never knew I'd like being called by another man's name."

"Jett!" the Texican shouted from down the hall. "We're rollin' out, brother!"

Jett confirmed with a nod and stood up straight from leaning on the wall. "Unfortunately, I do have to go. I'll be missing you like crazy."

"I'm already out of my mind mad about missing you," she unapologetically admitted. "Please be careful, Jett."

"As best I can, Doll. See you in a few days."

"Okay… Bye."

It took Jett longer than usual to end the call, he could've spent another ten hours just listening to her sweet voice.

21

"*Hey, foxy Moxie,*" Mr. Roman greeted on the phone later that week.

"Hi, Mr. Roman, how are you?" she cheerfully asked.

"Livin' the dream," he replied. "How's my favorite little gal doin'?"

"Oh, just peachy." She chuckled. "But also a little embarrassed, did I forget to call you for a meeting this morning?"

"I can't just call you?!" The man laughed. "Damn, I thought we had more than a client thing."

Moxie blushed and giggled back. "Of course we do! You know you're a forever favorite human of mine, Mr. Roman. And I *am* happy that you called, I've just been a little off the last day or so, so I wanted to be sure I didn't drop the ball."

"Everything alright?" Mr. Roman asked with concern rippling through his voice. They'd been watching the house, and aside from Trevor rolling by to check things out, everything had been quiet.

"I'm doing okay," she confirmed. There was no part of her that wanted to admit to Mr. Roman what a baby she was, lonely from not seeing Jett for over twenty four hours since meeting him. She would for sure sound insane. "Just out enjoying a little stroll with Mags." Moxie reached down and ruffled the top of the pretty girl's head.

"Well, I was actually calling to see if you have plans this evening?"

Mr. Roman promised Jett he'd keep an eye on her, and it wasn't unusual for her to have dinner with him and his family on occasion.

"I'm working for a bit this afternoon and then after that I'm pretty free for shenanigans."

A smile crawled across Mr. Roman's face. "Well, Ms. Estelle is preparing quite the spread for the evening and she asked me to call and see if you'd like to join us. It's just the kiddos, minus Sal anyway, and then a few other favorites of ours, so of course we need you here."

"I'd love to join! What can I bring?" She smiled.

"Just yourself, and if Mags would like to come along you're more than welcome to bring that lovely lady too."

"Thank you, she's always down to hang with the cool kids."

"Great, we'll see you around six."

"Can't wait, have a good one."

Moxie put her phone in her pocket and regarded the trail ahead of them. Having dinner with Mr. Roman's family was a very welcome distraction. She'd already planned to have lunch with Shane the following day, but this would get her through the long night. She hadn't slept much the last two nights. It was more difficult than she realized to sleep in the house without Jett there. His presence had been so comforting, and since they'd shared a parting kiss, she couldn't stop thinking about him. She tried her best not to dwell on what he could be doing—his job sounded terrifying. That unknown alone unraveled endless worries that made her stomach turn.

Mags perked her ears at a pair of seagulls who flew a little too close to them before landing in the water. Moxie snapped a picture of her with a gorgeous view of the sound beyond her. She smiled at the picture and decided to send it to Jett. She felt a little silly knowing he wouldn't even see it until he was home, but she was thinking of him, wishing he was there with them, so she sent it anyway. Her heart swelled staring at the text thread and before she could stop herself she dialed his number. She'd never heard his voicemail before, but was endlessly grateful to hear his voice. She hung up mid-beep before leaving a message and shamelessly called again just to hear his recorded greeting. This time, however, she did leave him a message.

After dinner that evening, everyone was out on the covered patio near the pool enjoying the wine that Moxie brought. Mags kept herself in close proximity to Moxie the entire night, but the loyal beauty took a break to explore Mr. Roman's expansive yard.

"So, how's the new place?" Mr. Roman lit his second cigar of the night.

Moxie fondly nodded a few times. "Pretty perfect actually. It's wild how the universe works," she admitted with a grin.

"Oh, sweetie, Tex told me he's good buddies with your new roommate," Ms. Estelle chimed in, pouring more wine into Moxie's glass just before filling her daughter's.

"Yeah, that was crazy to find out too!" She giggled. "Jett's been a really great guy, I'm just sorry he had to meet you the way he did." She grimaced at Mr. Roman.

"Yeah, what a psychotic piece of work that ex of his is." Mr. Roman shook his head. "I didn't tell Cerberus—because I'm not worried about it at all, and the last thing that man needs is another reason to hate that bottom-dweller—but she had her lawyer contact me about updating the terms of their divorce. You'll *never* guess what shit she tried to pull."

Moxie shook her head, unsure about knowing this information when Jett wasn't even made aware.

"She wanted to take Mags back or negotiate a larger chunk from the sale of the house."

Moxie's eyes widened and she looked across the yard at her dog who seemed to be on a scent trail.

"I dropped her cut of the house by ten percent for even asking. She's already getting more than I would've allowed, which is nothing. She and her lawyer are idiots too. Cerberus is—legally speaking— not Mags' owner. She couldn't have won her back even if she actually wanted her."

"Thank you for that. I told Jett you're an assassin in the divorce realm. I'm glad you're validating my claims."

Mr. Roman dipped his chin, smiling before Moxie continued, "Losing Mags isn't an option for either one of us… Which is why we've found ourselves in this very interesting position."

Mr. Roman couldn't help himself. He'd already seen a glimmer of it with Jett and now watching Moxie suppress her smile, he knew both of them were lying to themselves projecting this arrangement as *solely* for their love for the German Shepherd. There was clearly attraction from both sides.

"That's the only reason, huh?" Mr. Roman flashed a knowing smirk.

Moxie sipped her wine glass, hiding her playful expression and immediately felt Bianca, Mr. Roman's daughter, grab her arm, shaking it while Ms. Estelle gushed.

"Tex told us *allll* about Mr. All-American Hero, Jett Sharpe. Said he's a pretty good lookin' guy too." Ms. Estelle pumped her eyebrows.

"He's married," Moxie bashfully and quickly replied.

"Not for long," Mr. Roman reminded her.

The family decided to give the embarrassed Moxie a break and let up on the topic of Jett. Butterflies swirled in her stomach just thinking about him. While she'd hoped tonight would be a distraction from Jett's absence, her mind ended up being consumed with him—and she loved it.

22

Jett turned on his phone after four long days without any communication with Moxie. He'd wanted to call her while he was away—multiple times. He thought about her practically every second since their lips met. He worried when his phone finally lit up and he saw there were multiple voicemails from Moxie. He immediately played the first one. His face lightened and heart fluttered when it was just her sweet voice calling to check in. She had left a couple voicemails and sent him a plethora of Mags themed pictures. It was just after two in the afternoon so he decided to call her. She was ecstatic to hear that he'd made it back safely and couldn't agree quickly enough to pick him up in an hour. Before Jett unpacked his bags and showered, he continued checking the rest of the messages on his phone.

MR. ROMAN

I know you won't get this for a couple days, but wanted you to have it. You know this gentleman?

Mr. Roman sent along a picture of Trevor sitting in his car down the street, but within view of Jett's new house.

A second text followed up the picture timestamped a few hours later when Mr. Roman had discovered who'd been suspiciously sitting in front of the house.

> Disregard, just discovered he's your cousin.
> We're still keeping tabs on Mox, but that man
> stopped in front of your house a handful of times
> today. Seemed to be watching your house in
> particular. Didn't approach it at all though.

A day later, Jett had received another related text.

> Just updating, your cousin Trevor was at the
> house again today. Mox came out when he
> was there, but there was no interaction. We
> had her over for dinner tonight and it doesn't
> seem like she's noticed anything off around
> the house. Still watching and all's well. We
> won't hesitate to pick him up if anything looks
> more off than him sitting down the street.

> I just got back into town. I can't thank you
> enough for watching out for Mox. I'll have
> a chat with Trevor, he and I aren't exactly
> on great terms right now with the divorce.
> I don't know why he's around or how he
> found my place but that pisses me off.

MR. ROMAN
Not a problem at all Cerberus. You just
let me know anytime we can help out
with Mox, more than happy to.

> Will do. Thank you again.

Jett noticed another dozen missed calls and thirty-four text messages from his mom, Trevor, Julia, and Hallie. He knew all of them except his mom's calls would be some dramatic bullshit surrounding the divorce, so he left those on read. He did click into

Trevor's texts given he'd been seen loitering around his house while he was away.

Jett didn't have a lot of interest in speaking to Trevor. He planned to let him know he could stay away from him, his house, and Moxie when he saw him next, but he didn't want to do that now. All he wanted was to shower and see his girls—he didn't want to be in a pissy mood for that reunion. He'd been anticipating the feeling of her in his arms, her lips on his, since they last saw each other. Hearing her voice just ten minutes earlier had him even more excited to see her.

Mags rushed Jett the moment she sensed him. As she'd always done, she took a flying leap of faith just before reaching him. Jett caught her midair and quickly put the dog in a cradle hold while she licked his face. Once he set her down, he looked a few yards ahead of them where Moxie stood, clinging to the back passenger door she'd opened for Mags. She looked as perfect as she did when he last saw her four days ago. Her charmed smirk made Jett's heart stutter and his pace quicken knowing that glow was for him.

Moxie threw her arms around Jett's shoulders the second he was close enough, hiding her smile in his chest while breathing in his freshly showered scent. Jett held firmly to her waist, momentarily lifting her tiny frame from the ground to peck her temple. Relief flowed through both of them that Jett was safely back home and neither of them had simply dreamed up or regretted the affectionate farewell four days earlier.

Jett took a deep inhale as he held her. "I knew I didn't need confirmation, but that trip did me in." One of his hands brushed through her hair.

Moxie gazed up and waited for him to explain.

"You're definitely the missing damn puzzle piece to my happiness, Doll. We met for Mags *and* for this." He placed one of her small hands on his sturdy chest, right over his heart.

Moxie watched her hand as it rose and fell with every breath he took and couldn't fight the smile that was etched on her face.

"I sure wasn't a fan of being away from you, Dr. Brody. Your girls've *been* ready for you to come back home."

"Let me take my girls home then." Jett's index finger reached down to hook her chin and he placed his lips firmly against hers. His hands glided down her back, landing at her waist as he pulled her in even closer. Their kiss didn't last long after readjusting their lips because Moxie couldn't help but giggle. Jett chased her down for one more peck before he walked her to the passenger side of the Cherokee.

"You don't want me to drive? Aren't you tired?" Moxie asked when Jett opened the door and gestured for her to get in.

"You're the Passenger Princess, not me." He laughed. "I love your attempts at the independent and caregiver roles, but you're not doing those things for me—that's my job, my honor." He shot her a crooked smile before shutting her door. Jett opened the back for Mags and then set his gear down in the cargo area before he got in the driver's seat.

"You're going to allow *some* caregiving," Moxie protested and pulled out a container from a bag by her feet. "I think this batch might be better than the last." She popped open the tupperware to expose a lump of cowboy cookie dough.

"Damn, I missed you." Jett fondly shook his head but accepted a hunk. She was right. He didn't know how it was possible, but this batch was slightly better than the last.

"By the way"—he swallowed his first bite as he pulled out of the parking spot—"I got your messages." He smirked.

Moxie rolled her head away, almost embarrassed, but her eyes finally made their way back to his. Now that he was home, she hoped she wouldn't regret having left them.

"Yep." He reached for her hand. "I'm gonna have to tell everyone how I finally gave in one day because you followed me into a hotel one night and then our first time apart you called me eighty-eight times and sent me forty pictures." He winked at her while she giggled.

"Excuse me, Dr. Brody, I believe you tried to check into the hotel *after* us. And I'll be letting everyone know you ghosted me right after you were blessed enough to smooch on my lips."

Jett's head fell back as he laughed. He brought her hand to his mouth and softly pecked it. "We do have to talk about your messages."

She felt a heatwave of embarrassment.

"While I'm *very* grateful I got to listen to your sweet voice, I don't have even one picture of you and your beautiful face."

Moxie laced their fingers together, squeezing his hand. "You didn't leave me a picture of you either, but we can fix both of our complaints now that you're home. I know better for next time."

Jett had been craving Messina's lemon pepper wings for a couple days now. They decided to stop there on the way home to enjoy an early dinner on the patio so Mags could join them.

"Here you are." The server set down a couple of menus. "I'll be right back for your drink order in a couple minutes, happy hour is about to start."

"Thank you," Jett and Moxie replied in unison.

"Good girl," Moxie praised Mags who sat, unbothered, while observing a Maltese who continuously yipped at her since they'd been seated.

"So, how were things at home? Everything alright while I was gone?" Jett asked, really wondering how comfortable Moxie had been and if she'd noticed Trevor lurking around—not that she'd recognize him.

Moxie shrugged before responding, "It wasn't my favorite to not have you home, but we made it work. Right, pretty girl?" She looked under the table and scratched Mags on her furry head.

"Mox, I can make it even more comfortable next time I have to leave." He hated bringing up the topic again, but he had to be sure she kept hearing it until she gave up her ex's name. "I made a promise to you and I intend to make good on that when you're ready." He reached across the table and covered her petite hand with his tattooed one. "You just share that name and I'll take care of the rest."

Moxie studied their hands, Jett's thumb grazing back and forth along her wrist. "Thank you, Jett. I haven't heard anything from him"—she slowly shook her head and glanced away from the table—"I just want to believe he lost track of me since moving and you taking the AirTag from my Jeep."

Jett squeezed her hand, hoping she'd look at him.

It took her a minute, but she peered across the table. "Honestly, I wanted you home more because I missed you… and secondary to that, you do make me feel safer than I've ever felt."

Jett slid his hand under hers and intertwined their fingers. "I told you day one, you'll always be safe with me, Doll—that's a damn promise."

Moxie stood and made her way around the table to sit next to Jett. She'd quickly picked his hand back up once she sat down. Mags settled into a new spot between their chairs, reaching her head to rest on Jett's lap under the table.

Moxie took a deep breath and leaned against Jett's shoulder. "I really missed you."

Jett's lips curled, an adoring chuckle shooting out of his nose. He brought Moxie's hand up to his mouth so he could kiss it and with the other hand he gave Mags a good ruffle on the top of her head. Everything about that moment felt good—felt *right*. He'd been reunited with his girls and he couldn't be happier. This was the kind of homecoming he could get used to, and whether she was ready or not, Jett had already decided he wanted Moxie to *always* be the woman he came home to.

23

They made it back home that evening and settled into a movie marathon. Their previously established slumber party arrangement would leave them on different ends of the couch at the very least, but now that they'd kissed, cuddling was a given. Even if Moxie had been unsure, Jett playfully demanded it when he carried her to the couch and tucked her under his arm.

Moxie was snuggled under Jett's strong embrace, her head comfortably on his shoulder with one of her hands respectfully on his leg when she looked up at him. "Jett?"

"Yeah, Doll?" He dipped his chin to look at her, rubbing her arm.

"I'm sure you're not supposed to really talk about work, but are you okay?"

He brushed his middle and index fingers through a lock of her hair. "What do you mean?"

"I had lunch with Shane the other day and he said sometimes when Frank comes back he needs a day or two to… decompress." She glanced down, suddenly fidgeting. "I know you're a professional at compartmentalizing, and I've seen you… I *see* you, Jett. The version of you that's not a complete asshole is my favorite." She reached for his face, gently caressing his scruffy cheek. "I know I'm still a little sore, but if there's something I can help lift, please let me know. Mags and I are here."

Jett squeezed her hand and placed a soft peck to her palm. This woman had already lifted more than she'd ever realized for him and yet she offered more.

"Mox…" He leaned into her loving touch before connecting their lips as his hand glided down her side. He hovered just inches from her mouth, gazing into her eyes. "The dark and heavy is something I'll be carrying. I don't ever want you to have to worry about anything like that. Thank you for seeing me, but all I need is for my girls to stay soft and sweet to remind me to be gentle… So I don't turn into that complete asshole that I know I'm capable of," he admitted with a sly grin. "Me and my boys'll take care of my mind. Your job is to help keep that asshole out of my heart." He pressed their foreheads together. "Deal?"

"You got it," Moxie agreed with a sweet smile and initiated the next kiss. Jett went back and forth with her, both opening their mouths more and more after each time their lips readjusted against one another, exploring.

It was Jett who slowed them down before they fully exchanged tongues.

"And for the record"—he held her chin in place—"if you'll allow me to have it, I'll protect your heart as if it holds our very last breaths."

Moxie felt her chest swell at the sentiment, then melted at the confirmation that he likely felt the same about her as she did about him. "Jett, I gave you my heart a while ago. I just wasn't ready to tell you back then."

He carefully lifted her so she straddled him before he reached up and held her face. Moxie's hands held firmly to Jett's shoulder and the back of his neck as his tongue confidently plunged into her mouth. She caught it with hers and desperately exhaled as they found their rhythm.

They'd both wanted this for longer than either had been willing to admit and their passion didn't hide that desire. After a few exchanges Jett's hands descended down Moxie's back and landed just below her hips. He slowed his mouth, locking his gaze to hers and said with a steady voice, "Moxie, I love you."

She didn't respond initially. He felt her hands cling tighter to him as the sea of blue in her eyes settled.

"Shit, did I make it awkward this time?" Jett worried as he gently squeezed the top of her cheeks.

"Not at all," she assured while slowly shaking her head as her fingertips tickled the nape of his neck. "Because I love you too, Jett."

He smiled widely before pulling her in to meet his mouth.

Moxie slowed them this time and spoke softly when their lips separated, "Jett, is this okay?"

"What do you mean?"

"Is it okay that we love each other? We only just met. And are people going to be upset because your still marr—"

"Dollface." Jett gently placed his hands on either side of her face. "First and foremost, I wholeheartedly meant what I said—I love you. Secondly, we don't need to worry about what anyone else thinks. Unless it's your opinion, I really don't care. If there was anything I could do to speed up the divorce, I definitely would've done it by now." His thumbs rubbed the length of her cheekbones.

Moxie smirked and touched her forehead to his. "You and Mags have made my life better in every way imaginable. I love you *and* our pretty girl."

"We do owe our girl for bringing us together, don't we?"

"Forever in her debt," Moxie agreed.

Jett couldn't resist pulling her in again. Now that they'd opened the floodgates between them he didn't want to endure a second more of life without her love. This woman had turned an unimaginable clusterfuck into undoubtedly Jett's biggest win in life just by being her.

He rearranged them on the couch so she no longer straddled him. While he had jeans on, he had to believe she'd felt how tight they'd gotten on him. The nagging feeling that Hallie likely overlapped him and the wet noodle had him pumping the brakes with Moxie—yet another reason for him to be pissed at his ex. Despite wanting more, he'd instead soak in the welcoming consolation prize of his mouth exploring every inch of Moxie's.

The sound of the television woke Jett. A smile crept across his face when he opened his eyes. He lay on his side with his back against the couch and Moxie cuddled in his arms as she slept. One of her petite hands rested securely on his pec and her expression was peaceful. He loved the feeling of their bodies embracing one another.

Jett's heart and body were ready for all of Moxie, but his mind continued to nag him about his wife's cheating ass, encouraging him a little check-up first was in his *and* Moxie's best interests. He almost laughed at the thought of going into a clinic for STI testing at his age—he *never* imagined he'd be in this situation. Not to mention, he hadn't exactly prepared them with any kind of contraceptives. Still, Jett decided the trajectory of his life had changed for the better any way he looked at it.

The homecoming he experienced today was lightyears ahead of the one he'd been subjected to a few weeks earlier. He couldn't be happier to have Moxie's love. He brushed his fingers through her hair in an attempt to wake her up gently. Mags lifted her head off Jett's legs to eye him when she sensed him moving. He gave her a quick scratch before watching Moxie's sweet face twitch. A smirk tugged at the corner of his mouth before he leaned down to press his lips softly against her forehead.

"Sorry, is the movie over?" she croaked out in a tired voice.

Jett chuckled lightly. "I think it's been over, it's almost two." His hand caressed the side of her body. "Come on, Doll, I know we love our slumber parties, but we don't have to sleep out here. Let's go to bed."

Moxie cuddled closer to Jett and put her head on his chest. "I want to stay in your arms."

Her response made him grin. "Trust me, I still want to hold you. How 'bout we go down the hall and you can stay at my place?" He hooked her chin so she could watch him wink at her.

"Okay," she agreed with an adoring smile.

Once they were under the comforter, Jett invited Mags up to

join them. He hadn't bothered putting a bed in his room for her; he assumed she'd sleep with Moxie at night. Plus, Jett didn't mind his dog on the bed—it was always Hallie who'd insisted it wasn't sanitary. Moxie stroked Mags' head a few times once the German Shepherd settled into a comfortable sleeping position.

"If my bed isn't comfy enough we can always move to yours," Jett suggested as he positioned himself behind Moxie, engulfing her small frame in his strong embrace.

"I'm perfectly comfortable right here," Moxie assured him while squeezing his arms.

"Goodnight, Mox. I love you." He pecked the back of her head.

"I love you too, Jett." She turned her head enough to kiss just under his jaw. "Goodnight."

24

"*So…*" Hot Rod swaggered towards Jett in their squad room the next morning. "Rumor has it you may have more than a *roommate*, huh?"

Jett tried not to look surprised and didn't offer a verbal response either while he dug through one of his bags.

"Bro, don't leave us in fucking suspense over here when we already know. Plus, she's a fucking fox—so own that shit." Hot Rod looked around the room as the other guys pretended not to pay attention. "If nothing else, let us know how she wa—"

"You'll want to stop right there," Jett finally spoke up with a firm tone. "Not sure what rumor mill you've been listening to, but either way you're gonna be respectful to Mox."

"Okay." Hot Rod held up his hands in surrender. "I'll try to be more respectful." He quickly scanned the room again as Jett was preoccupied grabbing a few items from his locker. "Will you at least confirm if the fox is still just a *roommate*?"

The rest of the team subtly watched for Jett's response.

"What makes you even question that?" Jett asked.

Hot Rod laughed and blurted out, "Your ass got caught kissing her!"

The second Jett cracked a smile the entire room rumbled in encouragement.

"Ayyyy, that's my boy!" Hot Rod firmly patted Jett's chest a few times.

Once the chatter finally died down and the guys were going about their own business, Frank walked over to Jett.

"I'm happy for you, brother." He gripped Jett's shoulder for a brief moment. "I'm not like these idiots, I get it."

"I didn't think it was you stoking the gossip around here." Jett glanced down with a smirk on his face. "And I'm not embarrassed or whatever."

Frank laughed. "I know that!"

Jett knew Frank would let him express his thoughts and not immediately run around telling all the guys.

"It's new—well, obviously my feelings have been brewing for a while." Jett took a deep breath. "We got off to a very interesting start, and I know my current situation doesn't exactly allow me to offer her everything she deserves, but life just wouldn't be right without her." Jett shook his head, he hadn't looked up at Frank yet.

"You don't have to justify anything to me, or anyone else for that matter. I'm pretty sure I have an idea of what you may be thinking and can I just say, fuck everyone who wants to have a negative opinion about *your* life—especially right now." Frank took a seat on the bench near Jett.

"You can tell me to shut the hell up, but I'm gonna try anyway. You're always the calm and collected one around here—all business, sometimes a bit broody, just mental focus and toughness when we need it most. I'm not trying to say you're not a fun guy to be around, but everyone here knows you're the constant for our team. The few times I've been around you and Mox…" Frank smiled and shook his head. "That woman lights you up, Jett. You're going through some fucked-up shit, but that doesn't mean you can't let something wonderful in."

"Thank you for saying all that. Sometimes it feels like people are more worried about what *I'm* fucking doing versus the fact that my wife decided to get pregnant while I thought we were still happily married."

"If I was a straight man, that's the shit that would turn me gay," Frank genuinely admitted. "The fact that you haven't killed that guy is damn worthy of sainthood."

Jett chuckled. "I don't know about all that. I think it says a lot that I don't even care enough to do anything like that. Plus, the guy's a total wet napkin, it wouldn't be a fair fight. Shit, I honestly may be more embarrassed than anything being replaced by a fucking schmuck like that."

"I'm gonna be honest, and it's not just the situation, but based on looks and first impressions alone, you just got the biggest damn upgrade anyone could ever even dream of."

Jett nodded in agreement while a grin took over his face. He closed his eyes, holding the bridge of his nose, shaking his head when their personal DJ drowned the squad room out in Wayne Wonder.

Hot Rod held onto a magazine from his AR like it was a microphone and joined in the lyrics, "*Got somebody,*" he belted. "*She is a beauty, very special, really and truly. Take good care of me like it's her duty. Want you right by my side night and day!*" He jumped in front of Jett and gyrated his hips. "*No letting go, not holding back, because you are my lady…*"

He continued along with his solo performance until the Texican, and to Jett's surprise, Trip, both hopped in as back up dancers.

Jett covered his face with both of his hands and threw his head back while his team continued to perform. Frank eventually gave in and helped with the grand gesture of how proud and excited they all were that Jett was moving on. It was times like this that reminded Jett why he loved his job. Sure, it was life threatening and morally despicable more times than not, but he was damn good at what he did and loved having the brotherhood with the goons who were currently shaking and shimmying in front of him.

25

"Hey, babe!" Vera waved from across the lobby when Moxie walked into the shelter that afternoon.

"Hi, V." Moxie set a smoothie on the counter and leaned over to hug her friend.

"You're the best! Thank you." Vera took a healthy drink as Moxie walked around to sign in to the volunteer timesheet.

"Want to come walk with me for a bit?" Moxie offered before taking a sip of her orange-mango smoothie.

"Uhhh"—Vera looked at the time—"I can probably sneak outta here for a quick sec."

The girls walked down through the admin wing to get to the longest residents of the shelter. Moxie had been loving on a pit bull mix the last couple of visits and was delighted to see she wasn't there today—she'd been adopted. Vera freed one of the huskies from his kennel while Moxie prepared a shepherd-mix.

"How's GI Joe doing since coming back from their top secret shit?" Vera asked as they made their way through the exterior doors of the shelter.

Moxie tried to mask her smile by taking another drink of her smoothie before replying, "He's good." She nodded a few times before looking at her best friend again, fully exposing her smile this time so she could deliver her question, "Have you talked to Mankini?"

Vera's head fell back and she laughed. "*Stop* calling him that!"

"If I hadn't been visually assaulted by those big-girl panties I wouldn't have to call him that. I'm still disappointed in you by the way."

"You can judge all you want." Vera shrugged. "That man is so goddamn good in bed, I don't give a single shit what kind of underwear he puts on."

"I'll take your word for it." Moxie shook her head and bent over to give her four-legged mutt friend a few good ear scratches.

"So what's with you?" Vera's tone was accusatory but friendly as she watched her best friend lost in space with a charmed expression on her face.

Moxie's mouth gave its best efforts at biting down on her smirk but her eyes and the pink that rushed to her cheeks completely gave her away. Her teeth released her lips when a giddy giggle escaped.

"Babe!" Vera locked arms with Moxie's. "You have something to tell me, don't you?!" she asked excitedly. "That's why you wanted me to walk with you, isn't it?!"

"Well"—Moxie continued to giggle—"something happened…"

"Something *good* I'm guessing!" Vera squirmed.

"*Definitely* a good thing." She nodded.

"You slept with GI Joe, didn't you?!" Vera bounced around Moxie as her tiny bestie laughed.

"No!" Moxie rolled her head around. "I mean, kinda, yeah, but not what you're thinking—just the actual sleeping part." They took a few more steps for Moxie to try to keep her giddiness at bay. "Jett and I… We're definitely not just roommates anymore, we—"

"You kissed him!" Vera couldn't stop herself from interrupting.

"There's been a lot of that," she happily confirmed.

"Oh! Babe! I'm so happy for you!" Vera wrapped her arms around Moxie and rocked her from side to side. "I've been manifesting this shit since I first met him—I'm so glad you guys are going for it though! And the cherry on top is you don't have to worry about Nolie Girl."

Moxie chuckled. "Oh, our pretty girl is living her best dang life now."

Vera walked alongside Moxie instead of hanging on to her. "Am I still allowed to think he's hot?"

"Why in the world would I be mad about an observable fact?" Moxie shrugged, smirking.

Vera playfully nudged her.

"V…" Moxie's tone turned serious. "He told me he loves me."

"Of course he does! What's not to love?!" Vera practically shouted. "What did you say to him when he said that?"

Moxie peered up at her best friend. "I told him I love him too. And I don't doubt or regret that at all because the deepest depths of my soul truly feel that way for him." She fondly shook her head. "My heart had never known what it is to be safe or to be home until I met Jett."

Vera turned to hug her again. "Mox, you deserve this happiness and Jett is beyond perfect for you—I'm *so* pumped for you guys." She squeezed her, emphasizing her sentiment.

"Thanks, V." Moxie held onto her friend while also reaching for the mixed breed that was now jumping on her, feeding off Vera's excitement. "My life has felt better since meeting him."

"Embrace that feeling of home, babe—it's rare."

Moxie already planned to fully embrace Jett and everything he offered. The way in which she physically felt her body ease around him, and the blissful future she pictured ahead of them, left no room for any doubt in her mind or her heart.

Mags hopped around the door to the garage when she heard Jett's truck that evening. He opened the door and immediately greeted the furrier half of his favorite female duo with a few neck scratches.

"Hey, Doll," he said, looking across the room as Moxie approached.

Her face lit up as she quickly made her way to Jett. She didn't care how crazy she looked rushing him as if he'd been gone for several days; she threw her arms around his shoulders just before putting her lips on his cheek for a firm peck.

Jett caught her, spinning her in the air.

"I'm glad you're home."

"Me too." He set her down. "I've been thinking about those lips all day." He winked right before leaning down where she already eagerly waited for him. Jett's tongue dipped into her mouth as he lovingly held her head. Moxie indulged in their kiss, gripping his hip which slowed their lips when Jett smiled at the touch.

Moxie smirked when their mouths separated. "So, you don't think I'm crazy clingy for rushing you at the door?"

"Nope." He pecked the top of her head, affectionately holding her waist. "I was hoping you still kinda liked me."

"I *love* you, Dr. Brody."

"I love you too, Dollface."

"How was work?" she asked just before the kitchen timer caught her attention. "Dinner's ready." She reached on her tiptoes to press her plump lips to his before making her way to pull the lasagna out of the oven.

"Rushed at the door *and* dinner's ready?" Jett shook his head with an enamored grin while kicking off his shoes. "You realize I'm already in love with you, right?" He walked up behind her, wrapping his arms around her and pecking the back of her head. "And to answer your question, work was decent but obviously nothing compared to coming home to you, Mox."

"Well, I wasn't sure if you're even a lasagna fan—dinner was a bit of a gamble."

"I happen to love all Italian food," he happily informed her. "Honestly, after experiencing your cookie dough you could offer me anything and I'll probably love it."

"I'll keep trying my best with dinner options then and you just let me know when you've got a special request." She tossed garlic bread in the oven. "The only thing I've never tried is any kind of outdoor grilling," she admitted. "That'll need to be your department, Dr. Brody."

"Deal," he agreed, chuckling.

Living with each other the last few weeks made the progression into a more romantic relationship virtually seamless.

26

The Texican had been talking about his daughter's Quinceañera for several months, and the event was finally upon them. Jett had already RSVP'd during training that he'd be bringing the plus one his invitation included—he just didn't know at the time it wouldn't be his wife joining him. He was excited to be able to include Moxie.

She'd already met a portion of his team, but this setting would expose her to every member and their families. He appreciated that she had already formed a friendship with Shane, Frank's husband. He knew that relationship, and those with other members' spouses, would help her acclimate to the demands of his job. It wasn't an easy task to not know where your significant other was for days on end, or worse—if they were safe.

Upon notifying Moxie of the event, she requested a picture or copy of the invitation because the last thing she wanted to do was dress inappropriately. Guys didn't think about those things and she was overly grateful to have asked when she saw it was a semi-formal event. She managed to convince Jett they should be in cocktail attire versus the jeans he said he'd be wearing. He instead selected a very light blue slim-fit button down, graphite grey dress slacks, and even put on his mahogany oxfords and a matching belt. Moxie opted for a brand new dress as the ones she had were for very specific wedding occasions that had long since passed. The dress she selected for the Quinceañera was a dusty blue midi bodycon dress with spaghetti straps, an asymmetric neckline, and the shortest slit just above her knee. To round out her ensemble she wore a pair of nude, stiletto heels. She always loved wearing something with a four inch or higher heel to feel a bit more adult-size.

Most guests weren't invited to the religious ceremony for the Quinceañera, it was reserved for family. Everyone trickled into the venue where the reception would be held that evening. Jett and Moxie's hands were intertwined as they walked up the steps to the banquet hall when they heard a familiar voice flanking Moxie's left side.

"You're looking like a damn smoke show this evening, Mox." Hot Rod gave her a quick squeeze around her shoulders before reaching across her to bump fists with Jett.

"Thank you," Moxie politely replied as they climbed the final steps.

"I can't fucking wait for this party." Hot Rod strutted in front of Jett and Moxie to hold the door open for them. "Open bar, food's gonna be bangin', and I'm sure there won't be a shortage of women tryna get a piece." He rubbed his hands up and down his own chest as he followed them inside.

Jett and Moxie exchanged a quick and amused glance at their friend's expense.

"Now the party's here!" Frank called out when the trio approached the table that had been designated for the team.

Shane hopped right up to greet Moxie with a hug and then shook hands with Jett. He didn't let Moxie sit. Holding her hand above her head, he encouraged her to do a full spin.

"Foxy-damn-Moxie!" Shane complimented her. "I love this look on you—*so* elegant!" He turned his attention towards Jett. "You're a lucky man, Mr. Sharpe."

"Trust me"—he winked at his love interest—"I know." Jett smiled and rubbed Moxie's shoulder as he pulled out a chair for her with his other hand.

"Thank you." She affectionately squeezed his leg when he sat next to her.

"Well"—Hot Rod slapped Jett's shoulders—"I'm hittin' the bar, can I get you anything?"

"Mox, what do you want, Doll?" Jett turned to her as he stood to join Hot Rod.

"Mmmm, is it taboo to start with tequila?" She grinned after capturing her bottom lip with her teeth.

Jett chuckled. "I think this is the perfect setting to start with tequila, but I'll see what they have." He leaned down to peck the top of her head before following Hot Rod to the bar.

Shane immediately asked his husband to switch him seats so he could be next to Moxie.

"So…" he lowered his voice to get the tea from his new friend. "Things seem to be going well, huh?" Shane pumped his brows and gestured towards Jett.

Moxie giggled as her face turned pink. "Alright, what's the gossip you're confirming now?"

Shane shook his hand at her. "I'm just making sure he's been treating you right."

"Jett's always been a perfect gentleman to me," she quickly and confidently stated. He truly had been the most chivalrous man she'd ever known since the second she met him. That only intensified as they got to know each other.

"I knew that." He rolled his eyes. "But is this like the first offish public outing, or what?"

Moxie shrugged. "I mean, some details are complicated I guess—so, I'm not sure like what *official* really means. Of course, it's not nothing and not just a roommate situation now, but I don't really know, technically, what we can be labeled… with like—I mean, he's married." Moxie looked down after stumbling for words a bit. "I never thought this would be something I'd get myself into… So, I honestly don't know how we'd like introduce each other, if that's what you're asking?"

Whether he meant to or not, Shane laughed. "Mox, girl, who the fuck cares about a damn label?! That man may still be *legally* married, but I can assure you, his entire existence is focused solely on you. Feelings are more important than the title of the relationship."

"If we're talking feelings then I'm positive we're both equally as obsessed and there's no uncertainty there," Moxie happily confessed and leaned in when Shane put his arms around her in a congratulatory hug.

"The fox is lookin' so fine she's changing Shane's mind about the whole homo thing I see." Hot Rod returned with a predictably offensive greeting.

Shane flipped him off while Jett shooed him away from his chair next to Moxie that Hot Rod tried to occupy.

"You're such an alpha-*asshole*." Shane finally put his finger away.

"Oh, you girls can fuckin' get on me for being a dog and enjoying the company of women, but I can't say shit about how gay you two are for each other?"

Jett put his drink on the table so he could swat the back of Hot Rod's head.

"The shit you do is disrespectful, that's the difference," Shane pointed out.

"What the hell ever. I provide a service *all* the bitches beg for."

Shane rolled his eyes in disgust before turning his back to hang on his husband's shoulder instead.

"Stop being a dick," Jett discreetly commanded Hot Rod who threw back a healthy swig, rolling his eyes.

Jett didn't press him and instead turned his attention to his utterly gorgeous and patient date. "The specialty drink of the night is a dragon fruit margarita." Jett smiled as he set the drink in front of Moxie. He pressed his lips against the top of her head as he sat down next to her. "But if you don't want that they do have regular margaritas or shots."

Moxie's hand made a gentle pass along the top of Jett's quad.

"Thank you, I'll try this one out—I've never had a dragon fruit margarita." She took a sip and instantly perked her brows. "Okay, it's pretty dang good—you should try it," she encouraged, reaching the brightly colored drink to him.

He happily took her up on her offer and leaned over for a quick taste.

"It's pretty sweet." He smirked as his face puckered a bit.

Jett gave her a quick kiss to her temple before they were absorbed in conversation with the rest of the table.

They'd only been chatting for a few minutes when a familiar voice came up behind Jett and firmly patted his shoulders.

"Hey, Cerberus." Mr. Roman reached out to shake Jett's hand before he turned to Moxie. "Foxy Moxie sweetie, wow! You look great." He fully accepted the hug Moxie stood to give him.

"Hi, Mr. Roman, it's so good to see you," Moxie replied.

"Mr. Sharpe"—Mr. Roman still had an arm around Moxie—"I actually came over to see if you mind me stealing your lady for a quick second. I've been raving to a few associates about my secret little financial consulting weapon and now that you're in the same room I can't pass up this networking opportunity."

"I know I can trust you to keep her safe." Jett nodded with a smile as he reached up his fist to knock against Mr. Roman's.

Mr. Roman winked. "Always."

"Little pussy-ass." Hot Rod shook his head, laughing as Mr. Roman led Moxie away from the table with her arm linked on his. "Gonna just let the fox be whisked away with some Rico Suave in a three-piece suit, huh?"

"They've known each other for a long time." Jett rolled his eyes. "He's also a client of hers and he's my attorney, so fuck off with all that talk about me being a pussy."

"What *kind* of client?" Hot Rod was barely able to suggestively pop his brows before Jett delivered a healthy jab to his bicep.

Hot Rod continued chuckling while he rubbed his arm and looked around for the first lucky lady of the evening who'd be blessed enough to listen to a few of his horn dog pick-up lines.

Jett had his arm comfortably resting on the back of Moxie's chair when a slow ballad came on later into the night. He immediately leaned towards her ear. "Hey Doll, you wanna let me spin you around the dancefloor?"

Moxie smiled and reached down to the hand he had resting on her leg, intertwining their fingers. She was a little surprised he was so quick to ask—she didn't take him for the dancing type.

Jett confidently walked her out to join a dozen other couples. He started to sway them with one hand holding hers and the other on her waist.

"I'm ashamed to admit, I'm not much of a date dancer." Moxie blushed, gently tapping her forehead on Jett's shoulder upon her admission. "You'll definitely have to lead us around for this one." Dancing at concerts with her mom and with Vera at clubs were the only styles she'd ever done.

"In that case"—Jett readjusted the position of their hands with a smirk—"you're supposed to be holding me like this." He made sure her arms were securely around his shoulders so he could hold her waist with both hands.

Moxie giggled but thoroughly enjoyed the new placement.

"Dr. Brody, DDS, by day, professional dancer by night." Moxie smiled as Jett dipped her back.

Jett lightly shook his head and chuckled as he pulled her upright. "I'd hardly consider myself a professional dancer." He grinned, contemplating his next admission. "All the moves you're being subjected to are actually ones my nana taught me."

Moxie's smile curled higher and her eyes softened, her face begging for more of the story.

"I really wanted to ask this outrageously popular junior girl my sophomore year to the Fall Fling Dance at school." He laughed at himself, partially regretting even starting this story in the first place.

"I had no idea what I was doing on the dancefloor and I was too embarrassed to ask my mom. So, at Cousin Camp that year I asked one of my cousins, Elliot, about dancing and he was just as terrified and clueless as I was." Jett loved the smile on Moxie's face as she listened along. "So, we asked our nana to teach us—who was over-the-moon and honored to provide lessons for her most handsome grandsons," he was sure to clarify. "The other cousins made fun for a bit until they realized it was a skill they could all benefit from, so Nana and Papa put on a little clinic that weekend." Jett grinned fondly at the memory.

"That's like the most adorable thing I've ever heard." Moxie tucked her lip under her teeth as she beamed up at him, falling harder for Jett as each second passed. "So, you've just always been a perfect gentleman—this isn't a recent development, huh?"

He took a deep breath before answering, "I always try my best to be a gentleman, but I've always had that asshole superpower too. Just depends on the conditions, I suppose."

Moxie's fingers gently caressed the nape of Jett's neck. His hair was longer than when she met him. He said he'd maintained the buzz cut while in training, but his normal style was a medium tapered one. As it grew out, it made her even more attracted to him. "I'm appreciative of both the gentleman and the asshole—for the record."

Jett chuckled. "I'll never let that asshole hurt you"—he leaned his forehead down to connect with hers—"for the record."

"Oh, I know you wouldn't—Mags would disown you in a heartbeat."

He threw his head back, laughing. "You know what?" Jett was still smiling when he squeezed her waist. "If she ever had to choose a corner to be in, I'd actually prefer that it be yours, Doll."

"Nope." Moxie shook her head. "It's the three of us or nothin'."

Jett continued gliding them around the dancefloor, his heart full and mind at ease that life was just getting good.

"Frank, *pleeeease*," Shane begged. They'd only managed to dance to two songs all night and they were both slow.

From what Moxie could tell none of the guys on the team—aside from Hot Rod—were much interested in dancing. Jett had asked Moxie to dance both times they'd heard a slow song, but he was quick to lead her off the floor at the end of each. She didn't have a ton of slow-dancing experience aside from tonight, but she did know how to dance to the rest of the music that was playing.

"*Hell* no!" Frank shook his head. "You know what these guys'll do to me if they catch me out on that damn dancefloor for any of these songs? Why do you think we're all avoiding it?" He glanced around the table, laughing.

"Hot Rod's out there." Shane pointed at his least-favorite team member grinding on one of the more scantily dressed guests.

"I won't be mad if you go dance with Hot Rod," Frank offered and got an immediate, swift smack from his husband.

"I'd literally rather burn every last one of my Cher albums than dance with that asshole."

Knowing how serious his husband was about his Cher obsession, Frank laughed and massaged Shane's neck with one hand to apologize for his suggestion.

Shane whipped his head around to Jett. "Jett?" He pushed out his bottom lip in a pout.

"I'll echo Frank's *hell no* and raise you a *fuck no* for good measure." He chuckled and reached for his drink, having no interest in being Shane's dance partner for any of the songs playing that night.

"I was asking if you minded me taking your date out there since my husband's being such a buzzkill."

Jett rubbed Moxie's leg, smiling. "That's completely up to Mox."

A mischievous smirk tugged the corner of her mouth. Locking eyes with Jett, she held out her hand to Shane.

"Yaassss!" Shane kicked his feet, giddy that she accepted.

Moxie smacked a quick peck to Jett's lips before she and Shane scrambled out on the floor to get in on the *Cupid Shuffle*.

Jett's face lit up watching Moxie having so much fun dancing. He wasn't sure if she was normally like this or if the margaritas had given her the liquid courage she needed to dance with a room full of strangers. Either way, he could've watched her glowing, gorgeous face all night long.

Three additional songs had played and Moxie was still on the dancefloor with Shane. Their duo had grown; Mr. Roman's daughter, Bianca, shimmied her way towards Moxie and the ladies were going step for step with the Texican's daughter and all of her teenage friends. Shane had his own version of the dance that had all the girls squealing and Frank holding his head.

"Well, Cerberus"—Mr. Roman took over Moxie's seat next to Jett and gave him a good pat—"I've known Foxy Moxie to be a sweet gal, but I've never seen this side of her—good on you." He gripped Jett's shoulder a couple of times with a gigantic smile.

Jett chuckled as his gaze focused on his doll while she and Bianca were showing the kids they still had the stanky leg down like the song just dropped yesterday.

"I'm impressed she hasn't brought her shoes to me yet." He glanced at Mr. Roman. "There's no way those heels are comfortable right now."

"Yeah, and they say men are the stronger ones." He rolled his eyes with a grin. "It might be equally impressive that they have the balance they do in those shoes."

As if she heard them talking about her, Moxie made her way to the table for a break. She giggled along, wrapped up on Shane's arm as he came out for a rest too.

"Here." Mr. Roman stood. "Have your seat back, dancing queen."

Moxie smiled widely at him but didn't sit right away. She stood behind Jett and wrapped her arms around his neck before placing a soft kiss to the side of his face.

"Are you having fun, Dollface?" Jett rubbed her arms as they clung to him.

She leaned closer to his ear. "Much more fun if you joined us out there, Dr. Brody."

Jett chuckled and before he could respond, another slow ballad started. "Alright, I guess I'll get out there." He stood, reaching a hand to Moxie while looking at Mr. Roman. "Mr. Roman, excuse us."

They exchanged a friendly smile.

Moxie playfully rolled her eyes but accepted his offer.

"Are you okay that I've been out here dancing? I'm not embarrassing you, am I?" Moxie peered up at Jett who was already tossing his head back with a smile.

"Are you kidding me right now?!" He took a deep breath while shaking his head before his lips met her forehead. "I'll kick my own damn ass if I *ever* consider you embarrassing. I love watching you have a good time. If anything, I should be embarrassed for not joining you out here." He laughed. "Nana never taught me that kind of dancing."

"I'll teach you if you ever want to try." Her fingers caressed the nape of his neck. "And that can be at home—not out in front of an entire Quinceañera."

Jett's hands slid down to Moxie's cheeks and comfortably held her, resisting the urge to pull their pelvises closer than they already were knowing his slacks would expose his feelings.

"Thank you for the fun night, Jett."

"You're welcome. I wouldn't want to spend my fun nights with anyone else. I love you, Mox."

"I love you too." She reached up for a peck but Jett gave her more as his tongue slipped between the seam of her lips. It was quick given they were on the dancefloor, but what the kiss lacked in length it made up for in intensity.

Moxie bit her lip and gently laid her head on his chest when their mouths separated.

The team started going shot for shot towards the end of the night. Trip was the first to tap out—they only had their babysitter for so long—but the rest of the guys were going strong. The Texican looked like he'd be next, which was uncharacteristic of him because he held his liquor well. His precious little *mija's* Quinceañera, however, gave him a reason to drink even more than he typically would and he'd started well before everyone else.

Moxie had been chugging water to try to sober up when she noticed Jett wasn't going to be able to drive them home. He quickly assured her they'd be taking an Uber and further encouraged her to continue enjoying their night.

Hot Rod found a cougar in the crowd and took a break with her for a while. He decided an older woman was a safer bet after he'd dropped a line on who he later found out to be a high school sophomore. He caught the scolding of a lifetime from Jett and Frank when they found out. While Hot Rod enjoyed the company of many women, he had no interest in jailbait and took the deserved lecture.

"Well, the appetizer didn't disappoint." Hot Rod took his seat next to Jett while fixing the rest of his button-up shirt.

Jett shook his head at his buddy, laughing at how predictably promiscuous he was.

Hot Rod gave Jett a light elbow and leaned near him. "You see anything else out there I should pursue for my next course?"

Jett laughed again. "The only woman I've been checking out all night sure as shit isn't doing anything with you," he firmly stated. His gaze fell upon Moxie who'd made it back out to the dancefloor with Shane and Bianca.

"I have to tell you, bro, I'm a little hurt you didn't join me in the bachelor life for a bit before you got yourself all boo'd up again. I'm not saying you aren't a lucky motherfuck for landing the fox, I'm just sayin'… It would've been nice to have someone else on the team who doesn't have a leash."

"Oh, Rodney." Jett took a deep breath, putting his arm around his friend's shoulders. "One day—when you're all grown up—you'll understand."

Hot Rod flipped him off but laughed.

"Better not fuck it up with this one too. I'll *definitely* be around waiting for that one to be available." He pointed to Moxie on the dancefloor teaching the kids a respectable *Soulja Boy* routine.

Jett's inebriated chuckle led, followed by a hard jab. "You're an asshole." He shook his head "I'm gonna kick your fucking ass *very* soon, you dick."

"Everybody keeps sayin' that." Hot Rod tickled the back of Jett's neck, smacking his lips at him.

Jett swatted his hand away and delivered a much firmer jab to the same spot on his buddy's arm.

Hot Rod laughed but changed the subject to avoid another hit.

"What about that hot little number dancing with the fox? She's been drinking tonight—I'm sure she's over eighteen."

Jett shook his head as a corner of his mouth pulled back watching Moxie shimmy with Mr. Roman's daughter. "Good fucking luck with that—it'll be your goddamn funeral."

Part of Jett wanted his over confident pal to go over and make a fool of himself, but he offered a warning instead. He knew if the Texican didn't shut Hot Rod down immediately, Mr. Roman—or a handful of other men around the room who were clearly associates of his—would've notified Hot Rod that Bianca was off limits to him.

Hot Rod shook him off and pressed his shirt when he stood. "*Please.*" He rolled his eyes. "I need to lock something in to take home."

Jett smiled and watched Hot Rod make his approach. He wiped his mouth, finally grabbing the Texican's attention. "Yo, Tex!"

The Texican's buzzed gaze turned, focusing on Jett who sat, smirking.

"You and Mr. Roman want Hot Rod dancing with your little cousin?" He watched amused as his teammate couldn't rush to the dancefloor quick enough to grab Hot Rod.

Jett didn't enjoy being a rat, but he thoroughly enjoyed humbling Hot Rod.

27

Moxie clung to Jett's arm as they walked up the path to their house after getting out of their Uber. She was delightfully buzzed and decided it was safer to lean into him than trust her heels on the walkway.

While Jett had thrown down quite a few drinks he seemed to be in much better shape than Moxie—not good enough to drive—but he certainly wasn't stumbling and didn't have a problem with the key in the door.

"Maaaags!" Moxie sang out when they saw her racing to the door to greet them.

Both Moxie and Jett lowered to share in the affection while Mags hopped around, licking them. Moxie swayed off-balance in a squat so she plopped all the way down to take off her shoes. She worked on the buckles when Mags returned to her, begging for more ear scratches. Moxie smiled, smacking her lips against the side of Mags' head, using one hand for scratches and the other for her heels.

Jett scooted himself behind Moxie, his legs extended on either side of her as he wrapped his strong arms around her and buried his face in her neck.

"Do you need some help with those?" he offered before placing a soft kiss on her nape.

Moxie's skin prickled at the touch. "Thank you, but I've got 'em."

She tugged on the strap after unbuckling her second shoe to kick off the stilettos.

"I was getting jealous of Mags—she's taking all the kisses." Jett's hands worked along Moxie's skirt until he lifted it high enough to rub her velvety smooth thighs. He'd been mindfully working up to progressing their physical relationship over the last couple of days. He wanted her to feel the love he expressed before he pushed this step. Not to mention, he'd wanted to get a quick screening to make sure Hallie's skanky behavior hadn't left him with a parting gift from the wet noodle boy.

Moxie slowly turned her head towards him. "I'll always have plenty for you." She connected her pillow soft lips with his waiting ones. Their angle wasn't the best for what they wanted so Moxie turned and knelt, immediately going for the buttons on his shirt to remove it. Jett only held her head for a moment before reaching behind her for the dress zipper.

Once he had it down as far as it would go, his hands gently caressed her shoulders and slipped the spaghetti straps down to free her arms, her dress slowly falling around her waist. With the dress hanging around her hips, she crawled on top of Jett's lap to straddle him while she continued undoing his buttons.

Jett's hands found themselves at home on her backside so he could press their pelvises together. Moxie whimpered into his mouth upon the first contact and all he wanted was more.

She finally managed to unfasten the last button, her palms eagerly making a pass up the length of Jett's torso and along his shoulders to remove his shirt. Moxie wrapped her arms around Jett's neck so their chests could touch as they continued kissing.

Jett wanted to feel all of her so he reached up to unclasp the strapless bra she still wore. Moxie only created enough room between them for the bra to fall before she tightened her arms around him again, curing their need to be skin-to-skin.

Jett's calloused hands rubbed up and down her sides as Moxie settled her hips into a comfortable rhythm on his lap, grinding against him. She was grateful he'd worn slacks instead of jeans to the

Quinceañera, because the fabric allowed her to feel him as he hardened between her legs. Moxie whined near his ear when they reached a perfect cadence of her hips rocking while Jett clenched firmly to her cheeks helping to guide her along his lap.

Jett slowed to suggest their next move, "Doll, not that I'm complaining at all, but the entryway floor isn't exactly where I imagined all this." He trailed a line of soft kisses along her neck as one of his hands drifted to cup her breast. "I want to love on you in bed."

Moxie's head fell back when he reached the base of her neck and lightly sucked on her collarbone. "Jett, as long as you keep on loving me, we can go wherever you want." Her fingers lightly scratched through his short hair.

When he placed his hands on her waist and attempted to work his mouth from her collarbone to her chest, she unwrapped her hold from his neck, gently caressing down his strong arms. Jett pulled on her waist to help her sit up higher on her knees so he could be eye level with her breasts. His excitement made his first movement on her chest more frantic than he intended, but he quickly softened his mouth and hands as he acquainted himself with her exposed body.

"Oh, Mox, babydoll…" Jett's exhale ached with desire as his hands glided to her back. "You're perfectly damn stunning." He continued to drag his tongue along her breast until he sucked the nipple that stiffened under his tantalizing touch.

Moxie giggled from the sensation of his warm mouth until she looked down to watch him. Even with her tequila buzz she watched his sincerity as he worked her chest; he was on a mission and she loved it. Not wanting him to work alone, Moxie took Jett's head in her hands, she played softly with his ears before running her nails suggestively along the back of his head and down his neck to his shoulder blades. She wanted desperately to be on his lap again and started to lower herself.

Jett noticed and agreed it was time to move off the floor. Rather than let her sit back down, he lifted his head to catch her mouth and worked to stand them up. Their tongues were still tangled up with one another once they both stood. Jett's hands pushed Moxie's dress down over her hips and backside. It hit the floor before he stepped one of his feet in between her legs to walk her towards the bedroom. She took a careful step backwards to completely clear the dress and reached for the front of Jett's belt.

Jett quickly opened his eyes as their lips were still connected to be sure he wasn't going to run her into a wall. He held firmly to the small of her back with one hand while the other was at the base of her head taking a fistful of hair.

"Dr. Brody, I better not find any big-girl panties under these slacks," Moxie playfully warned as she worked on his buckle.

Jett smirked. "Do you really think I'd give you *any* reason to pump the brakes on me?"

"If I'm being honest"—Moxie unbuttoned his pants—"I'd probably forgive you for anything at this point. Your chest alone has me completely obsessed." She kissed and nipped where his tattoo covered his entire right pectoral muscle. "I can't imagine how much harder I'll fall once these pants are off."

"Allow me to help you with that." He unzipped his slacks, dropping them as they continued towards the bedroom. Jett chuckled when he felt Moxie's hands skim his backside until she felt the bottom of his boxer briefs, giving them a little tug.

Moxie threw her arms around his shoulders and smiled up at him. "I love you, Jett."

Jett grabbed her by the cheeks to lift her up and she immediately wrapped her legs around his waist.

"Mox, I love you too, Doll." He pressed their lips together and took another few steps before reaching the bed, pulling on the comforter to lay her down. Moxie scooted further onto the mattress and waited for Jett to get under the covers with her. He had just crawled on top of her when Mags hopped up to join them. She stood, looking over the couple, but Jett lightly corrected her.

"I don't think so, Mags." He snapped his fingers at his dog. "You get down for now—sorry."

Moxie giggled at the curious beauty, it was the first time she'd ever seen Mags hesitate when Jett gave her a command.

"Get down," his voice was a little more firm when he snapped again as he fought a grin.

Mags took another long second before she jumped off the mattress, trotting out of the room in search of another bed.

"Oh, poor pretty girl." Moxie smirked when Jett peered down at her.

"Did you want her up here?!" His eyes wide as he chuckled.

Moxie's petite arms swung around his shoulders. "Definitely not right now." She reached up for his lips. "Thank you for being the bad guy though, she's definitely gonna be picking my corner for a while."

"You're gonna pay up for my sacrifice then." He reached for her waist. "These are coming off before mine do." He tugged on the only article of clothing she still wore.

Moxie happily let Jett pull down her panties. Once they were off, Jett pushed her legs apart and completely consumed her body with his.

Even with his boxer briefs as a barrier, Moxie moaned when he gently thrust towards her. The sound triggered Jett to repeat the motion a few times while digging his fingers through her hair and kissing her neck. Moxie felt a hitch in her breath as she reached for the band of his boxer briefs—she needed them to come down because she was unraveling much quicker than she had anticipated.

"Mox." Jett's breath, warm and intoxicating, grazed her neck before she felt the scruff around his lips gently brushing against her. "You want those off?" he asked with his mouth hovering over her ear as she gently played with the elastic.

Her skin prickled, goosebumps taking over her entire body. "Yes, please," she nearly begged.

He didn't make her wait. He rolled to his side and removed the final barrier between their bodies. Once he was out of them, he rolled back on top of her, feeling her reach down to hold him. She was gentle with her soft hands and gave him a subtle, encouraging tug to line him up directly over her.

Jett steadily sank into her and they both blew out appreciative breaths, finally getting the connection they'd been craving. Moxie was even smaller than he'd anticipated so he was mindful with every inch. When he checked her expression, she had nothing but pleasure spilling all over her face, so with each intentional thrust forward, he attentively worked deeper.

Jett immediately noticed when Moxie's hips began to tilt in sync with his, each time more of him disappeared between her legs. Their breathing grew shallower and a sheen of sweat glistened over their bodies. As their pace quickened, Jett reached his mouth down for Moxie's and their lips ravished one another, their hips forging a rhythm that climbed perfectly.

Moxie broke her lips away when her head rolled back and she cried out, "Jett!"

"You like it right there, Doll?" He maintained the same angle, monitoring her face.

"Yes, baby," she whimpered. "Jett, yes." Her grip on him tightened.

Her desperate pleading resulted in Jett staying exactly where he was, picking up his speed and intensity, hitting the same spot until she let out a strangled cry. Moxie was still gasping to catch her breath when Jett felt himself bursting with ecstasy into her as she moaned.

"Fuck, Mox," he groaned as he felt the last few pulses shooting out of him.

They clung onto each other as if this was the last time their bodies would touch. When Jett felt himself soften, he rolled them over, draping Moxie's sprawled body over his. Her ear pressed against his chest, listening to his heartbeat working on its descent.

Jett wrapped his arms around Moxie and placed a firm but loving kiss to her hairline. "Doll, you are *incredible* and I'll love you even after my very last breath." He moved his hands down the length of her back, leaving one on her tailbone and his inked hand gripping one of her cheeks.

Jett, despite his buzz, knew he was holding forever in his arms. If finalizing the divorce was urgent before, he had no idea what to call it now. He was beyond ready to slam the door and throw away the key on that chapter to make room for the genuine love of his life. He enjoyed Moxie's delicate fingers drawing hearts on his chest, so he dipped his chin down to press his lips against the top of her head. He lingered there, taking in the feel of her petite body blanketing his and the floral scent of her soft hair.

His intoxicated mind forced his eyes to widen at the realization he hadn't worn any kind of protection. He'd discretely grabbed a box of condoms a couple days earlier—anticipating this very progression—and didn't even think to use one tonight. Surely Moxie, despite her slightly inebriated state, understood what they'd just done and hadn't said anything or been hesitant at all.

Jett wasn't afraid of any consequence from their love-making, he just didn't want to be an asshole if Moxie didn't want to get pregnant. His hand gravitated from her tailbone to her shoulders and he opened his mouth, but before he could vocalize his thoughts Mags came trotting into the bedroom and sat in front of the exterior door.

"Oh, pretty girl, you want outside?" Moxie asked, not wanting to leave Jett's chest.

Jett squeezed Moxie. "I've got her." He pecked her head.

"Trying to earn back some cool dad points after kicking her off the bed?" She smirked, sliding off his body so he could let their patient dog outside.

He couldn't help but lean back down and press their lips together before bringing Mags outside.

Moxie's entire existence reeled in the love she felt for Jett—he was more than home.

28

The next morning Jett was the first to wake up. His heart nearly exploded with the sight of Moxie lying next to him in his bed. While he'd gotten used to and enjoyed waking up in the same room over the last few weeks—and the same bed the last couple of nights—this morning in particular was special. She was on her stomach, her face turned away from him with her light mocha-shaded hair a gorgeous mess across her pillow. He watched as the comforter rose and fell with each of her peaceful breaths, the scene putting a smile on his face and permanently marking his heart.

Jett finally decided to reach for her just before he felt Mags sit up; she'd been curled up near their feet and was now ready to take her morning bathroom break. She stretched and hopped off the bed before turning around to make sure Jett got the message.

He exhaled a light chuckle at his dog and slowly sat up himself. He could feel the blood rush through his head and knew he needed to hydrate. Moxie likely would as well considering how buzzed she was the night before. He looked back to make sure his movements hadn't disturbed her slumber and then made his way to the bedroom door to let Mags outside.

Jett came back a few minutes later with water, ibuprofen, and Mags wagging her tail not too far behind him. He wasn't surprised to see Moxie hadn't moved at all. He walked around to her side of the bed to peek at her—she was as beautiful as ever with a serene look upon her doll-like face. Jett set the items on the nightstand before getting back into bed with her. He cuddled up behind Moxie with his arm securely around her torso and his head snuggly resting between her neck and shoulder.

"Mmmm, Jett love. Good morning." Moxie's sensual morning-after voice tickled his eardrums.

He smirked at her greeting and kissed her exposed neck just above her shoulder. "Hi, Doll. Did you sleep alright?"

Moxie spun her body as her arms reached up and around Jett's shoulders. She pecked him before answering, "Better than alright, it was the best sleep I've ever gotten in my entire life."

"How's your head feeling?" He gently brushed her hair from her face.

Her fingers softly rubbed the back of his head. "I'm a little dizzy, but that's probably just from the permanent high I'll be feeling from all your perfect loving."

Jett chuckled. "I brought you some water and ibuprofen." He gently pressed his lips against her forehead before leaning over her towards the nightstand.

"You're *so* good to me." She rubbed his chest while it was partially over her, tracing the feathers on the bald eagle's wing that covered a portion of the draped American flag tattoo consuming his upper body. She couldn't resist sneaking a quick, gentle nibble of his pec while he reached over her.

Jett smiled widely, enjoying the sensation of her mouth on his chest before he leaned on his elbow, facing her.

Moxie took the two pills from his extended hand and then sat up to drink from the water he gently tipped for her. The corners of her mouth slowly lifted before taking a quick sip. "I don't see a reason for you to *ever* have a shirt on in here—you should just be shirtless all the time."

Jett smirked. "I can get on board with that house rule. No shirts allowed for either of us."

Moxie swallowed the pills before her head rolled onto the pillow to watch him with a grateful smile. Her eyes only diverted from his face when she stared at his muscular, inked chest—for the millionth time that morning alone.

"No, just you." She couldn't resist connecting with him and rubbed his chest firmly. "I'm gonna be in trouble if you're ever shirtless while we're out in public."

Jett chuckled as his skin prickled. "Oh yeah?"

"Yep. The swooning and drooling and fondling is okay behind closed doors, but how am I supposed to just ignore all this out and about in front of people?" She peppered his pecs in soft kisses.

"Don't you own a mirror?" Jett smiled, caressing the side of her face while she was under his arm. "I'm gonna have to show the same restraint when it comes to your fine-ass chest."

Moxie's head shot up, laughing at him. "I *promise* you, I'll never be shirtless out in the open. So, *you*, Dr. Brody, can feel free to do whatever you'd like when I'm topless."

"You're topless right now," he seductively pointed out, intertwining his fingers with hers and rolling her onto her back.

"Topless and hoping you woke me up for more than just the ibuprofen."

Jett leaned down, breaking through the hold her teeth had on her bottom lip.

"I did mean to offer something up last night that yo—*we* may've thought about if we hadn't been drinking so much. I'm not upset or anything that we didn't use any kind of protection, but I—"

Moxie smiled warmly in her interruption, lovingly placing her arms around his neck. "Unless you've got some miserably incurable cooties you already passed to me, we don't need to worry about anything. Maybe we could've been a little more sober for that first time, but I don't regret being with you."

"Doll, neither do I—not at all." He shook his head, holding hers in place. "Nothing close to that because I love you with everything I've got."

"I love you too, Jett." She gently caressed the side of his face with her thumb. "And so you know, I don't need you to worry about anything. I'm not upset, I don't have any incurable cooties myself, and I've already got some precautions in place for anything else."

"Oh"—he smirked just before landing a quick peck to her lips—"so, you were planning to seduce me this whole time?"

"Just a happy coincidence that I was ready for you." Her fingers suggestively scratched the back of his head.

Moxie didn't want to kill the mood by telling him what scared her into birth control. When she'd realized her ex would make his unwanted visits a habit, she had to be sure she'd never have to carry his child if the beatings escalated into anything else.

Jett noticed her eyes were elsewhere and called her on it.

"Mox, baby, are you alright?" He brushed his fingers through her hair as he considered all the ways she could've taken his suggestion about them being more careful. "I didn't mean to come off as an asshole."

"It's not that," she assured, realizing her expressions weren't matching her words for him to say something like that.

"I'd *welcome* the consequences with you, Doll. I'm not upset at all—I wanted to make sure you're good." His gentle caress of her hair transitioned to cup the side of her face.

Moxie gently pulled his hand from her cheek and kissed it, gazing deep into Jett's hazel eyes that shone with sincerity. She knew, without a shadow of a doubt, she'd happily build a family with Jett. From the moment they'd met, Jett had felt like a safe haven and each day since, she only fell deeper for him.

"I think our pretty girl appreciates her only child status. So, let's just agree it's a good thing she doesn't have to worry about sharing."

Jett's mouth curled at both ends as he rolled on top of her.

"Her?" Jett's eyes widened. "What about *me* having to share?!" He smirked before lowering his head to place a soft kiss on her neck that trailed down to her collarbone.

Moxie's arms swung around Jett, giggling and wanting more than his lips.

"Dr. Brody, this kind of love and attention will *not* be shared with anyone else. You don't need to worry about that."

"You might need to worry about how you're gonna find time for all this love and attention from me."

"I'll add it to the list of reasons working for myself is such a great gig."

Jett didn't say another word, he busied himself with Moxie's body and a more sober roll in the sheets with the love of his life.

29

The team didn't train that day, they'd restocked their supplies and ammunition before Cappy decided to cut everyone loose early. Not only was their team next up for the on-call rotation, but they'd also previously been pulled ahead of their spot to be placed on select missions because of the team's success. He knew opportunities to give everyone extra time at home with their families would be limited now that it looked like theirs was the preferred team in Cerberus. Jett didn't wait around for that decision to change. He packed as quickly as possible and headed for his truck.

Hey doll are you doing your regular shift today?

DOLLFACE

Maybe a smidge longer today if that's okay actually. There was an awful animal abuse case the cops just busted, so lots of extra friends here today. 😢 💔 I might help with a few baths before I leave.

Sorry love. I'm actually done for the day, want me to come help?

Jett put his phone in the cupholder of his truck and headed for a couple stores before he went home. He and Moxie had spent a significant amount of time together since meeting, but they skipped an official courting-style dating phase before they moved in together and then declared their love for one another. Jett wanted to be sure Moxie still got the swooning experience. They had their whole lives in front of them now, there was plenty of time to continue doing things out of order.

Moxie pulled into the garage just before six that night, as predicted. It had been a long day at the shelter. It was one of those days where she really didn't love humans at all and realized how undeserving her species was to be blessed with dogs. The house that was raided had been keeping over thirty dogs and puppies in deplorable conditions and she'd cried multiple times watching the terrified animals as they were handled by over a dozen new humans and placed in an already crowded shelter.

Those were the excruciating days of volunteering that she really questioned how much her heart could take. It would be a lot easier not to go there at all, but the need was constant and if not her and people like her, then who? So, despite her own heartache, she continued to volunteer.

She got out of the car and looked down, her damp clothes were covered in hair and dirt. Her heart sure could use some goodness tonight, so she couldn't get in the door quick enough.

"Hey, Doll," Jett called out from the kitchen when he saw her.

She smiled despite her exhaustion. "Hi, love," she replied as she squatted when Mags trotted over to offer her greeting, followed by a full body sniff-down.

Jett was next as he walked over, leaning down to give her a kiss. "How was the rest of the afternoon?"

"Pretty tough actually." She scrunched her face. "People are awful and we don't deserve dogs." She hugged Mags around her neck, pecking the side of her furry face.

"Come here," he encouraged when she let go of Mags. Jett wrapped her up in his arms and kissed the top of her head. "I'm sorry you had to see the ugly part of life today. You're such a good person, Mox." He lovingly massaged his hands up and down her back.

"Would you be upset if I let dinner get a bit cold and hopped in the shower before joining you guys?" she asked from the comfort of his chest.

Jett's nostrils shot out a quick breath as he grinned. "Nope, because dinner isn't quite ready yet."

"Stop it!" Her head popped up. "Jett," she practically sang. "Are you serious?" Her eyes were near tears for the umpteenth time that day—this time they were heartfelt instead of heartbroken.

She walked over to Mags' feeding area. "Did you really build her a shelf so you could bring her flowers?" Her heart absolutely melted at the wooden shelf he'd constructed that hung above—and matched perfectly to—her feeding table. He had placed a glass vase filled with white magnolias on it.

"I did." He smiled before holding Moxie from behind.

They both stood facing Mags' wall, and as if they'd practiced all afternoon, Mags came over and sat next to her perfectly styled area. Moxie couldn't help but cry at the scene.

"You make my heart ache in the best kind of way, Jett."

He leaned down to kiss her neck and whisper in her ear, "Don't think I left you outta the mix." He turned her towards the dining room table where there was an oversized bouquet with an array of gorgeous pink magnolias. "I realized I committed the shameless offense of never having picked up a bouquet of flowers for you even though you've deserved them at least a million times since we met."

Moxie's heart swelled and she squeezed the arms he had wrapped around her tiny frame. "They're beautiful, thank you. And thank you for Mags' area and flowers—that is literally the most adorable thing I've ever seen."

"Yep"—he took a deep breath—"it's a tough job taking care of the two most beautiful girls on the planet, but someone's gotta do it."

"And you do it the best," she reminded him and thought about how crazy it was that they really hadn't known each other that long but life somehow felt complete now that he was part of her world. Not only complete, but she felt safe and genuinely loved—two things she assumed she'd only ever dream about.

A timer went off on the stove to interrupt their cuddling moment. Jett headed for the kitchen and Moxie for the shower she desperately needed.

"I can't believe we've done so much takeout when you've got this level of skill in the kitchen." Moxie thoroughly enjoyed the seafood pasta Jett prepared.

Jett chuckled. "We're gonna have to keep takeout in the rotation if you're thinking about tasking me with dinner duties. There's a *very* short list of things I'm proud of in the kitchen."

"It seems I'm home lots more, so I'm happy to keep you fed

regularly. But, I'll fully accept these surprise date nights where you cook too." She smirked.

"Oh, I already tried to play a bit of catch-up with the flowers—don't for a second think this is the extent of my gentlemanly ways. There's plenty more date nights in our future, Doll." Jett winked.

Moxie leaned towards him to connect their lips before she responded, "I'll happily accept any time I get to spend with you, Dr. Brody. Obviously, I have my favorite activities, but I'll do anything you want."

"You sure about that?" One of Jett's brows lifted. "I do spend a lot of time with Hot Rod running his mouth about all his laundry room activities."

"I'm not like V, I'll be shutting that down the *second* I see you in any kind of mankini," Moxie declared.

"I'll have to send you off to Hot Rod if you ever allow me to wear those big-girl panties," Jett teased her.

"Now you *really* never better be in those!" She laughed from her gut.

Jett loved the sound of her amusement, and even more than that, the look on her gorgeous face as her eyes sparkled and cheeks flushed. He could've watched her laugh all night, but his urge to connect his lips with hers was even stronger. Moxie's hand tracked the top of his thigh until it landed on the inside of his leg during their exchange.

Jett's nose drug along Moxie's cheek until his mouth hovered near her ear to whisper, "Mox, I picked up dessert for us too. You wanna try that, or is it bedtime?"

"I want both, please," she spoke softly into his ear before gently pecking his temple.

"Whatever you want, Doll." Jett stood, reaching for her plate.

"Nope." She attempted to scoop the plates. "I can get these, you prep dessert."

"Respectfully"—he lowered his loving but leading gaze at her—"hell no." Jett took both plates. "I'll take care of this and get dessert ready. You can relax, or pour us a second round of these drinks," he said over his shoulder as he made his way to the kitchen.

Moxie fought a smirk as her rolling eyes landed on Mags who sat obediently near the table. "Hi, pretty girl."

The long-haired beauty climbed her front legs onto Moxie's lap and enjoyed the embrace while she pecked the top of her head.

"Your dad flashes his culinary skills and thinks he can just make all the rules around here, huh?"

Jett could clearly hear and see Moxie talking to Mags from over the breakfast bar, he did nothing to hide the smile that tugged up one corner of his mouth. He'd just rinsed off their dinner plates when his phone notified him of a text.

TREV

Just checking in, I haven't talked to you in a
bit. I want to catch up to see how you are. Can
you give me a call when you've got a minute?

Jett shook his head. He'd wanted to have a conversation with his cousin since Mr. Roman sent him pictures of Trevor sitting on the block near his new house. He needed to make it clear he wasn't welcome anywhere near his new life—especially not when Jett was away. Right now wasn't the time, it was date night and Moxie deserved his undivided attention—he'd deal with Trevor later. He put his phone on silent and pulled out the cheesecake from the refrigerator he'd picked up from a local bakery on Frank's recommendation earlier that day.

30

The following day at work was marked with cross-training exercises with the entire Cerberus squad. Jett didn't mind those days. He'd always dreaded the idea of getting sent out with a completely different team, but knew the importance of the entire squad being familiar with one another. It was a necessary practice they all needed. Like any other night, however, he was ready to go home and be rushed at the door by his favorite girls. Moxie had even texted earlier that she had a special dinner planned, which only motivated him even more to shower and get out of there.

"What the hell, Trevor? What do you want?" It wasn't a treat at all to see his cousin lurking near his new truck, waiting for him.

"Jett, you good?" the Texican asked. Trevor's presence didn't make him question Jett's safety, it was quite the opposite. He wanted to be sure his teammate wasn't going to get in trouble for assault given the tone in his voice and scowl on his face.

Jett gave his buddy a confirming nod that he was fine to leave him in the parking lot with the uninvited company. The Texican's eyes delivered a harsh stare-down, memorizing every last detail of Trevor's face in case he needed to find him later.

Once the cousins were alone, Trevor shifted on his feet and started, "Look, I need to talk to you."

"I don't know how many times I need to repeat myself, or how long I need to ignore all of you before you just stop." Jett opened the door to his truck and tossed his bag inside. "Truth be told, my patience is running real damn thin with all this."

"I know." Trevor held up his hands. "I get it, I really do."

His cousin looked up at him with what looked to be grief-filled, tired eyes. Jett couldn't blame him for having that look, his wife constantly ran him ragged. If only Jett had seen how similar Julia and Hallie actually were long ago he could've at least avoided a lot of trouble for himself. He was fortunately able to get out in time, but Trevor looked like he was being consumed with the delayed realization of what he'd gotten into.

"We've had Hallie staying with us a few nights here and there lately," Trevor disclosed.

"Why the hell would that concern me?" Jett asked pointedly, he didn't care in the least bit. He didn't know why that information was relevant to him and he was even further confused as to why they'd all need to shack up together since Jett's house was still available for the homewreckers to blissfully live in.

Trevor shrugged, but cautiously continued, "I'm pretty sure Billy still lives at thei—yo—the house. Like I said, Hallie doesn't always stay with us, but yeah. Everything goin' on's just been a lot."

"You guys keep telling me things as if *any* of it's my problem." Jett put his hands on his hips. "I don't give a fuck, so you don't have to keep me up to date on shit. Crazy how suddenly you wanna fill me in when you know damn well you kept your mouth shut about things I *should've* been informed of."

"They're having a girl, in case you wanted to know." Trevor shrugged again, kicking a rock, hoping that breadcrumb would soften Jett up a bit.

"Great." Jett threw his hands up. "Perhaps they can use Ivy, or one of the other names we'd discussed. In fact, I'm sure she still has the locket I bought her after that loss—it's got that name engraved if she chose to forget. I'll offer my blessing for any of those options to be considered—I'd never even think about using them again." His tone didn't hide his disgust. "I get the feeling Billy boy enjoys assuming my life rather than making one of his own with her."

Trevor nodded, realizing Jett may be beyond repair when it came to him and Hallie. But he promised himself he'd try, if for no one else but that baby.

"Jett, you may not want to hear this, but I need to say it anyway… For me. And I know I don't deserve the opportunity, but you've always been a better man than I am, so I know you'll at least listen to the words so I can say them out loud."

Jett took a deep breath and shot irritation through his nostrils, but nodded once. He would listen.

"Billy is *not* a good guy. I think Hallie sees that now too. There's something off about him—I think he's likely running around on her." Trevor paused for a brief second when he caught Jett rolling his eyes and almost laughed at the irony. "I'm afraid how Hallie's going to manage. She's already struggling—we all are, really. He says it's work stress, but Hallie works there too and doesn't have an explanation. He goes out at odd hours, comes back completely closed off—it's like he's lost his damn mind. This isn't the same guy I met a year ago."

Jett barked out a dry laugh, scratching his scruffy chin with the back of his thumbnail. *A year ago, huh? So, they met in some type of romantic way at least a year ago—nice. Nothing like the feeling of overlapping with some beta bred noodle boy to really reinforce my damn decision of filing for divorce.*

Trevor realized what he'd just said and knew exactly what was going through Jett's head. "I'm sorry."

"It's all good, I've been telling you I don't give a shit. I'll offer some free advice though since that seems to be why you came to me. Because I *know* you weren't ambushing me thinking I'd suddenly be willing to help you." Jett leveled his stare but Trevor wouldn't make eye contact. "Tell Hallie to sign the damn divorce papers already so she can use some of that money and hire a PI. You guys can get all you need that way, and even better, you won't have a reason to contact me anymore."

Jett looked down at his watch, he was already a good twenty minutes later than when he told Moxie he'd be home. It wasn't a favorite of his to disappoint that woman. "Anything else?" He grasped the door handle of his truck.

Trevor considered how brave he wanted to be, but didn't have anything to lose at this point. "I know where you've been staying, Jett… And I know you're living with someone. Julia told me a couple weeks back she saw you out with a woman at a bar, and I had to find out what was going on… I'll admit, I've been by your new place, and I saw a woman there with Mags."

Jett huffed out an irritated breath. "You have to be some kind of goddamn idiot if you think I didn't know that you'd been by. I don't know how you found out where I live or why you're doing that, but I'd strongly urge you to knock it the fuck off before my patience runs out completely." Jett still had the surveillance photos sent to him by Mr. Roman of each instance Trevor had found himself not-so-subtly parked down the block of his new house.

"I haven't told the girls—I mean, I *won't* tell the girls," Trevor assured him.

"I'm not ashamed or trying to hide anything." Jett shook his head, pursing his lips with scrunched brows. He stood taller and took a half step towards his cousin. "What I *am* trying to do is keep the peace I found, so I'm gonna need all of you to stay clear of me and everything around me."

Trevor swung his hands by his sides, shoving them in his pockets while he sucked in a healthy breath. "Jett, just be careful."

Jett scrunched his brows, having no idea why his cousin was cautioning him. Trevor's tone wasn't an attempt at being threatening, it was more of a plea.

Trevor realized he needed to elaborate. "I have to ask." He hesitantly met Jett's unwelcoming expression. "When did you meet this new gal? Was it before training? Because it seems pretty sudden to live with someone and trust her with Mags like that. I mean, you even said, you didn't know Hallie wa—"

Jett's eyes darkened and his face turned cold. "First and foremost, stay the *fuck* away from her and keep her out of your mouth." He firmly poked two strong fingers against Trevor's chest. "You don't need to worry about anything or anyone in my life—it's none of your fucking business. I was *never* unfaithful in any way towards Hallie. I was *always* a loyal partner."

Trevor's mouth opened but Jett wasn't finished.

"I don't give a fuck how sudden you think anything in my life is happening. Hallie is the only one who fucking cheated."

Trevor held up his hands, palms toward Jett. "Look, I'm just trying to make sense of things and help out, okay? I know I fucked up before, but I'm just trying to help now."

"Help?! How? By trying to spin some bullshit about me being the bad guy?"

"No!" Trevor's head shook vehemently. "No, I know you're not a bad guy, Jett. Look, no one knows if this whole thing with Hallie and Billy's gonna work out, I'm just trying to make sure you don't do anything that'll end up hurting any chance to rebuild your marriage."

Jett's entire body leaned back. Holding his midsection, he belted out a disbelieving laugh.

"Trevor"—Jett gripped his shoulder, harder than he needed to—"I mean this in the most disrespectful way possible. *Fuck. You.*"

The men stared at each other for a long minute, there wasn't a single shred of evidence showcasing Jett's amusement anymore.

"I have absolutely zero fucking interest in *ever* being with Hallie again. Keep your goddamn nose out of my business and stay the fuck away from me, my house, and my girls."

Jett didn't wait for a response, he angrily hoisted himself into the driver's seat of his truck.

He blazed through the parking lot, working on regulating his breathing. He sat at the first traffic light and grabbed his phone, his thumbs flying across the screen.

Jett let his head fall back to the headrest as he smiled. She always came at him with the soft and sweet to keep his heart gentle with her.

He watched bubbles pulsing through two more lights, suddenly a little nervous about his southern hemisphere comment until she finally sent a response.

Jett smirked and accelerated through a yellow light.

Jett 'hearted' her text and set his phone in the cupholder. He'd never get tired of how quickly Moxie could boost his mood. It didn't matter what he was upset about, the mere thought of her reminded him all he had to look forward to. That future with his perfect girls trumped everything else in his life, and he'd do anything to fulfill that destiny.

He *did* end up slipping into a mini broodfest thinking about Trevor's skeezey ass. The audacity to even allow a thought to take space in his idiotic brain that Jett would be interested in helping or mending anything at all with Hallie left him dumbfounded. He thought about where he and Hallie'd been a year ago—when Trevor said they'd met the wet noodle—and it made him hate her even more.

Nearly a year and a half ago they'd had a very quiet miscarriage—their second. The only other people who knew were Trevor and Julia. He knew that loss ate at Hallie, and she dove into work like never before, claiming it was better than to have her mind hyper-focus on the miscarriage. Jett had taken family leave for a couple of weeks after that just to be with his wife. He even managed to peel her away from work for a vacation, just the two of them. He'd actually been thankful for Julia, who'd been such a supportive friend to Hallie and helped get her through that loss.

While those couple of months following their loss were tough, he never suspected cheating was the reason she spent so much time at work. Now that Trevor provided enough breadcrumbs to put a timeline together, he felt sick at the likelihood his wife had been with both him and Billy for a few months. He'd removed himself from any overtime at his job and even declined a mission—the first time in his career—because it would've taken him away from his healing wife for over a week. Despite also being broken about losing two babies, he'd set his emotional wreckage aside each time in favor of doing what he thought was best for Hallie.

She'd begun pulling away from him, intimately, around fall which continued through the holidays. He'd had to pry the reasoning for that change in behavior out of her. Her explanation was she wanted to be careful and take a break from trying to have a baby until

Jett was done with training for Cerberus. He not only accepted that, but supported his wife without reservation when she disclosed those feelings.

In his mind, he'd done everything right—all the things a supportive and loving husband should do. He tried communicating, took time off work, revisited the conversation about joining Cerberus, and through all of that, Hallie acted as if they were still happily married to his face while cheating behind his back. It pissed Jett off because she could've simply said something versus being so conniving and disrespectful. He never imagined he'd be blindsided so badly by someone he thought he knew better than anyone else in the world.

He stewed in his anger regarding the betrayal for a beat until he heard his phone and saw another text from Moxie.

Jett was thankful for the traffic light he got stopped at because he wanted a quality look at the picture she sent. He'd take Hallie's betrayal a million times over if that's what it took for him to find Moxie. There wasn't a single thing about her he wasn't obsessively in love with. The racy picture she sent was no exception, and he felt that sensation from his brain to his heart to the tightness in front of his pants. His thumbs hovered over the screen of his phone right as he got a courtesy honk from the car behind him. He pressed the gas while activating his talk-to-text to reply, "*I love you too, but you might as well take that the hell off because we're having dessert before dinner tonight.*"

His smile widened as he glanced down to her immediate reply bubbles in their chat.

"Goddamn, I fucking love her." Jett chuckled to himself, shaking his head at his good fortune while another light stopped him.

Those last four blocks were torture; Jett couldn't wait to get in the house. He decided what had really been eating at him with Hallie was the why. He realized now that the why was at home waiting for him—Moxie was always his destiny.

31

Jett attended his great-grandma's birthday without Moxie or Mags the following Sunday afternoon. They'd been able to meet the guest of honor and select members of Jett's family earlier in the week, in a more private setting. Jett knew the company that would likely be present didn't have tact enough to show Moxie any kind of respect which would result in a scene he didn't want at GG's birthday.

He was already mentally preparing himself to be subjected to Trevor again. Jett shook his head at his cousin's endless attempts at whatever it was he wanted. Despite their brother-like relationship that'd formed since they were kids, Jett did his best to cut Trevor out of his new life since his betrayal.

Jett had greeted his GG right when he arrived, followed by his parents shortly thereafter. When his mom started questioning him about how he'd been doing, he decided he needed to find a family member who may not put him through an interrogation. Just as Jett located his grandpa to find a quiet moment with one of his favorite people, an unwanted voice came up behind him.

"Didn't bother bringing your child bride, huh, Jett?" Julia was ready for blood since running into Jett at the bar. "Don't tell me that teenage fling is over already?"

He didn't so much as look at Julia so he could avoid a scene. He made sure to scratch the back of his head with his middle finger and continued walking towards his grandpa. He knew she got the message when he heard a not-so-subtle *fuck you too* in her spiteful voice.

"Hey, Papa." Jett reached out and gripped the old man's broad shoulders a few times before sitting in a lawn chair next to him.

"Jettster, how are ya, buddy?"

Jett shrugged. "Not too bad. GG's looking like a movie star today, it's hard not to have a smile about that, right?"

His grandpa snuck a loving look at his mom. "The only criticism I have is that I can't go near her because of that god-awful perfume she bathed herself in. I'm not sure who gave her that Tabu, but when I find out, I'll be shoving the bottle up their ass." Papa took a swig of his beer while Jett laughed.

"I think it was Trevor and Julia," Jett offered, having no clue who actually bought it for her but wanting to send him their way first.

His grandpa looked around the yard and landed on a group of his grandkids, which included both Trevor and Julia. He narrowed his eyes when he realized who approached that crowd; it was a pregnant Hallie and her new beau, Billy. Papa took a deep breath and glanced at his grandson to see if he'd turned his head towards the new guests. Jett thumbed away on his phone with a smile, blissfully unaware of what was going on behind him.

"I heard you were here the other day, huh?" Papa tried to rope him into a longer conversation in hopes that he wouldn't find it in him to look up and decide to rearrange Billy's face for having shown it at a Sharpe family event.

"Yeah, we wanted to have a chance to celebrate with GG on her actual birthday. Plus, my schedule's all over the place, I wasn't sure if I'd be able to make it today."

Papa took a deep breath. "Look, I know there's been a lotta drama going on." He reached out and patted Jett's leg. "I'm proud of you though, buddy. Not many men would be carrying themselves the way you have. I hear a lot these days, but one thing I've always known is what a good man you are, Jett."

"I try." Jett exhaled and in that sigh inadvertently looked towards the area he'd left Julia. To his utter dismay he saw Hallie *and* Billy. "Some days I'm better than others on that front."

"You plannin' to go over there?" Papa asked.

Jett scrunched his face. "I've got no interest in greeting anyone over there. Besides, today's about GG—not any of the issues I have with those assholes."

"Well, as a heads up, Trevor's weasley dad made a self-appointment for the job of keeping an eye on you today," Papa delightfully informed Jett who laughed and rolled his eyes at the ridiculous intel. "That was my reaction when I heard that too."

"Papa, you know me—I've never been the one to start anything. I *am* the one to finish shit though. Uncle Pat better keep that in mind if he thinks he's coming at me in any kind of way."

"So when you say you're not doing too bad, you mean you're good with all that?" He made a subtle nod towards Hallie.

"I've always been able to manage," Jett reminded him. "And with that whole thing, I think I'd be hurting if I truly lost something." He looked fondly at his grandpa. "To be honest, I gained something I never knew I was missing. By all accounts, my life's gotten significantly better over the last several weeks."

"Glad to hear it, buddy." Papa nodded. "The grapevine did mention that as well." He winked at his grandson.

"Yeah, I'm sure everyone has their own versions about what's going on and their own opinions about *my* life. Good thing my papa taught me about opinions at a young age."

Papa chuckled. "Oh yeah? What wisdom did he drop on you?"

Jett smirked, knowing full-well the old man just wanted to hear him say the words. "He said opinions are like assholes, everyone has one and they all stink."

"Damn straight, buddy." Papa reached out his beer to Jett so they could clink bottles.

"The rumor mill hasn't been all bad. GG and your mom seem to love Moxie."

Jett peered over at his papa and smiled. "She's got a lot to love about her. I knew GG would instantly fall, but I figured Mom might take a minute because of Hallie."

"Your mom puts on a good show around the family, but I'm telling you, she wants *blood* for what Hallie did to you." Papa checked Jett's expression that didn't change much. "They shouldn't have been invited here today—you and Moxie deserved to be here together."

Jett shook his head. "Mox and I talked about it. We're happy GG was available on her birthday to do something special to celebrate away from everyone. If we'd come here together today Mox wouldn't have been able to spend quality time with her." He took a deep breath. "Based on what Julia's already said to me today, I would've definitely caused a scene if Mox was sitting here being subjected to it. And the last thing I want is Hallie having a go at her. Today's about GG. I have to control what I can control so not having Mox here being bombarded with the bullshit was our best play for keeping this a nice family event. Trust me, Mox isn't getting boxed out of my family functions. We'll play the game for now, but this isn't how it's gonna continue. She'll be at the next one."

"Like I said"—Papa eyed the group of cousins again—"you're a good man. I woulda kicked the shit out of that little pissant over there. How the hell Hallie's standards dropped so low is beyond me—what a damn dweeb."

Jett laughed and decided to get a good look at the group Papa now stared at. "Eh, it wouldn't feel all that great beating up someone who's clearly no match for me." He waved at Julia with a smug smile when she glared at him for looking. "Honestly, I'll probably end up thanking each of them to their faces one day real soon. Once that divorce is finalized my life'll be perfect."

Papa smirked. "I can't wait to meet her, buddy."

Jett had a fond grin when his doll's sweet face flashed in his mind.

"Hey." Trevor hesitantly approached Jett later that afternoon.

"Trevor," Jett acknowledged.

"How are you?"

"Are we gonna do this?" Jett asked pointedly while popping the cap off another beer.

"Do what? I'm just trying to make things right."

"Last time I saw you I told you to stay the fuck away from me. My mind hasn't changed."

"I know I've got a lot of work to do between us, Jett. I'm willing to at least try, especially at family events because I know we both still want to attend."

Trevor stood by, waiting for any response from his cousin.

Jett knew completely ignoring him wouldn't be possible, he'd have to find a way to tolerate him, and unfortunately Trevor's wife. He took a deep breath, finally answering his spineless cousin, "Aside from a couple *uninvited* guests showing up today, and that fucking divorce not being finalized yet, I'm doing pretty fantastic. Thanks for asking."

Trevor shoved his hands in the pockets of his chinos and nodded. "I'm really glad to hear that—really, I am. I'm happy for you."

"Thank you."

"Listen… I know I've been so shitty to you. I wanted to genuinely apologize for that. I could've done so much better and I just didn't—I don't even have an excuse for it."

They stood in silence and Jett noticed Hallie watching them. Not too far from her, good old Billy boy jawed away with Uncle Pat and Aunt Bea like he was family. It pissed Jett off because Hallie wasn't even family anymore; the audacity to show up to *his* great grandma's birthday *and* bring the baby daddy seemed like an especially despicable thing to do. Not that her ratty-ass behavior surprised him after what he'd experienced with her the last couple months.

"Hallie send you over here?" Jett asked.

"No." Trevor shook his head. "No, this is from me."

Jett remained skeptical. "If you're standing here thinking I'm gonna go back on my word about anything between us, you don't have to worry about that. I'm not that kind of man."

Trevor had not only been unfaithful once to Julia while they were engaged, but he'd also lost his job at one point in their marriage. Jett had vouched for him when Julia came digging into a drunken night she'd suspected her fiancée of cheating and just three years later had covered their mortgage when Trevor lost his job and didn't want to tell Julia. Based on those things alone, Trevor definitely owed Jett more respect than what he gave.

"Thank you, Jett. That's not why I'm apologizing, but I do appreciate that. I know it might not make sense to everyone, but I do love my wife."

"Yeah, a husband and wife should love one another—and at minimum *respect* each other," Jett pointed out.

"Look, I don't want you blindsided by anything else. Like I said, I've been shitty enough." Trevor scratched the back of his head. "Just so you know, Hallie and Billy are engaged."

An acidic grin cracked on Jett's face. "Before signing the damn papers she's had for weeks, huh?" Jett nodded a few times. "Busy year for them. I'm guessing whatever you guys were stressing over wasn't an actual issue. Odd she's not wearing a ring—you'd think that'd be something they'd want to show off seeing as she's very obviously with child."

"Honestly, I still don't know what he's hiding, but they seem to have moved beyond it." Trevor shrugged. He knew why Hallie wasn't wearing a ring but he didn't want to tell Jett it was because Hallie and Billy decided to use the engagement ring Jett had given her. "I know you're already aware, but Hallie really messed up losing you."

"This was probably the best thing she's ever done for me, honestly. Not wild about how it was done, but like I said, I'm doing pretty fantastic myself. I don't give a shit what she's got going on. I'd prefer not to see her at my family functions, but I'll manage."

"Hey, kiddos," a sturdy voice called out.

Jett's demeanor lightened when he turned around to see his cousin, Elliot. Elliot was a former Division I linebacker, but the biggest ginger-baby teddy bear anyone had ever met. He didn't live close, but he and Jett had always gotten along nicely whenever they were together. They shared a manly embrace before Elliot put his arm around Trevor's neck and gave him a quick knuckle sandwich.

"You ass." Trevor laughed and smoothed his hair back down.

"Did you bring the family today?" Jett looked around.

"No, Miles had soccer this morning and Nash is goin' to a birthday party later, so Bri stayed home to get 'em to all that."

"It's been a minute, tell the fam I said hi." Jett took a quick sip of his beer.

"How've you been, bro? My dad was telling me some shit the other day. I didn't believe it, but now I'm here and, uh…" Elliot gestured towards Hallie who happily rubbed her belly with Billy perched right behind her.

Jett shrugged and tried to look unbothered while having the conversation in front of Trevor. "I'm just waiting for the damn divorce to be finalized—she's struggling to sign the papers for some goddamn reason."

Trevor looked uncomfortable as he fidgeted, but Jett wasn't interested in offering him any relief. "Trevor actually knows much more than I do since he's known about them for at least a year now—I'm sure he can fill you in. He just informed me today that Hallie's engaged."

Elliot's eyes widened, his brows chasing his hairline, looking at Trevor for confirmation.

"I'll see you later, El—I wanted to catch up with GG a bit." Jett didn't wait for a response from either of his cousins as he walked away. He'd only made it a few steps from them when he felt his phone vibrate and he grinned down at the text.

Moxie sent a short video of Mags playing fetch with two small children.

I'm sorry doll. I can slide outta here and meet
you at home, we'll do something fun tonight.

DOLLFACE

Thank you baby, but you should celebrate GG -
she's never gonna be this young again. 😊🤍
We can hang here for a bit. I was going to see
if my mom's nap will help her mood AND Mags
isn't even close to being ready to leave. lol

Moxie sent a photo this time and the younger of the two girls
playing with her was puckering her lips at the gentle dog who bathed
her face in kisses. It made Jett smile.

Look at our pretty girl with the manners.

DOLLFACE

I've never seen her around kids, she's
doing so amazing with them. Makes me
love our perfect girl even more. 🐾🤍

Is everything going okay today, love?

GG is lookin amazing and seems to be having a
good time, my Papa is excited to meet you, and
a few cousins I haven't seen in a while are here.
So that's been good. But then Trevor's still a little
skeeze, his wife is a bitch, and the ex decided to
invite herself and bring her fiancee today in front of
my entire family so the rumor mill is in full swing.

DOLLFACE

I'm happy to hear about the glimmers, and of
course I'm excited to meet Papa too. 😊🤍 But
I'm sorry about the shitty stuff… Engaged now
and they both showed up?? I wish you didn't have
to be around them today. 😒☹️ We're definitely
doing something fun tonight, but you don't
have to worry about any of that planning. I'll be
doing something special for YOU. 😈🤍😈🤍

Whoa whoa, I don't know about that. I'm
supposed to be taking my lady out.

Then you can plan the next date night,
I already called dibs tonight. 😏

We'll see about that…

😏

"Jett, nice to see you could make it today," Uncle Pat called out.

Jett tried to keep his irritation at bay and took a deep breath before he responded, "I wouldn't miss a chance to celebrate GG—no matter the circumstance." He looked pointedly at Hallie who was part of the small group.

"Trev was telling me you're living your dream now with the whole elite undercover force operations thing." Uncle Pat had completely different world views compared to Jett and had never been one to acknowledge any of his military accomplishments; Jett couldn't help but wonder if he was mocking him.

"Yep," was all he offered in response before he watched Billy attempt to formally introduce himself.

"Jett"—he cleared his throat on his approach—"I'm Billy."

He stared at the man's extended hand that looked soft and sweaty, calling on his composure to keep from slapping that limp gesture away from him. "You and I don't need intros." Jett shook his head before meeting Billy's eyes with disgusted ones of his own. "Introductions are for people who may become friends and I can tell you right now, I'm not fucking interested."

"You don't have to be a dick," Hallie hissed.

"I'm not the one who brought my wet noodle homewrecker to my *ex*-in-laws' party, but sure, *I'm* the dick," Jett scoffed while rolling his eyes.

Uncle Pat took a step towards Jett. "We don't need a scene, you need to calm down." He had his palm up, ready to push it into Jett's solid chest if he needed to separate the men.

Jett's head tilted as his icy gaze landed on his uncle. "Lucky for all of you, I *am* calm. If I wasn't, I promise you, there's nothing you or anyone else here could do about it," he tersely reminded his uncle.

"That's *enough*," Uncle Pat tried to assert himself.

Jett didn't back down. "I think it's quite pathetic for you to act like I care enough to do something. I can assure you all, I would've done it by now. I don't give a single shit about anything going on right here besides that divorce getting finalized." He glared directly at Hallie. "If you'd go ahead and sign the damn papers, we could all get on with our lives."

Hallie looked down at her fidgeting hands. Billy put an arm around her, squeezing her shoulder to relax her. He took a breath and looked at Jett with one of his palms rising to the side of his body. "Jett, come on, you don't need to—"

Jett didn't let him get another syllable out. "I'm gonna go ahead and give you the opportunity to shut your fucking mouth before I shut it for you." This was the closest he'd ever been to his replacement and he took in every last detail. The guy was nearly a head shorter than Jett and had a much smaller frame. If he had an active lifestyle, it certainly wasn't from lifting weights at the gym. His hair was a caramel blonde that he spiked with gel and his permanently flushed face had freckled accents and a porn-style mustache. Jett was unimpressed right down to the most feminine pair of thong flip-flops he'd ever seen.

Uncle Pat sharpened his tone at Jett, "I think it's best if you found a different crowd to converse with."

"It was your petty ass that stopped me," Jett pointed out with a sneer. "I would've been more than fine not seeing or speaking to *any* of you," he added before stalking away from the group.

Jett felt his blood pressure rise at the audacity of his family. As if it wasn't enough to be subjected to Hallie, Trevor, and Julia that day, Billy had to be there too, with his own uncle defending the slimy schmuck.

He knew the irritation and anger was projecting from his face when he caught eyes with Nana who looked worried. Jett took a deep breath and decided to find GG to wish her a final happy birthday before he left—he needed to get some distance between him and a few of the guests at the party.

Jett found his great-grandma enjoying a lemonade under the shade with a couple of her grandkids, including Jett's mom. He smiled at his mom before putting his hand on the frail birthday girl's shoulder.

"GG, I gotta head out." He pecked her wrinkled cheek. "Happy Birthday."

"Oh, buddy, are you leaving already?" She grabbed his hand and lightly slapped the tattoo covering the back of it.

"Already?" Jett laughed. "GG, I've been here almost four hours."

"No amount of time will ever be long enough, you know that." Her crooked, arthritis re-shaped fingers rubbed his hand. "I'm really happy to see you today, Jett. You be sure to bring Mags and Moxie by for another visit really soon, okay?"

"I promise, GG." Jett smiled before wrapping his arms around her. "And I know Mox loved cooking with you, so we'll definitely be back soon."

"Me too, buddy."

Jett's mom got up from her chair, grabbing his attention as he took a step from his great-grandma. "Son, are you really leaving?"

Jett nodded. "Yeah, it's not a good idea for me to stay here much longer. You know I don't do the petty bullshit and I've had my fill for the day."

His mom rubbed his shoulder. "I'm sorry, Jett. I didn't realize Hallie'd feel comfortable enough to show up today—especially not with that… that man."

"Yeah, that wasn't my favorite surprise." Jett quickly shook his head and clarified, "Not that I'm bothered they're still together or anything, but this *isn't* her family. And your brother-in-law is a total shithead."

"Is Pat being an asshole?" She rolled her eyes, one of the many family text chats had blown up the last few weeks over Jett and Hallie's drama.

"Nothing I can't handle." He shrugged. "But unless you want to watch me knock a few of his teeth out, it's probably best I leave. They've all taken their turns today letting me know how shitty *I* apparently am."

His mom shook her head with a deep sigh. She knew her son to be a great man and hated the hand he'd been dealt. While she knew he'd never forgive or mend anything with Hallie, she did want to know where he stood with his cousin who used to be a really close friend. "Have you and Trev talked?"

Jett held the bridge of his nose between his closed eyes and took a controlled breath before looking at his mom. "Mom, I really don't want to talk about him right now. He pisses me off."

"Jett, I'm sorry. We don't have to talk about him, or anyone else for that matter." She didn't press him on the topic, her son had been through enough. She reached up and rubbed his arm. "Thank you for hanging out for a while today. I know it meant a lot to your GG."

"I wouldn't have missed celebrating with her today." Jett hugged his mom. "I'm gonna go tell Dad and Papa bye, then I'm outta here. Good to see you today, Mom."

"You too. I love you, son."

"Love you too."

Jett made brief goodbyes to his dad and Papa before heading for his truck. It hadn't been long since he talked to Moxie so he thought he may try to catch her at Golden Ridge.

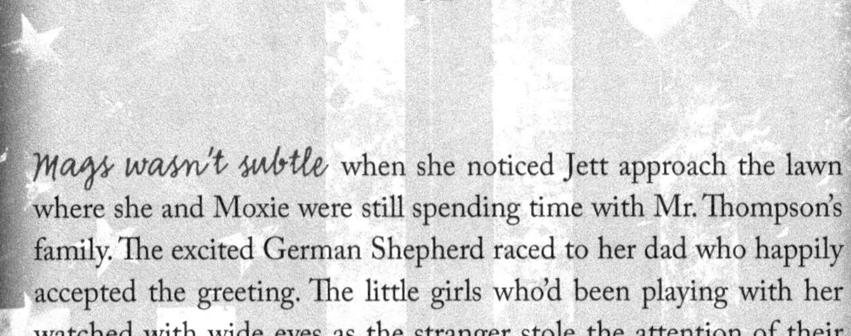

32

Mags wasn't subtle when she noticed Jett approach the lawn where she and Moxie were still spending time with Mr. Thompson's family. The excited German Shepherd raced to her dad who happily accepted the greeting. The little girls who'd been playing with her watched with wide eyes as the stranger stole the attention of their new friend. Moxie wasn't too far behind Mags, ready for her greeting as well.

"Hey, Doll." Jett smiled, opening his arms to engulf Moxie in his sturdy embrace.

"Baby, you didn't have to leave GG's." She rubbed her hands along Jett's lower back as she squeezed him.

Jett took a deep breath. "Eh, it was time to leave." He pecked the top of her head. "Plus, I was missing you like crazy."

"You already know I do nothing but miss you when we're apart, Dr. Brody." She let herself be rocked in Jett's strong arms. "I'm really happy you're here, I didn't like some of what you were subjected to today. I'm sorry, love."

Jett dipped his chin, trying to catch Moxie's eyes. "Seeing you turned my mood right the hell around." He touched his forehead down to hers. "And, you've got nothing to be sorry about."

"A little." She giggled. "I didn't know you'd be ready so soon, I haven't gotten everything for our date night yet."

"What do you need to go get?" He lovingly brushed a lock of hair behind her ear.

"A full carton of eggs and some toilet paper for one. We've got some houses we need to visit tonight since people want to be skeezes and bitches to my man." Her arms tightened around him.

Jett's knees bent as he leaned back, laughing. "Doll, you want to have a date night egging and TPing some houses?"

"*Very* specific houses," she informed him.

"I'm down, but mine is in escrow right n—"

Jett was interrupted by one of the care staff. "Moxie, your mom is up and seems to be in a better mood. Do you want to give it another try with your visit today?"

"Oh, thank you." Moxie smiled, still clinging to Jett. "We'll go check—is she in her room?"

"Nope, she's actually in the sunroom right now. We brought her down because dinner is in about ten minutes. You guys are more than welcome to stay for that if you'd like." The woman offered a warm smile and headed back inside.

"Do you want to come say hi, or do you prefer to hang out here?" Moxie gazed up at Jett.

"Wherever you're gonna be is where I'd like to be." He grazed her cheek with the back of his knuckles.

Moxie smirked, intertwining her fingers with Jett's to lead him to the sunroom with Mags closely behind them.

"Luna!" Alison immediately got out of her seat, remembering a version of the sweet German Shepard who trotted toward her. "That's a good girl," Alison praised when she sat for ear scratches.

Moxie cautiously approached with her hand in Jett's, noticing Harry not too far from her mom.

"Your son's here," Harry's grumpy voice notified Alison.

Alison glanced up and stared at the couple for a split second before recognition flashed in her eyes. "Brody, honey, what a nice surprise!" Her arms flung wide to capture Jett who couldn't help but grin at Moxie during his greeting embrace.

"Hi, Mom," Jett's voice was full of cheer.

She squeezed him a few more times before backing up to shake his arm. "You little rascal, surprising me like this." Her focus turned to Moxie. "And you brought your wife again too? So nice to see you dear." Alison hugged Moxie.

"Alison, I'm so happy to see you again," Moxie replied with her arms around her mom, grateful to visit her.

"Brody, honey, your father and I were going to have some dinner. Do you guys want to join us?"

Jett looked at Moxie. He knew she'd been waiting all day to see her mom, so he happily agreed to dinner at Golden Ridge and followed Alison to the patio with both of his girls on either side of him.

The facility coordinated outdoor dinners on summer Sundays when the weather allowed and today was no exception. There were a handful of resident family members joining their loved ones for dinner on the slow evening.

Harry and Jett helped their ladies to seats at a small picnic table for them to share with Mags lying comfortably near her dad's feet. They were each given a salad to start with. Moxie smiled, noticing her mom picking all the mushrooms out of her greens and piling them on Harry's plate. She and Jett were doing the same, shoveling their mushrooms onto a napkin between them. Small talk around the table left no room for silence during their shared meal. Moxie attempted to get a few words out of Harry, but the old man was predictably grumpy and rarely looked at Moxie despite her sitting directly across from him.

When Moxie whispered in Jett's ear during dinner, Alison didn't hide her curiosity in the least bit.

"Well, Brody, honey, I've been wanting to see you two again." She gave him a knowing smirk.

Jett's charmed grin from Moxie's last suggestion lingered on his face when he turned his attention to Alison.

"It's been a while now since you opened the practice… Any more talk about starting a family?"

"Ma—" Jett caught himself and said, "Luna still isn't enough, huh?" He chuckled.

"Oh, honey, you know what I mean." Alison playfully rolled her eyes, lightly swishing her hand across the table at Jett.

He put his arm around Moxie's shoulders. "Mox and I did find a house, so we've got more space now."

"That's so great!" Alison wiggled around in her seat and bumped into Harry. "Did you hear that? That's one step closer to *grand-babies!*" her voice sang. She peered across the table at Moxie. "Moxie, I remember when I was pregnant with Brody. Initially, I was terrified and completely unsure, but then I felt him kick for the very first time…" She brought her hand over her heart, gazing at Jett. "I just knew that little life inside me was going to be the light of my entire existence."

Moxie swallowed hard. It was conversations like this that made her miss her mom most. She knew the memory of those feelings were very real for her mom, she just got the details a little mixed up with her son who never was. Jett rubbed the small of her back and Moxie took the opportunity to lean into his strong and comforting embrace.

"You're going to feel that one day too, Moxie. You won't have to be scared or unsure like I was; there's so much love radiating between the two of you. Brody's going to be an amazing father."

"Luna would already agree he's the best dad around." Moxie kept her head resting on Jett's shoulder, gazing into his hazel eyes. "He *is* the light of our existence and we love him endlessly."

Jett held the side of Moxie's face and connected their lips, dipping his tongue into her mouth as his hand gently slid around to the back of her head.

"We don't want to watch you make any grandbabies here at the dinner table!" Harry's curt voice nearly shouted.

The curling of their mouths into grins halted their kiss. Jett turned his head to Harry. Smiling, he apologized, "Sorry, Dad." He rubbed Moxie's thigh and dug back into the barbecue chicken on his plate.

"Harry," Alison quietly scolded her assumed husband for stopping such an adorably loving moment.

Harry's tolerance quickly deteriorated after dinner and Alison spent more time tending to him than chatting with Jett and Moxie. They only lasted for about an hour after dinner before they called it a night.

Jett and Moxie's hands were intertwined as they made their way out of Golden Ridge and to their cars.

"I'm sorry your day was kinda sucky, but you sure made the evening pretty wonderful around here—thank you."

Jett took a deep breath but had a mischievously crooked expression painted across his face. "I dunno, seems like I could've had a bigger impact around here today." He swung their hands up so he could kiss Moxie's knuckles.

Her enchanted eyes begged for him to continue.

"I think Dr. Brody's mom wants some damn grandbabies." He pumped his brows at Moxie who felt her face burn before she rolled her head onto his shoulder. "Who am I to deny her that?"

Moxie slowed them down as she giggled. She spun on the ball of her foot to be chest-to-chest with Jett. Her large blue eyes gazed up at him with her bottom lip trapped under her teeth. Mags made herself part of the crew when she obediently sat next to Jett, studying her crazy-in-love parents.

"Well, we can't always get what we want," Moxie informed him with a coy smirk.

Jett's fingers sank into her hips, suddenly wondering if Moxie actually wanted kids. She hadn't outright said she *wanted* them when they'd referenced the topic before, but he'd assumed she meant kids would be in the future. He couldn't imagine not having a family with her, kids were absolutely in the life he saw with the woman standing before him.

He decided to settle any uncertainties. "Mox, do you want kids someday?"

Moxie's gaze drifted from his eyes to his chest. He watched her slowly shake her head, the hesitation made him nervous until her bright eyes and adoring smile peered back up at him.

"We're gonna have to deny Dr. Brody's mom for a little bit longer. We can keep practicing in the meantime, if you'd like." Moxie reached higher on her tiptoes, tugging on the back of his neck, knowingly closing the space between their mouths until she was hovering just under his lips. "But to answer your question, I don't just want kids someday—I'd like to have *your* babies, Jett."

Jett consumed her mouth with his, not able to get enough of her. His mind still tried its damnedest to catch up with his heart on rationalizing how one person could be so utterly perfect in every way imaginable. Loving her was effortless. They allowed their passionate exchange to slow naturally before breaking.

"Mox, I'll happily keep practicing with you until the day you're ready for me to make you the mother of *our* babies."

She didn't hesitate connecting their lips again, her hands making a firm pass up his chest that she was so obsessed with.

"Not that I'm trying to slow us down from getting into bed, but do you wanna make a couple pit stops to correct the day's shitty parts on our way home tonight?" she offered, knowing full well she still wanted to toss a little rain cloud on a few of Jett's family members for being so awful to him.

The corners of Jett's mouth reached for his ears. "*Hell. Yes.* I want to go act like a teenage rebel with you before we go home and practice baby-making!"

Moxie giggled. "Let's go then, Dr. Brody."

Jett realized Moxie wasn't bluffing about wanting to egg houses. She did let him know the toilet paper wasn't necessary because the eggs would be more fun, but once they dropped off his truck at home they made their rounds to correct the wrongs of the day.

The impromptu date night left Jett feeling lighter than he had all day and it was yet another reason for him to fall deeper for Moxie. He couldn't imagine her ever disappointing him and any time he felt down, he knew he could count on her to turn his mood around.

Jett and Moxie hosted a game night for the team shortly after they'd moved in and had been craving another. It was hard for the guys with kids to come so tonight it was only Frank, Shane, Hot Rod, and Vera—undoubtedly the most fun of the bunch.

Messina's turned into the go-to spot for food when they all got together; of course Jett had his lemon pepper wings and Moxie made some of her cookie dough to share for dessert. Vera and Hot Rod weren't exclusive, but when they got together with the team they acted like an official couple. Frank and Shane always brought the games, this time, however, they went with a classic and planned to play charades. To mix things up a bit they pulled random teammates versus coupling off.

"Okay, I put numbers one through three in the hat twice, so find the person who pulled the same number and that's your partner for the night," Shane instructed everyone.

They each pulled their numbers and moved around the living room to find their partners.

"Yup, let's go Mox the fox!" Hot Rod slapped his hands together, noticing Moxie wiggling a peace sign in search of her partner. "The rest of you can get ready to take the L, bitches."

Moxie giggled but looked over to see who Jett got paired up with.

He and Frank sat in the chairs on the opposite side of the coffee table and he winked at her when they caught one another's gaze.

Shane stood to prepare the scoreboard. He wrote *THE GIRLS* for his and Vera's team in their column, *THE BOYS* in the next for Frank and Jett, and when he got to the area for Hot Rod and Moxie's team, he wrote *FOX & THE HOUND*.

"Hell yeah!" Hot Rod hollered his excitement for the team name.

Shane and Vera ran away with the first couple of rounds—no one came close to their score. Jett was great at guessing, but Frank was the better actor. Moxie did her best to keep up with Hot Rod demanding partner shots the entire game.

Moxie had crossed the buzzed line a few rounds in and now dipped her toe into the waters of complete and utter intoxication. Besides her impaired state, Hot Rod's filthy mind always suggesting a sexually related answer for every act Moxie attempted decreased the team's point accumulation even more. Her face burned their entire first round as Hot Rod watched her attempt to act out *Knocked Up*. Jett delivered a healthy punch the second time Hot Rod yelled out an obnoxious guess that wasn't even a movie title. After he'd already shouted 'fine ass,' he got hit for 'nice tits.'

Team Fox and the Hound was dead last going into the final round. Moxie was, fortunately, back in the guessing seat but had only managed to make out one of the movements Hot Rod offered when they heard the timer go off.

"Mox!" Hot Rod leaped into a tuck jump, holding his head in defeated disbelief. "How did you *not* get that one?! It was *The Hand that Rocks the Cradle*."

Moxie slapped her palms over her flushed face, then removed them to scold her teammate, "Then *whyyyy* were you thrusting at me the *entire* time?! What part was the hip thrusting for?!" She couldn't stop giggling when she flung her finger towards the coffee table. "And why the *hell* were you on top of the table *twerking*?!" Her small, inebriated body rolled to the arm of the couch.

"That's some baby-making moves! I was trying to get you to guess baby cradle!" Hot Rod was beside himself that she didn't guess such an easy movie. "Shit, do I need to teach you some new positions?!" He glanced at Jett. "Bro, I'm happy to do some hands-on tutoring with her if you've been strugglin'."

Moxie watched Jett deliver a firm jab to Hot Rod's bicep before she slid onto his lap, her back against one arm of the chair and her legs over the other, while wrapping her arms around Jett's neck. She gazed suggestively into his eyes before reaching for a quick peck. Jett could taste the booze Hot Rod had been pouring her all game long and he couldn't help but adore the overly tipsy version of her.

"I promise you, Jett does *not* struggle in the bedroom," she informed Hot Rod. Blood rushed to Jett's cheeks so she kissed his neck while gently scratching the back of his head.

Hot Rod continued his sales pitch, "I guarantee you, I'd teach you things his domesticated ass could never even fathom."

Moxie turned to Hot Rod. "Your confidence is so stinkin' cute. I guarantee *you*, you couldn't possibly compete with *or* fathom the heavenly perfection Jett provides—*especially* not with your big-girl panties that have me drier than the Atacama Desert, sir."

The entire living room howled at her statement. Shane literally fell to the floor squealing as he held his stomach. Vera covered her mouth to suppress her chuckling and Frank slapped Hot Rod's shoulder, laughing in his face.

Jett couldn't resist squeezing Moxie even tighter and gently guiding her by the jaw to press his lips against hers. Their kissing stopped when neither could hold back from joining the group chuckling at Hot Rod's expense.

Hot Rod nodded, the corner of his mouth curling up as he looked around the room at his friends' amusement. "Here I am offering my services and you got jokes, huh?"

"Oh, Hot Rod, I still love you." Moxie stretched from Jett's lap to pinch Hot Rod's cheek, smacking her lips at him before sitting upright on Jett again.

Jett's cheeks had cooled off while he laid soft kisses to the side of Moxie's head. "That little burn was your fault, bro. You're the one who's been pushing alcohol on her all night."

Hot Rod didn't care, he was having a good time and his choice in underwear wouldn't stop Vera from staying the night with him. He poured himself and Moxie another drink. Despite her making fun of him in front of everyone, he still reached it out to her and clinked glasses before downing his double shot.

The game had been over for a while and the friends eventually got chatting about work. Hot Rod had been going on for—what everyone agreed—far too long, incorrectly ranking their team, conveniently always putting himself at the top of the list.

"Stop fuckin' lying to yourself—it's embarassing." Frank rolled his eyes. "We'll all bow down to you being the explosives expert and the tallest, but when we're talking best all-around warrior, you know Jett wins by a landslide."

Hot Rod still wanted to state his case as the superior teammate. "Please. I'm *always* willing to rush into the fuckery."

"So does Jett. The difference is you do the dumb shit that'll get us all killed one day. Jett *tactfully* rushes into the fuckery."

Jett wasn't contributing to the debate, he comfortably lounged on the couch with his feet on the coffee table and his girls on either side of him.

Hot Rod stood, to command the attention of the room in an animated way. "Okay, so let's look at all the categories you're using to be all up on Jett's dick right now."

Frank rolled his eyes, dismissing Hot Rod with a wave.

"I'll give it to you, he's superior with tactical skills," Hot Rod conceded. "What else are you basing your decision on though? You're the best sniper, I'm best with explosives, Cappy's the fastest, I'd say when it comes to raw strength that's a toss-up between me and the Texic—"

"Bull-*fucking*-shit!" Jett finally cut in, laughter roaring out of him.

"Yeah," Frank agreed. "I call bullshit."

"We're settling that shit next time we're in the weightroom," Jett promised. "You're goddamn delusional if you think you're stronger than me." He laughed. "Being two inches taller doesn't mean you're stronger."

Hot Rod flipped him off.

"To answer your question"—Frank looked at Hot Rod while reaching his hand to rest on Shane's knee—"Jett's the teammate I trust over everyone else to complete the mission *and* get me back home to my husband every damn time we get called." Frank, like the rest of them, was drunk so they were all freely spewing thoughts they may otherwise keep to themselves. "Truth be told, I think Jett should be the team leader."

Jett's gaze shifted from staring at Moxie's leopard print socks playing footsie with his calf to Frank as he continued along on his intoxicated campaign speech.

"He's got a natural warrior mentality. You're goddamn blind if you don't see that. No one else has the focus he does; the ability to compartmentalize. He keeps his composure better than literally anyone I've *ever* met, and I can't think of a circumstance where he'd leave any of us behind. Don't get me started on the way in which he'll perform the most heinous of acts to get the mission done knowing full well the rest of us would wear that shit for months—if not years. He could be completely hands off on one mission and the next, slit the throats of fifty men and you'll never see a visible difference in that man." Frank jabbed his index finger towards Jett, standing on his very high opinions. "And maybe he's not the best sniper on the team, or as skillful as you with explosives, or whatever other bullshit you wanna say anyone else is better at, but I promise you, whoever holds the top spot has that mother fucker *right* behind him. You can't deny that."

Hot Rod rolled his head around, considering there wasn't anything Frank just said that he could realistically argue.

"Yeah, what about that fucking trip to that Middle East shithole last month?" Hot Rod couldn't even finish his sentence before Frank was shaking his head. "Your Mr. Fuckin' Warrior would've been coming home in a goddamn pine box if you hadn't saved his ass."

"Whose fault was it that he was even in that position?!" Frank shouted in disbelief. "And don't sit there like I wanted to take that shot! We all know if I was even a millimeter off it would've killed the insurgent *and* Jett."

"Yeah, don't put that shit on me," Jett agreed. "I told you assholes what would happen if we tried to shortcut that shit—why even have a fuckin' recon man if we're not gonna listen to him?" Jett still questioned Cappy's hesitation in that situation, *especially* since their recon man was Trip.

"Don't get me started on Colombia either," Hot Rod warned.

"Oh, fuck all the way off." Jett laughed. "Trip's ass got lucky Tex had my damn back on that one—we *know* what we fucking heard."

"I dunno, brother, you'd probably enjoy a prison camp just as much as Frank would," Hot Rod teased with a slight single-shoulder shrug.

Jett threw a couch pillow at him and Hot Rod caught middle fingers from both Frank and Shane.

Moxie's feet slowly stopped rubbing against Jett's leg. Listening to the guys talk about life-threatening situations like it was just another relaxing day at the office made her realize there was much more danger associated with his job than she ever wanted to recognize. She was lost in thought of what it really meant to have Jett out on missions she knew nothing about, and most of the time had absolutely no contact with him to know if he was even still alive. A wave of sobriety washed over her as she considered the number of times she'd unknowingly almost lost Jett.

Jett picked up on the change in Moxie's demeanor so he slowly rubbed his fingertips up and down her arm. When she didn't move after the fourth gentle rotation of his fingers circling her shoulder, he leaned down and pecked the top of her head. It broke her focus enough to where she quickly gripped his solid thigh, sitting up a little taller as if she'd just been woken from an unfavorable dream.

Frank and Hot Rod continued arguing, while Moxie sat in silence, attempting to drown out the words and suppress the growing fears her mind now hyper-focused on.

34

Jett thought about Frank's speech that seemed to change something in Moxie earlier in the night. She looked visibly shaken and her overall demeanor seemed distant. Even as they now laid in bed, he could tell there was something in the air that fought the typical comfort and light he felt when he was around her. He'd seen her drunk before, and this didn't track. There was something lingering on her mind and he couldn't go to sleep without trying to talk to her about it.

"Mox, are you okay?" he finally asked.

Her head rolled on her pillow to look at him but she didn't answer right away. "Yeah," she eventually muttered in a tone that lacked a shred of confidence.

Jett turned on his side and put a hand on her stomach. "Doll"—he reached up and held her face so she would meet his eyes—"do you want to talk about what Frank and Hot Rod said about work tonight?"

Moxie didn't respond. She gazed up at the bedroom ceiling, not even sure what she was thinking.

Jett felt enough time of silence had gone by so he tried again, "Are you upset with me?"

"No," she immediately answered and finally looked at him, tears welling.

Jett pulled her head to his chest, wrapping both of his strong arms around her and immediately stroking her back. "Mox, what's wrong? Will you talk to me? Please?"

She tugged on the front of his cotton shirt while tears rolled down her flushed cheeks.

"Jett, I know your job is terrifying. And I'm genuinely proud of you—I really am." She wiped her eyes. "I just don't think I was ready for details like that. It's easier while you're away to pretend you're just on a normal little errand versus rushing into danger and making sure your team's safe. I want *you* safe, Jett." Her voice trembled. "I'm glad Frank has someone who makes sure he comes home to his husband, but who makes sure you get home?" She couldn't even look at him, her face was buried in his chest and he could feel her fighting the tears. "All I heard tonight is you're tasked with the scariest parts of the missions, you make sure others get home, and you've almost died like a million times. That's all I'm going to be thinking about every time you leave us." She sobbed, unable to stifle any more tears.

Jett blew out an exhausted breath, he'd wondered if this time would come. A time when Moxie realized exactly what she'd have to accept by loving him—he wasn't even close to ready for this. The last thing he wanted was her to pull away because all he'd been thinking about lately were all the ways their future together was going to give him a happier life than he could've ever imagined.

This job was something he'd wanted for a long time and after all his hard work and sacrifices, it was finally his. On the other hand, he'd also recently realized what it truly meant to have a soulmate, someone he wholeheartedly loved more than anything he'd ever known. *Of course, I won't be able to keep both—what a fucked-up delusion,* he thought.

"Mox." He squeezed her as he placed his face on the top of her head to inhale the sweet scent of her hair. He didn't know what to say to her, but he wanted to savor the feeling of her in his arms because he started to realize this might not be what she wanted and he'd have to figure out a way to live with letting go of the career he'd worked so hard to achieve. There wasn't a scenario in the universe where he'd allow himself to be the cause of her unhappiness—he'd give her whatever she wanted.

"I love you," he whispered near her ear as his throat tightened. "Forever, Doll."

Moxie shifted so her arms could wrap around Jett's neck as she straddled his body.

"I love you too." Her broken voice tried to continue, "I never want to let you go, Jett."

"Then *please* don't let us go." Jett tried not to beg.

His statement made Moxie's head pop up from his chest to look at him.

"What?" she choked out with tears collecting in her thick lashes.

He gently wiped underneath her eyes with his thumbs. "Moxie, I know I've done nothing but ask you to trust me since we met and I'm sorry. I'm sorry my situation isn't ideal for us and I'm sorry my job places a ton of emotional weight on you. Most of all, I'm sorry that I'm so selfishly in love with you that I just want you to continue trusting me and give us a chance—*please*, Doll. I promise I'll make you so happy. That's a mission I refuse to fail because I can't lose you—we have too much to look forward to together."

"Jett!" she cried, her arms tightening around him. "You don't have to be sorry, you've already made me the happiest I've ever been." Moxie couldn't stop the tears from streaming down her face. "I wasn't planning on leaving, I'm just scared that one of those missions could take you away from me."

His chest released all the pent up, anxious air in his lungs as a dizzying wave of relief hit him. His fingers entangled themselves in her silky soft hair while he held her.

"Oh, Mox"—his hands massaged her scalp—"I didn't want to lose you." He placed a prolonged kiss on the top of her hair.

She shook her head as he held it firmly against the canyon between his brawny pecs. "I promise I'm not letting go—I don't want to lose you either. I just selfishly need to know how you're gonna get home every single time you go out. It doesn't make me feel comfortable to know everyone relies on you to bring them home—what about you? Who's bringing you home to me, baby?"

"Dollface, *you* bring me home—you're all I need to get me out of any of those missions, no matter how impossible they seem. The life you give me with Mags—that's the pull I'll always have. I can't fail because I want and need this life with my girls."

"But baby, Frank said the team relies on you for like everything. I never doubted you being a superhero, but why can't it be someone else?" She rubbed his chest as she was finally able to slow the tears. "Who's watching your six while you're out there doing all the scary shit?"

"Mox, my team takes care of each other. I swear to you, I'm not the only one who demands that everyone makes it home. I'm not gonna sit here and lie to you and tell you that you have nothing to worry about when we get called. I *know* what I do is unpredictable and lots of times dangerous, but all six of us do everything we can to get each job done with no casualties on our side. No one's leaving anyone behind."

She tilted her head to meet Jett's eyes as he continued reassuring her.

"Cerberus is already elite and I'm telling you right now, my team is number one within that squad. I'm not just blowing smoke—we're honest to God that good. There's a reason they pick guys like us to do things they don't want anyone knowing about. While I *obviously* agree with Frank's assessment of who our best member is"—he tried to get a laugh out of her—"I've been refining my skills since I was eighteen. I know what I'm doing, and not in a cocky way where I think I'm invincible—I know I'm not."

She gripped him tighter.

"That acknowledgement suits me, because without it I'd be like Hot Rod out there just acting like shit can't touch me. I train the way I do, both physically and mentally, so I can be the best—that's the only way I'll give myself a shot at always coming home. I control everything I can control—the rest is fate." He rubbed his sturdy hands up and down her petite back. "You know what though?"

"What?" she asked in her sweet voice while cuddling her head under his scruffy chin.

"I think fate's on my side because how else do you explain us meeting?"

Moxie finally smiled. Jett didn't see it, but he felt her body ease for the first time since they'd started on this topic.

"You're right," she agreed and rubbed her palm on his chest.

They laid holding each other in silence while Moxie's head started to spin. Between her alcohol consumption and the crying, her mind was exhausted. She knew she didn't have a choice but to trust that Jett was skilled enough to survive this career. She wanted to share a life with him for every last second fate would allow and prayed she'd never have a broken heart over that job taking Jett from her. To get her mind off losing him, she asked him about something specific Frank had said. "Jett?"

"Yeah, Doll?"

"Have you really slit someone's throat before?"

He closed his eyes, taking a deep, uncertain breath. "I'll always tell you anything you want to know, but do you truly want the answer to things like that?"

She slowly nodded without looking up at him.

"Moxie, I promise you, I'll never be violent towards you—*never*," he repeated with finality. "I don't do stuff like that out of rage and I could never be so angry with you I'd hurt you in any way. I know how to leave work at work."

She tilted her head up to peer at him and confidently replied, "Jett, of course I know you'd never hurt me." She knew what psychotic rage in a partner looked like and Jett had never shown anything remotely close to that.

He brushed his fingers through her hair a couple of times, fully enjoying her beautiful face gazing up at him. He took a quick breath before responding, "But to answer your question, I have. Not with this team… but in the past."

She wasn't surprised to hear this admission, and she didn't love him any less knowing what he'd done. "Do you always kill people on your missions?"

"No, Mox—it just depends."

"Jett?"

He pressed his lips against the top of her head before replying in a tender voice, "What, Doll?"

"Will you promise me something, please?"

He wove his fingers through her hair before answering, "Anything you want. What is it?"

Moxie looked into his eyes when she made her request. "I'm not asking you to quit your dream job, but if Cerberus ever gets to be so much that it starts to change you, will you please choose me and Mags?"

Jett cupped both sides of her face and gazed deep into her blue eyes, projecting pure devotion from his heart.

"Moxie, there's nothing in this world that's more important to me than my girls. I love the two of you more than you can ever imagine and I promise I will *always* choose you."

35

Jett was in the kitchen just before the sun came up the next morning. Moxie had put quite a few drinks down the night before and he wanted to put a Liquid IV drink on her nightstand for when she woke up.

"Oh, hey…" Vera's voice trailed off, unsure if she wanted to be face to face with Jett since she and Hot Rod had spent the night together.

"Good morning." He tried not to grin too widely at her; he'd give Hot Rod a hard time, but he didn't want to make Vera uncomfortable.

"You're up before Nolie girl, that's unusual isn't it?" She helped herself to some orange juice.

Jett's face lightened. "She and Mox aren't awake yet. I'm sure poor Mox's head's gonna be spinning when she gets up though—I'm just making sure she has a drink and some ibuprofen nearby."

Vera sat down at one of the kitchen bar stools. "You're really good to her. Thank you, Jett."

"She deserves the world and I intend to give it to her." He opened an upper cabinet to grab a bottle of ibuprofen.

"So, it must be safe to say I was right about you." She took a sip of her juice but didn't elaborate.

Jett stood with his hands on the breakfast bar opposite where

Vera sat. "You gonna share what you think you're right about?" He was intrigued.

"When I first met you, I knew there was something about you. You have no idea how badly I wanted Mox to agree to meet you." She lightly shook her head, chuckling at her admission. "I'm sure I don't need to even say it, but she's my babe, so I'm gonna say it anyway. Don't ever hurt her, Jett—she's more than worth it."

Jett laughed. "You don't think I know this?"

"I didn't say that," she clarified with a smile. "Mox's had her fill of life being shitty, just don't add to that list by hurting my babe."

"Anyone willing to hurt her has a fucking death wish." Jett held Vera's stare to let her know he absolutely meant that.

"Boy do I wish you were around before she met her absolute yeast infection of an ex." Vera's brows lifted to her hairline while taking a sip of juice.

Jett watched Vera, hoping she'd have more to share because he had a good idea she was talking about the same ex that had relentlessly and ruthlessly beaten Moxie. The same ex Jett planned to take care of.

"He was so damn lucky to land her. He *never* deserved to even breathe the same air." Vera rolled her eyes. "I tolerated him…I regret that now and would've done more had I known how that one was gonna end."

Jett hesitated, wanting to be sure he didn't show his hand through his tone or expressions, but he wanted some damn clues to find the depraved piece of shit. "What happened there?"

"Like I said, the guy was a damn yeast infection. On looks alone you'd think he would've worshiped the ground she walked on because he was clearly dating way out of his league." Vera regarded Jett from under her sleek obsidian brows. "Mox was, and still is, a damn Olympian and he wasn't even on the tee-ball field."

He smirked despite the anxious rage he felt throughout his body to be so close to finally getting intel to find the guy—this was perfect. Moxie never had to feel any guilt for leading the sleaze straight into a death trap because Vera would do it. To conceal the fury, he forced a light tone and attempted a longer, more detailed conversation, "So, I don't need to worry about competing with the guy? Or her having any lingering feelings?"

"*Fuck* no!" Vera's head shook as she slapped her palm on the countertop to solidify her point. "Shit, there's *no* damn competition, and I'd argue she wasn't all that physically attracted to that shitstain anyway—you've got *zero* worries about wanting and lingering or any-goddamn-thing with babe having any feelings for him besides nausea." Vera wanted to be very clear Jett had nothing to worry about; she'd never seen her best friend as utterly happy as she was with Jett. "I'd be lying if I didn't admit to having encouraged her to date him in the first place—which I *thoroughly* regret and still feel like shit about."

Jett knew as much, he didn't take Moxie for the type to act how she was with him while pining for some useless ex. All he wanted was clues on how to find the damn guy.

"And listen," Vera continued. "I don't want to tell all my babe's secrets, but her mom never let her date. The crotch stain was likely the first guy to ever show her persistent attention once she realized she was allowed to be an adult and make her own decisions. I didn't know he'd be such an awful person. I just thought it was perfect because she could get a feel for dating and when she realized how amazing she was and there were plenty of trophy fish in the sea versus his pint-sized, wannabe ass, she wouldn't be so heartbroken." Vera shrugged and let a short stint of silence hang in the air.

Then a scowl darkened Vera's face. "I'll *never* forget the night she left him. That was the night Will had—" Vera was interrupted when Hot Rod marched down the stairs.

"What the hell, V?" In true form he'd donned a mankini and had his arms stretched over his head, yawning as he made his approach. "You take off knowing full well I've got needs first thing in the morning?"

Jett was even more irritated at Hot Rod for interrupting and quickly put up his hand to look away from his friend. "Goddamn, can you put on some fucking pants?"

"Don't tell me you don't wake up like this too?" Hot Rod gestured to his mankini, that was even tighter than usual. "If you're not consistently waking up with morning wood you need to go get a check-up, brother. It's a fact that this is a good indicator of men's health. And not only that, but if you're not waking up next to that little fox hard as hell, you've got bigger problems."

Jett let out an irritated exhale, warning Hot Rod about Moxie was already getting old—he'd have to kick his ass sooner than later if it continued. "We're *not* going to talk about any of my erections." Jett shook his head and plucked the glass he'd filled off the counter. "I'm just asking that you at least try to hide yours—I don't want to see that shit."

"Oh, I plan on hiding it." He stood behind Vera and wrapped his arms around her before doing a few thrusting motions.

"Rodney!" Vera swatted at him but laughed.

"Stay off the couch until that thing's good and gone," Jett warned as he walked down the hallway to his room.

The corner of Jett's mouth lifted when he walked in the bedroom and saw Moxie still sleeping with Mags sprawled out near her feet. He set the cup on her nightstand and went back to his side of the bed to hold her for a couple more hours.

Mags decided the bottom of the bed was too far from the pack and got up shortly after Jett settled. She plopped down behind him with her head on his pillow. It made him smile the second he was the cream filling of a Mags and Moxie Oreo. His arm reached behind him to pat Mags a couple of times and he placed a kiss on the back of Moxie's head before wrapping her up in a loving embrace.

"Good morning, love," Moxie greeted when she felt his lips.

"You're awake?" He kissed her again.

She rubbed the arms he had around her.

"I brought you some Liquid IV and ibuprofen, Doll."

Moxie's gaze zoned in on the nightstand where he'd left both of those items, he was always so damn caring. She felt guilty for being so dramatic the night before; drunken crying wasn't her favorite attribute.

"How did I get so lucky landing you?" Moxie smiled before her face turned serious. "I'm sorry for being a drunken mess last night. I shouldn't have be—"

He didn't let her finish. "Mox, please don't apologize. I'm glad you didn't keep those feelings from me, and I'm not mad at you at all for being what you call a drunken mess. If anything, it makes me feel good to know you love me that much." He leaned closer to her ear. "And that you want to stay with me."

"Forever," she confirmed.

Despite her head spinning, she carefully rolled over so she could cuddle into Jett's chest. She closed her eyes and immediately began drifting off to sleep while Jett laid contently between the two most important girls in his life.

36

Jett reached over to hold Moxie's hand as he was behind the wheel of his truck later that week. They'd just picked up a bouquet of peonies for her mom and were about ten minutes from Golden Ridge when Jett's phone signaled a text. He squeezed her hand before letting go to check the message.

"Dammit." He rolled his eyes. "Doll, I've gotta be at command in two hours."

"Mmmm," Moxie pouted and her face soured. "Do you know how long you'll be gone?"

"Doesn't say. We probably won't know until the briefing." He quickly replied to the text with this thumb. "We can still visit, I'll just have to cut it short." He set his phone back in the cup holder, irritated that they got called in again when he hadn't even been home for two full days since the last mission.

Moxie picked up his hand to play with Jett's fingers. She slowly and softly circled his index and middle fingers before tickling his palm. She rested her elbows on the center console of his truck, leaning towards him, and nearly put her mouth in his ear.

His lobe received a gentle peck before she whispered, "Or I can come back out here later after dropping you off… Why don't you turn this truck around and we can spend some time in bed before you have to go?" She giggled when Jett took an immediate right to head back towards home. "I sure hope your bag's already packed because I want every last second of your undivided attention until you have to leave." Her hand roamed until it found the front of his pants and she nibbled his earlobe.

Jett clenched his teeth and let out an appreciative grunt. His hand couldn't make it to her thigh quick enough. He hastily gathered as much of the skirt of her cotton sundress as he could to expose her legs before his hand dove along the bare skin of her inner thigh.

"Doll, I'm gonna need you to help me out with those panties so I can start loving on you. Just lift that sweet little ass of yours," he encouraged after his pinky had hooked the elastic band of her skimpy undergarment.

She obediently and seductively shimmied out of her panties as he pulled. Once they were down far enough, she placed his hand at her entrance and finished pulling the cheeksters down herself.

"Depending on your efficiency here, we may be able to complete a couple tours before you have to go."

Moxie rolled her hips to the side when his fingers opened her up and slid themselves vertically between her legs.

Jett softly chuckled. "I'm only doing reconnaissance right now—showing off my land navigation skills." He drug his fingers around until he landed on her favorite bud of nerves and watched her bite her lip before turning his head back to the road. "I've located the high value target, I just need to get you to a secure location now so I can complete the mission." He continued to explore.

Moxie's giggle over his explanation turned into a whimper to the sensual route he took as her core was heating up.

"Mmmm, Jett," she sighed as her back arched off the seat, her hand putting more pressure on the front of his pants as she slid her palm against his zipper.

He felt himself pulsing under her hand and wanted to pull the truck over right then and there but they were just about to get to their house.

"Doll, we're almost there." His fingers were soaked, working inside of her. "You want me to finish this one for you and start another tour when we get home?"

"I'm almost there," she admitted through shallow breath and slowly put her hand on top of his to move it down to her inner thigh. "Get us in the garage, love. We're finishing this one together."

As Jet pulled into the garage Moxie unhooked her seatbelt and twisted around to reach for Mags' door. She flung it open as Jett put the truck in park; the German Shepherd made herself scarce and used the doggy door to go into the house. The bay door worked on its descent as Moxie crawled over the center console and into Jett's lap. He realized she intended to finish the tour right there in the truck so he pushed his seat backwards to give them some space from the steering wheel.

"I'm gonna need you to lift that sweet ass of yours," Moxie encouraged after she had his button and zipper undone.

Their mouths smiled against one another at her request but Jett happily complied so his bottoms could come off.

Moxie had her knees on the seat and began unbuttoning her dress so she could uncover her body, Jett held the back of her head until their mouths ravaged one another. He wanted her on his lap so he helped with the buttons, going for her bra when the dress started to fall.

She wiggled her arms out of the dress. Now completely exposed, she pulled on the bottom of Jett's shirt to get it up over his head, immediately sinking down on his lap and taking him into her body. They both exhaled into each other's mouths on the initial sensation of Moxie sliding down every inch of him.

"Oh fuck"—Jett helped lift and lower her hips as she rode on top of him with ease as fluids built—"this is so goddamn hot."

Moxie let him control their pace when her mouth began working on the base of Jett's neck. He thrusted under her, his thumbs digging into her hips and fingers pressing firmly just over her cheeks as he picked up the speed in which he bounced her. Moxie's head rolled back, her small hands gripping Jett's shoulders, and all she could do was cry out his name until they peaked at the same time, sending shockwaves between them. Her thighs tightened around him and she leaned down to gently bite the base of his neck as she felt the warmth of him finishing inside her.

They stayed connected to catch their breath, even after the pulsing stopped.

"Two hours is *not* enough time with you." Moxie planted her lips on Jett's, pressing their exposed chests together.

"Eternity isn't even enough time for all the things I wanna do with you, Mox." Jett sucked her neck just under her jaw.

She giggled and pushed away when she felt his tongue feverishly flicking along her skin.

Once she freed herself from his mouth she gazed into his eyes. "I love you."

"I love you too." He kissed her and then slapped her backside a few times before he got them both out of the truck to spend a bit more time in bed before he had to leave for work. "Now let me keep paying up on that undivided attention I owe you." Jett pushed the door open to the house with Moxie in his arms.

Jett held firmly to Moxie with his head nestled in her neck. He'd considered bringing up this topic multiple times with her in the last week alone. His patience was running thin with getting her ex's name. Thanks to Vera, he had a first name, Will. He also had a couple of leads, but they hadn't produced enough to find the scumbag. Jett was still waiting for the legal paperwork Mr. Roman had submitted— it appeared to be the only way to obtain the identification of the AirTag user. He did lie on the paperwork that the AirTag was on his property, not Moxie's, because he didn't want her name to be on anything that may get back to her ex.

He'd also broken the ice a bit with Vera on the whole ex topic, but since that initial conversation she'd been pretty distant and he figured it had something to do with Hot Rod. Moxie told him Vera was stepping back from that whole arrangement, but she didn't say why. His chances of getting information from Vera were now pretty limited.

The ex issue hadn't escaped his mind since that first night with Moxie, but he tried not to bring it up too much because he knew it upset her. The number of times the team got called away increased his worry. He hated leaving her home alone knowing that shithead was out there somewhere. It was beyond time for him to deal with that waste of a human. He looked at the alarm clock perched on his nightstand and knew he didn't have much time before he'd need to report to work, so he made another gentle attempt at the name.

"Doll, I know you haven't wanted to bring it up, but I really don't like leaving when your shitty ex is still out there somewhere."

He waited to see if she would respond, which she didn't.

"It's hard enough to leave you in the first place, I'd feel so much more settled if I knew you were not only safe, but that you didn't have to carry around the weight of that worry." His hands tenderly worked their way along her arms. "The dark and heavy is mine to carry, Mox. Please let me give you the happy life you deserve, baby."

Moxie slowly twisted her body to face Jett, her hands making loving passes up and down his chest with her fingers spread before she looked up at him. She didn't doubt it would take Jett minimal effort to put the beating of a lifetime on her ex, he had an advantage in height, weight, muscle mass, combat skills—that list could go on and on. She had to acknowledge, part of the reason for gatekeeping was due to the fact that she was so embarrassed of her ex—for multiple reasons. Her ex couldn't hold a candle to Jett, it was shameful they were allowed to walk on the same planet. Moxie knew she couldn't just ignore him, she had to respond in some capacity.

"Jett, I've never been happier in all my life and that's all I want to focus on."

"Doll"—Jett held her face in his hands—"it's my job to keep you safe too. I feel like I can only do so much right now. You don't even have to say his name then, just give me some clues—please, Mox."

"It's not that I want to protect him… that's not it at all." Her throat tightened but Jett didn't let up on his loving hold on her face. "You have enough on your plate—let's just keep focusing on the good stuff."

"You know me better than that. Not only can I manage all of this, but I'll clear the damn plate for you if need be. You're more important to me than anything else."

"I know that, thank you." She adoringly rubbed his chest. "Please stay focused on whatever mission you're headed on versus some bottom dweller. I want you to have a clear head for that."

Jett took a deep breath. His head would be much clearer knowing that piece of shit wasn't around at all. He'd be forced to settle with the protection Mr. Roman offered while he was away for work. For as sweet as Moxie was, she sure had a stubborn streak. He sincerely didn't understand why she wouldn't just relinquish her safety and security to him completely.

37

The squad was out on a heavily wooded obstacle course a week later, Jett slapped Hot Rod's back as they were the first to make it through the gauntlet.

"While we wait for the slow pokes you wanna fill me in on what you did to piss off V?" Jett caught his breath.

Hot Rod took a few steps with his arms folded and resting on his head.

"Shit, Grizz can't follow the boundaries we established for our little arrangement. She got all pissy that I declined her company the other night for something a little lighter so I could partake in two at a time."

"Goddamn, you're such an asshole." Jett shook his head but couldn't help chuckling at his buddy who was never anyone but his true self.

"It's not actually my fault, I fucking followed the rules we *both* established. That's her ass who read into what we were doin' so I've had to find more to occupy my time." He shook his head.

"You wanna elaborate on that?" Jett hesitantly asked.

"Well, as you know"—he pumped his eyebrows at Jett—"we're quite the conversationalists when we're benefiting together."

Jett threw his head back, wiping his face trying to suppress his smile, regretting the fact that he needed to ask about this to figure out why Vera was ignoring him.

"I had the Grizz all twisted up ten ways to Sunday ov—"

"Fast forward to the part about the words, please." Jett circled his wrist.

"She was…" Hot Rod rolled his head around trying to find the correct words for Jett. "*Thoroughly* enjoying what we were doing when all of the sudden she's panting and moaning, *begging* for me to say I love her. I'm about ten seconds from busting and don't wanna stop from gettin' mine so obviously I say it. A few times actually since it made her even we—"

"I get it, I get it, I get it, I get it." Jett stopped him, holding up his hand.

"I think she thought I actually meant it when we were done, because then she was all cuddly and telling me she loved me and shit." He shrugged and reached out his hand to slap with Trip and the Texican when they made it through the finish. "It's not the first time we've prompted each other to say certain things while fooling around—that shit's supposed to be part of it. I didn't know she wanted me to mean it. Had I known that, I wouldn't have fuckin' said it. It's always just been an arrangement. Grizz knows better—or should anyhow."

Jett nodded, looking around—this made perfect sense. He was being punished by association. The only reason it pissed him off was because of the timing.

Moxie had told him countless times she wanted to simply continue enjoying their bliss and not have Jett stalking around for her ex. They were both on a fresh road of happiness and she didn't want to think about the past. She wasn't opposed in the slightest to Jett taking care of her ex *if* he crossed their path, but if he was gone for good then there was no reason to bring him back in the fold. With that, she'd kept any indication of a name or any details a complete secret from him.

Even with help from Mr. Roman, and having possession of the

AirTag, Moxie had done a fabulous job of erasing that rat bastard from her life as if he never existed.

Jett knew the key to unlocking the information he wanted was Vera. He'd approached her to establish their own friendship a few times since he and Moxie decided to be official. He thought it was going pretty well and he and Vera were at a point where he could ask her things privately that wouldn't get back to Moxie if they both felt it was for her own good, but then Hot Rod had to fuck it all up.

"So why do you ask? Did my fuck-up get you cut off from plowing into that sweet little Moxie muff of yours?" Hot Rod laughed.

Jett shoved him but tried not to be completely hostile about it. "I swear to God, I'm gonna kick your fucking ass one of these days."

"Fuck dude, can't take a damn joke?" Hot Rod shoved him back and Jett didn't think twice before he returned the gesture with an even harder push, going chest to chest with Hot Rod.

"Come on, fellas." The Texican made his way to separate them, knowing Hot Rod was always toeing the line to one of them making good on kicking his ass.

Hot Rod saw him coming, so he decided to continue pushing buttons just inches from Jett's face. "Goddamn, all fucking wound up—is that tiny little fuck box not doin' it for you?"

The Texican didn't have time to grab either of them before Jett threw the first punch; he knocked Hot Rod square in his jaw and didn't let up after that. Hot Rod was able to keep his feet under him but crouched down to tackle Jett's torso and the men hit the ground. Jett may have been two inches shorter than Hot Rod but he was quicker, and when it came to their hand-to-hand combat oltillo, it wasn't even a contest—Jett bested him on every level. Hot Rod landed on top of Jett and returned a healthy jab to the face before Jett used his entire body to get off his back and reverse their positions.

"Knock it off!" The Texican attempted to grab Jett but they were moving too much and fists were flying. "A little help over here?" He looked at Trip and Cappy who gave simultaneous sighs and slowly made their way to the men.

"Let them be!" Frank had just finished the course and watched the commotion. He tried to catch his breath but ran next to the Texican to stop him. "They need this, let 'em be for a minute."

They all watched Hot Rod get hit in the face a few more times and then finally decided to jump in when it didn't look like he was going to get out of the choke hold Jett locked him in.

"Alright, alright!" Cappy yelled. "You're done, *both* of you!" The Texican and Frank wrapped Jett's arms up, pulling while Trip and Cappy made sure Hot Rod didn't make a move to retaliate. Both men glared at one another, panting with blood on their faces.

"You two get that out of your system, or what?" Cappy asked.

Neither replied.

"The four of us are taking the truck back to the compound. You two figure the rest of your shit out on your *walk* back." Cappy stared down both of the men. "Grow the fuck up, *both* of you. We're not doing this again," he warned before stalking off towards the truck.

Trip and the Texican immediately followed Cappy; Frank hung around for a split second before he patted Jett's shoulder and then joined the rest of their team to get a ride back.

Neither of the men looked at the other when they started their nearly ten-mile trek back towards the compound.

"You didn't have to hit me in my fucking face like that." Hot Rod finally broke the silence a quarter of the way into their punishment hike.

"Yeah. I did," Jett tersely countered, still brewing.

"You could've broken my goddamn jaw."

"But I didn't." He didn't turn to address Hot Rod directly.

They walked another mile and Jett finally started to cool down. "You done fucking disrespecting Mox, or are we gonna have to have that conversation again?"

Conversation? Hot Rod thought and rolled his eyes. *That was hardly a conversation—that was Jett losing his damn head.* "You know I'm an asshole."

"I've asked you a thousand times not to be an asshole about her.

I'll never understand your obsession with being such a dick. I never hear you saying that shit about anyone else's wife."

"She's not your wife," Hot Rod shot back.

"You know what I mean." Jett glared down as he marched through the woods. He'd finally snapped. After all that had gone on the last couple of months, he met his limit. He'd be lying if part of him didn't feel better after having hit Hot Rod a few times.

They were less than a mile from joining the team again. They both knew they needed to resolve their spat before they saw Cappy. Hot Rod decided to break the ice. "Look, I know I sound like an asshole about her, but I do genuinely like Mox. I'd never do anything to hurt her or disrespect her to her face."

Jett took a deep breath. He knew that—Hot Rod seemed to say the dumbest shit just to get a rise out of him. Perhaps now he'd at least have to think about it before being disrespectful. "I should actually be thanking you for letting me get that out of my system," Jett admitted.

Hot Rod cracked a smile and choked out a chortle. "Look who's the fucking asshole now."

"Just don't push me there anymore and I won't have to kick your ass again."

"*You* kicked *my* ass?!" Hot Rod barked out a laugh. "*Please*, I'd hardly call it that."

"You're lucky they grabbed my arms when they did. Plus, my nose already stopped bleeding an hour ago—I'll have a busted lip and nothing else. You're waking up with some bruises on your damn face tomorrow, I guarantee you."

Hot Rod flipped him off before slinging his arm around Jett's shoulders. "All bullshit aside, I *am* glad you and the fox are together. I'll do my best not to be a dick about her—she's an angel. And despite you being an asshole, you're my brother and I love you."

Jett returned the one-finger sentiment with a grin. As they got closer to the compound they saw Cappy waiting for them. They knew they were in for a lecture—at least they'd figured out their shit before that happened.

Jett was steps from his truck when he felt his phone vibrate so he grabbed it from his pocket.

FRANK
Jett you good man?

> Yeah. Everything just finally came to a
> head. My bad bro, I shouldn't have brought
> all my shit to the team like that.

FRANK
Don't apologize for that, Hot Rod deserved
what he got. I'm surprised it took this long for
you to finally notice the weight enough to do
anything about it. You've been unnervingly
steady since everything, it needed to be let out.

> I appreciate that man. Hot Rod and I are good,
> I'm gonna have my head right from now on.

FRANK
Just let me know if you need anything.

> Thank you.

Jett put his phone in the cupholder of the truck's center console and finally headed for home after a long and trying day. He was always ready to be home with his girls, but today felt like an absolute necessity versus his usual yearning and desire to be with them.

Mags and Moxie made it a habit of happily rushing Jett each time he came home from work. No matter what they were doing they'd always drop it when they heard the bay door to the garage open.

Tonight was no exception but Moxie's bright face dimmed when she got closer to Jett and noticed his lip. "Baby, are you okay?" She gently held the side of Jett's face.

"Just a little scuffle. I'm totally fine, Doll," he assured her when he leaned down and pressed his lips to hers.

Moxie's hand softly rubbed his chest when they repositioned their mouths on one another. She slowly opened her eyes as they separated. "Do you want to talk about it?" Her arms reached up and rested on his shoulders, her fingertips rubbing the nape of his neck.

"Hot Rod and I just took things a little too far today. We're good though." He stroked his hands up and down her back before settling on her cheeks.

Moxie could see the exhaustion on his face and didn't want to dwell and nag for an answer that may or may not be there. He was an expert at compartmentalizing, afterall. She couldn't help but feel something was weighing on him, so she made one more attempt.

"And this was just a 'you and the boys' kind of thing that's all good now? Or do your girls need to hop in and make things better?" She peered up at him with her chin resting on his strong chest. She felt a breath shoot out of Jett's nose when he chuckled.

He tilted his chin down to press his lips against her forehead. "My head's straight, Dollface," he tried to assure her, even though he still felt a tingle of the brooding that had come to a head that afternoon. "And you girls have already made my day better; I can't tell you how much I love getting rushed at the damn door every night."

"Oh, you better love it, Dr. Brody, because we're never gonna stop with that routine." Moxie bit her bottom lip to stop her smile. "Come have dinner with us, I made some Philly Cheesesteaks *and* homemade crinkle-cut fries."

"Moxie fuckin' Hall, you are a dream come true." Jett hooked her chin and planted another kiss on her before they ate dinner.

Jett had devoured dinner, telling Moxie multiple times it was the best Philly Cheesesteak he'd ever had. Mags was currently content with them on the couch as they'd also taken her on a pretty long walk along the waterfront after dinner.

Jett smiled, he'd been waiting for this text—it always came at the last minute because they all knew to plan for the same weekend every year. He was excited that he'd be able to go this time. He missed last year's event, the first one in eighteen years. Moxie plugged away at her laptop next to him on the couch but he leaned over to share the phone screen with her. He squished himself between the back of the couch and Mags who groaned at him for disturbing her sleep.

"Hey, Doll, look what we're doing this weekend." He held out his phone to her.

Uncertainty cast through Moxie's smile, but she was intrigued. "Cousin Camp, huh?"

"It's tradition." Jett shrugged, thumbs flying across the screen of the phone with an excited grin on his face. "Have you ever been camping?"

"I actually haven't." Moxie giggled. "Is this like tent camping or is this *glamping*? Like how many amenities will we be without?"

"Oh, it's all about roughin' it on this trip," Jett proudly informed her. "But, you'll be with a top notch survival expert; if you wanted to bring your laptop and hairdryer I'd find a way for you to use both." Jett reached up for the back of her head to pull her down to kiss him.

Despite the excitement in Jett's voice, Moxie's tone exposed her worry when she asked, "And you're sure it's okay for me to be there?"

"Are you kidding right now?" Jett sat up, chuckling. "Mox, of course you can go—it's Cousin Camp. It's Nana and Papa with all the cousins and their significant others. We don't even invite the kids— first gen cousins only—and none of our parents go. It's the best."

She rubbed her fingers on the back of his head. "Yeah, so since it's so exclusive, I just want to be sure there isn't anything weird about me being there. Are your cousins okay with that? And I haven't met Nana and Papa yet, are they—"

"Doll." Jett put his arm around her and Mags finally decided Jett was getting in her way too much so she got up to reposition herself on the other side of Moxie. "I think I know what's going through your head right now, and you don't need to worry about any of that. There's a shit-ton the extended family's been saying, but the cousins are different." He rolled his head. "Except Julia, I'll admit that, but she may not even show this year. She knows I'm not doing shit to make her comfortable in the elements and Trevor isn't exactly a boy scout. They may opt to stay in a nearby hotel and only hang out during the day. Papa told me himself he can't wait to meet you, *and* Mags gets to come."

Moxie gazed back into Jett's hazel eyes. She inhaled his encouraging demeanor, knowing she could trust him. "So what kinds of things do we need to pack for Cousin Camp, love?"

Jett didn't hide his excitement. "Well, Camp Sharpe is on a pretty secluded lake, there's no electricity, Nana and Papa have a little shack-like cabin where they sleep, and then all the cousins construct a tent city in this little grass patch off to the side."

"So, no electricity…" Moxie mentally prepared for the likely answer to her next question. "What's the bathroom situation like?"

Jett smiled widely to admit, "Roughin' it means an outhouse, and while there aren't any showers there, they do sell camping showers and I'll get you one if it'll help you be more comfortable on your first camping trip."

"No one brings a trailer or anything?" She reached for any suggestion to modern living, and at the very least running water or some version of indoor plumbing that she could take comfort in.

"The road in and out barely fits my truck, so nope—no trailers," he confessed.

She took a deep breath before her smile slowly developed from her eyes to her mouth. "Well, I trust you, so I'm obviously in." She rubbed his leg. "Thank you for inviting me."

"Are you outta your mind?! I wouldn't dream of going without you." He laughed. "We're gonna have so much fun."

Moxie couldn't help but be excited right along with him. It was like life just started since Jett walked into hers and she was in love with what he'd been creating for them.

"Okay, why don't you give me a nice little rundown of everyone I get to meet?" She encouraged Jett to put his head on her lap and began stroking his hair with one hand and holding his chest with the other. He fully appreciated her loving affection and returned her smile before he launched into a full report about each of his cousins.

38

"I knew you'd be here way earlier than everyone else, you ass!" a large, ginger-haired man yelled from his truck not too far from Jett as it pulled up to the secluded Sharpe cabin.

Jett chuckled at his cousin, Elliot, who he was closest to in age.

"You know me, gotta scope out the best spot and be done with my camp so I can help all the rookies like yourself when they finally show." Jett shrugged with a grin.

"Nana and Papa here yet?"

"Nope," Jett confirmed as he walked up to the driver's side of the truck. "Hi Bri," he greeted Elliot's wife in the passenger seat.

"Hey, Jett! So good to see you."

Elliot looked towards the lake where he saw Mags and who he assumed to be Jett's new lady. "So, we all get to meet her, huh?"

Jett wiped his smirk and fondly looked towards Moxie who wasn't paying attention to anything but Mags swimming back to her from retrieving a stick.

"That's Mox," he proudly declared with a charmed grin.

Elliot couldn't help but smile when he watched his cousin's smitten face. "I'm happy for you." He waited until Jett met his eyes. "Trevor told me pretty much everything at GG's—well, his version of everything anyway—and I'm really sorry, Jett. That's fucked up what Hallie did, and you definitely deserved better from Trev."

Jett shrugged. "At this point I'm only pissed that the divorce isn't finalized yet. They all deserve each other."

Two more cars appeared through the break in the brush, and Elliot didn't want to lose out on a good spot.

"On another note, I'm glad to see you're all set up so you can help me with all my shit now." Elliot winked before parking his truck behind the cabin.

Moxie decided she and Mags should head over to see if there was anything they could help with when she noticed more cars joining them. Jett playfully shooed her and Nana away to join Bri for drinks while he and the guys got camp organized.

Moxie couldn't help it that her eyes were glued to Jett while he worked—he was in his element and she loved watching him. He looked relaxed and content, running around to help his cousins unload, and construct their tents, using his creative ingenuity to establish the perfect set-up to enjoy the rustic camping weekend.

Jett had assured Moxie his cousins would all be accepting of her and their relationship, and they'd have a great time—that's all she's experienced so far and it helped her settle in even more. None of them made her feel unwelcome at any point, despite them being used to seeing Hallie as Jett's other half for the last ten years.

39

"We can all thank Jett." Elliot slapped his mammoth-sized hands together, rubbing them a few times. "For the first time in four years, we've got a virgin among us." His devious grin scanned the group around the late-night campfire and landed on Moxie who was propped comfortably on Jett's lap. "Mox, are you ready?"

Moxie suddenly felt all eyes on her as Jett rubbed her waist and thigh. She took a quick peek at him but his eyes were fixated on the crackling fire with a smirk on his face.

"I'm scared to answer that," she admitted with a giggle.

"You told me you've never seen a snipe before." Elliot perked his brows at her.

"Yeah, I don't even know what that is, so I can't tell you if I've seen one," Moxie replied grinning bashfully.

"She's never been camping, give her a break," Jett chimed in with a light smile, knowing full well how they were setting her up.

"Oh, Mox, you're a lucky girl though," Papa entered the chat. "This group right here?" His finger scanned his grandkids around the campfire. "Best damn snipe hunters this side of the Mississippi. You'll be catching at least one on your first trip."

"So, you just catch it? We don't have to kill any, right?" Moxie was an animal lover at heart and had no interest in killing anything, especially not for pure sport.

"Some people eat 'em." Elliot shrugged. "I don't like the taste, so we usually just fuck around, catch a few, get some pics, and then let them loose."

Jett's youngest cousin, Sterling, offered her two cents next. "I remember my first hunt, the guys were really no help at all." She rolled her eyes. "They sit here and tell you all this stuff and then once we're out there they make the newbie do all the work."

"We only made you do all the work because you were such a brat back then," her brother, Gabe claimed.

"Are you kids heading out soon? Do you want me to go grab the sacks?" Nana offered, she always loved a good snipe hunt.

There was a bit of chatter floating around the campfire now so Moxie took the opportunity to whisper to Jett, "Baby, I don't even know what we're looking for. What do these things look like and do they bite?"

Jett's head fell back. "Doll, do you think I'd put you in any kind of danger? Not only will I be right there with you, but Mags is coming too—you'll be the safest one out there. Snipes are really small, I'm talking like the size of a large squirrel." He looked at Elliot who had picked up on their conversation.

"Yeah, Mox." Elliot's brows furrowed a bit with an unworried expression. "They're technically a bird, but they don't fly long distances and they're nocturnal. The best time to find them is on a full moon and we've got one tonight."

"I can't believe I've never heard of them before," Moxie admitted, watching as the group got up to assemble for the hunt.

"Let's go grab some flashlights and put on some tennis shoes, we've gotta walk a bit to find them." Jett picked her up off his lap so they could head to their tent. "We probably need to grab Mags' leash too, just in case."

"Are we all going? They don't get scared of people?" Moxie looked around at the herd of cousins who planned to join them.

"Like Papa said, we're professionals." Jett winked. "We've gone with larger groups and we know how to be just quiet enough."

They'd been walking for about ten minutes straight through trees and along the bank of the lake in search of these animals Moxie had never seen or even heard of. A few times a cousin would claim to pick up on one, but they always just missed them. Mags had been on full alert and after the first time she tugged on Moxie, Jett had taken over the leash.

Unfortunately for Moxie, she was in the front of the pack because, of course, everyone nominated Jett to lead the way. She couldn't deny he was undoubtedly the best candidate to brave the dark wilderness ahead of everyone. *Dang him and his sexy alpha manhood*, Moxie thought. As she had her arms wrapped around one of Jett's, there was rustling in the bushes to the right of them. It didn't last long but it was enough to make her jump and Mags stop, hackles raised and tail stiff.

"Did anyone see anything?!" someone called from the rear.

"I think it's a flock!" another suggested before there was collective 'shushing' going around the crew.

Flashlights pointed in the direction of the noise. It just looked like a bunch of bushes, no one could even see the ground. There was another short burst of movement and the flashlights followed.

Jett held firmly to Mags and put his arm around Moxie. "You have your pillowcase?"

"Yeah, but I don't think I'm going to be grabbing anything. I'm ready to piss myself."

He laughed. "What are you scared of, Doll? I'm right here."

"I don't know, I think because I've never seen o—"

"Holy shit!" Gabe squealed and then there was a lot of noise in the bushes. When everyone turned their lights towards the sound they saw Elliot diving into the brush.

"El, you good?!" Jett called out and turned them to face Elliot's direction.

"Ugh! Swift little bastard!" He got up, brushing himself off. "I thought I fuckin' had it." He flung his pillowcase around to shake off the dirt and leaves. He hustled towards the front of the group and was only steps from Jett and Moxie when he pointed to her feet, yelling, "Mox! Get him! He's right by you!"

Moxie immediately screamed, her feet scrambling as she climbed onto Jett who chuckled uncontrollably. He held firmly to her as Elliot ran by them—he was the best showman when it came to snipe hunting. When Moxie realized what she'd just done, and everyone around her was laughing, she covered her face but still clung to Jett with her legs around his waist.

"I promise, I won't let a snipe get you, Doll." Jett pecked the side of her head to hide his laughter.

"I don't think I want to be the one to catch it." She motioned to get down so Jett set her gently on the ground. "I *do* want to see one, but I'm obviously too scared to be the one to grab it."

"We'll find you one." Just as he assured her they weren't giving up, they heard both Gabe and Elliot running up behind them to take off into the darkness ahead of the group.

"Gabe, go left!" Elliot yelled and all anyone could see were their flashlights flailing about as the guys hollered back and forth at each other. The group slowed and soon heard Gabe and Elliot congratulating each other—they'd caught a snipe.

Moxie's grip around Jett's waist tightened when Elliot proudly marched towards them with what looked like an occupied pillowcase. The cousins' flashlights scurried all over to slice the darkness around him as he closed in on Jett and Moxie.

Jett held firmly around Moxie's shoulders as she watched Mags stiffen and sniff the air once Elliot stood next to them.

"Mox, you get the honors." Elliot held the pillowcase up closer to her face. "You can pull it out of here and we'll get your picture."

"What?!" Moxie's eyes widened. "You want me to pick it up with my *hands*?!"

"Their teeth are so tiny, plus this one's terrified and playing dead. I think it's a weanling."

"A what?" Moxie asked while still tucked cautiously under Jett's protective arm instead of walking over to look inside the bag.

"A weanling—just a baby snipe," Elliot clarified. "Their biggest predators are owls, so they typically don't bite unless they pick up on that scent. Just stick your hand in here and let it smell you."

Moxie gaped at Elliot who confidently held the pillowcase out at her.

"What if I just put my hand right *by* the pillowcase?" she suggested instead.

Elliot shook his head. "You want them to have a clear path to your scent. Uncertainty could cause them to bite."

Jett rubbed her shoulder. "I'll be right here with you, Doll. You can stick your hand in there, the weanlings are pretty damn cute actually," he encouraged.

The group waited in anticipation for Moxie to trust Jett and stick her hand in the sack. She peered up at him and saw a beaming smile. It was a different smile than usual, but she trusted him either way so she took a step towards Elliot.

"Just slow and steady, Mox," Elliot coached as he lowered the sack so she could reach her hand in. Once her arm was about halfway into the pillowcase Elliot grabbed it and shrieked. The entire group joined him in their high pitch screeching rant.

It didn't take long for Mags to pick up on the terror behind Moxie's screams as she struggled with her arm and clung to Jett. Jett had one of his arms wrapped around her but loosened it to grab Mags when she lunged for the pillowcase and shook it around in her mouth. The screaming chorus the cousins had started slowly stopped while Mags violently attacked the pillowcase. Elliot had let go of Moxie's arm when Mags lunged because the dog was on a mission to completely eliminate any threat.

"Oh, no!" Moxie started crying. "Jett, did she kill it?" She covered her face as tears fell.

Jett let Mags continue mauling the pillowcase, knowing full well what was inside, and wrapped his arms around Moxie. He couldn't help his chest from bouncing as he tried to suppress his laughter. He glanced around at his cousins who were doing the same. Jett didn't want Moxie to continue feeling bad, he'd already felt a little guilty for sending her into this trap.

He rubbed his hands up and down her back. "Doll, I'm so sorry— we're assholes." He bit his lip and tried to wipe the smile before he reached for her chin to tilt her face to look at him. "Mags didn't kill anything."

Moxie blinked up at Jett. They could barely see each other's faces in the darkness of the night, despite the multiple flashlights among the group.

"Snipes aren't real," Jett finally admitted.

"What?" Moxie's tears slowed.

Elliot put his hand on her shoulder. "Mox, you're a trooper." He barked out a laugh. "That was fucking great!" He gripped her shoulder a few times. "Welcome to the club."

Mags sat next to Moxie and nudged her hip until she rubbed the top of her head—her only ally that night, she decided.

Jett leaned down, praising their guard dog, "Good girl." He ruffled the hair on her neck and then stood to put his arms around Moxie's waist. "Mags wasn't in on the ruse either. She definitely would've killed whatever was in that bag for you though."

The cousins were patting Moxie and laughing as they passed her.

"That was all fake?" Moxie stared up at Jett. "What was in there?"

"Dollface, I'm sorry." Jett let out his final chuckle. "Snipe hunting is tradition, but there's no such thing as snipes." He picked up the destroyed pillowcase Mags had left ripped on the ground. "See, look." He opened it.

Moxie let out a sigh of relief when she shined her flashlight in the bag and saw a stuffed Woody Woodpecker.

"You guys are children." Moxie shook her head, covering her eyes before planting her face in Jett's chest.

Jett laughed again, stroking her back and peppering the top of her head with soft pecks. "We only act like this towards the ones we love." His hands softly glided up the sides of her body. "And you know damn well I'd never let anything bad happen to you." He held both sides of her face and leaned in to press their lips together.

Moxie's heart rate was finally coming down again and she lightly gripped Jett's wrists as he cupped her face.

They were wrapped up in each other when Elliot shined his flashlight back at them. "You two coming or what?"

Jett slowed his mouth first and then smiled at Moxie. "I love you."

Moxie popped up on her tiptoes to place one more quick peck to his lips. "You're lucky I still love you too, Dr. Brody—that was mean."

Jett chuckled and slung his arm around Moxie as they walked towards Elliot who still waited for them.

"And honestly, I know who *really* has my back at the end of the day…" Moxie reached down to scratch Mags' head. "My girl loves me the most."

Mags stopped and licked Moxie's hand so she leaned down to hug the loyal dog and give her a few quick kisses.

Jett had a grateful smile as he watched their loveable canine; Mags was just as adamant in protecting Moxie from the slightest amount of harm as Jett was. The fact that his girls loved each other so much made his heart warm.

Nana and Papa had already gone to bed when everyone got back to the cabin. A handful of people stayed up to sit around the fire, but Jett and Moxie didn't last long before they headed for their tent to turn in for the night.

Moxie was *surprisingly comfortable* on the bed Jett set up for them. He told her they'd be roughing it, but he also made preemptive adjustments to make Moxie as comfortable as possible on her very first camping trip. He'd brought an air mattress and an additional pad to keep them completely off the ground. She'd never slept in a tent but quickly decided she loved it. One of her favorite things was how seemingly relaxed Jett had been since they got there. Sure, he was typically in a good and certainly steady mood around her, but this environment left Jett weightless.

Since their arrival at the cabin, it seemed as if he didn't have a worry in the world—no shitty divorce terrorizing him, no stressful job pulling at him, and no ex-boyfriend of Moxie's threatening to resurface. She'd happily watched Jett enjoying life that entire day and night. Her smile grew as she laid next to him in their tent, finally breaking their silence when Jett sat up to remove his shirt.

"Even though you guys are all super jerks"—she whipped her head towards Mags—"except for my girl, of course." She turned back towards Jett after giving Mags a few good strokes. "I had a lot of fun today, love." Moxie rubbed her hand back and forth across Jett's bare chest once he lay on his back again.

He couldn't help but allow a grin to take over. "They wouldn't have taken you snipe hunting if they didn't love you. Only newbies they deem good enough to stay are taken out on a snipe hunt. *And* not every newbie gets to go on their first Cousin Camp experience—sometimes they have to wait a summer or two to see if they're keepers. Julia didn't go for four summers—the longest we've ever iced someone out," he happily admitted. "In fact, her maiden voyage was when Gabe brought his wife out here for the first time."

Jett made sure he met her eyes when he delivered his next line. "You, ma'am, have been the quickest one accepted. Based on our short dating timeline, you should've been held over for consideration until next summer. Not only that, but historically, snipe hunting happens on Saturday night. El made the call right after dinner though and no one objected."

Moxie smirked at this new information. "Are you okay with all that?"

"*More* than okay, I knew they'd love you."

"Should I be expecting any more pranks this evening, or is it okay for me to love on you for the rest of the night?" She placed a feather soft kiss on the base of his neck.

Jett's lip curled into a devious smirk before rolling on top of her. "You'll just want to keep your volume down, if you can help it." He pushed her legs apart to make room for himself in between. "These tents aren't exactly the best for soundproofing."

"No promises tonight." She put her arms around his neck as their mouths found each other, silencing their conversation.

Jett's hands slid under Moxie's top to relieve her of it when they heard Elliot calling Jett's name. They paused to see if he'd go away.

"Jett!" His loud whisper sounded even closer this time.

Jett took a deep, reluctant breath, not wanting to stop even a little with Moxie. He decided to answer when Mags growled at the footsteps headed their way.

"Yeah?"

"Oh, good—you're not asleep yet. Hey, one more just showed up and I don't remember how to get that generator going so we can have some extra light. Can you help real quick?"

Irritation surged through Jett's body. Everyone was already

accounted for aside from one couple he'd gladly have missing this trip.

"Who's here?"

Elliot hesitated, knowing Jett would be less than thrilled. "Trevor."

"He can sleep in his car," Jett replied very matter-of-factly.

It was quiet for a long moment before Elliot was brave enough to respond, "I get you two are going through it right now, sorry to bug you. We'll grab some flashlights."

"El, seriously, tell him to bunk with Nana and Papa tonight. I'm not in the mood to see him right this second—I didn't think he'd show."

"No, I get it. We'll get it figured out."

They heard Elliot walking away from them and when Jett peered back down at Moxie's face he could tell she was hoping for at least a short explanation.

"Trevor's my cousin—Julia is his wife."

Moxie remembered the terse woman from the bar a couple weeks ago.

"Do you think she's here too then?" Moxie secretly hoped not.

Jett blew out an irritated breath but then smirked. "We'll find out soon enough if we hear her damn mouth. She doesn't love when things don't go the way she demands. But, El did say *one* more showed, so I'll hang on to that sliver of hope."

He brushed the side of Moxie's hair and then leaned down to reconnect their lips. Neither wanted to worry about the added company at that moment, they were only interested in each other.

Both Jett and Moxie woke up a couple hours later to Mags growling. Jett calmed her down when he realized it was only someone zipping a nearby tent.

"Is everything okay?" Moxie asked in a tired voice.

"Yeah, just someone going to bed or to pee." He kissed the side of her face before lying on his back, staring through the top of the tent that had mesh exposing the clear night sky.

Moxie rolled over to rest her head on Jett's shoulder, her fingertips immediately finding his exposed chest to mindlessly create heart-shaped patterns.

"Are you alright?" he asked as his arm squeezed around her shoulder.

"Much better right here." Her lips briefly met his pec as she caressed his chest. "There are so many stars," she commented when she followed his sky-focused gaze.

"I love it out here." Jett took a healthy breath.

"I'm sure you've seen a million more stars than anyone else—traveling and all." She rolled onto her back but reached up to interlace her fingers with Jett's hand that held her. "What's the most beautiful place you've ever been?"

Jett didn't take long before he leaned close to her ear to reply, "Every time I've been in your presence is the most beautiful place I've ever been."

Moxie's face lit up and her smile burned, turning her head to connect their lips. Their tongues danced until she slowed their pace. "Okay, how about *second* favorite place then?"

Jett snagged one final peck before he thought about her question and all the places he'd been; he couldn't even keep track at this point since the military had sent him to nearly every inch of the globe. Being on specialized teams kept him moving a lot on various assignments versus being deployed and stationed to any single post.

"A few years ago I was still in the Marines and we were out on a mission to stop a weapons deal." He kept the details of the assignment very basic. "We were camped out in a jungle the night before we planned to intercept a convoy that was carrying everything, and I was on watch. I remember the view when the sun came up that morning... It was definitely the most beautiful sunrise I've ever seen. I was only about a half a klick from the team—we were in some mountain range in the Congo. It didn't even look like I was on the same planet anymore, it was just so peaceful and the sun popping up over the mist of the jungle was like nothing I've ever seen before."

"That does sound beautiful." Moxie squeezed him. She could imagine how surreal that must have felt while he was on what was likely a very dangerous mission filled with hate and the ugly side of the human race.

"What about you, Doll? Where's the most beautiful place you've traveled to?"

Moxie chuckled, having to admit, "I haven't really been any-where." She slowly shook her head while under Jett's arm. "We didn't have a ton of money when I was growing up. The only time I've even been on a plane was when I went as V's date to her brother's wedding in Texas. Flying in, it looked pretty and all, but I didn't really get to do much sightseeing."

Jett couldn't believe she'd managed to go twenty-six years and had only left Washington state maybe once. He'd probably spent more time away from home than not and almost always to a new destination.

"I'd love to help you find beautiful places, Mox. We'll explore together." He turned his head to place a prolonged kiss on her temple.

"This place is already a pretty amazing start." She melted under the touch of his lips.

Jett stared up at the night sky. "What did your mom do when you were younger?"

"The first job I remember her having was as a waitress. I think her first office job was when I was still in elementary school. She started doing just general data entry and some reception duties at a large medical facility part time. When my grandma passed away, my grandpa wanted some of the life insurance money to help my mom go to school, so she got her medical coding certificate. That's what she did until she was too sick to work anymore."

"What about your dad?" Moxie had never spoken a word of him.

Moxie was quiet for a long moment before her soft voice broke the silence. "I don't know my dad," she disclosed, taking a large breath. "My mom would never respond anytime I asked about him and all I got from my grandparents before they both passed was the very age-appropriate answer that my mom would tell me one day when I was old enough to understand."

Jett rubbed her shoulder. "She never got around to telling you, did she?"

Moxie shook her head and Jett stayed silent to see if she had anything else she wanted to share.

"I've made a few assumptions based on how my mom was while I was growing up. She *never* had any guy around until her friend Harry at Golden Ridge. I was also always under strict curfew hours, wasn't allowed to date or go to dances, and she scrimped and saved to make sure she'd be able to pay for college if I lived at home those years. Besides my grandpa, she'd always been weary of men. I truly believe I was the product of something that completely broke my mom."

Jett clenched his jaw, pulling her in tighter. When she slid her arm across his chest to hug him he tugged on her until she was lying on him. His sturdy hands worked a massaging pattern on her petite back, easing her into telling him more.

"My childhood wasn't like a sad, depressing time or anything. I only know we were poor because I look back at how I grew up, but my mom always provided me with the things I needed and I don't remember ever being unhappy. Summertime was our favorite because of all the free activities at the local parks." Moxie smiled as she thought about dancing barefoot in the grass with her mom on countless occasions. "We must've been to over fifty concerts growing up—there was always live music at the park events. She was my very best friend until she ended up having to share with V when I met her right after high school."

Jett's hands never stopped their rhythm when he leaned in, kissing her forehead just below her hairline.

"Did you two meet in college?"

"No, we met at the Humane Society. I'd always wanted a dog and my mom always told me no, which I understood as I got older and realized it was probably because it would be another expense for her. So, she'd suggested I start volunteering at the shelter because that way I'd always have multiple dogs. I met V day one, about eight years ago, and we've never looked back," Moxie happily admitted.

"You've been volunteering there for that long and just adopted your first dog?" Jett was a little surprised.

"I had school, a part-time job, and volunteered while I was getting my degree. I didn't think it would be fair to have a dog then because no one was home during the day—plus, we lived in a really small apartment. I had a lot on my plate when my mom started getting sick, so I couldn't take on a dog then either. When I felt like I could handle one because my business was doing well and I'd be home whenever..." Her voice trailed off, hesitant to bring up the topic. "I started seeing my ex." She took a breath. "He wasn't a huge fan of dogs, so I just planned to wait for a bit to see if he'd come around. Honestly, that should've been the only red flag I needed; not many good people dislike dogs."

"Mox, it's not your fault that guy's a piece of shit." Jett was quick to jump in on that topic. He drew closer to her ear. "I'm so damn grateful the timing for you to be ready to adopt was when Mags needed you. There weren't any doubts before, but this just further solidifies the fact that we belong together, Doll. You and I were always destined—the three of us were always going to be a family."

Moxie knew he was right. While those feelings of shame and regret would probably linger forever, she took comfort in the fact that it was all behind her and her bright and hopeful future was with Jett and Mags.

41

"*Good morning, Dollface,*" Jett whispered when he noticed Moxie stretch from her fetal position.

They were on their sides and Jett pulled Moxie until her back was pressed against his chest. She smirked when she felt his lips on the back of her neck as he tilted her hips even closer.

"Baby, it looks like it's still dark out." She rolled her pelvis against his, grateful they each only had a thin layer of clothing between them. "I think we've got a bit more time before morning starts for us."

Jett watched her skin prickle when he kissed the base of her neck. "Mags wants out and I thought I'd wake you up to come out there with us."

Moxie chuckled. "After being subjected to a literal wild goose chase in the dark where I nearly peed myself, you'd like me to agree to get out of this cozy spot and be outside at o'dark thirty?"

"Yep." Jett's hands glided in between Moxie's legs. "I want you to grab one of these blankets so we can go watch the sun come up together—we're gonna work on that list of beautiful places. And I'll build us a little fire… It'll be even cozier than this, I promise."

She rolled over, her arms landing around Jett's neck. "I definitely can't say no to that."

They exchanged a few quick pecks before putting on a couple layers to go outside.

Jett had a healthy fire burning for them in no time. Moxie couldn't help but swoon over the new level of masculinity she got to witness since they'd gone off the grid. She settled comfortably perched on Jett's lap with her legs hanging over the arm of the chair, watching the sun make its appearance. After her morning duties, and a perimeter check, Mags situated herself between them and the bonfire.

"You were right, Jett, this is beautiful. And while this *is* pretty cozy, I don't know about cozier than where we were." She kneaded his shoulder with the arm she had around him.

"Well shit," Jett scoffed, amused. "Did I need to build you a better fire?"

Her free hand reached for his thigh, squeezing it before she turned her head to softly whisper in his ear. "Your fire's perfect, but if we were still in our cozy tent spot I could do something about my favorite part of you that's bumpin' into my leg right now."

Jett rolled his head back, chuckling at her. "Both he and I will painstakingly wait for the sun to come up as long as we get *some* action out here."

"Dr. Brody, you're out of your mind if you think I'm doing any-thing like that out here where anyone can see." Her flirtatious grin was suppressed by her teeth that caught her lip.

"Good thing I was just talking about helping you move to a cozier location." He situated Moxie on his lap so her back could rest against his chest. Jett readjusted himself a bit before whispering in her ear, "There, I'm not poking your thigh anymore."

"Mmmm," Moxie pouted, fully enjoying what she felt between her legs, rolling her hips on his lap to show him her appreciation for his placement. "I'm thinking the sun needs to hurry it up." She stretched one of her arms behind them, rubbing the back of Jett's head.

He pulled on her hips eliciting a flirtatious giggle from her.

"Wanna know what else I'm thinking?"

"Of course I do," Jett's mouth worked on her neck, waiting for the answer.

"We should come up here on a *private* weekend to have cozy time in front of this sunrise."

Jett smiled. "So, you've already decided you're a fan of camping, huh?"

"I'm a fan of this extra-rugged version of you, baby. As if I wasn't already head over heels, you bring me out here to watch you slayin' man shit left and right. I knew when we met I'd been missin' out, but *damn*." Her head rolled onto his shoulder and she placed a quick kiss under his scruffy chin.

He couldn't help but chuckle, holding his love even tighter.

"I don't love that camping means no bathroom and tons of bugs though—those two things could use improvement out here."

"I'm glad you're having a good time, Doll."

The sky transitioned from a purple haze to a blazing pink as the sun made its way to the horizon.

"Thank you for bringing me out here, Jett."

"Of course." He set his head next to hers. "I love you."

"I love you too." She smiled, squeezing the familiar arms that held her.

"Who's that out there?" Nana noticed her husband had been standing at the door for a long minute instead of making his way outside. When she looked out the window she could see someone sitting in a chair on the bank of the lake.

"It's Jett." Papa put his arm around his wife when she stood next to him.

"Why don't you go join him? I know you'd never say it outloud, but he *is* your favorite."

Papa smiled. "I thought I'd give them their moment—I'm pretty sure his Moxie's out there with him."

As they observed, they soon saw Moxie's bun as it poked above the back of the camping chair next to Jett's head. Nana held her husband's hand a little tighter when they heard subtle laughter, warming both of their hearts. When they watched Mags get up and head to the water, they decided to join the serene and scenic morning.

"Good morning!" Papa called out, not wanting to sneak up on them.

Jett turned his head to see his grandparents walking from the cabin. "Good morning." He waved.

"We're not crashing the party, are we?" Nana asked as her husband helped her onto one of the double camping chairs for them to share.

"Of course not." Moxie smiled. "There's plenty of room by Jett's amazing fire."

"You two are up early," Papa commented.

"Jett was up early, I was just an innocent bystander," Moxie clarified with a light chuckle.

"Do you guys want some coffee?" Nana asked.

"Why don't you just enjoy the rest of the sunrise—no need to get up," Jett assured her.

"I heard you kids caught yourself a snipe last night, huh?" Papa smirked, watching Moxie cover half of her face with the blanket that was draped over her and Jett.

"Mox did good." Jett hid his grin when he kissed her temple.

"They did inform you that's the initiation for officially being accepted, right?" Papa leveled his gaze at Moxie.

"Jett told me I'm in the cool kid club now. They're all still rude though." Her smile widened. "But I'm pretty grateful for their approval."

"I think I'd be disappointed if they ever gave up that tradition," Papa admitted.

"Did you start the snipe hunting tradition?" Moxie asked Papa.

Nana cocked her head towards her husband with a knowing grin.

"I did, but it was before the kids created their Cousin Camp. It was the second summer we had the cabin—almost thirty years ago now." He gestured in his grandson's direction. "Jettster was in that first snipe hunting class. He was about seven at the time I think. The youngest one of that bunch—but the bravest—weren't ya, buddy?"

Jett grinned and agreed with a nod. "I'm *still* the bravest, Papa."

Papa chuckled. "Oh, we know."

Mags waded in the water just enough for her feet to get wet when she leaned down to take a drink out of the lake. They all watched as she looked towards the horizon where the sun made its first official appearance of the day.

"I wish I had my phone on me." Moxie snuggled closer to Jett. "Look at our pretty girl right now."

Jett reached into the pocket of his sweats to hand her his phone. Moxie took several pictures while Mags watched the sun rise.

"Here, let me take a few of you guys." Nana rose out of her chair, eager to photograph her grandson's happiness.

They smiled for the first couple of snaps until Jett turned his head to peck Moxie's cheek as Nana continued to click away.

"Thank you, Nana." Jett fell in love all over while scrolling through the photos she'd taken. The pictures showcased what a natural and effortless love he and Moxie had. He was so addicted and in love with her it truly made him wonder how his heart ever settled on Hallie. Sure, at some point they were happy, but he'd *never* felt the way Moxie made him feel. It was like his soul was unlocked and freed because it was finally exposed to its other half—the counterpart it was always destined to be with. Jett put his phone in the cupholder of the chair and wrapped his arms around Moxie. She melted into him as they watched the rest of the sunrise with Jett's grandparents.

"Hey, Jett." Trevor put up a hand to wave when he joined the small group roasting breakfast sausage over the fire later that morning.

Everyone got quiet, wondering what the tone would be like for the rest of the day given Trevor's rumored part in Jett's divorce.

"Trevor," Jett flatly replied but didn't look at him. He and Moxie had been the only cousins who weren't up for Trevor's arrival the previous night. Unlike the rest of his family, Jett didn't offer him an introduction to Moxie.

A couple people, including Moxie, noticed when Trevor studied Jett's new lady where they shared an oversized camping chair.

His inhale was deep before he reached out his hand to the new face. "Hi there, we haven't met. I'm Trevor."

Moxie was predictably polite when she returned the gesture and smiled. "I'm Moxie, it's nice to meet you, Trevor."

The awkward silence became too much for Elliot so he tried to lighten the mood. "Mox, did you sleep alright? Or were thoughts of snipes running through your nightmares?"

Moxie whipped her head towards him with narrowed eyes until she broke into a smile.

A couple of the cousins snickered and Jett slung his arm around her, chuckling himself before he placed a kiss on her hairline.

"Despite your less than desirable skills as a hunting guide, I slept quite nicely, thank you," she stated with her head held high.

Elliot laughed. "If it makes you feel any better"—he lifted the leg of his flannel pajama bottoms—"I did end up with a nice little scrape when I dove into the bushes."

Everyone laughed at him.

"You guys went hunting last night?" Trevor asked, his voice full of shock, eyes frantically scanning the group around the fire for confirmation.

Jett's smile turned smug. He was overjoyed when his cousins accepted Moxie to the level of breaking tradition to indoctrinate her as soon as possible into their exclusive club.

"We were gonna wait until tonight, but this one"—he wiggled his finger at Moxie—"there was just somethin' about her. We needed to add her immediately." Elliot's oversized body shook with laughter. "It was worth the damn show she put on too."

"I wasn't scared." Moxie attempted nonchalance with a grin on her face, avoiding all eye contact.

"Bullshit!" Gabe barked out a laugh as everyone else hollered their friendly disagreements as well.

The pitch in Elliot's voice increased as he mocked her, "*Jett! Jett! OMG I'm gonna piss myself!*"

Everyone, including Moxie, was laughing as Trevor gawked. Cousin Camp rarely deviated from tradition; to snipe hunt without all of the cousins *and* on a Friday night was definitely breaking tradition. He remembered the second summer he'd brought Julia, everyone used that exact excuse for not snipe hunting. One of their cousins was in a wedding that weekend and couldn't make it, so they assured him they'd try again the following summer... which also didn't happen.

"Knock it off, El." Sterling tried to catch her breath. "I'll give it to Mox, she was willing to put her hand in that pillowcase without seeing the snipe first." She had to give credit where it was due because not many of the girls, Sterling included, blindly stuck their hand in the sack to pet the snipe before seeing it.

Moxie's adoring eyes gazed up at her love. "Jett wouldn't have let me do that if I was going to get hurt."

Jett pulled Moxie impossibly closer. "Never," he confirmed.

"No"—Elliot continued laughing—"but he sure as shit let you walk right into that snipe hunt for *our* entertainment."

"Why don't we talk about how you scream like a little girl?" Jett leveled his accusatory gaze at his cousin. "You sounded like you were about to piss *your* pants when Mags jumped on that bag."

"Jumped?!" Elliot quickly stood, jerking his head around. "That dog was fucking coming for my whole entire arm!"

"Please!" Jett rolled his eyes, firmly swatting a hand at him.

"You did shriek like a little girl," Sterling agreed.

Moxie caught Mags' attention and then slapped her legs to invite the pretty girl onto the chair with them. Mags only put her front half on top of Moxie's lap, but when she did, Moxie hugged her and gave her a couple kisses as the dog's fluffy tail flew around.

"Mags is the *best* girl, huh?" Moxie continued showing her affection.

Jett watched them with a smile in his eyes and then looked at Elliot. "That was your bad, bro, you were messin' with mama."

"Yeah, yeah. I learned my damn lesson." Elliot shoved another sausage into the bonfire.

Trevor regarded the group as so much had changed since Moxie entered the fold. His cousins tossed tradition out the window, Jett completely abandoned any ties with Hallie, his relationship with Trevor was seemingly over—or headed that way anyhow—and even Mags, who was Jett's velcro dog, had a new human that she favored just as much as Jett. He was happy to see his cousin was moving along, but deep down he was full of regret for not doing a better job to at least maintain his relationship with him.

Trevor knew if there was ever going to be another chance for him to repair his relationship with Jett, he'd have to learn to embrace Moxie. Getting to know her and managing to show Jett he could be respectful of her was going to be difficult given Jett warned him to stay clear of her. Not to mention, his wife would be showing up later that day and he knew she wasn't going to be as considerate of the situation. Rather than give Jett the heads-up that Julia was on her way, he decided to again keep quiet and let things simply unfold how they would.

"Ow ow ow, Nana!" Gabe whistled, interrupting Trevor's thoughts, when he saw his grandma walking towards them in her swim suit. It was a stereotypical grandma one-piece that had a ruffled skirt attached to her waist that dropped to the middle of her thighs. To top it off, it was a royal purple shade with a tropical flower print.

Nana did a little strut and spinned to show off her new suit. The cousins joined Gabe in their friendly catcalling towards their grandma.

"Damn, Papa, you're brave letting her out of the house wearing that," a blonde cousin sitting next to Jett commented.

"My little pearler's still a dreamboat even after decades of life have captured us both." Papa gave his wife an enchanted smile as she made her way to the lake with a simple inflatable ring floatie and her oversized sun hat.

The cousins loved watching their grandparents still obsess over one another after all this time. It was a dream relationship they all strived for.

Mags perked up, ready to spend her day in the water now that someone was getting in.

"You ready to float on the lake all day, Doll?" Jett squeezed Moxie's thigh.

She beamed up at him. "Of course."

It didn't take long for everyone to start making their way back to their tents to change into swimwear for the day.

43

Jett, Elliot, and Gabe sat in short lounge chairs out on the giant inflatable dock Papa had purchased for this Cousin Camp when a car pulled up to the cabin. Jett looked over at the Sunchill float that was tethered to their dock where Moxie and Mags were floating with a few of his cousins. She was tossing back seltzers and appeared to be having a good time. The smile his heart projected on his face watching her was instantly turned upside down when he noticed whose car it was that had arrived.

Jett took a healthy swig of beer. "Here we fuckin' go," he mumbled to Elliot.

"Trev didn't mention she was coming. I would've given you the heads-up, you know that."

"It's not yo—" Jett stopped dead in the middle of his sentence. "What the *fuck* is she doing here?" His jaw clenched as Hallie got out of the passenger side of Julia's Tucson.

"Shit," Elliot groaned.

"El, I'm gonna fucking lose my shit. What the fuck is this?"

"Bro, please give me a minute to go over there and figure it out— look, Papa's already talking to Trevor."

"Trevor better pray that fucking wet noodle didn't show up too." Jett's eyes scanned the Tucson, waiting for the slimy schmuck to slither out of the car.

Elliot got up and grabbed the paddleboard that was tethered to their floating dock so he could get to shore. Jett seethed, he and Moxie were having a genuinely good time and he knew the mood of the entire camp was about to shift with Julia there. It only made things that much worse that she brought Hallie. Apparently not all of his family was able to cut Hallie off as easily as he was. Her belly was even larger now and she did nothing to hide it, which should've been enough for everyone to at least spare him from having to physically be around her. Of course Julia had always been a unique breed of heinous snatch, so the fact that she brought his cheating ex along didn't surprise Jett.

"Damn," Gabe cautiously started. "Trev couldn't even give you a heads-up about those two, huh?"

"That little asshole didn't say shit about everything Hallie was doing behind my back. I'm not shocked at all he failed to mention they'd be showing up today." Jett shook his head in disgust.

"I'm sorry man." Gabe reached over and gripped his cousin's shoulder a few times. "You know the only reason we were all ever nice to Julia is because of you and Hallie, right? Now that it's over with that wench, none of us give a shit about offending either one of them. Those two just made the biggest mistake showing up here, *especially* after what Hallie's done to you."

Jett didn't reply right away. He peered back at Moxie to see if she was watching the shoreline at all. To his relief, she was now lying nearly on her back with Mags rolled up right next to her, giggling away to whatever Sterling was telling her.

Gabe followed his gaze before he said, "And you know we all genuinely love Mox, right?"

Jett peeled his focus away from Moxie and looked at his cousin.

"We're not just embracing her because we feel bad for you and your situation," Gabe assured. "I thought you'd be an angry ball of fury when I heard about everything, but she's got you walking around this weekend like life's just begun."

"I didn't know life could be so good," Jett finally responded. "I'll admit, I was fucking pissed when I came home, and to find Mags gone put the goddamn icing on the cake for me. Mox saved Mags and then she saved me. This isn't to spite Hallie or some rebound… I'm in love with Moxie."

Gabe cackled. "Obviously! Shit, none of us thought that—okay, none of us *cousins* thought that. You know how some of the family is though."

"Yeah." Jett took a deep breath. "Look, I'll try to be on my best behavior, but Mox is having a genuinely good time and I won't sit by and watch that smile get chipped away because those two showed up." He stabbed a hand towards the cabin.

"As far as I'm concerned, keeping a leash—and a muzzle—on those two is Trev's problem." Gabe shrugged and finished his beer. "Godspeed to him with that one, we're all gonna have to start placing bets on how long it'll take for you to kick his ass this weekend." He laughed.

Jett didn't want things to get to that point. Cousin Camp wasn't the place for those issues, but he wouldn't allow Moxie to suffer any kind of discomfort when it came down to it. He decided he'd at least give her the heads-up and if she gave him any indication this wasn't going to work out, he'd make a move from there. For now, he was going to soak in the afternoon on the lake with his favorite girls.

"I'm gonna go chill on that float with her before I have to make any ass-kicking decisions." Jett lightly slapped his cousin's back. "You wanna join? Looks like there's plenty of room still."

"Let's go," Gabe agreed before standing.

Trevor watched Elliot pull up to the shore on his paddleboard. He figured someone was going to come be the buffer. Hallie and Julia had cornered Papa while Trevor was getting their bags out of the car.

"Hey." Elliot made a slow approach towards Trevor and grabbed a cooler from Julia's car.

"Look, I didn't know Hallie was coming—I'm sure that's what

you're over here to talk to me about. Please just let me get this figured out with them before you do anything."

Elliot scrunched his eyebrows. "Do anything? Trev, we're not ten, what are you afraid of me doing?"

Trevor sucked in a deep breath. "I didn't mean it like that, sorry. I'm just as surprised as everyone else and there isn't much I can do about the situation now."

"All I wanted to come and say to you is that Jett's been through enough. We all know this isn't exactly helpful so just keep that in mind while those two are here. I'm sure things will be tense, but we're all gonna still try to have a good weekend. It's no secret what's gone down. And at the end of the day you and Jett are family, but outside of that, we all know what's right and what's wrong. Don't blame people for acting accordingly."

Trevor only nodded.

"You might wanna give them notice that Moxie's here," Elliot suggested. He wasn't sure if they knew about Jett's relationship, but he would bet his last dollar they had no clue she'd joined them for Cousin Camp. He hadn't spent as much time around Julia as others, but based on what he'd seen and heard of her over the years, he knew she'd be the one to start a war that weekend.

Trevor filled his lungs with air, making a full rotation with his head—it was going to be a long weekend.

"I'll help you get the rest of your tent set up for the girls," Elliot offered, knowing Trevor was going to be on the outs now.

"Thank you, El."

The two men inflated a couple of air mattresses when Julia and Hallie approached.

"Hi, El," Julia was the first to greet him.

"Hey, Jules." Elliot was friendly and opened his arm when Julia stepped up to hug him.

"Thank you for helping out, we were just catching up with Papa." Julia pecked her husband.

Hallie stood a couple steps away from the group but noticed Elliot glance down at her belly.

"Hey." Hallie hesitantly waved at Elliot.

"Hallie." He offered a flat smile and a dip of his chin.

"Hey, babe"—Trevor looked at his wife—"why don't you girls get your suits on and grab the tubes from the car. I'll blow them up and we can go float for a while before dinner."

"Sounds good." Julia took Hallie's hand and they headed for the car to grab the tubes.

Trevor faced Elliot once the girls were far enough away. "Jett may not rearrange my face if we're all out there floating for the initial meeting… It'll be harder to do anyway."

Elliot laughed. "No one's ever accused you of being stupid." He plugged the air mattress he'd just inflated and tossed it into Trevor's tent. "I'm gonna grab a few drinks and snacks and then make my way back out there. Just remember what I said—everyone just needs to take it easy."

Trevor nodded along, agreeing but knowing he wouldn't have control over others' emotions or their actions.

A speaker blasted music from the inflatable dock and all the cousins, along with Nana and Papa, were floating and enjoying the late afternoon sunshine.

Jett had commandeered a double float for himself, Moxie, and Mags. The girls sat on each of the tubes within the inflatable while Jett was in the water holding onto the side to keep them near the rest of the group. He was sure to maintain a position on the opposite side of Trevor, Julia, and Hallie—they hadn't even so much as greeted each other.

Moxie and Sterling had become close, they had quite a few similar interests and were almost the same age. Sterling didn't miss an opportunity to tease her cousin with cradle-robbing jabs when she found out only two months separated her and Moxie. A handful of cousins were having fun with the eight year age gap.

"So, Jett, is it weird that you joined the military when Mox was still in elementary school?" Sterling lifted her heart-shaped sun-glasses and pumped her brows at him.

Jett flipped her off with an easy smile. "It's only weird when you think about it like that. It hardly seems like that many years apart since we're both grown adults."

"It must be so nice going to the movies cheap as hell." Gabe pointed between his cousin and Moxie. "One senior and one student."

Sterling added another thought, quickly shouting over the amused group, "Jett you'll have to be on the paperwork for renting a car on vacay, Mox isn't old enough yet!"

"Shit," Elliot barged in their conversation. "Every man's dream is to snag a younger woman." He braced himself for a friendly swat from his wife who was a few months older than him.

"And every *woman's* dream is to snag a super hot, older man." Moxie leaned back to cup the side of Jett's face and kiss him. She took full advantage of their mouths touching because she'd been fiending for him since the second he'd removed his shirt—his chis-eled chest was enough to send her over the edge. Jett also fully indulged in her lips, and tongue, as he held one hand up to flip off his cousins who'd been teasing them for the better part of the day now. They finally separated not wanting to get too carried away in front of everyone.

"Shit, a few more years and you could've been her dad." Elliot chuckled and lifted the top of the floating cooler to exchange his empty beer can for a new one.

"Keep chirpin', asshats." Jett's light tone led a hand roll to wel-come them for more if that's what was going to entertain his cousins. "I'm not embarrassed, you're the ones spewin' a bunch of bullshit right now."

"Shit! Embarrassed?!" Elliot shouted. "If anyone's gonna be embarrassed in that equation it's Mox having to wipe your geriatric ass one day—probably soon with that ten-year age gap."

The small group around them all cackled again.

"You're just jealous, El," Moxie teased and stuck out her tongue. "One, I'd *never* be embarrassed of Jett. Two, it's not even ten years"—she grinned at her handsome love interest—"and three, Jett takes *amazing* care of himself, he's never gonna be geriatric."

Jett couldn't get up on the floatie quick enough to connect with Moxie's lips again. She caught his face between her petite hands and melted in the familiar feeling of their mouths moving against each other.

Cousins in the immediate area began both ew'ing and whistling at them before Elliot chucked a Nerf football at Jett. He ended up missing but the ball flew right over his head and plopped into the water just beyond Mags.

The German Shepherd perked her head as she fixated on the neon blue ball that floated in the water not too far from her. Moxie and Jett's lips separated just in time to watch the dog launch off the back of the double floatie.

"Oh shoot!" Mags had sliced the plastic headrest on the floatie with her nails. The inflatable tube hissed as air raced out of it. "This one's toast." She smiled at Jett as she pointed at the hole. "Good job, El!" Moxie playfully scolded him.

"I can paddle us back to shore, we're not gonna last long out here." Jett chuckled. It was getting late anyway and he was hungry.

Mags had retrieved the ball and swam back to the float. It was much easier for her to climb on now that it was losing air. Moxie called her over to her side of the inflatable and then she slipped into the water with Jett.

"I'll tow you guys, Doll, you don't have to get out."

Moxie giggled. "I don't mind." She watched Mags sprawl out with her head propped on the side of the float. "Obviously our pretty girl wasn't about to help any."

Jett joined her laughter and they continued kicking towards the shore as the float steadily deflated.

"You guys coming back out here?" Elliot shouted after them.

"Nope!" Jett responded and then winked at Moxie for a private reply, "I'm starving and ready to get out of these trunks."

"Me too," Moxie agreed. "Plus, I need some water—I'm buzzin' a little more than I'd like to be right now."

"We're camping, Doll, you can be buzzed all weekend if you want," he assured her.

"I think it's a good idea to take a break so I can enjoy some tequila with you at the fiesta tonight."

"That was a given for us," he confirmed. "I also can't wait to get ahold of your Texas Caviar and that ceviche—you're gonna have everyone begging for those recipes."

Moxie giggled, her eyes sparkling.

"Alright, you're gonna need to swim now too, Mags." The float spewed the last bits of air and the confused dog was trying to stand. Jett gave her a gentle push so her legs didn't tangle and the three of them finished the swim to the shore with Jett towing the deflated float behind him.

"Yikes." Moxie stumbled a bit after getting out of the water. "I didn't realize I was that tipsy—floating makes the actual state of drunkenness quite deceiving." She giggled at the slight swaying she felt.

Jett's large palm slapped her butt before he wrapped his arms around her. "I won't let you fall." He pecked the top of her head. "You know what might feel good right now?" he asked while holding her.

"I know what would positively feel *phenomenal* right now." She bit her bottom lip, her hands gliding up his defined abs and landing on his pecs. "I've been terrorized all day only getting to gawk at your perfect chest… It's definitely time to touch now."

Jett's head fell back as he chuckled. "I'm more than happy to make that happen too, but I was gonna suggest a quick little shower and then change into something cozy."

Moxie glanced towards the water, it didn't look like anyone was on their way to follow them. "We'll have to go for record time since that shower doesn't have an endless supply of water."

"We better get started." Jett flashed a toothy grin and scooped Moxie up in his arms to hustle them behind the cabin where he'd set up her portable shower next to his truck, her giggles music to his ears.

44

There was a pleasant commotion as everyone either helped cook meat or set up the tables with the rest of the fiesta spread. Jett grilled with a few of the guys but kept a watchful eye on Moxie—not trusting Julia or Hallie in the least. He noticed and appreciated that Sterling had been maintaining a close proximity to Moxie since everyone had come out of the water.

Moxie had assured Jett she'd be okay with the added company when he tried again to talk to her about it after their short shower. He trusted that she'd tell him the truth about her feelings, but wasn't convinced she didn't have some liquid courage going on when she told him things would be fine. Either way, he wouldn't accept Moxie being uncomfortable in the slightest.

Sterling dipped another chip into Moxie's Texas Caviar, continuing to gush about the taste as Julia and Hallie found themselves across the table from them. When Sterling noticed, she did her best to quickly chew and swallow her bite so her mouth was free to step in if needed. Hallie rubbed her swollen belly on their approach while Julia had her venomous eyes locked on Moxie, who didn't seem to notice.

"Hal, let's move a few of these around, you know how much Jett *loves* your guac." Julia pushed a container of salsa away from the tortilla chips to make way for a bowl of homemade guacamole.

Moxie didn't respond or look up at them, she continued giving her ceviche a final mix to set it out.

"No." Julia reached over the table, her hand shooing Moxie's bowl from the intended placement. "Meats don't go over here."

"Nana actually asked us to put this by all the chips," Sterling announced, narrowing her eyes and throwing Julia an equally spiteful expression.

"Well, we don't want to go around upsetting Nana now do we?" Julia offered a scrunched, acidic smile.

"Julia," Sterling's voice was a pleasant version of terse, "have you had the *absolute* pleasure of meeting Mox yet?" She slung her arms around her new favorite cousin.

"Not formally," Moxie answered, recalling the time Julia barged over to make her disgust of Jett known at the bar in front of Frank and Shane.

Julia's lip sneered, but Moxie didn't look at her. "You know, I was actually hoping to introduce her to Jett's *wife*." Julia put an arm around Hallie, glaring at Moxie, to emphasize the rest of her statement. "The one I already tried to tell you he has. This is Hallie."

"*Ex*-wife," Jett very firmly corrected as he joined them. Sterling's hold around Moxie retreated when Jett's hand landed on the small of Moxie's back. "If you wanted to formally meet Mox you could've done that while we were on the lake all afternoon. You didn't need to try to trap her when I wasn't nearby—not that I'm surprised this is the approach you'd take." His hand settled around Moxie's waist.

"You didn't exactly come over and greet anyone when we got here, Jett," Julia hissed.

"Why would I?" he scoffed. "I've told you I don't have anything to say to you, that includes any kind of greeting." Jett shrugged before his tone darkened. "This isn't the time or place for whatever you two need closure on. Even more than that, you'll *both* be respectful of Mox or you'll regret having shown up here."

"Babe—" Hallie started, but Jett was quick to cut her off.

"Don't fucking call me that," Jett snapped.

"Jett," Hallie tried again. "We didn't know she'd be here."

"Yeah. Right," he responded in a hateful tone. "Sure as shit didn't know *you'd* be here. You lost the privilege of being here the second we were over. I have no idea why you keep inviting yourself to *my* family functions."

"I thought maybe we could talk…" Hallie trailed off.

"You and I have nothing to talk about. Whatever you have to say can be relayed through my attorney."

The previously bustling group around them was now quiet as nearly everyone had turned their attention to the toxic interaction. Jett's stance was eerily still, his hold on Moxie tense. She decided to make a move before things got any worse than they already were. Her hand found Jett's, and the second they touched he interlaced their fingers. Moxie slowly spun towards him so they could be chest to chest.

She spoke softly after lifting her chin to meet his gaze and offered a neutral expression. "Baby, it's about time for Mags' dinner. I was gonna go feed her, do you want to come or are you stayin' out here?"

Jett affectionately squeezed her, his muscles relaxing slightly. "Let's go, Doll." He maintained his gentle hold on her hand while they walked toward his truck to feed Mags.

Once they were out of sight from the rest of his family, Jett apologized, "Mox, I'm sorry about them. Are you still okay with things or do you—"

She interrupted him with a sweet smile, "You don't have to be sorry—I'm not upset." Moxie softly placed her hand on Jett's chest just over his heart. "You told me my job is to keep that asshole out of your heart. I was just making sure he wasn't trying to make an appearance on my behalf."

Jett held Moxie's head before connecting their mouths. His tongue plunged over hers and she held tightly to his body as they continued.

"My heart may burst completely one day from loving you so damn much, Doll," Jett warned when their lips slowed.

Moxie giggled. "Oh, Dr. Brody, I think you can handle it." She slowly reached up on her tiptoes to peck him. "And for the record, I love you *and* the asshole. I just don't want you to do or say anything you'll end up regretting. We're having a good time and I don't want that to change for you."

Jett took a deep, grateful breath and Moxie rubbed her hands up and down his back. He wasn't exaggerating, his heart pumped full of love whenever the mere thought of Moxie crossed his mind. The surge of love wasn't in spite of seeing Hallie that weekend—he truly felt an inexplicable connection to Moxie. She was, without a doubt, his soulmate.

"Jett." Moxie encouraged him to look at her. "You haven't really had a ton of time to decompress from everything she's done to you. I'm right here if you want to talk about it."

"I'm not having any feelings of regret for leaving her or filing for divorce. And I sure as hell don't have any reservations about you and me being together. I love you, Dollface. All I want is a future with you and Mags."

"I wasn't suggesting any of that at all." Moxie gently cupped his cheek, smiling softly. "That future is absolutely yours, baby, because that's all I want too," she assured before tapping his heart again. "If there's anything on your mind that's chipping away at that amazing heart of yours though, I need you to tell me so I can make it better."

Jett put her hand in his, kissing it before he acknowledged, "Thank you, Mox. I just get pissed having to see her. I've done what I can to cut ties and yet she continues to surface at *my* family events. She's pregnant and engaged to her little wet napkin baby daddy but insists that we still need to talk. I don't get why she can't just let me go my separate way at this point. And I'll admit, the asshole begs for an escape when I see you being subjected to all this bullshit. I can deal with being pissed at her, but I can't deal with even the thought of you being hurt in any kind of way."

Moxie wrapped her arms around Jett and squeezed him before she lifted her head off his chest, gazing into his hazel eyes.

"Jett Dr. Brody Sharpe, you are—without a doubt—the very best man I've ever known. I don't love that we've both been subjected to plenty of awful things from toxic partners, but you know what?"

Her adorable smile was so full of love that Jett's face softened. His hands slid around her waist and down to land on Moxie's cheeks to pull her closer. "What, Doll?"

"You and I have shown each other what we do love and that's all we're going to allow from now on. No one gets to ruin our weekend or get in the way of the life we want."

Jett pressed his lips against Moxie's forehead and held them there for a long moment while he held her. He loved this woman. She'd heard him and was keeping up her end based on the conversation they had a couple weeks ago about his heart. "Mox, thank you for being the soft and sweet. I needed that reminder."

"I don't want to deter you from any kind of healing—so you say what you need to, Jett. I just wanted a private moment to remind you I love you and I'll still love you if the asshole wants to settle some scores—just know you don't have to do that on my behalf. If anything, I feel bad for her. I can't imagine the regret she must feel from losing you. Anyone crazy enough to take your love for granted never deserved it in the first place."

Jett fondly shook his head and smiled widely. "I promise I'll be making up for the ten years her undeserving ass stole from us." He brushed the side of her face with the back of his knuckles.

Moxie's lips curled to a devious grin as she continued to gaze at Jett. "I mean, I was only sixteen ten years ago—I don't think it would've worked out for the two of us then." She giggled.

Jett joined her laughter as he lifted her off the ground to hold her. "I'm gonna have to start limiting your time around Sterling," he joked. "Let's get Mags her dinner and then go enjoy that bomb-ass Mexican spread we've got goin' on out there."

"Deal," she agreed. "I'll grab the tequila out of the cooler too."

A few minutes later Papa walked around the back of the cabin to check on them. He found Jett sitting on the tailgate of his truck bed while Mags ate and Moxie was in the tent putting on more layers.

"Hey, buddy." He slowed his approach.

"Hi, Papa." Jett turned around when he heard him.

"You guys doin' alright?" He glanced around. "Is Moxie okay?"

"We're good." Jett nodded. "We wanted to feed Mags before we eat and Mox is getting cold so she's bundling up before we come back out there. Is everyone eating already?"

Before Papa could answer, Moxie came out of the tent carrying one of Jett's hoodies. "I wasn't sure if you'd want this for later."

"Thanks, Doll." Jett leaned over to peck her when she handed him the sweatshirt.

"Papa, are you taking a pre-dinner shot with us?" Moxie smiled.

"What do you two have over there?" Papa cranked his neck to see what Jett had sitting next to him.

Moxie picked up the bottle and gave it a little shake. "Tequila."

"Oh, shit." He shook his head, chuckling. "Don't tell Nana I took a pull before dinner."

Both Moxie and Jett made zipper motions over their mouths and shared the bottle. Each of them took a quick swig from the honey-colored liquid before they headed back out to join the fiesta.

45

Everyone was pretty well into their first round of food as they sat around the fire. Jett got up for another helping and Trevor followed him.

"Hey, thanks for the heads-up." Jett didn't bother to look at his cousin when he noticed him standing next to him grabbing more chips. "Can't say I'm surprised."

"Jett, I didn't know she was bringing Hallie." Trevor shook his head, truly blindsided just as much as everyone else had been.

"It's all good." Jett turned so he could face his cousin. "You better hope your wife has enough sense to be respectful for the rest of this weekend because I won't hesitate ripping her a new one. It's clear she has no damn respect for the guest list we've established for almost twenty years."

Trevor thought better than to point out the weekend had already deviated from tradition with the snipe hunt. He also held his tongue pointing out the divorce hadn't been finalized yet, so technically speaking Jett's wife, Hallie, was still part of the guest list. He didn't have time to contemplate his response any longer as Jett went back to sit with Moxie without another look.

"Alright, listen up kiddos!" Elliot slapped his hands together before wiping crumbs off his shirt as he stood. "Next year is the *twentieth* anniversary of Cousin Camp! What're we doing to celebrate?"

"I say we start bringing the kids so they can learn the traditions to pass along," Gabe's wife suggested.

A chorus of groans and immediate disapprovals made its way around the campfire.

"Don't get me wrong, I love the kids," Sterling made her opinion known, "but why subject those of us without kids to have to be around them all weekend when this has been our thing for years? We already have an established family weekend—this one's just for us."

"Yeah, well there are only like two of you without kids anyway," Gabe's wife countered.

"Three," Sterling corrected.

"You and Trevor are the last ones standing. Jett and Hal—" She'd begun gesturing towards Hallie before she regretted everything that just came out of her drunk mouth.

"That's *not* my fuckin' kid." Jett didn't look at anyone in particular but his terse voice made it crystal clear in case anyone missed the memo.

Gabe and his wife offered Jett an apologetic look.

"We're not inviting the kids to our weekend," Elliot declared. He tried to divert the attention from his cousin who'd already received more grief than he ever deserved. "Who wants to hear *my* epic idea for celebrating?"

A few hands went up and several other people silently begged for him to continue just to move beyond the awkwardness.

"I propose we extend the weekend to a whole week *and* I think it's time we add to the old cabin a bit."

"I don't know about that, El," Papa was the first to comment. "You know we love our little cabin."

"I get that, but you two need a few updates and some accommodations so you can keep coming out here with us for another twenty years."

Everyone tried to put in their two cents at the same time and eventually a few side conversations took place.

Jett had already talked to Elliot about helping out with some updates for their grandparents, so he didn't bother arguing with the group. He decided Elliot was a big enough voice for the both of them. Instead, he directed his attention to his two favorite girls.

"You need a bath, girlfriend." Moxie giggled as Mags climbed up on the double chair with them. "I'll still cuddle you though, pretty girl."

"Lay down, Mags." Jett snapped his fingers at her while she stood with her front paws on Moxie's thigh.

The clingy dog settled on the opposite side of the chair but her top half laid across Moxie who snuggled on Jett's lap.

Hallie watched them from across the bonfire and decided Moxie genuinely loved Mags. The new woman had fully embraced the protective beauty on her lap by putting her arms around her neck to kiss the dog's head. Hallie loved Mags, but she surely never let her cuddle up after camping all weekend, her long hair had a tendency to pick up all kinds of foreign matter.

Hallie made the mistake of peeking at Jett. Her ex-husband's eyes were fixed on his new woman and she saw nothing but pure love and adoration. She watched as Moxie turned her head and whispered something to Jett which elicited a smile and him kissing on her neck. Hallie only broke her gaze when Julia noticed her staring and put her hand on her leg.

"You doing okay?" Julia asked her best friend.

Hallie put on a fake smile and nodded. When she looked towards Jett again he was watching Moxie and Mags make their way toward the outhouse. It surprised her to see Jett's velcro dog leaving him to follow Moxie. Jett finally turned back to the bonfire when Moxie closed the outhouse door. Hallie got caught looking at him and immediately received a scowl.

She hated being iced out like that. If she was being honest with herself, she still loved Jett. While Jett was away, she'd decided letting go of him in favor of Billy was the right move. Jett would always have work taking him away from her and she'd lived through that lifestyle for longer than she was comfortable with.

Hallie loved Billy and was genuinely excited for the family they were building. Sure, he'd been acting off lately, but the worst of it had been recent—since Jett got home. Hallie had to admit the divorce and how Jett had been treating her likely contributed to Billy's moody demeanor. She was willing to overlook that since he promised things would be better now that they could officially be together with no restrictions.

Hallie recognized Billy wasn't the same man Jett was—they were two very different lovers. Jett's balance of effortless model masculinity and the chivalrous and fearless ways in which he loved remained unmatched; Billy was physically smaller than Jett and his masculine energy had an edge to it Hallie couldn't place. Her mind and heart twitched and stung every time she watched her ex-husband interacting with Moxie. She wondered if Jett felt the same when he saw her and Billy together. Her heart stung as she took a deep breath and stared into the crackling embers of the bonfire in front of her.

Moxie really hated the outhouse, so she always tried to make her trips super quick. It was a much harder task in the dark but she managed. When she came out she decided a sweet treat was in order and headed for the truck to grab the multiple tubs of cookie dough she'd made for the trip that they hadn't broken into yet. She was just about back to the firepit when she stopped and waited for Mags who was on a scent trail near the cabin. Moxie had her hands full with a blanket and three tubs of cookie dough when she heard stomping feet rush towards her and a loud '*rah*' style scream before someone was lifting her up. She immediately screeched and threw the tubs of cookie dough in the air. The voice behind her, Gabe's voice, chuckled as he set her down but he soon started yelling again when Mags charged him, barking and growling. He grabbed Moxie's shoulders and used her as a shield until she could calm the dog down.

Jett raced toward her when he heard the scream. She was still rubbing Mags' neck to assure her things were fine when he made it to them.

"Gabe, you dumbass." Jett shook his head, squeezing Moxie's shoulder to check if she was alright.

Gabe picked up the blanket Moxie dropped and shook it off. "My bad." He tried wiping his smirk. "I forgot she gets testy around Mox."

"I'm glad I *just* peed." Moxie stuck out her tongue at Gabe.

Jett helped by picking up all the cookie dough tubs that were luckily still closed. "We're not sharing any of this cookie dough with you," Jett claimed before giving Mags a few healthy pats to her head and then tucking Moxie under his arm to return to the fire.

"Did she bite him?" Elliot's grin glowed by the fire.

"No, but he's still a dumbass." Jett looked back at Gabe who threw up his hands, still convinced the almost-bite was worth scaring Moxie.

"You *are* a dumbass, Gabe," Elliot agreed. "You didn't see her try to rip my arm off last night?"

"I tried to warn you guys—keep testing her." Jett shook his head and patted his dog again before commanding her to lay down by their chair. "Here Papa, try this." He handed over two of the cookie dough containers for him to choose from and kept the third for himself.

"Is Mags okay?" Elliot's wife, Bri, asked. "She's never been so protective, not to mention she hasn't been attached to your hip all weekend." She chuckled because everyone knew Mags was basically another limb on Jett.

Jett took a deep breath and put his arm around Moxie, his eyes finding her gaze as he responded, "Mox saved Mags when she was scared and alone after being dumped at an animal shelter while I was gone for work." He glanced at Bri and rubbed Moxie's shoulder. "There's nothing wrong with Mags, she's doing exactly what she's supposed to do—she's keeping her mom safe."

Bri had snuck a quick peek at Hallie when Jett made reference to the animal shelter but nodded in response to his explanation.

"Where did you guys get this damn cookie dough?" Papa had chunks from both containers, hesitant to pass the treats around the fire. "And what kind are you hiding over there, buddy?" He wanted to sample all of them.

"This one's my special recipe Mox makes for me. I won't be passing this around the fire, but I might share a chunk with you, Papa." Jett winked.

"Hand that over here, Jettster," Papa commanded, his hand laid flat with his fingers encouraging the pass. "Is it another chocolate chip?"

"That's cowboy cookie dough." Jett rubbed Moxie's shoulder. "What other ones did you make, Doll?"

"There's a loaded peanut butter chocolate chip cookie dough and then a white chocolate macadamia nut one. So, hopefully no one's allergic to boy cookies because they've all got nuts."

"Boy cookies?!" Elliot howled, taking a bite out of the loaded chocolate chip. "Goddamn, this is bomb!"

"Did you run out of time to bake the cookies, or what?" Sterling laughed, reaching for a chunk from the white chocolate macadamia nut container.

"Nope, we like the dough." Moxie flashed a grin at Jett who offered a chunk of the cowboy cookie dough toward her to share.

"You could probably put some of it on a roasting skewer and bake one if you wanna ruin it," Jett suggested to his cousin with a friendly warning look.

Most of the group settled in to enjoy the fire and the company. Julia and Hallie whispered to one another throughout the night as they got tired of watching the family become enamored with Moxie.

46

A couple hours had passed and half the camp had turned in for the night including Nana and Papa. The much smaller crowd drew closer to the fire Jett and Elliot continued to feed to keep everyone warm as the pleasant summer evening turned into a dark and chilly night.

"Hal, do you need a pillow or something?" Trevor asked as she slowly readjusted her position on the camping chair she sat in, holding her stomach.

"Would you mind, Trev?" She looked almost apologetic to have him go back to Julia's car to grab her the seat cushion she'd been living on lately.

Trevor rubbed his wife's shoulder as he stood and smiled at Hallie. "It's not a problem."

"Nice to see someone around here cares about helping the one growing an entire human right now." Julia shot a quick and narrowed glance at Jett.

Jett wasn't paying any attention to her. He and Elliot were in a deep conversation about college football. Moxie sure heard and saw her gesture though. She shared a double camping chair with Jett that had foldable leg rests, his legs were stretched out on one of them and Moxie had hers curled with her knees resting on him. She squeezed his thigh to gently interrupt his conversation.

The amusement immediately vanished from Julia's face as she snarled, "Do what?"

"He already told you this isn't the time or the place, so please quit trying to bait him by taking digs at Jett in front of everyone. He's been tolerant enough to take it, but it's super disrespectful and I don't like it."

Julia practically salivated at the opportunity to put Jett's new pet in her place. "Can't take the fact that he's got a *long* history with Hallie?" Her vile grin taunted Moxie.

"Julia," Jett warned in a sharp, threatening tone.

Her tongue swiped across her teeth with closed lips, assessing how far she'd test Jett. "Or is the child bride getting upset liste—"

"Watch your fucking mouth when you talk to her. And she's right, this isn't the time or the place." Jett glared daggers when he interrupted her. The only thing that kept him seated was the fact that Moxie sat between his legs.

"Keep a muzzle on that one then—*she* started it." Julia jabbed her finger towards Moxie as Trevor begged her to stop talking.

"I don't think she did. I believe she very politely asked you to quit being a bitch." The arm Jett had around Moxie tightened.

"Jett, come on, shit's not worth it," Elliot tried to shut down the argument by reasoning with the level-headed one.

"Oh, you haven't heard the half of it yet," Julia threatened. "How dare you walk around here like the better person when you can't even give Hallie enough respect to have a conversation." Her focus fell on Moxie. "Something to look forward to because your little honeymoon phase won't last."

Moxie slowly shook her head and Elliot joined Trevor in asking Julia to stop.

"Oh, you don't think so, huh? You've known him for five seconds and think you're anything more than a rebound?" She belted out an evil laugh.

Jett shifted as if he was going to stand. "I won't hit a female, but I'm not above tossing your ass in the lake if you don't knock it the fuck off," he gritted through his teeth. His finger violently gestured towards Julia and her only two supporters when he continued, "And you assholes don't even know what respect means. Don't go tossing that bullshit around me."

Moxie felt Jett's rigid body behind her and reached for his hand under their blanket. She was soft in her caress to try to get his attention, suddenly wondering if she should've just kept her mouth shut. It was hardly fair for Julia and Hallie to continue talking about him like he wasn't sitting right there though. Not to mention everything they spewed was completely ridiculous given what Hallie had done to him. She was relieved when her fingers stretched out for a second rotation on his hand and he matched her tenderness when he interlaced their fingers. Moxie mindfully caressed his hand with her thumb under the blanket as the arguing continued.

Trevor held up his hands. "Look, it's been a long day and we've all been drinking. I think we should just call it a night." When his wife wouldn't even look at him he hesitantly glanced at Jett and knew no one would take him up on his suggestion.

"Fuck both of you for thinking I owe either one of you shit," Jett sneered. "I get you two are fucking joined at the hip, but this is really none of your goddamn business, Julia. You can fuck all the way off with ever talking to me again. I don't need or want any kind of conversation with you either—and you've known this." He stared right at Hallie. "There's nothing to mend, I don't have anything to apologize for, and I sure as shit don't want an explanation or apology from you."

Moxie maintained her gentle rhythm on his hand.

Tears fell from Hallie's eyes and Trevor now stood behind his wife trying to gently coax her out of her chair.

"And you can go ahead and start wearing your ring from Billy boy. I'm aware you're engaged, you don't need to hide that from me in fear I'll be upset or whatever the fuck."

"You are *such* a *dick*." Julia was disgusted as she watched Hallie cry. "You're really gonna sit here and yell at her while she's already crying?"

"First off, I'm not fucking yelling. And those have to be the most pathetic crocodile tears I've ever seen. Since we're already in the thick of it, let me just air it all out now in front of everyone since this is clearly what the two of you have been begging for."

"Jett, please," Trevor pleaded as the rest of the group watched, engrossed.

They'd all heard rumors, but they'd be getting the facts straight from the horse's mouth now, so everyone else preferred to let Jett continue.

He completely ignored Trevor and glared at his ex from across the fire. "Hallie, you actively chose to end our marriage. It's not an accident that you started cheating—that was a *daily* choice you made. You had plenty of time to rethink that fucking treachery before you got yourself pregnant. I'll take some of that blame since apparently it'd been going on since *before* I left." He looked pointedly at Trevor who'd never bothered to let his cousin know Hallie had been seeing someone for that long and even been friendly with the prick. "That's on me for not filing for divorce much sooner. Not that I'd forgive you for getting pregnant from your affair, but then you went ahead and made sure a conversation would never need to happen when you brought my dog to a fucking animal shelter. As if she's ever done shit to you—that was some next level fuckery right there. Ignoring my phone calls while I was away, not returning texts, changing the locks to the damn house, *and* letting your pint-sized fuckin' baby daddy drive my truck while I was gone were also really great indicators for the kind of person you truly are. So you can sit there and throw yourself a pity party. I'd be crying too if I was about to spend the rest of my life with a wet noodle boy."

"Jett, I know I hurt you, I—" Hallie whined before he cut her off.

"Hurt me?" Jett choked out a laugh. "Shit, I'll admit the initial shock stung—maybe more of an embarrassed sting when I saw what you traded me in for. What actually hurt me was finding out Mags was gone—that was fucking devastating. But you know what?" He squeezed Moxie's hand. "If you hadn't done that I wouldn't have met the love of my life. So I'll take back what I said about not owing you shit. I owe you an endless amount of gratitude for doing what needed to be done to bring me to the woman I was always meant to be with."

Julia fumed and Jett watched as Hallie wiped the constant stream of tears rolling down her face.

"Don't be sad that we both got what was truly meant for us in life. Trevor tells me you're expecting a girl soon. I'm sure—if nothing else—you're happy about that," Jett added. Moxie's thumb resumed the soft circles it'd been doing before he'd squeezed it.

"You'd know if a baby girl would make her happy, wouldn't you, Jett?" Julia put her arm around her teary-eyed best friend. "I remember how ecstatic Hals was to find out that the second one was a girl."

Elliot and Gabe exchanged a quick glance with wide eyes, they didn't realize Jett and Hallie had a second pregnancy.

Julia seethed as Jett's face maintained its scowl, she wanted to hurt him for not being more sympathetic. To elicit the desired reaction she continued sharing Hallie's darkest secret, "Too bad that third one wasn't around long enough to know." She shrugged with an unapologetic grin.

"Jules!" Hallie's tone broke and her distraught eyes showed she wished Julia hadn't said anything at all.

"What did you just say?" Jett's sharp question sliced over the flames of the fire. He hoped he misheard her, he knew nothing about a third baby—besides the one currently in Hallie's belly.

"Please don't," Hallie begged under her breath, gripping her best friend's hand. Unfortunately for her, Julia's talons had sunken too deep and she wanted to go for the kill.

"Another thing you get to look forward to." She narrowed her spiteful eyes at Moxie. "Jett's gone so much you'll have to make the same decision if he gets *you* pregnant at a less-than-ideal time." She shrugged lazily. "No one wants to deliver a baby alone while your husband's off *training* for some ridiculous job offer he shouldn't have taken in the first place. Who can blame her for what she did? She made the right choice." Julia's triumphant sneer never strayed from Moxie.

Moxie's entire body surged with nervous heat when Jett's voice thundered right behind her.

"What the *fuck* is she talking about, Hallie?!"

"Jett, please! Not here," Hallie cried.

"You two've been foaming at the fucking mouth to do this here all goddamn day! What *third* baby is she talking about?" he repeated with more anger this time.

Moxie wanted to puke. Her stomach was completely unsettled at the mere thought of what Hallie had done on top of her adulterous pregnancy, not to mention the tone of Jett's voice and the building energy she felt behind her scared her to the point of her body trembling.

"This is private, Jett," Hallie's voice was nearly impossible for anyone to hear.

"Your bestie just made it public." He gestured at her swollen belly. "I'm assuming that's not number three, huh?"

Hallie slowly shook her head as her chin tilted down in shame.

"Why don't you fucking enlighten the rest of us on when this all happened? And better yet, why you never told me?!"

She sniffled, hesitating to respond and refusing to look at him. "I'm sorry. I-I—"

"Was it even mine?!" Jett demanded.

"Of course it was, Jett!" She couldn't verify that fast enough and met his fury-filled gaze, her expression pleading for him to believe her.

He rolled his eyes. "Don't act like that should've been obvious to me after what you've fucking done."

"The due date was while you were in training. I didn't think it was the right time for—"

Now undoubtedly yelling, Jett cut her off, "Not the right time?! What did you fucking do?!"

Moxie went from semi-controlled trembling inside her body to visibly shaking. Mags immediately climbed the top half of herself onto Moxie's lap. They could both feel Jett's rage and neither of them were comfortable.

"Stop yelling at her! You're the one who left!" Julie stood, shaking her finger at Jett.

"Shut the fuck up, Julia—you have no idea what you're talking about."

"Come on"—Trevor stood behind his wife, holding her shoulders—"everyone just calm down."

"Fuck you too." Jett swept his hand toward his cousin. "I won't be surprised to find out that you knew about this all along—you've been such a dutiful little husband and all."

"I knew about it because I'm around more than you are," he responded with more confidence in his voice than Jett could ever recall.

Jett leaned forward, finally realizing Moxie was shaking. He tried not to yell, "Don't let her fucking lie to you that this job was some secret I signed up for behind her goddamn back. She's known this was my goal for *years* and we talked about it *at length* before *she* signed off."

He tried to calm himself and both of his girls by taking a deep breath and holding tighter to Moxie's hand. "Besides the training piece, this job's gonna keep me home more than I have been. She's known *all* of this."

"You still would've been gone for her due date," Trevor pointed out.

Jett sat up taller. "I can't believe what I'm fucking hearing right now." It took him a minute to look at Hallie again. "Did you have an abortion while you were carrying my child? After two goddamn miscarriages?" Air harshly blew through Jett's nostrils as he waited for her inevitable response. Based on the conversation and Hallie's reaction he already knew the answer, but he wanted her to admit it out loud, not hiding behind her ruthless bestie.

Moxie's second hand left Mags and wrapped itself around Jett's that was already interlaced with hers, squeezing from both sides. She felt tears rolling down her cheeks at the pain Jett must be feeling. Finally, the silent tension around the fire consumed too much of her so she slowly inched her way down the chair to get up.

"Uh oh," Julia sarcastically sang and put her hand on her heart. "Doesn't look like you ever informed the child bride about the babies you made with Hallie. I wonder what else he's kept hidden from you?"

Jett was off the camping chair in record time and shouted once he stood, "You always manage to out-bitch yourself, but you'll keep your smug-ass comments the fuck away from Mox or I'll beat the shit out of your soft little husband over there."

Mags scrambled to Jett's side, standing at attention, the loyal dog looking up at him.

"Calm. Down." Trevor put up his palm.

Jett harshly wiped his face with both hands.

"You have no fucking idea how goddamn calm I've been throughout this entire clusterfuck, Trevor. I don't know if that line or the fucking apologies are worse. For your own safety, I'd suggest you quit fucking saying both."

He felt Moxie's timid hand touch the back of his waist and it made him take another breath.

Julia was uncharacteristically quiet and Hallie continued to cry.

"I don't know how I ever loved you." His disgusted gaze landed directly on Hallie. "You make me *sick*."

"Jett, please!" Hallie sobbed, taking a step in his direction as he stormed for the lake.

Mags trotted after him but stopped to look back at Moxie who was preoccupied, glaring at Hallie through tears of her own.

Hallie took a couple more steps to follow Jett before Moxie stopped her.

"No." She shook her head, her finger warning her. "You're done hurting Jett."

Julia tried to step in on Hallie's behalf and Moxie interrupted her as well.

"You're *all* done hurting him. You have to be some of the most disgusting people I've ever met. None of you ever deserved his love," she choked out as the flow of tears cascaded from her eyes. She made sure the three of them stayed put before turning around. Elliot and Gabe stood sentinel not too far behind her.

"I'm really sorry guys." She wiped her eyes and offered a flat smile before her worried face turned to the darkness near the lake to locate Jett.

Mags waited for Moxie with her low tail sifting nervously through the air. Together they followed the direction Jett had stomped off in.

"You all should spare them from having to see you for the rest of the night. That was so fucked up." Elliot's disappointed eyes moved across the trio and landed on Trevor to let him know he needed to make sure all of them headed for bed sooner than later.

47

Mags caught up with Jett first. She maintained his pace, bumping into his legs and lifting her head to look at him. It took him a moment, but he reached down and scratched her ears as he slowed.

Moxie watched Jett squat to pet Mags as she quietly continued her approach. Her tears still flowed steadily when she made it to him. He pecked Mags' head just as Moxie placed her hand on Jett's shoulder. He didn't hesitate, he immediately got up and folded his arms around her. Moxie buried her face in his strong chest, allowing herself to cry freely as Jett's steady hands rubbed up and down her back. After the fourth descent, she looked up at him.

"Jett, I love you *so* much. You didn't deserve any of that—I'm so sorry."

"Mox, I love you too, Doll." He rocked her while placing a firm peck on top of her head. "None of that's your fault, you don't have to be sorry."

"Baby, I do." She gazed into his eyes, trying to stop her tears. "That just blew a crater through my heart, I can't imagine how you're feeling."

"I'm sorry you had to hear about the babies like that—I should've told you."

Moxie's brows tried to reach each other and she shook her head. "I'm not upset about that. I understand you've been married for a long time. You get to decide what you want to share from that part of your life," she assured him. She couldn't bring herself to outright say she was sorry he'd been through two miscarriages, just found out his wife aborted a third, and now had the displeasure of seeing her not too far from labor with a child that wasn't his.

"I'm upset that anyone could ever intentionally set out to hurt you like that. All three of them are *monsters*—I don't like any of them." Her tears were re-energized so she planted her face in his chest again, placing a palm on his strong pec.

"Jett, are you okay?" Her petite hand brushed over his heart and she felt the rise of his chest as he filled his lungs to take an exhausted breath.

"I'm actually pretty fucking pissed off right now," he admitted, blowing out another huff of air.

"I can head back if you want to be alone for a while?" she offered.

Jett's arms squeezed her as he shook his head. "No, Doll, I'd prefer it if you stay here with me. I'm sorry for yelling like that, I know it made you uncomfortable."

Moxie feverishly disagreed with her head this time. "Your reaction was completely warranted. I'm not upset at you at all. Jett, you've been carrying so much—too much, in fact." She reached up to caress the side of his perfectly scruffy face with her soft fingers. "You don't owe anyone an apology, but you *do* owe yourself peace. I know you're strong, Dr. Brody, but you don't need to carry this alone. Mags and I are both here and we love you more than life itself—anything you need is absolutely yours."

Moxie peered up at him. She could see the devastated heartbreak in his eyes and it killed her. Jett was always strong and steady, but tonight he was definitely under emotional duress. She wanted nothing more in that silent moment than to completely heal his aching heart.

"Let's walk for a bit," she suggested.

Jett nodded, reaching for her hand to lead them along an overgrown trail near the lake, just barely lit by the moon.

The couple walked in silence with Mags leisurely sniffing her way ahead of them. Jett had traded holding hands with Moxie for curling his arm around her. They were approaching a more wooded area when Moxie slowed them down and turned towards Jett to be chest to chest.

"Jett, I honestly didn't mean to initiate all that, I just couldn't handle how disrespectful they were being to you."

He tilted her chin up before pressing his lips against hers. One of his hands brushed through her hair and landed on the base of her skull as their tongues massaged each other. They went back and forth, building more passion through each exchange, and Moxie's hands rubbed Jett's sturdy chest. An owl hooting in the distance finally slowed their kiss.

"Doll, I'm not mad at you for speaking up." Jett put his hands around her waist. "It makes me love you even more that you stepped in—you didn't have to do that."

"I did," she disagreed. "No one gets to treat you like that."

"Mox, don't ever be worried about that. I will *always* have your back no matter what you're doing or saying." He grinned at her before projecting more sincerity in his face and his voice. "We'll have our moments to disagree *without* an audience—in front of everyone else I'll always support you above everything. At the end of the day it's you and me, Doll."

"Dr. Brody"—Moxie smiled up at him—"that makes me feel invincible. Thank you for that."

"You're welcome." He swayed them gently under the moonlight and took a quick second to check on Mags who wasn't too far from them, sniffing the brush. "Mox." Jett took a deep breath. "I'm also sorry you had to be subjected to their bitchiness." He hooked her chin, his expression open and honest, "You're *not* a rebound. If it'd been Trevor saying that shit, I would've broken his fucking jaw."

Moxie lifted her small hand up to his hairline and brushed her fingers through his short hair. "Baby, I know that. And I'm way too grateful for our love to be worrying about anyone on the outside who wants to be jealous of it."

Jett cracked a smile.

"We should make everyone buy tickets for the show they're gonna get if they keep hanging around like they do." She tilted up towards his lips but stopped just before they connected. "You and I haven't even finished the opening credits yet."

Jett didn't let her say anything else or move away, his mouth consumed hers as his tongue ran along her bottom lip before sliding into her mouth. He maintained a secure hold on her backside until one of his hands grazed her body to reach for the back of her head where he held her in place as they blissfully continued.

"Well, shit." He smirked when their lips separated. "Not that I want to skip anything, but what else is on the agenda for our opening credits?"

Moxie began to blush. "I feel like a title is something you find in the opening credits… And we haven't exactly dropped the girlfriend-boyfriend thing." She quickly shook her head, embarrassed for having shared that and not wanting to appear ungrateful or push him. The way he made her feel was more than she could ever ask for, it was simply being able to openly refer to him as her boyfriend that she shamefully yearned for.

Jett couldn't help but throw his head back, laughing. He held her around her waist before capturing her gaze. "So, when I called you the love of my life in front of everyone, that wasn't the title we should've used in the opening credits?"

Her head fell into Jett to hide her giggles. "I'm happy to accept that title anytime." She finally looked up at him, her smile still burning. "Is that how we're going to introduce each other though?"

"Is that what you're worried about, Dollface? You want to be sure you can introduce me as your boyfriend?" His thumb traced her chin.

Moxie shrugged, flirtatiously tilting her head to the side. "I mean, is that what we are?"

Jett took a deep, adoring breath. "I know my *legal* situation has muddied the waters a bit for us when it comes to titles," he admitted, gently cupping her face. "But, Moxie Hall, you are undoubtedly the love of my life—you're my doll, my lady, my partner, and my soulmate. I'll happily agree to the girlfriend-boyfriend titles on one condition…" His mouth curled into a sly smirk while his hands glided down her hips and reached around to squeeze her cheeks.

"Name your terms, Dr. Brody." Moxie held Jett tighter, sucking her bottom lip into her mouth.

"Those titles have to be placeholders because I have a feeling our show is gonna include more than girlfriend-boyfriend."

Moxie reached up to hold the back of her boyfriend's head. She was giddy and wanted for his lips to weave with hers. They went back and forth, sparking more desire with each caress. Jett cupped the bottom of her cheeks and lifted her to hang securely around his waist as they continued kissing. Moxie's legs tightened around him which elicited an appreciative chuckle from Jett.

"I'm ready for my boyfriend to take me to bed," Moxie whispered before she sensually sucked his neck. She was ready to drag her tongue towards his ear but felt a rush of heat when Jett began to harden under her. "Boyfriend, you could probably be hands-free right now—I feel like I've got a perfectly delicious perch that'll hold me up here just fine."

Jett couldn't contain the guttural laugh that was triggered by her words. "Moxie fuckin' Hall, I'm so goddamn in love with you it hurts."

"Take me back to the tent, baby—I've got the perfect painkiller for you." She smirked.

"Anything you want, Doll." Jett gave her a few flirty slaps to her backside before pecking the side of her face. "You wanna piggyback ride back to camp?"

"Of course I'll help you cover this up." She bounced lightly in his arms to tease him.

Jett made sure she slid down the front of his body as slowly as possible to feel her against the throbbing that was calling out for her just below his waist. He wished they had a blanket at the very least because he didn't want to wait. There wasn't a comfortable spot for Moxie where they were though; her back would've been dragging along the forest floor or her knees digging into the sticks, stones, and dirt around them. Neither of those options were worth Jett getting what he wanted so desperately at that moment. Instead he quickly walked her and Mags back towards their tent. Both allowing the entire fireside incident to slowly fade as they made room for the plans they had for the rest of the night.

"Seriously." Elliot grew a generous level of resentment towards Trevor and the girls since Jett and Moxie left the fire. Reasoning with them in a neutral tone had done nothing to urge them to be out of sight when his cousin returned. "I think everyone's had enough for one night. There's no reason to go another round with Jett when he gets back—I think you've all done plenty to him already."

"Fuck you, El." Julia rolled her eyes. "You don't even know what happened."

"We all just heard exactly what's been happening to him," Elliot reminded her. "And I know Jett's *always* been a great guy." His accusing eyes shifted to Hallie. "Not to mention a devoted husband. You guys are being dicks, honestly. They were having such a good time before you started spewing your bullshit—even ignoring your pettiness out on the water today. I'd venture to guess Jett's had a pretty stressful time since coming home, he deserved to have a carefree weekend."

"Perhaps he should've told his little child bride to keep her mouth shut then." Julia waved her hand. "*Her* immature ass started that shit tonight."

Elliot shook his head, completely dumbfounded at the hatred. "You act like none of us heard what you were already saying about Jett the entire night. It was disrespectful as fuck and someone needed to tell you that."

Harsh breaths shot out of Julia's nostrils and she crossed her arms. She wasn't steaming for long when they heard giggling in the distance. Despite the darkness of the night, the group around the fire noticed Jett, Moxie, and Mags making their way back from the brush along the lake.

Elliot was relieved to see a smile on Jett's face—it was obviously from Moxie who was wrapped around him as he effortlessly carried her on his back. It looked like her lips were glued to his ear as she whispered to him.

"Babe"—Trevor put his hand on his wife's leg—"Just look at me, don't even worry about them."

Jett let out a quick whistle to divert Mags' attention away from the water to avoid having a sopping wet dog in their tent.

They were only steps away from passing the fire when Moxie turned to smirk at Elliot.

"El, you better go wake up Nana to get you a pillowcase—we just saw a whole flock of your little snipe friends."

Elliot grinned and offered her a friendly bird.

Jett's head rolled back as he laughed and rubbed his hands on Moxie's legs that clung to his waist. He didn't even slow down as they passed the bonfire—he was on a mission to get Moxie to bed like she requested.

"Goodnight, El—Goodnight, Gabe," Jett called out over his shoulder, completely ignoring the fact that Trevor, Julia, and Hallie were still sitting around the fire.

"Goodnight," Moxie echoed and went back to whispering in her boyfriend's ear.

"You took her fucking snipe hunting?!" Hallie sneered at Elliot; she knew the significance of that hunt. It was also Saturday night, so they must've broken their precious tradition to include her.

Gabe and Elliot both nodded in unison, unashamed.

"That's actually pretty shitty—they've been together for a milli-second." Hallie's throat swelled. This pregnancy and the drama surrounding her and Jett made her especially emotional.

"Yeah," Julia agreed, also irritated and offended she'd had to wait four years to be invited. "You don't even know if they'll last. You guys just wasted that initiation on some impulse, sub-par rebound situation."

Elliot had his fill of the trio for the evening. He had only stayed up to be sure nothing too crazy went down when Jett and Moxie came back anyway so he stood. Gabe followed right behind him.

"Aside from the irony of *you*"—Elliot looked pointedly at Hallie—"telling me that's a shitty thing to do"—he tossed his beer can in the bonfire—"Moxie's really fuckin' cool if you all would just give her a chance. You're punishing both of them for finding each other when you didn't even want Jett anymore, Hallie. You tossed him right to the fucking curb behind his damn back. You should be thanking her; without her I guarantee you Jett would've gone off on all three of you the second you two showed up today." He pointed at Hallie and Julia before he stared at Trevor.

Trevor could feel the disappointment in Elliot's eyes. He took a deep breath and stared at the fire, not interested in heading to bed until everyone was fast asleep. A large part of him wanted to leave camp that night.

48

"I've never really been a morning person, but you, Dr. Brody, are slowly converting me," Moxie admitted the next day when they returned to their sunrise spot. She sat on Jett's lap, wrapped in a large blanket, softly tickling the scruff beneath his jaw with her fingertips.

"I told you I'd make getting out of bed worth it." He squeezed her, placing a peck to the side of her head.

Moxie giggled. "Don't go making that bold claim when I would've happily stayed in bed this morning for a continuation of last night."

Despite the terrorizing conversation that swirled around the campfire, Jett and Moxie eased the emotional pain by loving on one another throughout the night. Connecting on a deeper level than they ever had through every touch, breath, and sweet word spoken.

"I never said we can't go back to bed." Jett kissed her neck as both of his hands gravitated down her torso, on a mission to her inner thighs. "You know damn well I'd love nothing more than to—"

"Love birds turned early birds!" Elliot's loud voice initiated a reactive scramble by Mags until she realized who approached them.

"Goddamn, you're up early." Jett laughed, stopping his hands from diving any further in between Moxie's legs.

"That Mexican spread expedited my regularly scheduled morning shit time." He plopped down into a chair not too far from them.

Moxie covered her face, unsure if she should be disgusted or amused.

Jett noticed Moxie's reaction and it made him chuckle. "Let's add a second outhouse when we're updating the place next year."

"You're right, I need my own." Elliot put his large feet up on the rocks that surrounded the bonfire.

"I meant for the girls," Jett clarified, shaking his head with a smile. "We oughta let them have their own."

"Fuckin' beyond love birding over here." Elliot chortled at his cousin. "I never heard you try to modernize or make this place any more accommodating than it is now before we had a virgin camper among us."

Moxie's head rolled into Jett's shoulder and she squeezed the arms he had circled around her.

Jett shrugged, not caring that he wanted to do something to make Moxie's transition into the camping lifestyle a little easier on her.

"For the record"—Elliot lowered his voice—"I'm glad there's only one outhouse right now." He jerked his head towards the little wooden shack.

When Jett and Moxie followed the motion they saw Hallie opening the door. She only took half a step before she covered her nose, quickly turning around to head behind the outhouse. All three of them snickered.

"I'm sorry about last night." Elliot interrupted the chuckling. "I should've said something when I heard the shit too… You guys didn't deserve any of that. I did try to talk to them when you guys left."

Both Jett and Moxie shook their heads but it was Jett who responded, "Don't get me wrong, that all pissed me the fuck off. No matter what though, I'm sure I'd get the same treatment, with or without Mox here. It's a joke they're mad at *me* for this. Like I was supposed to fucking stick around in a marriage when she's carrying some prick's baby?"

Elliot nodded. "I get it—you don't have to convince me it's fucked up." He hesitated, but had to know. "So, the cheating was goin' on for a while, huh?"

Jett turned his attention from the fire to his cousin. "Apparently. I'm not completely stupid, when I saw her I knew it'd been going on for months at the very least. But Trev slipped up a couple times with when they met him and a few other comments that led me to believe they weren't just fucking co-workers. Based on what I've gathered, she's been seeing the wet noodle for at least fourteen months or so." He rubbed Moxie's legs when she curled them to be propped on the chair instead of the footrest. "My best guess is something started at that annual company anniversary celebration last year. I didn't go because I had that last fucking op before heading into training. According to Trev, baby daddy had just gotten out of a relationship or something. They all claim it was tough on him because the woman was a total psycho—I obviously have my suspicions about that though."

"Can I ask about the wet noodle reference?" Elliot tried to keep his amusement at bay.

Moxie had wondered the same thing after hearing him say it a few times.

"I don't know what else to call a guy like that. He's not fat, but he's damn soft." Jett shrugged. "Looks pretty bland overall. He's got a sheen of sweat living on him either permanently or just when I'm around. Absolutely no spine whatsoever—a bit like Trevor, only more conniving. I don't think Trevor has the balls to do what this little fuck's been up to."

Elliot had his head back laughing. "Alright, the wet noodle thing sounds legit then."

"Hey, Papa," Jett greeted his grandpa upon his approach.

"Good morning, early birds." He patted Elliot's shoulder just before reaching for Jett's and then gave Moxie another greeting. "Making you get out of bed before dawn two days in a row, huh?"

"Yeah." Moxie peered up at Papa with a small smile. "The sunrise here does a good job of making up for Jett's demanding morning schedule though."

"No one else is up yet?" Papa looked around. "Did you all have a late night or what?" He was met with silence from the group.

Moxie's eyes quickly found Mags on the ground next to them, while Elliot watched Jett for a half second before joining his cousin in staring at the fire. Papa took their reactions as an indication that no one wanted to talk about it. As he contemplated if he should push for anything else, Hallie approached the group.

She reluctantly waddled her way to the coolers for bottled water. Papa scanned the trio who didn't so much as look up, and Jett's face morphed into a scowl that had Papa unsettled.

Their grandpa decided to be cordial with a greeting, "Good morning."

"Hi, Papa," Hallie spoke softly, but showed her appreciation for his kindness with a flat smile before unscrewing the cap to her water.

"How're you feeling?" He made small talk, in response to her rough appearance.

She was visible to the entire group, standing in front of Papa, when she replied. Moxie felt a tight, reflex-like squeeze from Jett's strong hand. Her boyfriend's breaths were harsh, noticeable through the rise and fall of his chest right behind her.

"Just tired… I'm gonna go back and sleep for a while longer before we leave."

"Well goodnight then—or good morning." Papa chuckled at his joke, but he and Hallie were the only ones.

The silence was so thick when she left that everyone could hear Jett breathing.

"That was *fucking* rich," Jett finally said.

"Buddy, I'm sorry, I—"

"No," Jett quickly cut him off. "I'm not mad at you, Papa. She's a goddamn piece of fucking work."

Papa fidgeted in his seat. "Look, buddy, I'm not trying to be condescending, but you're doing a really great job. You could be doing a lot of damage to her right now and you're choosing the high road instead. I'm really proud of you."

"I'm not sure how much longer I'll be able to take that road," he admitted. "She just came out here wearing the goddamn ring *I* gave her. As if she hasn't been shitty enough, she thinks that shit's funny?"

No one wanted to speak, there wasn't anything to say to make his situation more digestible. Moxie decided she'd try though. "Baby"—she leaned deeper into his chest and spoke softly into his ear—"why don't we take Mags on a little walk? We can get all the angles of this beautiful sunrise before we have to leave today."

He took a deep, grateful breath and pecked her forehead. He'd typically prefer to brood, but since meeting Moxie, all her efforts at keeping him in a good mood had been welcomed. He couldn't get over how easy it was with her. Sure anything right now was better than Hallie's snatchity-ass, but Moxie was so much more. Even at the peak of dating Hallie and their honeymoon stage, Jett never remembered feeling so loved. It was his duty, as Hallie's husband, to take care of her; with Moxie, it was his *honor* to not only take care of her, but to love her.

"Let's go, Doll." Jett opened the blanket they'd had wrapped around them and they both felt the slight sting of crisp morning air.

Mags didn't need an invitation when she hopped up, ready to join them wherever they were headed. Moxie reached for Jett's hand when they both stood, immediately interlacing their fingers and Jett tossed their blanket on the back of the chair.

"Hey!" Moxie playfully smiled at him. "I'm bringing that, it's cold out here off your lap, Dr. Brody."

He grinned at her before pulling her in for a quick embrace. Just over her head, he caught his papa nodding at him with a heartfelt smile.

After Moxie cocooned herself in the blanket, Jett snaked his arm around her and led his girls towards the lake.

"How'd he ever manage without little Mox?" Elliot watched his cousin disappear into the distance holding close to the girl who had literally been made for him.

Papa shook his head. "I don't think we'll ever have to worry about him managing without her now. That seems like forever right there."

"Damn straight," Elliot agreed.

"Hey, boyfriend," Moxie spoke in a quiet but flirty voice as she swung their interlocked hands.

Jett's short chuckle escaped through his nostrils. Squeezing her hand he gazed down at her and replied, "Yes, girlfriend?"

"Do you know of a good, out-of-sight spot from the cabin we can go to for the rest of this sunrise?" The morning had already made its appearance, but hadn't completely taken over the sky quite yet.

"If we keep heading down this path for a bit, I'm sure I can get us through the brush to something by the water where we don't have to look at camp."

"Well, let's do that, please."

"Whatever you want, Doll—it's yours."

Mags sprinted ahead of them, barking and diving into bushes opposite of the lake. Jett let her chase whatever she saw until he lost sight of her and blew out a quick, sharp whistle for her to check in. She charged through the foliage, heading straight for them with an array of leaves and twigs caught in her long hair.

"Oh, pretty girl!" Moxie laughed. "Come here"—she squatted to pull pieces of the forest from their dog—"you're going to the groomer when you get home."

"What were you chasing anyway?" Jett smiled and leaned down to help get the larger debris off of her.

"Snipes," Moxie offered with a shrug.

Jett snuck a quick peck to the side of her head. Moxie turned to press their lips together, gripping a handful of cotton from the chest of his hoodie. Their squatting position wasn't sustainable for the speed and intensity of their kiss so Jett stood them up, ensuring Moxie stayed securely in his arms.

"Oh, you didn't want a sunrise view—you're going for a continuation of last night, huh?" Jett's brows perked as his girlfriend's hands scaled the waistband of his sweats and boxers. His tongue continued to sweep the inside of her mouth as she reached into his pants to hold him. Her petite, soft hand made him want her even more as she began gently tugging.

"Damn am I glad you brought that blanket," he admitted, blood rushing toward his girlfriend's sensual touch.

"Oh, Dr. Brody, just wait 'til you find out why I brought that blanket," Moxie teased against his lips.

"I think I have an idea…" Jett reached for the back of her high waisted yoga pants.

Moxie broke their kiss, grinning as she pulled the blanket from around her and dropped it on the ground between them. She gazed into her boyfriend's perfect hazel eyes and lowered herself to the ground, bringing his sweats and boxers with her until her knees rested on the blanket. Jett's heart slammed within his chest watching her irresistible face make its way below his waist.

"Mox," Jett exhaled her name, his head falling back, completely and pleasantly surprised at what his girlfriend prepared to do.

Her moist mouth wrapped around him, enveloping him in warmth and comfort just before her hand glided up his leg to gird his throbbing erection. It'd been so long—over six years, in fact—since he'd been given this particular sexual favor. He assumed anything would've felt perfect, but his girlfriend was a damn mind reader while she worked. Each time he'd settled in for a motion that would make him explode, she slightly adjusted her hand or her tongue in a way that made his eyes roll back even further. She may have been the one on her knees, but he worshipped the woman before him— Moxie's existence had entirely eclipsed Jett's world.

"Fuck, Mox." Jett had a fistful of her hair and knew if she kept at it with her mouth, he'd burst within seconds. Her delicate hand intentionally wrapped around him, stroking to the rhythm her mouth pumped along his shaft. He gently pulled back, preparing for his approaching release, but Moxie gripped him with slightly more pressure, moaning as her mouth worked to cover as much of him as she could. His balls tightened at the sensation, predicting he had two more of her stroke-suck combos left in him, at best. Jett's tattooed hand gripped her hair tighter as he fought his head from rolling back so he could watch his gorgeous girlfriend lap up every ounce of his orgasm.

Moxie didn't have it in her to take her mouth off him yet. Her tongue flattened, slowly patting along what she decided was her favorite vein. Jett's hips jerked, eliciting a giggle from Moxie who reluctantly showed him mercy by putting her tongue back in her mouth. She placed a feather-light kiss to his tip before gazing up at her strapping boyfriend from under her lashes.

"I love you, Doll," Jett declared, catching his breath and helping her stand. "You're so damn perfect it's scary." He squeezed her tighter, tracking the full length of her spine with his sturdy hands.

Moxie smirked. "Well, now, boyfriend, I thought you were the bravest of them all?" She burrowed into his strong chest, inhaling his rugged campfire-marked scent.

"I *am* brave"—he hooked her chin to make her meet his eyes—"I've just never had the privilege of calling something so special mine. I don't ever wanna mess up." He pressed his mouth against her plump lips.

"I know you won't because you make me happy. I feel so loved, Jett—every single day—and you keep me safe. If anyone's perfect, it's you," she assured. "I love you." The corners of her mouth curled higher as her eyes softened, peering up at him. "Plus, your body's hot as hell—I can't get that taken away from me."

Jett chuckled. "You're fuckin' *wild* if you think I'm the hot one."

Moxie allowed the smirk to creep across her face while her hands traveled suggestively up the hard chest that she was utterly obsessed with. "*And*," she emphasized, "you're really great in bed—I don't ever wanna mess *that* up."

Jett threw back his head, laughing from his gut. His hands drifted down to cup her spandex-covered cheeks that fit comfortably in his grasp.

"*I'm* good in bed, huh?" Jett swayed them.

"I said 'really great,'" she corrected.

"Okay." He lifted her because just being in his arms wasn't enough, he wanted to feel the full weight of her in his embrace. "So, you're incredible in bed and together we're phenomenal then, how 'bout that?"

"That's not limited to bed, baby. We're phenomenal together—period."

"I agree, Dollface, I agree." He reached his lips to her and she lovingly gripped the sides of his face before they connected.

Moxie leaned back from their kiss and caught sight of Mags out of the corner of her eye. She softly shook her head, smiling at their pretty girl.

"Dr. Brody, your dog got herself covered in brush again."

Jett took a healthy, adoring breath, shaking his head at both of his girls who he loved more than anything else in the world.

"I say we let her swim all that off this time." Jett pecked Moxie's forehead before setting her down, pulling up his pants and grabbing the blanket they'd been standing on. "My mind was a little preoccupied… I wasn't paying attention to her doing all that again."

Moxie interlaced her fingers with his and bit her bottom lip, looking down as they made their way back to camp.

"Mox, that was hot as shit—and it's not even my birthday or anything."

Moxie laughed, playfully bumping her head into his shoulder. "It doesn't have to be your birthday to get one of those!"

"Okay, well, it wasn't a special occasion, is what I'm sayin'."

Moxie halted their progress down the trail they'd made it back to. "Do *not* tell me you think that's only for special occasions?!"

Jett squirmed a bit, his face souring. "Don't get me wrong, I'm damn grateful for that—I just don't expect it. I know not a lot of women… It's—you know—it's not something everyone likes to do." His face filled with color as he struggled to explain. "I know they're far and few between and—"

"I'm gonna stop you right there." She put up her hand, palm facing Jett, and giggling just before meeting his uncertain eyes. "I don't know about other ladies, but after what I just experienced and with how much I freakin' love my boyfriend, you don't need to wait for special occasions for that treat again. I'll be correcting your view of how you deserve to be loved. In fact, I'm more than happy to do it again right now if you need reassurances that it'll be a regular thing moving forward."

Jett barked out a laugh. "Mox, you're the best damn thing that's ever happened to me." He positioned them to face each other and held both of her hands. "Thank you for always being the soft and sweet to pull me out of asshole mode." He leaned down to place his forehead against hers.

"Baby, you know I love the asshole too, he for sure has a place. I didn't know I could hate her any more than I already do and then she just keeps piling on. I'm so sorry, Jett."

"It's not your fault, Doll. And like you said, they're all gonna have to buy tickets to our damn show."

"Damn straight, Dr. Brody," Moxie confirmed. "Just so you know, this is how you deserve to be treated all the time. Our first few weeks are only a glimpse of how I'm gonna be loving on you for forever. This honeymoon stage will *never* be over."

"It better never fuckin' end." Jett's eyes widened, projecting a friendly and ardent warning as he dipped his girlfriend back, suspending her in his muscular arms. "I don't want to live in a world without Moxie *fucking* Hall cookie dough, being rushed at the door after work by my two favorite girls, *and*"—he pumped his eyebrows—"your goddamn perfect blow jobs." His mouth playfully attacked her neck.

Laughter rumbled throughout Moxie's body. She loved Jett more than she'd ever be able to express. They both had some baggage, but when they were together the load was nearly impossible to feel. She had no idea how Hallie could ever want anyone else, Jett was the definition of perfection from every angle imaginable. She was guiltily grateful for Hallie's disinterest in her marriage because Moxie's life wouldn't be right without Jett.

Shortly after Jett's neck-gobbling routine started, Mags interrupted them by nudging his backside. Jett popped up, pulling Moxie with him. Mags barked before giving him a final warning nip.

Moxie's eyes widened in shock, but she wore an ear-to-ear grin. "Did our pretty girl just declare her unwavering allegiance to Team

Mom?!" She reached for the protective canine, scratching the top of her head.

"That's fucked, Mags—I can't believe you bit me." Jett chuckled but couldn't deny the pride he had for his dog's protective nature. He gazed into Moxie's eyes and informed her, "We're *both* Team Mom, thank you very much."

"Happy to have you on the squad." She wrapped her arms up around his shoulders. "Let's go get you and our pretty girl some breakfast."

"You're not eating with us?"

"I just enjoyed sausage for breakfast." She barely choked out her last syllable before giggling consumed her tiny body.

Jett scooped her up and effortlessly threw her over his shoulder, slapping her cheeks once she was perched safely and securely in his grasp. "I *can't* with you, Dollface." He shook his head, beaming. His heart was full of gratitude for the perfect future he saw in front of them.

49

When they got back to camp, Jett and Moxie decided to pack up while some cousins were still sleeping. He would be on-call for work later that evening and they wanted to be able to enjoy the lake for the remaining hours before having to drive home.

They blissfully ignored their least favorite trio as much as possible, despite the girls' attempts to bait them. Moxie held nothing back in showing Jett the affection he deserved—no matter the audience. She didn't sit in her own chair despite sideways accusations about her "insecure needs" to always be on Jett's lap, and she certainly did nothing to dissuade Jett's hands from squeezing her backside or maneuvering their way to be sandwiched between her thighs when they sat together. It wasn't until Gabe wrangled a few of the guys' attention before they physically separated from one another for the first time since they'd packed.

"Yo, we gotta pull that dock in, who's down to help?" Gabe shouted around the fire where most of the cousins sat.

Jett placed a kiss to the back of Moxie's head before standing them up.

"El and I'll help—we know your weak ass can't pull that thing," Jett teased and accepted the finger Gabe shot at him.

A few of the guys gathered down by the shore to get Papa's new prized possession, his floating dock, stored closer to the cabin.

Trevor and Gabe ended up paddling out to free the dock from the anchor and attach a longer rope for everyone to pull.

"You know, I could probably just hook this up to my truck and get the dock here in no time," Jett suggested.

Elliot shrugged, watching Gabe and Trevor paddling back. "Eh, a little teamwork never hurt anyone. This'll be more fun."

"You're not wrong," Jett agreed.

Moxie and Mags stayed near Sterling and Nana, but Moxie needed to use the outhouse so she walked over and patiently waited her turn when she saw the door was locked. She was bent at the hips placing kisses on Mag's face while scratching her ears when a snide voice sounded behind her.

"Jett's really great and all, but I hope you're ready for the lifestyle he'll drag you through."

Immediately realizing who it was, Moxie tensed but didn't respond.

"It may feel like bliss now but just wait, he'll start taking off for days and weeks on end. It'll get to you too, mark my words."

Moxie shook her head, still stroking her loyal German Shepherd. "Aren't you already ashamed enough of how you've treated him?"

Hallie didn't answer right away. She studied Moxie, making comparisons to Jett's new pet as she continued rubbing Mags' head. Of course Hallie was larger than usual since getting pregnant, but Moxie was much smaller than she was—pregnant or not. She also noted her lighter brunette hair which surprised her—Jett had always leaned towards blondes. Hallie would never admit it outloud, but Jett's new lady was quite pretty, even after a couple days of roughing it camping.

She shook that observation off very quickly so she could respond to Moxie's question. "You don't even know me! How dare you say something like that."

"I don't have to know you to see how horribly you treated him and how wrong it is."

Hallie crossed her arms, scowling.

"Not that I have any care or concern for your feelings, but you should probably find someplace else to be before Jett sees you lurking around us," Moxie suggested when she noticed her boyfriend not too far away. He'd already begun stalking over when he saw who was talking to Moxie, his expression ice cold.

Hallie's back was to Jett so she didn't see the approaching storm. "That's real damn classy of you, threatening a pregnant lady."

"That wasn't a threat," Moxie clarified. "You don't strike me as someone who knows anything about class, and I wouldn't give you the title of 'lady' either. But, again, please just leave us alone. I don't need or value any of your opinions."

"Jules warned me about your smug-ass mouth. Does Jett already know what a bitch you are?"

"I *better* have fucking misheard you." Jett's tone was sharp.

Hallie whipped her head around, shocked to see him.

"You can start your apology right fucking now." He sliced her with his eyes.

Julia flung open the outhouse door and stepped out hissing, "She won't be apologizing, and why don't you watch *your* fucking tone with her?!"

"Fuck off," Jett snapped and glared when Trevor scurried his way to the small group. "It's one thing to be shitty to me, but you'll *both* knock off this disrespectful shit towards Mox." His rigid finger flung aggressively toward Julia.

"Calm down, Jett," Trevor urged, sliding next to his wife with his eyes on his angry cousin.

"Tell me to calm down one more time, Trevor—see what happens," Jett warned, closing the gap between them.

Julia's eyes widened, Jett looked like he'd happily make good on his warning of beating her husband.

"Okay, well take a breath," Trevor tried in a shaky voice.

"That's the same goddamn thing you weasley little fuck."

Elliot stepped between his two cousins, delivering a few healthy pats to Jett's chest with his other arm around him, squeezing his shoulder.

"Why don't the three of you go get packed up?" Elliot stared purposely at Trevor.

"Us?!" Julia complained.

"Jett's already packed," Elliot pointed out. "It's time for you to do the same."

"I still need the bathroom." Hallie walked right by Moxie, who'd been waiting longer.

Moxie huffed out a laugh, shaking her head. She wasn't surprised that Hallie would be so blatantly rude.

"You're all a bunch of fucking bottom-dwelling assholes," Jett growled.

Julia had to open her mouth to get the last word. "Don't get all pissed, Jett." Her calculated grin curled as she folded her arms and side-eyed Moxie. "I think it's common knowledge the child bride prefers her turn *after* Hallie anyway."

No one had time to blink before Jett launched a heavy blow to Trevor's midsection that sent him stumbling backwards and landing on his tailbone.

"What the actual *fuck*, Jett?!" Julia screamed.

"That's on you." His fury-filled eyes landed on Julia. "I told you I'd beat his ass if you kept up the disrespectful shit towards Mox. You're lucky all I did was hit him." Jett kicked dirt their way as Julia crouched down to help her husband stand.

"You're such a dick!" Julia spat at Jett.

Jett reached for Moxie's hand, leading both her and Mags down to the lake. He wanted to let Mags have one final swim before they took off. He also knew if he stayed to entertain anymore of the bull-shit, Trevor would end up black and blue.

Moxie made sure they were well out of earshot from the group. "All hail, the asshole." She fondly rested her head on his shoulder and interlaced their fingers.

Jett cracked a smile and squeezed his girlfriend's hand at the sentiment. He accepted the bewildered stares from the cousins who didn't catch anything but him hitting Trevor.

Papa watched his favorite grandson walk away from camp and looked over at the scene by the outhouse. Trevor was finally getting up, gripping his stomach. Papa had an idea of what may have happened, he'd heard Julia screaming just seconds before he walked out of the cabin.

"Julia, you need to watch your damn mouth," Elliot interrupted her frantic rant. He'd had enough the night before. Listening to her freak out over the exact thing Jett had warned her about—multiple times—only increased his irritation. "You wanted this, you've been harassing Jett since the second you got here. Put yourself in his damn shoes for the last few weeks before you say some other shit to him—*especially* after that shit you two dropped on him last night. Give the man a goddamn break!"

Papa glanced around, wondering what exactly he'd missed out on after he went to bed.

"Fuck you, El!" Julia flung her finger toward Jett and Moxie. "*She* started that shit *again!*"

"Oh, like last night when she apparently started it by politely asking you to quit talking shit about Jett like we weren't all sitting there hearing the same bullshit?" Elliot shook his head. "That's your choice if you wanna keep bullying Mox. I promise you, Jett'll have Trev paying tenfold for your mouth though. That hit wasn't shit compared to what Jett's capable of. That was just a warning—the tip of the fucking iceberg if you keep pushing him."

"So, we just let her smug mouth fly and we have to sit silent?!"

"I've gotta believe she was minding her own damn business before one of you started in on her," Elliot accurately predicted. "Stop pushing that bullshit on her because you want to hurt Jett—you've all done plenty to him."

"Do you and Hallie actually feel good about yourselves for how you've been?" Gabe had joined the small gathering and stood with his hands on his hips. "And honestly, what the hell did Mox do to either one of you? She sure as shit didn't steal Jett from Hallie. What the hell is your obsession with being so damn mean to her?"

"He's been out of control since he met her!" Hallie shouted, standing in the doorway of the outhouse. "Jett would *never* turn his back on Trevor like this before—certainly never get violent with him."

"Since they met? Or since he came home to find you pregnant with another man's baby?" Elliot very pointedly asked. "Better yet, do you think he may've lost some control last night when he found out you took it upon yourself to abort one of *his* babies?"

Papa's face deflated. The old man felt pain tear through his chest, like his heart had never experienced. He needed them out of his sight.

"It's time for everyone to pack up. *Now*." His voice left no room for objections, it demanded immediate compliance. Everyone, including Gabe and Elliot, rushed for their campsites to break down and pack up.

Hallie made the mistake of looking at Papa. The old man wasted no time in making his feelings known. "I think it's best if we don't see you at our family functions anymore."

Hallie's stomach dropped. She'd known what she'd done to Jett was shameful, but seeing the untamed disgust on Papa's face made her want to disappear completely. It was a different kind of pain to be deemed unworthy by the old man. She turned quickly, and made herself scarce before Jett's grandpa had anything else to say.

Nana cautiously approached her husband after catching his demand that his grandkids all pack up. She'd missed his parting comment to Hallie, and all the drama that had caused. She placed a concerned hand on his forearm. "Honey, what happened?"

"That woman is *not* welcome here anymore. I don't want to see her *ever* again. Trevor and that wife of his are on thin ice too." Papa stormed off to the cabin.

Nana watched as Jett and Moxie made their way along the lake again, the rest of her grandkids scattering to clean up camp. Her husband would get angry with their kids from time to time, but generally the grandkids were all angels in his eyes and could do no wrong. Something major must've happened to set him off.

Cousin Camp had never ended so abruptly. The majority packed up before Jett and Moxie even made it back to the cabin, so they only had a chance to say bye to his grandparents and a handful of cousins. Trevor lingered by the fire, and Jett didn't care to stick around for another minute.

50

Jett and Moxie were finally close enough to civilization for their phones to pick up service so a symphony rang out from the messages they'd missed all weekend.

"FUCK! YES!" Jett emphatically shook his head. "Doll, look." He held his phone over to her.

Moxie's face lit up before she leaned over the center console to peck his cheek.

Jett pulled the truck over and threw it in park so he could give her a proper kiss.

"Congratulations, baby," Moxie managed in between kisses.

"We're celebrating tonight," Jett decided.

As of Friday night, he'd officially been a free man and had no idea—his divorce was final. Hallie had to have known, yet she hadn't said a word when she invited herself to another one of his family events. Regardless, nothing could bring down the current high he was riding.

"Tonight?" Moxie murmured suggestively. "Why don't we start celebrating now?" She rubbed the inside of his thigh.

"Just off on the side of the highway here, Doll?!" Jett chuckled while shaking his head. "You're gonna be my favorite damn thing for the rest of my life."

"Bet your ass I am." Moxie smirked and unclipped her seatbelt when a familiar truck pulled off the road in front of them.

Jett smiled just before his phone rang. "Hey, El," he greeted. There was a pause before he responded, "No, we're good. I dropped my phone under me and needed to grab it. Thank you for stopping though." Another short pause went by. "Yeah, you too man—it was great to see you guys this weekend… Later."

He watched Moxie settling back into her seat, assuming Elliot and Bri were looking back at Jett's truck when they pulled over.

"So… perhaps you were right about the side of the highway," Moxie conceded with a giggle.

Jett reached for her jaw to gently hold it in his strong hand. "I'll go for record time getting us home." He winked and put the truck in drive.

They didn't even make it two minutes down the road before Jett's phone did its best to ruin his mood.

"Ah, fuck." He blew out a sigh, rolling his eyes.

"Work?" Moxie tried not to show too much disappointment.

Jett reached for her hand to lace their fingers together. "Sorry, Doll. We'll get a couple hours at home but that's about it… and that's assuming we don't hit traffic. I've gotta report at 0200."

"Two in the morning?" Her frown arched.

"Yeah." He grimaced.

Moxie took a deep breath but maintained a loving hold on her boyfriend's hand as he increased his speed along the highway. "This part is my least favorite about our life together, baby, but I do love and appreciate how you make up for lost time when you come home," she assured him with a suggestive smile.

"The silver lining with this one is we're only projected to be gone for a day. Sounds like a quick thing which means it's likely closer than usual."

Moxie's neck relaxed and she rolled it around on the headrest. "You're gonna let me be alone for twenty-four hours thinking of all the ways we're gonna celebrate your amazing news? I always knew you were a brave man, Jett." She pumped her eyebrows.

Jett chuckled, kissing the back of her delicate hand. He couldn't deny his girlfriend's sensational ability to flip his mood anytime he felt even a sliver of negativity.

51

Moxie and Mags dropped Jett off at command just before his required reporting time, so they had to exchange quick goodbyes.

"I already miss you, Doll." Jett squeezed Moxie, planting a firm peck to the top of her hair as she clung to him.

Moxie lifted her head off his chest to look up from under her lashes with a flirtatious grin on her face. "I'm super grateful we shared a weekend of uninterrupted time together."

"Me too," he couldn't help but agree.

"I love you, and please be careful out there."

"I always do my best, *girlfriend*." He winked. "I love you, and I'll see you soon." He gave her one final passionate farewell kiss before he unwillingly let her go and headed in to work.

Moxie and Mags went back to bed when they got home from dropping off Jett in the wee hours of the morning. She caught another five hours of sleep before her shrill ringtone interrupted the dream she was having.

"Hey, V," Moxie greeted her best friend in a tired voice.

"Hey, babe—what are you up to?"

It's barely eight o'clock in the morning." She chuckled, rolling to her side after putting the phone on speaker. "I was snoozin'."

Vera didn't offer to let her go back to sleep. "How was living like you're traveling to Oregon in a covered wagon catching a case of dysentery?"

An amused breath shot from Moxie's nose. "Overall, it was a really good time, but also had a few moments I'd prefer to forget."

"What happened?"

"The CliffsNotes version is that Jett's ex-wife showed, and a particularly wretched cousin-in-law of his as well—so, that was less than ideal. V, these people are *monsters*. My heart hurts for Jett and what they've done to him. But"—she beamed, excited to share the best news—"Jett's officially single—well, not married anymore anyway," she clarified, still giddy from establishing titles with him.

"It's about fuckin' time!" Vera practically shouted into the phone. "I'm glad her sorry ass got to see you with him all weekend. What a homestyle-size twatwaffle to do what she did to our GI Joe."

"You don't even know the half of it…" Moxie was still in heartbroken disbelief from everything revealed of how Hallie treated Jett. "And if you think she's bad, you should meet his cousin's wife. I'm convinced they're both actual spawns of Satan, if not Satan himself."

Vera laughed. "Sounds like they're lucky I wasn't there too."

"Definitely!" Moxie agreed, rubbing Mags' head when she rested it on her hip bone.

"So, I'm playing hooky from work today. Are you too preoccupied in bed with your man to come have a girls' day with your bestie?"

Moxie rolled her eyes in a predictively friendly fashion. "Jett got called in when we were heading home yesterday—they had to report at two this morning." She yawned.

"Bittersweet then, because that means you're freeee!!" Vera sang. "Let's go grab coffee and carbs so you can give me the fully detailed recap of what exactly went down this weekend. Plus, I have a date tonight so I need to find a couple new date night fits. We can also hit the bookstore, lunch, and if we're still out, Happy Hour to prefunk before my date, of course."

Moxie had to agree, after roughing it for a couple days it would be nice to relax and do girly things with her best friend. She was also excited to hear about a date that had Vera calling out of work. She hadn't really been seeing anyone since meeting Hot Rod and that whole arrangement they made. This date gave Moxie hope her bestie wouldn't be subjected to removing those big-girl panties for the rest of her life.

"I'm down for all of that. I do need to drop off my gorgeous, but stinky dog at the groomer while we're out, *and* I won't be sad if we add the nail salon to the list."

"Deal! I'm on my way to your place."

Moxie flung the comforter off, chuckling. "I guess I'll get out of bed and get ready."

They hung up and Moxie let Mags outside so she could strip the bed and wash everything before taking a shower. She thought about Jett and wondered what he was doing, always hoping whatever it was, the other half of her heart was safe.

52

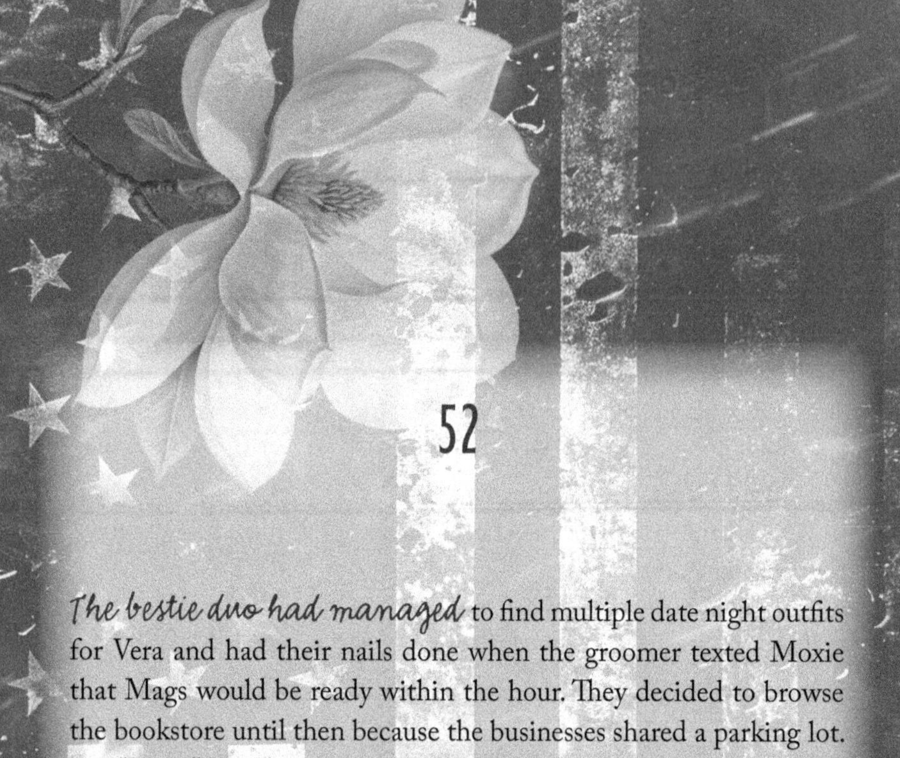

The bestie duo had managed to find multiple date night outfits for Vera and had their nails done when the groomer texted Moxie that Mags would be ready within the hour. They decided to browse the bookstore until then because the businesses shared a parking lot.

"Here." Vera handed a small black book to her best friend. "This one was a fantastic smutty little read, you should try it out. It's a series and they're all pretty short."

Moxie read the back cover, jumping slightly when a scornful voice interrupted her perusal.

"Didn't expect to run into *you* again so soon." Hallie stood just a few feet away from them.

Moxie didn't respond. She stared at Jett's ex-wife for a long moment then went back to thumbing through the book Vera had handed her.

"So quiet now? Your keeper must not be around to save you—I'm guessing he's away for work *again*. I told you that lifestyle's going to get to you one day. You'll be choking on your judgmental-ass thoughts real soon," she sneered.

Vera made her presence known, standing firm at Moxie's side while glaring at Hallie. She'd never seen pictures, but based on her greeting, Moxie's reaction, and the fact that this woman was pregnant, Vera accurately predicted it was Jett's toxic ex-wife. "Well, if it isn't the skankiest twat-o-potamus from the trenches of the cheating-ass lagoon. You know, based on Jett's amazing taste, I didn't expect you to be as raggedy as you are." Vera gave Hallie a long, disgusted inspection from head to toe. "And don't come at my girl starting shit you can't finish." Vera's head shook.

Moxie reached for her friend to let her know it was okay.

"You either. You don't know me, bitch." Hallie's brows furrowed.

"I know you're a particularly heinous breed of FUPA fungus who never deserved someone like Jett." Vera shrugged.

Hallie's face transformed into a full-on scowl. Before she could say anything, Moxie gripped Vera's arm hard enough to bruise when someone else strode down the aisle toward them.

"I was wondering where you went, Mama." The man walked up behind Hallie, his palm sliding from her hip to her underbelly. He kissed her cheek while shooting Moxie a quick wink.

Moxie wanted to vomit, her body shook violently as she shrunk behind Vera.

"Mox." His wicked grin terrorized her. "It's been too long, wouldn't you say?"

Hallie was confused and turned her head to look at her fiancée.

Vera jumped in, immediately recognizing Moxie's abusive ex, "Will, you have less than two seconds to get the *fuck* away from her."

He clicked his tongue. "V, always so hostile." He slowly shook his head but had a smug smirk plastered on his face. "I didn't realize you two were friends with my fiancée. That'll complicate things if you want me to stay away now, won't it?" A wave of frenzied satisfaction for having found Moxie again rattled throughout his body, settling weeks of frustration since his AirTag tracking had somehow failed.

"We're *not* friends," Vera firmly educated Moxie's nightmare.

Hallie couldn't agree quickly enough. "Yeah, the pint-sized one who's hiding right now is just Jett's little rebound tramp," she snarled, flapping a hand towards Moxie.

Will tried to hide his surprise, swallowing a nervous lump in his throat. His minimal interactions with Jett provided him enough information to know Moxie wouldn't be easily accessible for his violent visits. Fortunately for him, he also knew Jett left for work quite often. He'd navigated that schedule flawlessly with Hallie; he could try the same with Moxie.

"Just because you're realizing what a big fucking mistake *you* made doesn't mean she's a rebound. Congratulations on finding this infected crotch stain though." Vera gestured towards Will. "You two are gonna be *real* happy since you're both such shitty people." She used her taller stature and confident voice to give the couple even more encouragement to disappear. Moxie hid behind her now, shaking so badly Vera heard her teeth chatter.

"I think you should leave the store entirely before we have to get security since you're in *violation of a restraining order* right now." Vera's boisterous voice caught the attention of a couple women who looked at the small group and scurried the other way.

Hallie did her best to hide her confusion. She didn't want to expose her ignorance of the full story in front of Moxie, so she gripped her baby daddy's hand and encouraged him to leave. They were only a few steps away when Will turned around.

Vera glared at him while Moxie's terrified body still trembled behind her.

"It was a pleasure running into you ladies." He waved. "I'll be seeing you again *real* soon, Moxie."

Will strutted off with Hallie under his arm. He and Trevor had been getting closer and through that friendship he knew he'd located Jett's new place. Now that Will knew Moxie was the woman Jett had been shacking up with, he couldn't wait to talk to Trevor to get the address.

Once the couple was completely out of sight, Vera quickly turned around to inspect her best friend. The book lay open and crinkled on the floor and tears streamed silently down Moxie's cheeks.

"Babe, he's gone." She wrapped her arms around her quivering bestie.

"I—I—I… I have to go." Moxie struggled with the words, distressed. "I need to go home."

"We're not letting that stray pube ruin our fantastic girl's day." She rubbed Moxie's shoulders, trying to look at her face. "Okay?"

"V…" Moxie sobbed. "I need to get Mags and go home." She looked down as her wet face blazed crimson.

Vera's features shattered when she saw why her best friend demanded to leave. She immediately took off her hoodie and wrapped it around Moxie's waist. She'd known things were bad, but she never imagined her best friend's fears of her ex ran that deep— especially to elicit such a severe response.

Vera sent Moxie to shower the second they got back to her house. She threw Moxie's pants and the hoodie she'd lent her in the washing machine and checked her phone. She'd have to decide soon if she was going to cancel on her date. That was the last thing she wanted to do after falling pretty hard for this guy over just their chats online, but she'd do anything for her best friend. If this guy was as special as she thought he was, he would understand. Rather than jump the gun before reassessing Moxie post-shower, Vera went into the kitchen to prepare Mags' dinner.

"Hey, babe." Vera smiled when Moxie walked into the kitchen, fully showered and wrapped in a robe with a towel on her head.

Mags left Moxie's side, trotting to her bowl for the dinner Vera put out.

"Thank you," Moxie said in a soft voice, catching eyes with Mags when the loyal shepherd turned to check on her before eating.

Vera put her arms around her best friend. "I'm gonna text Ray and reschedule, we can't end our girls day yet. How 'bout pizza and a trashy rom-com?"

"V, you've been gushing about the guy all day, I don't want you to bail on him."

"You're not okay, Mox. I'm not leaving you by yourself."

If Moxie was being honest with herself, she didn't *want* to be alone. Of all the people Hallie could've cheated on Jett with, why did it have to be her ex? She felt a sting of regret for gatekeeping his name. Her boyfriend would've taken care of it the first night they'd met. She tried to ease her mind with the fact that Jett got rid of the AirTag from her car, they moved to an address Will didn't have, and Hallie didn't even know where they were living. Plus, she wouldn't be separated from Mags at all and Jett said they'd only be gone about a day. It was already seven in the evening, he'd surely be back sooner than later. On top of all that, V had never seemed so genuinely excited for more than just hooking up; this guy had even made reservations to take her to eat at a nice restaurant. She wanted that for her best friend, no matter how unsettled she felt.

"V, I don't want you to cancel."

"Don't pull that brave bullshit on me, babe." Vera held onto her shoulders, trying to get a grin out of her. "Our GI Joe is brave, not you." She laughed. "You may be strong, but bravery is buried at the bottom of your little toolbox."

Moxie finally cracked a half smile.

"See!? I'm right!" She shimmied her shoulders.

Mags quickly abandoned her food and rushed over, nudging Vera.

Moxie reached down to let Mags know it was okay, but the protective dog sat next to her and they locked eyes. She knew she could let V go for a couple hours because Mags was there. Mags understood Moxie's moods and demeanor—the vigilant guard dog wasn't going to let anything happen to them tonight.

"Jesus, Nolie girl." Vera scratched the top of Mags' head. "I know you love your mom, but you're gonna warn me like I'm Rodney or something?" she playfully accused the dog.

Vera's phone lit up on the counter as she bent over, making up with Mags. Moxie couldn't help but read the text that came through.

RAY

Are you gonna stand me up if I admit
how excited I am to see you tonight?

Moxie couldn't keep Vera from this date, *especially* after seeing that. "Can we compromise for the night?"

Vera stood from petting Mags. "What do you mean?"

"You have everything you need here to get ready for your date, and the team should be back in the next few hours… What if you get ready here and then check in with me after dinner?"

Vera narrowed her eyes at her best friend, not believing for a second she'd been miraculously freed from her fears.

"I'll get ready here," Vera finally conceded, "but that doesn't mean I'm still going."

"V—" Moxie tried before being interrupted.

"Hold on"—she politely put up her palm—"*if* I still go, I'm also asking him if we can change our reservations to be closer to you, *and* I'll have my ringer on and expect you to reach out if you're uncomfortable *at all*."

Moxie considered her friend's proposal and knew she'd have to accept or Vera would cancel completely. She drew in a slow, steady breath before answering, "Okay. Thank you."

Moxie and Mags set themselves up in her old room while Vera completed her finishing touches. She figured it may be smarter to be upstairs versus the master that had an exterior door. She missed Jett much more than usual and needed him home. She'd apologize and come clean about the name he'd been asking for too. Guilt consumed her knowing he'd soon find out the guy who broke his home was also the one who stalked and beat her. Coming face to face with Will earlier solidified any reservations Moxie'd had with her conscience surrounding what Jett would do to him. She didn't think her boyfriend would have access to his phone, but she tried him anyway.

I love you Jett

Vera was dressed to perfection and ready for her date. She sashayed into the room, offering a couple of spins for Moxie and Mags.

"I have a feeling you're not coming by after dinner…" Moxie cuddled with Mags but smiled at her best friend.

"Babe, you know me better. I'm gonna call you the second dinner is over to check in."

"I think we'll be okay. We're just gonna stay up here and watch a few movies."

Vera plopped on the bed next to her. "Are you *sure* I should leave? I really don't like this."

Moxie nodded, refusing to meet her eyes.

"I can always see if Ray'll just come over here? We can order in—you'll get to meet him too… That might be fun, right?"

"V, I'm not going to be lurking around while you meet your future husband for the first time."

Vera blushed and gave Moxie a friendly shove. "You're stepping on the gas *way* too quickly!" She let out a giddy chuckle.

Moxie sat up and hugged her best friend. "I love you. Have an *amazing* time tonight. I think he's gonna be a keeper, and I'm *so* happy for you."

After the girls swept the entire house to be sure all the windows and doors were securely locked, Vera finally left to meet Ray. Right after she started her car, she shot off a text to Hot Rod.

53

The Hounds of Hades had completed their mission unharmed and in record time. The team boarded a C-17 to catch a ride home, and like usual, Hot Rod was the first to settle into a seat. He turned on his phone while waiting for the rest of the guys to join him.

He hadn't talked much to Vera since the whole 'I love you' mishap during their friends-with-benefits trial period. He knew they wouldn't be able to avoid each other because of Jett and Moxie's relationship, so he didn't mind that she texted. Based on the timestamp, she'd texted a couple hours earlier, and it was after midnight back home. Jett would likely be pissed if he found out Hot Rod didn't share his number when the topic was Moxie, so when Jett walked up the ramp with his phone in his hand, he hollered at him. "The Grizz wants your digits, brother."

Jett's head snapped up. "Is Mox okay?!"

Hot Rod shrugged. "She said she wanted to talk to you about Mox before you got home."

"Did you give her my number?" Jett's jaw clenched almost pain-fully as he waited for his phone to turn on. "When did she send that text?" He checked his phone once the home screen finally lit up, immediately flicking to Moxie's last text which seemed completely fine: a simple, quick message saying she loves him.

"A couple hours ago. I'm sending your number now—I just wanted to make sure that was cool." Hot Rod dipped his chin.

Jett's worry eased when he saw the timestamp on Moxie's text was from a couple hours ago too. He had a plethora of other texts and as he was opening one from Mr. Roman, an unknown number popped up on his phone.

> Hey Jett - sorry to text so late, it's V. Was hoping to just give you a heads up about what happened today. Mox and Nolie girl are fine, but babe may need a little extra love and assurance when you get back.

> What happened?

Jett didn't offer any other greeting and his heart rate climbed again.

> We were out on a girl's day and had a bit of a run-in with her yeast infection of an ex.

The rage in Jett blazed throughout his body like wildfire—his teeth were clenched and knuckles blanched as he gripped the phone, nearly cracking it.

> Did he fucking touch her?

> No! I would've kicked that guy's weasley-ass if he did.

Vera thought about his question for another millisecond before she realized Jett may know *exactly* why Moxie left Will.

She must've told you why those two didn't
work out if you're asking me that though.

Yeah. I'll kill that fucking guy. Did he
talk to her? What happened?

Can I call you?

Where's Mox right now?

Jett stared at his phone waiting for a text, but it rang instead.

"V." Jett's lungs released all their oxygen, but his leg bounced anxiously for Vera to get to the point and tell him what happened to his girlfriend.

"Hey, Jett. Don't worry, Mox is as good as can be expected after seeing that creepy crotch itch today."

"Are you at the house with her?" Jett wouldn't be settled at all until Moxie was safe in his arms.

"No, I left them a couple hours ago. I had a date tonight that she *insisted* I still go on. I checked in after dinner and she said she can manage and that she's got Mags to keep her company. I'm just having a couple drinks now, but still plan to go over there if you're not home when I'm done. We made sure the house was all buttoned up before I left too. I'm not sure if you know, but she tried to get a restraining order against that guy when she ended things. I have no idea if it's still effective—I sure as hell reminded him about that order today though."

Jett appreciated Vera's protective nature related to her best friend, but he knew the full scope of what her ex had done. He needed to get off the phone and call Moxie.

"V, I need to—"

"I should tell you that she did have a pretty bad reaction to seeing him… I know she's still scared of him, but I've *never* seen that kind of terror in my babe—not even the night she left him." Vera wasn't sure about sharing all the details, so she left it at that. "I just wanted to warn you that she still may be a little shaken when you get home.

I got her calmed down and she seemed more settled once we got to the house and she had Nolie by her side, but it was still really bad… Like I said, I've never seen her that scared before. I felt shitty leaving her there, I know she's still upset."

"I need to call her, I'm sure she's on edge at the very least and I don't want her to—"

Vera interrupted him again. "Real quick—before you call her—there's one more shitty thing." She squeezed the back of her neck as she continued, "The reason we even saw him was because your ex was also at the bookstore today."

Jett shook his head, confused on why that would matter. "What? So you ran into both of them?"

"Technically, your ex ran into us. She had a couple things to say to Mox before I cut her bitch-ass off and then Will walked down the same aisle we were all in."

"I don't give a single shit about her, but thank you for putting her in her place. Did that fucking asshole talk to Mox?" His breaths were sharp and he was anxious to get back, there was no way Moxie felt safe at home alone right now. He was equally as disturbed to not be there when she'd just run into her ex.

"Just a smug greeting that would've made your skin crawl." Vera rolled her eyes in disgust. "But Jett, it's a small fucking world because that yeast infection is actually the guy your ex is having a baby with. Those two were there *together*. That little pube proudly claimed her as his fiancée."

Heat surged through Jett's body and he choked on his gasp. The wet noodle Billy and Moxie's ex, Will, were one and the same.

Jett's unusually rattled demeanor alerted his team that something was very, very wrong. They'd all been watching him since he'd picked up Vera's call. He took the phone from his ear and put it on speaker while his fingers opened the texts from Mr. Roman. He needed to get someone over to the house as soon as possible, just to be safe. His heart practically stopped when he saw the latest message. Mr. Roman had sent a picture of Trevor's car in front of his house again, but this time he had a passenger—it was Billy.

"V, I gotta go, I need to call Mox. She's *not* safe to be alone. I'm sending someone to her."

"What?" Vera tried. "Wait, what do you mean? Wh—"

Jett cut the line to Vera and dialed Moxie. As it rang, he jerked his head up to lock eyes with the Texican, who was lounging across the plane from him with his legs propped on his tactical bag. Desperation filled his voice as he nearly begged, "Tex, can you call your cousin? Can you get Mr. Roman on the phone *right now*?"

"What the fuck's going on?" Hot Rod asked while the Texican immediately sat up and made good on Jett's request.

Jett held his forehead, praying to every God he knew that Moxie was okay while he waited for her to answer.

Moxie was frenzied, throwing a few essentials in a bag so she and Mags could leave the house. She was kicking herself for having shoved Vera along on her date because Will had just texted her. Like every other time he'd terrorized her via texting since their break-up, she hadn't recognized the number, but she knew a visit *always* shortly followed his messages. The context was enough to let her know it was him, and he was coming for her. Thankfully her car was in the garage so they didn't even have to go outside until she and Mags were both securely in the car.

She'd contemplated multiple plans to bide time until Jett got home: either sit in the parking lot of the bar where Vera's date was, stay with Shane until Vera's date was over, or simply sit at command until Jett was back. When her phone rang her heart raced even faster, thinking it may be Will calling. Relief swelled when she saw Jett's picture flashing across her screen—she couldn't answer fast enough.

"Jett, are you home?" she cried into the phone.

"*Mox*," he exhaled her name, full of solace to hear her voice. "No, love, we're in the air though. I'm on my way to you. Are you okay? Are you at the house?" Jett's head jerked to the right when he heard Mr. Roman's voice on the Texican's phone. "Doll, I'm sorry, one second—please stay on the phone with me, okay?"

"Okay," she croaked.

"Mr. Roman." Jett leaned over towards the Texican's phone after muting his call with Moxie.

"Cerberus? Everything alright?" Mr. Roman's voice was slow and raspy, like he'd been sleeping.

"No, nothing's alright. That picture you sent of my cousin"—Jett's breathing shot from his nose and mouth, irregular and harsh—"I just found out that man in the passenger seat is the fucking problem—that's who I need to keep away from Mox and now he knows exactly where she is. Is there someone close who can go over to my house right now? I'm going to fucking kill that guy, but in the meantime please help me keep her safe," he begged.

"Shit, I'm sorry, Jett." Mr. Roman fumbled around on his end as he got moving. "I'm heading over there now and I'll send one of my guys who's already close."

"Thank you." Jett cleared his throat of the lump that had taken root. "Please protect her, Mr. Roman. If you see that fucking piece of shit don't kill him unless you have to. I'm gonna take care of him once I get ahold of his fucking ass."

"You got it."

Jett took Moxie off both mute and speakerphone. "Doll, Mr. Roman and one of his guys are heading to the house to be with you. Stay on the phone with me until they get there, okay?"

"Jett," Moxie stammered, panic threading through her tone.

He could hear her breathing, it was beyond frantic—she was hysterical now.

"He's coming for me. I *know* he is! He just texted me he's coming to see me *tonight*!" She ran down the stairs to find her keys. "I packed a bag, I have to get out of here before he finds me. Jett, he'll *kill* me this time!"

Her entire body shook at the thought of enduring another beating, sure that Will wouldn't stop until Moxie was no longer breathing.

"Doll…" Jett folded over in the chair, holding his head and fighting tears himself. "Doll, listen to my voice. I need you to stay in the house, please—don't go anywhere, Mox." He didn't wait for her reply before he relayed directions. "I want you to get into the big safe. Do you remember the code?"

All he could hear was crying, so he gave her a second before he tried again.

"Mox, baby, listen to me. *Please.*"

"I'm scared," she sobbed.

"I know." He tried to take a breath and felt it catch. "Go to the safe in the bedroom closet. Can you do that for me?"

"Okay," she choked out.

"Do you remember the code?"

"Yes."

"I want you to grab the shotgun, okay?"

She struggled to take full breaths.

"Mox, are you okay with that? Can you handle the shotgun right now?"

"I don't want to die, Jett," she admitted, voice shattered.

Jett's emotions finally got the better of him and the tears that had welled finally escaped, sliding down his face. "Mox, no—no, you're not gonna die. You hear me?" He did his best to keep his tone steady. "Mr. Roman's on his way, I just want you to have the shotgun ready. Help's coming, you're not gonna be alone, okay?"

The Texican waved to get Jett's attention then whispered, "His guy is on your street right now, tell Mox he's gonna be in a navy hoodie. He's another cousin, so a jumbo-sized, sand colored man with a bald head is coming to the door. Rome's gonna let me know when Big Teo's in the driveway."

Jett wiped his eyes and sucked in a breath before talking to Moxie again. "Mox, you're alright. Grab Mags and go let Mr. Roman's man in, okay? He's there to help you, and Mr. Roman's on his way too—they'll stay with you until I can get to the house. They're not gonna let anything happen to you. I'll tell you when he's in the driveway so you know it's him."

Moxie listened, attempting to unlock the safe with teary eyes and shaking hands.

"I'm so sorry." Jett knew it wasn't necessarily his fault, but he'd also told Moxie that guy wouldn't touch her again. To hear the terror in her voice while he was thousands of miles away shredded his insides—he'd never felt so helpless.

"Are you close to home?" She could barely get the question out, voice splintering at the edge.

Jett's chest deflated in disappointment. He grabbed his temples with one hand and delivered the unfortunate reality, "I'm a couple hours away. I'm *so sorry*, Doll. I'm coming though, and I'm gonna make sure this never happens again. On Mags, this is getting taken care of the second I get home."

"Jett"—the Texican quickly snapped his fingers—"he's there. His name is Big Teo. He'll tell her Ms. Estelle sent him so she knows he's there to help."

Jett gave him a grateful nod. "Baby, Big Teo's gonna be at the door and tell you Ms. Estelle sent him, okay? If that's not what comes out of his mouth, *do not* open that door."

"Okay." Moxie trembled as she and Mags made their way to the front door.

"Mr. Roman is a few minutes out. We've got you, Mox. He's not going to lay a finger on you." Jett knew the weight of his words would be limited until he was able to physically get to her. He felt guilty for not making a sharper point on the topic of her worthless fucking ex. How fucked up was the world to not only allow that degenerate to repeatedly harm the uncontested love of his life, but also allow him to take Jett's wife? If he didn't already hate the guy before, he was bloodthirsty now.

Jett reluctantly hung up with Moxie once Big Teo, Mr. Roman, and Vera had made it to their house. He'd never been so powerless and vulnerable. Staring at the floor of the airplane, he couldn't place a time where he'd ever felt so completely out of control—his emotions were in a full-on battle with one another.

He was having a hard time coming to term with the facts. *Of all the fucking people on the planet, wet noodle Billy was the main character of Moxie's living nightmare—Will, the undisputed woman-beating leader of all degenerates.*

Jett had settled fairly quickly with the fact that Billy got Hallie pregnant and essentially replaced him while he was away, but he sure as shit wouldn't simply overlook and forgive him for what he'd done to Moxie. Those crimes would absolutely not go unpunished—Jett was going to kill him.

He didn't even realize how visibly upset he looked until Frank grasped his shoulder. It wasn't until that concerned touch that Jett felt his rigid body rocking from the harsh air that heaved out of his nostrils as his chest fully contracted with each rage-filled breath.

"Jett, brother"—Frank's hand tightened around Jett's shoulder—"you wanna fill us in?"

Jett finally looked up and found each of his teammates surrounding him with uneasy expressions. He held the sides of his head with both hands, attempting a deep breath as his elbows rested on his thighs.

The team surveyed each other, all thinking the exact same thing. Something major had to have happened to rattle their most steady and stoic teammate. No one had seen Jett like this before, not even in the worst of circumstances out on a mission.

Jett finally sucked in enough air, feeling as if he must've cleared the plane of oxygen. "Alright…" he started once his tone was even enough. Then he outlined the situation, breaking it down with the cold clarity of a tactical summary.

The men scanned each other's reactions when it seemed like Jett had told them everything. The pause was long enough for them to realize it was time to formulate a plan.

Hot Rod spoke first, "We're all in agreement this guy's as good as fucking dead, right?"

Jett never doubted Hot Rod's willingness to be onboard with any job, no matter the risk. He did, however, catch the slightest glance between Trip and Cappy. He assumed they both worried how their wives may react given this wouldn't be some secret, *sanctioned*, and overseas mission.

"Look, I should've taken care of this myself weeks ago… Should've pushed Mox for that name." Jett shook his head. "I don't want anyone putting themselves in a situation that'll jeopardize anyth—"

Hot Rod cut him off, "Don't start that bullshit. This isn't just a team—we're fucking family." His voice was firm as he slapped his hand on Jett's shoulder before looking at the rest of the guys. "Right?"

The Texican and Frank were the first to reinforce the gesture as they firmly gripped Jett's shoulder.

"You're not going down for what needs to be done," Frank assured him. "We're doing this smart. We're doing this together."

"We're gonna make sure this is nice and quiet," the Texican added. "Any one of us would lose our fucking head—let us make sure you keep yours."

Jett offered a grateful nod at his teammates, that damn lump crawling back up his throat.

Trip finally took a step towards the group, silently making his intention to join.

Cappy didn't move, but he watched his team with a keen, assessing spark in his eyes. "You guys know I can't officially sanction anything, but I'll personally endorse the hell out of taking care of this. *No one* threatens our family, but the Texican's right—you need to keep your damn head, Jett."

"So it's settled." Hot Rod did a little jig, giddy to put their skills to use on a problem that was personal for them. Typically their team dealt with enemies of their country, not personal enemies. Moxie's perpetrator and the man who wrecked Jett's home was the most intimate opposition they'd ever come across. "We're going home to rid the world of that sick prick."

When everyone nodded their approval, Jett met each of his brother's eyes, one by one. "Thank you."

54

The girls had a movie playing while Moxie lay horizontally across the bed. Her head rested on a pillow in Vera's lap with Mags curled up in front of her. Vera brushed her fingers through her best friend's hair as she had been since they'd gotten comfortable.

Mr. Roman and his cousin, Big Teo—who had arms the size of Moxie's entire body—were out in the living room and sporadically performed rotating patrols around the house. Big Teo had cleared the backyard a few times since they'd settled in the bedroom and Mr. Roman popped his head in to check on them every so often.

Vera had shown up about ten minutes after Mr. Roman and they all assured Moxie no one would leave before Jett got home. Vera hadn't pushed for details when she arrived after hanging up with Jett, but she knew that either there was much more to the story, or Jett was the kind of overprotective boyfriend that she should be concerned about. She threw out the latter option the second it crossed her mind, convinced Will was even more of an actual threat than she originally understood.

"Babe, you should try to sleep a bit. Rodney texted me and said he's bringing Jett straight here when they land. You can sleep for a while and when you wake up, your man'll be home, okay?" Vera sat with her back against the headboard.

"V, I can't sleep," Moxie shamefully admitted.

"I'm sorry I left you tonight." Vera continued stroking her best friend's hair.

"I'm not upset at you at all." She was aware that she'd never shared the ongoing abuse she'd endured from Will. That wasn't something she wanted to talk about at the moment, so she attempted to change the subject completely. "Why don't you tell me all about your date?"

Vera immediately had an ear-to-ear grin thinking about Ray and their evening, and Moxie couldn't help but smile listening to Vera's voice—her best friend had never sounded so giddy. Her date, Ray, appeared to be a perfect match both physically and emotionally for Vera. His larger frame would allow her to feel comfortable and confident in even the highest heels, which only made her fall deeper for him. Vera complained on countless occasions that she couldn't wear the heels she wanted on a date because most guys were uncomfortable with an unfavorable height difference. She always tried to remind her best friend that the guy wasn't it if that was a problem for them. It sounded like Ray had been a complete gentleman and offered more than the appropriate amount of first date swooning.

Moxie brushed her fingers through Mag's freshly groomed fur, listening to Vera's overly detailed account of her first kiss with Ray, when her phone signaled a text.

"Is GI Joe back?" Vera asked, although she already knew the answer by the way Moxie's muscles finally relaxed.

Moxie nodded, still resting her head in Vera's lap. Vera rubbed her best friend's tiny shoulder, knowing relief was settling into her for the first time that night since she'd soon be wrapped up in her boy-friend's arms.

55

Jett didn't even wait for Hot Rod to stop his car completely before jumping out. He rushed into the house, leaving his buddy in the truck. Mr. Roman and Big Teo sat at the breakfast bar when Jett burst through the door.

"She's in the bedroom with Vera and Mags." Mr. Roman pointed down the hall, knowing full well that's all Jett cared about at the moment.

Moxie and Mags both popped up when Jett bolted inside the room. Mags, of course, made it to Jett first. He gave the loyal canine a quick rub when she jumped up but caught Moxie in his other arm once her body collided with his. She threw her arms around his neck and wept the second they touched.

Mags read the room and her front feet hit the ground before sitting obediently next to Jett as he picked up Moxie completely, wrapping his strong arms around her.

After placing a firm peck on her head, he spoke softly into her ear, "Oh, Doll." He blew out a relieved exhale. "I'm sorry." One hand held the back of Moxie's head as she sobbed into his shoulder. "I'm here, baby, you're safe."

She cried through her jagged reply, "Jett, I'm so sorry I didn't tell you his name." She choked on a few tears. "I should've told you that first night and I'm sorry—I'm so sorry—I didn't know."

"Shhh…" Jett swayed with her clinging to him. "Mox, I'm not mad at you at all. It's okay." He rubbed his fingers through the back of her hair.

Vera felt like they needed a minute, so she gave Jett a flat smile and left the room to catch up with Hot Rod. She knew there was definitely more to the story for Moxie to be as upset as she was.

"He texted that he's gonna see me soon. Does he know I'm here?" Moxie's voice broke and strained to get her question out.

Jett's body burned at the thought of that degenerate anywhere near his girlfriend. "I swear, on everything, he's not seeing you *ever* again." He held her tighter knowing his next disclosure would scare her even more. "Mr. Roman showed me a picture of him with fucking *Trevor* on our street tonight. Now I'm sure that he knows where we live."

Moxie's grip tightened and she cried even harder to know how close her ex had been to her that night. Jett readjusted his hold so both of his hands supported her, moving to set his forehead against hers.

"Moxie, now that I know who he is, I'm gonna follow through on that promise I made to you. He won't be around anymore, period." He held her watery gaze, looking for any indication that she wasn't okay with his plan—that reaction didn't come. "I'm also going to kick Trevor's fucking ass."

Moxie sputtered, removing her forehead from his and straightening her back. "Jett, you can't k—"

He knew where she was headed and cut her off before she could finish. "I'm not going to kill Trevor, but he's getting a grown-man beating though; that's for damn sure."

Moxie's crying slowly reduced to sniffles but she didn't release her boyfriend. Her hands made their way to the back of his head to run through his short hair that was barely long enough to get caught between her fingers.

"I love you, Doll. You and I are making it through these opening credits because we've got an entire show ahead of us still. I'll never stop giving you everything you want and more."

Moxie created just enough space between them to gaze into Jett's eyes, catching specks of chestnut in his irises. "It's you I want, Jett—having you is having everything. I love you."

Jett couldn't help but smile at her. Despite the tears and sleepless night on her face, his doll was there—his world clung safely to him and his heart was grateful.

While he was committed to fulfill his vow to rid Moxie of her worst nightmare, his determination to provide her a happy life filled with more love than anyone had ever known was stronger. Even with her securely in his arms he couldn't get enough of her, and he knew he never would.

"Babe!" Vera cried, wrapping her arms around her best friend who somehow felt smaller than ever. "Why didn't you tell me what he's been doing? I'm *so sorry*, Mox."

Another wave of crying consumed Moxie.

"I would've helped," Vera assured her best friend. "You didn't have to go through that alone."

"I'm sorry, V."

"You don't have to be sorry." She rubbed comforting circles along Moxie's back.

"I should've said something but he said he'd kill me."

Vera couldn't hold her best friend tight enough.

Jett kept an attentive watch over Moxie from a close distance, but caught up with Mr. Roman. He noted how the typically clean-cut lawyer dressed down—no suit jacket in sight—with the sleeves of his button-down rolled up and his firearm not so discreetly tucked in a hip holster.

Mr. Roman gripped Jett's shoulder. "Cerberus, how're you holding up?"

Jett couldn't speak initially as he observed his girlfriend crying with Vera.

"Just so you know, the plan's already in *full* motion," Mr. Roman confirmed. "I just talked to Tex."

Jett finally turned his focus to face Mr. Roman. "I can't tell you how appreciative I am that you guys got here so fast—thank you."

"I told you, *anything* for Mox. That's family right there." He gestured toward her and continued, "And so are you, Jett."

Jett offered a flat smile and a slight tilt of his chin. "I've never wanted to protect something so fiercely in all my life," he admitted. "She's never gonna be in fear of that piece of shit ever again. He's fucking dead."

"Agreed." Mr. Roman squeezed his shoulder one last time before spinning on his heel to take the call that buzzed in his pocket.

Jett couldn't take his eyes off his girlfriend. He hadn't exaggerated his feelings, he'd give anything to have Moxie never feel an ounce of fear again in her life.

56

Jett couldn't sleep. He couldn't even close his eyes, despite reassurances from Mr. Roman that Will was detained. He looked over for the umpteenth time in the last hour and noticed Mags wasn't sleeping either. The fiercely loyal and protective guard dog lay facing the closed bedroom door. She rarely relaxed enough to set her head down and her ears stayed perked listening for even the slightest disturbance in the house.

Moxie hadn't moved a muscle since curling up with Jett in an attempt to finally catch some sleep. Jett's strong arms wrapped around his girlfriend the minute they laid in bed. Half of her body rested on his chest with her head snuggly under his chin while one of her legs twined in between his. Her delicate hand clutched his shirt and he knew she'd been falling in and out of NREM sleep for the better part of an hour. When she gently squeezed the cotton, Jett knew she was awake.

"Mox," Jett whispered just before pressing his lips to her soft honey-brown hair, "close your eyes and try to sleep, Doll—you're safe."

Mags stood, her nose in the crack of the door and her tail straight out. She didn't wait long before letting out a guttural growl. Moxie's hold on Jett tightened while he carefully observed their dog. Less than a minute into her threatening rumble, the upstairs toilet flushed. They both relaxed at the sound, knowing it was just one of the houseguests they'd acquired that morning. Vera predictably insisted on staying on the futon in the office. She locked herself in to be crystal clear that she wouldn't be reviving her situationship with Hot Rod, who camped out on the living room couch. Frank and Shane stayed in Moxie's old room and Shane planned to spend his day with Moxie when the guys had to go back to work.

"Have you slept at all?" Moxie finally asked.

"I'm alright, Doll," Jett replied while squeezing her.

Moxie crawled on top of him, placing a leg on either side of his hips and wrapping her arms around his neck. "That's not what I asked," she pointed out.

Jett's mouth curled in one corner. "I'll sleep when you sleep." His sturdy hands glided down the length of her back before they ascended into a massaging rhythm that soon included her neck and shoulders.

She was no match for Jett's hands, he'd have her falling asleep in no time. Before she closed her eyes, she whispered to her boyfriend, "Thank you for making me safe again."

"Forever."

Jett had no regrets about what he planned to do to Moxie's ex. He'd already wanted to murder the guy *before* he found out he was Hallie's baby daddy. The realization that Billy was also the worthless piece of shit who terrorized and abused Moxie only increased his thirst for revenge. He considered what he'd be taking from Hallie. Her behavior didn't warrant the consideration, but Jett wasn't a complete monster. While he still hated her for everything she'd done to him, her child didn't deserve the same treatment he knew Billy was capable of. A man like that couldn't be trusted with a wife and certainly not a daughter. Above all else, Jett had zero confidence that he wouldn't resurface around Moxie. He wouldn't leave that to fate— he'd take control.

57

The only reason Jett managed to leave Moxie at the house that morning was because Mr. Roman had sent him visual proof that Moxie's ex was handled for the moment. He left her in the care of Vera and Shane, and under the capable protection of Mags. For their plan to work, Jett had to report to work—the *team* had to report. Jett left his phone at command, as planned, and rather than joining the team on a remote range, he and the Texican got picked up by one of Mr. Roman's men to meet up at his office.

"Jett." The Texican held both of his teammate's shoulders, peering at his eyes until Jett met his stare. "He'll get his, but not here—can you handle that?"

Jett's chest rose and fell with each harsh breath that escaped his nostrils. He honestly wasn't sure if he could handle that. Just on the other side of the door from where they stood was Will, Moxie's deranged and abusive ex—the man he formerly knew as Billy, the man who wrecked Jett's marriage.

The door cracked open and Mr. Roman slid out so as not to give Jett a peek inside yet. He noticed the uncertainty painted on his cousin, the Texican's, face.

"Cerberus, I'm good keeping him until you guys get called out and can take him," Mr. Roman offered Jett an out for having to see him. The guys already planned to take care of him somewhere besides home, Mr. Roman's place was always meant to be temporary so Jett and the team could show face prior to anyone discovering Will was missing.

"I want to see him." Jett's sharp tone matched his dark eyes and tense muscles.

"Can you handle that right now?" the Texican asked again.

Jett's eyes made a slow and deadly track before locking onto the Texican's. He didn't say a word.

The Texican took a deep breath, gripping Jett's shoulder. "I'll be right there with you, brother. You're not losing your head right now—I won't let you."

Jett only tipped his chin down, barely noticeable.

Mr. Roman nodded at his cousin before opening the steel door to what used to be a walk-in cooler. There were two men in the dimly lit room: one standing guard and the other seated in a metal chair, Moxie's walking nightmare.

"Damndest thing happened," Mr. Roman unapologetically explained why Will had blood crusted on his nose and a swollen eye. "*Will* here had a very unfortunate misstep getting into the car." He emphasized the man's name, having learned he typically went by Billy only at work since there was another, much older, Will in their office. Naturally, Hallie continued the use of Billy beyond the office and that's why her friends and family knew him by the nickname.

"That eye's gonna be the least of his fucking worries." Jett forced his heavy steps to stop a few feet from the degenerate.

Will's eyes widened, his heart rate skyrocketing.

"Jett?" he choked out. His confusion from being abducted was laid to rest the second he caught sight of his fiancée's terrifyingly intimidating ex-husband.

The room was eerily silent besides Will's trembling and rapid breathing. Jett looked so different to him. He'd always seen him in relaxed clothing—jeans, cargo shorts, tee shirts—this was the first time seeing him in what he determined to be tactical gear. The man looked absolutely lethal. Will always had more than a sliver of fear concerning Jett. He acknowledged the danger in having impregnated this man's wife, but now, as his harrowing presence stood directly in front of him, likely with Moxie on his mind, he knew his life was in danger.

Jett had always been disgusted by the sight of wet noodle Billy—*Will*—but staring at him in this moment, he didn't want the sick piece of shit to take another breath on the same planet as his soulmate. The urge to beat the life out of him right then and there consumed Jett's thoughts. He didn't know how long he stood, glaring with jagged breaths and clenched fists before Mr. Roman squeezed his tense shoulder.

"Cerberus"—his hand tightened—"*say* whatever you need to, but Tex's getting you back to work soon—alright?"

Jett didn't acknowledge Mr. Roman. He stood in the center of a storm of swirling fury, calculating exactly what damage he'd be able to inflict before Mr. Roman, the Texican, and their Hulk-sized guard could stop him. His composure had never been so painstakingly tested.

He forced himself to take another step and intentionally lowered at his waist to be eye-level with Will. His calloused hand came up and pointed just inches from Will's face. In a deadly tone he delivered his promise, "I walked away from you impregnating my wife, but I sure as shit won't be letting you go after what you've done to Mox. Mark my words, you're a *fucking dead* man."

The chilling threat in Jett's tone made Will's insides shrivel and before he could even attempt to control his bodily functions he felt warmth spread throughout the seat of his dress pants.

Steady droplets of liquid dripped noisily beneath the chair and Jett shifted his focus to watch several sprinkles of urine pooling under Will.

"I'll be paying you back for every threatening text, each time you bruised, cut, and broke that beautiful body, every frantic move you've forced her to make, the sleepless nights she's had completely terrified that you'd resurface—all of it. You have no goddamn idea what pain is, but you're about to fucking find out." Jett didn't think twice when he hurled out a precise shot of saliva directly to Will's injured eye.

Will undoubtedly deserved the beating of a lifetime, but he wasn't worthy of getting hit just yet. Jett preferred the bastard sit in angst and distress over when and where that inevitable pummeling would take place.

Jett turned on his heels and angrily strode out of the room.

The Texican followed less than a step behind his buddy. "Jett—"

"I need a fucking minute." Jett violently slapped the bathroom door. He wanted a private moment to hopefully cool off.

The bathroom door swung several times before closing. The Texican took a deep breath and returned to the room where they held Will captive. His cousin was fussing with a hose in the corner of the room.

"P-please," Will pleaded. "I can pay you—all of you. Whatever you want, I'll pay it. Please just let me go. I won't say anything to anyone, I swear."

"Rome, we're gonna get outta here in a minute, you guys good?" The Texican, and the rest of the room, completely ignored Will's pathetic negotiating tactics.

"Yeah," Mr. Roman confirmed, "we're good here. Someone's about to get a bath though, I'm not gonna have the place reeking of piss."

"I'll let you know when we're ready to move. You just holler if you need anything here."

"Please!" Will tried again. "I'll leave! You won't see me ever again! I swear—on everything! Please! I have a daughter on the way!"

Mr. Roman turned the hose to the jet setting on full blast and pointed it at the front of Will's pants. "You need a burner, or you want me to reach out to your cell?" he asked nonchalantly, spraying Will as he begged for relief from the harsh and frigid spray.

"Actually, a burner's probably a better idea, let's do that," the Texican agreed, disregarding Will's cries for help.

Mr. Roman released the nozzle and walked to his man in the corner, who'd been covering his face to hide the smile from watching Will struggle. "Take this for me?" Mr. Roman handed him the hose.

"Let's wash that eye for you too, guy."

"AH!" Will screamed as the water jetted directly into his already aching eye. "Please!"

"C'mon, I'm just trying to get the spit out."

Mr. Roman and the Texican walked out of the room, taking joy in Will's misery.

"We should probably wait for Jett." The Texican's voice was low but his eyes warned his cousin that Jett may be tempted to walk back in there and settle a few things with Moxie's tormentor.

There was a thump on the bathroom door right before it swung open. Jett hadn't cooled off completely, a deadly scowl still darkened his face. The cousins knew better than to ask Jett how he was.

"I just need to grab a burner from Rome real quick and then we've gotta roll." The Texican gripped Jett's shoulder a couple of times.

Jett followed his teammate without looking back at the door Will sat behind. He knew he could count on Mr. Roman to keep the degenerate secure and uncomfortable while they waited for their plan to fall into place. He'd never been more anxious to catch an assignment.

58

One of the benefits of Jett's clandestine unit was the fact that they had a long leash and questions about what they were doing were not only far and few between but rarely answered. The team was only ever held accountable for whether or not the mission was completed, not how. Being as their unit operated under a black ledger that only a handful of high-level government officials were even aware of, they had endless resources at their fingertips.

Jett's team was given a quick mission in Turkey three days after capturing Will. Their assigned task was executed swiftly and flawlessly. Cappy let the air cargo crew who brought them to their official mission location know they needed a ride to Syria once they were done. The wooden crate they'd stored Will in was anything but inconspicuous, but again, the crew knew to never ask questions. They weren't grilled about it by the troops at the covert base hidden in the foothills of the Anti-Lebanon Mountains where they borrowed a cargo truck either. Everything they'd planned fit like pieces to a puzzle and every minute that ticked closer to Will's ending, Jett's eagerness intensified.

As the cargo truck rumbled along the rural roads, Frank, without a word, reached into the pack on Trip's bag and handed the satellite phone to Jett.

Jett gave Frank an appreciative dip of his chin, immediately dialing Moxie. The team tried to give him as much privacy as the open-air cargo truck would allow.

"Hello?" Moxie's hesitant and slightly raspy voice reflected the fact that it was well past one in the morning back home. She'd been more open to answering unknown calls any time Jett was away, knowing he couldn't always have his cell on him.

"Hey, Dollface." Jett's chest relaxed hearing her voice. "Did I wake you up?"

Moxie smiled. "Yes, but I'm glad you did." She rolled to her side, noticing the time on their alarm clock. "Baby, are you okay?"

"I just needed to hear your sweet voice," he admitted.

Worry fell on Moxie, it was loud on Jett's end and the connection didn't seem strong. She sat up, flicking on the nightstand lamp. "Jett, are you sure everything's okay? Can you tell me where you're at?"

"Everything's all good—I promise. We've got one more thing to do before we head home. I can't say where we're at right now, but I do plan to have you in my arms by this time tomorrow, okay?"

Moxie took a deep breath, she trusted Jett with her entire being and accepted that the unknowns were for her own good.

"I really can't wait for that. I love you, Jett."

"I love you too, Mox—forever."

"Forever," she confirmed.

"I'll see you tomorrow, okay?"

"Okay," she agreed, already counting down the minutes. "Be safe, baby."

"I always try. Bye, Doll."

"Bye."

Jett stared at the phone in his hands well after they ended the call. He would never regret what he was about to do, and hearing her voice further solidified his decision. Moxie wasn't just the love of his life, she was the love of his entire existence—both in this lifetime and any that came before or after. Life had never felt as good as it did until his world collided with hers. He wouldn't allow the one thing that shadowed her days to continue. The threat of Will would end today.

After driving about twenty miles from the outpost, they stopped. Cappy and Hot Rod hopped out of the cab of the truck to help the team lift the wooden crate from the bed.

"Wake the fuck up, shithead." Hot Rod gave Will a harsh nudge with his booted foot once they opened the crate. He'd been on his side, his arms and legs still bound.

Will struggled to sit up, unable to see through the dark canvas they'd draped over his head. He'd given up on his efforts hollering for help after hours of begging and countless beatings to shut him up. He had no idea how long it'd been since he was ripped from his car in the parking lot at work. He sucked in a breath when the canvas bag was yanked off his head, blinking rapidly as his eyes readjusted to the light. He didn't know where he was, but they were surrounded by a forest with terrain much different than anything he'd seen.

"We've got about twenty minutes," Cappy notified everyone as he scanned the area.

Hot Rod slapped his heavy hand on Will's shoulder, jerking him to his knees. "Hear that, fuckface? You've got about twenty minutes left of your useless life."

"Jett, you want any of this?" The Texican flashed a small set of knives from his leg holster.

"I don't want anything other than about ten minutes alone with this asshole." Jett hadn't lifted his glare from Will since the second that crate had opened. He removed the shoulder strap and handed his AR off to Frank, unholstering the two handguns from his body as well as the rest of the team put the crate back in the truck and loaded up to give Jett the privacy he requested.

Jett held his breath when he squatted down to free Will from the ropes they'd restrained him with. Will's response to fear was releasing his bowels, and despite the multiple times they'd allowed him time on an actual toilet, he'd made a mess of himself during the most recent flight.

"Y-y-you're letting me go?" Will's voice trembled once he was free.

An acidic chuckle passed through Jett's sneered lips. "You wouldn't make it two fucking feet if you fled right now, but go ahead and test it."

Will knew that wasn't a challenge. He stayed on his knees but rested his soiled backside in the dirt, timidly awaiting the inevitable punishment.

Jett knew he didn't have time to draw this out, so he got started. "Not that it'll save your pathetic fucking ass, but why don't you tell me why the fuck you ever harmed a hair on Mox?"

"Jett, I'm sorry! You have no idea how sorry I am that I ever hurt her," Will cried. "She was always too good for me, I should've never hit her."

"I don't give a shit how sorry you are—I want to know *why*." Jett moved closer, the looming threat of his heavy fists making the cowering man wince.

Will shrugged, not offering an answer.

"I *know* you never hit Hallie. She would've beat your ass if you ever raised a hand at her." Jett still hated his ex-wife for what she'd done, but he knew he'd taught her how to defend herself. She would've given Will a run for his money if he tried to lay a hand on her.

"No, I promise, I never hurt Hallie," Will confirmed in a rush.

"Just Mox, huh? Why? Because she's tiny and you could finally pretend you were some kind of man?"

"I can't explain it. And it was only a couple of times!"

Jett kicked him in the face, using the full force of his leg and the bottom of his boot. "I saw her fucking face after the most recent time, it wasn't fucking nothing."

Will rolled on the ground in agony.

"You broke her fucking ribs too—I can't imagine what the rest of her body looked like."

Jett's foot repeatedly connected with Will's torso. Each blow harder than the last with images of Moxie's battered face a slide-show in his mind. Not only had Will physically abused her on several occasions, but he'd mentally terrorized her with his stalking and texting—Will deserved the pain.

Will screamed in misery. He'd thought the random, short beatings he'd received at the hands of Mr. Roman and the other guys had been bad, but they'd been nothing compared to Jett's unleashed rage.

Jett let up after kicking Will's jaw, blood spraying across the dirt as two teeth flew from his mouth.

"You know what else makes me fucking sick?" Jett asked, squatting closer to Will's bruised body. "The fact that the last beating was probably because you knew that was the day I was coming home— the day when your little fucking honeymoon with my wife was about to get complicated." He spat on Will's face.

Will couldn't catch his breath. He'd been coughing up blood and couldn't decide if he needed to hold the rest of his jaw together or reach for his torso that throbbed with excruciating pain. He found enough self-preservation to roll onto his back, holding his jaw as he pleaded, "Please"—his hand shook against his jaw and barely assisted him with his muffled speech—"please, don't do this." He took a couple of sharp inhales, doing his best to suck in air to his lungs. "I know I deserve this," he sputtered, "but I'm sorry. It'll never happen again."

"I know it fucking won't!" Jett gave his legs a rest and backhanded Will's broken jaw. "I promised her you wouldn't lay another hand on her, and I'll never break a promise to her."

"Jett!" Will begged, his words barely discernible as his jaw no longer worked. "If you ever loved Hallie, you won't do this—we have a daughter on the way! Don't do this to them!"

Jett had considered the impact on their unborn child of removing Will from the equation, but decided it wouldn't stop him from what needed to be done. No daughter, or wife for that matter, deserved an unpredictably violent batterer in their life, and his girlfriend deserved to step out from under the shadow that Will cast upon her the first time he hit her.

Resolved and at peace with his decision, Jett dropped to his knees and delivered heavy blows, unrelentingly, to Will's face.

"I think we oughta check on him." Frank looked down at his watch, it'd been just under ten minutes since they'd left Jett alone with Will.

Hot Rod was sprawled out on the tailgate of the truck, a wicked chuckle erupting when he responded, "I know you're not worried that little prick bested our boy."

"That's not what I said," Frank clarified with an eye roll. "I'm just sayin' we don't have that much longer before we need to be back."

With a heavy sigh, Cappy agreed. "Why don't you and Tex go back up there? We'll make sure we're ready to roll." He gestured to the truck.

"What the fuck?" Hot Rod threw up his hands. "I don't get to go see what kind of damage Jett did?"

"You have a way of pushing his fuckin' buttons and I don't know what state of mind he'll be in, so no, you'll stay with me and Trip."

Hot Rod flipped him off, but would follow orders. He didn't have to whine for long because Jett stormed toward the truck.

The team assessed the rage still scorching Jett's face. The black clothing he wore didn't completely mask the blood splattered, and he'd covered up his hands with a pair of tactical gloves so they had no idea what condition they were in.

Cappy shot Hot Rod a warning look to keep his mouth shut; it didn't look like Jett needed one of his dumbass comments.

Jett didn't meet the eyes of his team. He went straight for the back of the truck and climbed into the seat he'd previously claimed. His chest rose with one healthy breath before he finally returned their gaze. "Thank you."

There was a chorus of chin dips and acknowledging nods before Cappy broke the silence. "Let's roll." He twirled his finger in the air.

Without hesitation the team piled in the truck and headed back to the outpost so they could get home. This was just another day at the office for the men—they knew not a single word of this would ever be spoken and none of them would have to answer for Will's disappearance. It would take an act of Congress, the White House, and God himself before Jett or the Hounds were held responsible for anything that happened to Will.

Jett had always been able to compartmentalize his mind of the heinous acts he and his military brothers had carried out in the past. While this one would be no different on his conscience, he wouldn't be able to completely settle from this trip until he held Moxie in his arms. Killing Will wasn't about how he'd broken Jett's home, it was about how he'd tormented Moxie, his soulmate. He'd resolved the disappointment of his ex-wife's infidelity pretty quickly, and now he'd be able to confidently continue his life with Moxie knowing she never had to agonize about her nightmares coming to life again.

59

Mags and Moxie sat in the Cherokee just outside of command, waiting for Jett to come out. Jett was the only one who consistently had a ride versus driving his own car, and Moxie had gotten used to Frank or Hot Rod walking out with him on occasion. Tonight was different. She'd never seen the entire team walk to their cars together. Even more unusual, the Texican and Hot Rod flanked Jett's sides, each with a hand on his shoulder while the Texican spoke in Jett's ear. Despite the elation of seeing her boyfriend, this scene—along with the memory of his phone call the day before—had Moxie a little unsettled. Regardless, he still deserved his typical homecoming greeting so she got out to open the door for Mags who raced to her dad. A short puff of relief blew through her chest as Jett caught their dog with a smile.

"Hey, Mox," Frank greeted while Jett and Mags said their good-byes to Hot Rod and the Texican.

"Hi, Frank." She hugged him. "How are you?"

Frank took a deep breath. "Glad to be home." He offered a quick smile, his hand lingering on her shoulder.

He glanced back at Jett with concern and Moxie picked up on it. "Frank, did something happen that I should know about?" She looked up at him, noticing how his lips tightened at her question. "Jett called me yesterday and it—I just—he sounded a bit off."

Jett made his way towards them.

"Your man's good, Mox. It was just one of those trips—we all go through it." Frank squeezed her shoulder once more and made room for Jett's approach.

Moxie's face brightened, her feet scurrying to reunite with her boyfriend. He matched her smile and hoisted her into his arms when they connected, Moxie's limbs wrapping around Jett as their lips crushed against one another.

He felt all the built-up angst in his chest completely release its death grip on his heart as he held her. He'd never have to worry about harm coming to her again—her nightmare was gone and their happily ever after bloomed ahead of them.

"Oh, Doll…" Jett exhaled his sentiment and a relieved breath into her neck. "I needed your sweet touch."

Moxie's extremities tightened around her boyfriend. "I'm so glad you're home—we missed you so much." She lifted herself up, separating their chests so she could gently cup Jett's face in her soft hands. The initial wave of relief for his safe return settled into unease when she met his eyes. "How's your head, baby?"

Jett took a deep breath, knowing she deserved the truth. He simply didn't want that truth to include all the details. His thumbs stroked her backside as he held her. "My head *and* my heart are already better now that we're together again." He stretched his neck for a kiss that Moxie immediately indulged in. His team had only lingered for a minute before they started piling in their cars; they'd done their job and it was Moxie's turn now.

When their kissing slowed, Moxie opened her eyes and locked onto Jett's gaze to assess the validity of his response. Something was still off, so she gently placed her forehead against his. "Dr. Brody, I feel like there's room for improvement in that response. You wanna take me home to work on that?"

Jett chuckled, nestling his head in her neck and holding her even tighter. Their embrace came to a halt when Mags hopped in the Cherokee—it was time to go home. He walked Moxie around the jeep and set her down just outside the passenger door. When he reached for the handle Moxie gasped, placing a hand on his forearm.

"Baby, what happened?" She inspected Jett's hand with horrified eyes. Even with the ink masking some of the injuries, she could see the open wounds and swelling.

The tears welled in her eyes as her fingers delicately caressed his arm but he didn't respond.

"Jett, you said you'd always tell me if I ever wanted to know anything."

"I did say that, Mox. I promise, I'll always be honest with you."

"Then are you going to tell me what happened?" A tear escaped Moxie's eye as she gently held his injured hand, reaching for the other to see if both were mangled. They were, and it filled her with even more dread. "Baby, I'll never judge you for anything you do out there. I'm just asking because I know something's weighing on you. This isn't the same as the other times—something *feels* different. I know you said I don't have to worry about the dark and heavy, but I'm worried about you, Jett."

Jett's chest rose, his lungs completely filling with the heavy air that surrounded them. Part of the reason he loved her so much was her ability to see him and know exactly what he needed. To keep that love he had to find a way to put her mind at ease, despite what she saw in his eyes. His fingers brushed through her hair a few times as he took another deep breath before speaking.

"Mox, I'm only gonna say this once, Doll, and please don't ever ask me about it again." His voice was gentle but firm. "On Mags, I'd never lie to you and I certainly won't keep anything from you unless it's necessary for your own safety. You know that, right?" He cradled her face, every accent color in his hazel eyes pronounced as he focused on her. He waited for her agreement before continuing, "Will won't be following you, he won't call or text you, and he'll *never* touch you again."

Moxie's cheeks were wet as she peered up at her boyfriend. She threw her arms around his neck and squeezed before the shaking in her legs could take her down.

Jett easily swept her trembling body up into his strong arms.

Moxie wrapped her legs around him, trying to snuggle closer even though there was no space left between them. "I'm so sorry," she cried, holding him tighter.

He stroked her hair, his hand finally landing on the base of her neck. "I'm not."

"I love you *so much*, Jett. Thank you."

"I love you too, Mox—forever."

He'd said enough for Moxie to know Will was dead. Jett would never make that kind of statement if there was even a sliver of a chance that she'd see or hear from him again. Moxie couldn't help but shiver, despite the relief she felt that Jett had fulfilled his promise of Will never harming her again. Jett's devout embrace assured her everything was going to be more than alright.

60

The next couple of days went by slowly. Moxie may not have known exactly what happened to Will, but she knew if anyone ever found out, Jett would have to answer for that crime. She'd already tried to come to terms with the fact that his job was dangerous and the threat of him not coming home from any one of those missions was always looming; now she worried about this new possibility of him being taken from her.

She wasn't surprised that Jett settled back into their life together as if he hadn't just performed unspeakable acts that he wasn't even willing to share with her. The comfort of having him home and never having to worry about her ex resurfacing should've been enough for her to fall completely into her happily ever after with Jett, but to fully embrace that, she needed to know he'd be free and clear from being held responsible for what he'd done.

Jett physically and mentally felt the weight of the world lift from his shoulders once he'd gotten back from the mission where he ended Will's life. His girlfriend would never be harmed again, he wouldn't have to see the piece of shit at any of his family events anymore, and he could finally live the life he wanted with his soulmate; chasing down beautiful places, loving on their pretty girl, and eventually turning practice into reality by having a couple of babies. The only thing holding him back was the sense that Moxie still clung to worry of Jett's fate for what he'd done. Part of that was his fault for not sharing details with her. Being held accountable for his actions was the very last thing he was worried about. No part of him wanted to share with her *how* Will died, or where they left him. It was safer to keep her unburdened from that knowledge in the off-chance anyone asked her about it.

Shane worked in IT and had a flexible schedule, so he happily started a routine of spending time with one of his favorite friends while Jett was at work. He'd made himself at home that day working from Jett and Moxie's, sharing her second-story office.

"Mox, I'm gonna make a smoothie, do you want one?" Shane stood, stretching his lengthy arms above his head, leaning back.

"I'm good. I'll probably start dinner soon so it's ready when the guys come home, but thank you." She plugged away at her computer with Mags lying at her feet.

Shane walked down the staircase and just before he got to the landing where the steps turned, the doorbell rang.

Mags shot up, dashing down the hall from the office to beat Shane to the entry. She took deep inhales, sniffing the cracks of the front door while groaning.

"Are you expecting anyone?" Shane called up the stairs.

Moxie poked her head out of the office. "No. Do you think we should answer it?"

"I'll take a look." Shane confidently made his way to the front door. Mags hopped her paws onto the windowsill to peer over the bushes by the front door to see who stood on the porch. He took it as a good sign that the dog simply watched the guest with her tail slowly swishing behind her.

Shane looked through the peephole and didn't recognize the man but noted he waved at Mags in the window and called her by her name. He decided to unlock the door to see what the man wanted.

Shane left the storm door locked but greeted the stranger as Mags sat attentively next to him. "Can I help you?"

"Hi." Trevor put up a friendly hand. "My name's Trevor, I'm looking for Jett."

"Is he expecting you?" Shane reached for the top of Mags' head and stroked the dog.

"No," Trevor admitted. "I'm his cousin. I was just in the neighborhood, but I've been trying to get a hold of him. Do you know, is he around? I know work takes him away sometimes—is he gone for that?"

Shane wasn't interested in sharing any information with this guy, he didn't even know if he was truly Jett's cousin.

Noticing Shane's hesitation, Trevor tried a different tactic. "Is Moxie home?"

Jett's approaching truck caught Shane's eye before he replied. Based on the slamming of the brakes and the manner in which Jett jumped out of the truck he knew he wouldn't have to answer Trevor.

Shane pointed. "Looks like your cousin's home now."

"Oh shit," Trevor mumbled when he turned around and saw the scowl on Jett's face as he stomped closer.

"Jett." Trevor held up both of his hands. "Take it easy, I tried calling first. This is serious."

"Didn't I tell you to stay the fuck away from my house?!" Jett made heavy steps towards Trevor with his heart pounding and his fists clenched, thoughts still fresh in his mind of the danger Trevor had put Moxie in by bringing Will to their house.

Trevor scrambled off the porch, his hands still raised. Mags jumped and scratched the storm door, yelping at Jett's arrival.

"Jett, please—just listen for like thirty seconds. Please!"

Trevor's begging encouraged Jett to deliver the first blow. He wanted the beating to last so he strategically hit him in the lower rib cage and sent pain like Trevor had never felt throughout his entire body. When he folded over Jett spat out, "Less than thirty fucking seconds now. So what the fuck do you want?"

Trevor managed to lift his hand again, wincing. "Okay, okay!" He held his torso. "Shit..." Trevor tried to catch his breath. "Jett, Hallie's freaking out." He folded over again and took a couple of deep inhales.

"Why the fuck would I care about my *ex* freaking out?"

"Let me explain—you'll want to hear this," Trevor pleaded. "Will you just *listen*? Please?!"

Jett stood steady, fists clenched, but allowed Trevor to continue.

"Hallie's freaking out because Billy's missing."

"What the *fuck* does that have to do with me?" Jett's poker face was rock steady. "I stepped right the fuck over for them to go ahead and live their lives together. It sure as shit isn't my fault if he got cold feet on her. That goddamn divorce was basically my blessing for them to be together."

Trevor knew his next question may set Jett off, but he had to ask, "Jett, how well do you know Moxie?"

Jett grabbed Trevor's collar with a snarl, yanking him up to be within inches of his face, and threatened his cousin through his teeth, "You better tread fucking lightly." He shoved Trevor away from him.

Trevor stumbled and swallowed hard, looking down when he got his footing under him. It took him a minute to be able to have the courage to continue, "Jett, there's some shit you need to know about her. I know you're not Billy's biggest fan, but the guy's been through some shit. He had to run from a psychotic ex…" He peered up at his cousin. "That ex was Moxie."

Jett didn't hesitate, his solid fist collided with Trevor's face, connecting with his left eye. He kicked Trevor into the side of his house and had to restrain himself from anything else before he got too carried away.

"Fuck!" Trevor held his face, leaning against the siding. "What the fuck?!"

"How *dare* you try to spin some shit about Mox."

"Ask her!" Trevor squinted, rolling his head back in excruciating pain. "If she doesn't admit to Billy being her ex, she's lying! I've seen receipts, Jett."

"Careful," Jett warned with his thick fingers slamming into Trevor's chest.

"I'm trying to warn you! She's not who you think she is. Hallie already told the cops about her when she filed the missing persons report."

"What?" Jett seethed.

"Moxie tried to get Billy in trouble when he dumped her. She went out and got a restraining order and everything."

"Are you that fucking stupid, Trevor?"

Trevor moaned and tried to stand up straight, battling stars in his vision. He had one hand over his eye and the other struggled to hold his torso.

"They don't hand out restraining orders for nothing."

"She went *psycho* on him, ended up with marks on her body when he tried to stop her. *She* called the cops and spun it around. She didn't even show up to court to get the full protection order in place, so what does that tell you?"

Jett's fist slammed into Trevor's jaw and cocked back to hit him again in the nose.

Trevor dropped to his knees and Shane opened the storm door but left Mags inside, barking and pacing.

"Jett!" Shane took a couple hesitant steps towards the men. He'd already texted his husband to hurry his ass up and get over there before Jett beat the shit out of Trevor with the neighbors watching.

Jett didn't acknowledge him. He loomed over his cousin who rolled on the walkway in agony, grabbing his face.

"You're such a piece of fucking shit. You, your wife, Hallie, and Billy boy deserve each other."

"Jett, please—"

"Fuck you! Did you really come over here to accuse Mox of doing something to that wet noodle boy?!"

Trevor sobbed, wiping blood from his face. "You don't know what she's capable of."

"I know he's a dainty little dickhead, but have you seen Mox? What do you conniving little fucks think she could've possibly done to him?"

"I don't know"—he laid on his back, pinching his nose—"but Billy's missing and he just ran into Moxie the other day. It's not adding up. You need to be careful with her."

Jett's dominant foot kicked Trevor's ribs multiple times before Frank rolled into the driveway, parking and rushing to the men.

"Jett!" Frank practically tackled him. "C'mon, get your damn truck out of the street, I'll take care of this."

Jett kicked his cousin once more for good measure. He bent down, his tone harsh as he vowed, "If I ever catch you around this house again, I'll kick your fucking ass so bad you'll prefer death. Keep Mox out of your fucking mouth. I know *exactly* who she is—it's you I'm just finding out about, you fucking piece of shit." Jett held his glare for a moment longer before taking a fury-filled path back to his truck that was still idling in the street.

Frank put a hand on his hip and the other held his chin. It was obvious Trevor wasn't going to be able to get up alone. When Frank glanced up at his husband, who stood near the front door, he caught a glimpse of Moxie in the house behind him with a horrified look on her face.

Moxie covered her mouth as Trevor rolled on his side in agony. She couldn't quite see his face, but knew it wasn't good based on the blood she saw on their walkway.

Frank's eyes gestured at Shane to take Moxie in and shut the door before Jett came back to deal with the clean-up.

Shane didn't need more than that look from his husband to tend to Moxie. Jett's truck shut off inside the garage so Shane quickly turned on his heel and opened the screen door. "Mox, c'mon, let's get you and Mags settled inside." His comforting hands held her tiny-framed shoulders. Shane shut the door behind them and ushered Moxie to the kitchen.

Outside, Frank braced himself for Jett's approach, wondering if he'd need to stop him from another round on Trevor. A woman walked by with two smaller dogs, and Frank was grateful Jett caught sight of her because it lightened his glower just enough.

"Get your ass up and sit in the garage for a minute," he spat. "And you'll want to hurry up because I'm hosing this walkway down whether or not you're still lying here." Jett walked to the spigot to turn on the water and grab the hose. He rinsed his hands first, a few of the healing cuts he already had on his knuckles from Will had reopened.

Frank reluctantly reached down to help Trevor. "C'mon."

Trevor groaned with every movement, attempting to get off the ground. His head spun and he couldn't decide what part of his body was most injured—he had unbearable pain shooting throughout. He was barely to his feet when Frank got under his arm and pulled one of Trevor's around his shoulders to help him walk.

Frank was less friendly in finding a place for Trevor to sit in the garage. Once Trevor leaned against a wall to slide down to the floor, Frank took his arm off him, letting him hit the concrete.

"Ah!" Trevor shouted in pain.

There wasn't much blood on the walkway, so it didn't take Jett long to join them. He headed straight for his cousin, standing over his body that was slumped against the cinder block wall.

"If you get *any* fucking ideas in your goddamn head about pressing charges for this well-deserved ass beating, just know I have receipts too, Trevor." Jett pulled his phone from his pocket and began scrolling through photos. "These pictures show multiple instances of your pathetic ass stalking my house while I'm away for work and Mox is home alone. This is all I'll need. I'm sure your wife will be pleased to know you've been lurking around for an opportunity to see Mox."

"It wasn't like that," Trevor mumbled under his mangled face.

"That's not what it looks like to me." Jett shrugged. "Fucking test it, because I've got *zero* fucking patience when it comes to her safety."

A long moment of silence passed. Frank glanced back and forth between the cousins, unsure of what his role should be.

"I don't know what I'm supposed to do here, Jett," Trevor said in a defeated voice.

"As long as you're far away from me and everything that's mine, I don't give a fuck what you do, Trevor. I hope I've made myself clear about your goddamn accusations too. Don't fucking wrap Mox up in whatever shit Hallie's little wet noodle got himself into. Mox and I have steered clear of all of you. *You* guys keep coming for us and it's getting fucking old."

Trevor peered at his cousin through battered eyes. "I really did come over here tonight with good intentions. I genuinely thought for once in this whole mess I could help you avoid another heartbreak."

Jett shook his head. "Don't sit there and try to spin that bullshit or you're gonna piss me off again. I seem to remember you worried about his janky ass just weeks ago—specifically telling me he's not a good guy, accusing him of being into something shady, and asking for *my* damn help. Then you want to show up at *my* goddamn house and point your finger at Mox?! She hasn't done shit to anyone, yet here you are acting just like your spiteful, petty-ass wife."

Trevor tried to nod, realizing just how lost he was to Jett. He'd completely destroyed their lifelong relationship by backing Hallie.

"I'm sorry," Trevor finally said.

Jett stared at his cousin, feeling no guilt for the injuries he'd caused—it was well deserved.

He took a few deliberate steps towards the door leading into the house before he paused, not looking back at Trevor when he spoke, "You have ten minutes to get yourself out of my fucking house. You don't want to know what I'm going to do to you if I come out here and you're not gone."

61

Jett slammed the door behind him and Mags dashed through the living room to greet him. He caught her and then looked across the room to see Moxie cautiously standing on the threshold of where the tile kitchen floor met the hardwood. She'd obviously been crying, and one of her hands covered her mouth while the other held tightly around her midsection.

Jett wasn't sure if she'd witnessed him beating Trevor and it triggered her trauma or if she was just upset at the situation in general, but she didn't look like she'd be rushing him at the door in her traditional routine. Either way, he hated seeing her upset. Just as he set Mags down, Moxie made her way to him, speeding up the last few steps to crush into his familiar hold.

Jett's arms held tightly to his girlfriend, securing her against his strong body. He planted his face in the hair on top of her head and worked his comforting hands along her spine as she cried.

"Mox, Doll, I'm sorry if you saw or heard any of that." He cupped the back of her head firmly against his chest. "I'd never hurt you."

"Jett, I know that." Moxie subdued her tears and took a quick breath. "Are you hurt anywhere?" She couldn't imagine he was, but needed to ask anyway.

"Not at all," he confirmed in a gentle tone, caressing her back in a comforting rhythm. His hands were a bit of a mess, but that was mostly because he hadn't let them heal before he used them again for the justice he felt his girlfriend deserved.

Jett's ability to shut down certain emotions was unmatched. The tenderness he showed Moxie when the world had been weighing so heavily on him was something she never expected but was endlessly grateful for. She closed her eyes, gripping the front of his shirt and allowing herself to sink deeper into his devout embrace.

The door to the garage opened behind Jett just before a hand clasped his shoulder.

"He's gone," Frank said, squeezing Jett's deltoid a couple of times before making his way to his husband.

The men took a deep breath together before their short embrace. Jett could hear them whispering, but didn't know what they said and he didn't mind. His trust for his teammate was unwavering.

"Is Trevor going to tell anyone what you just did?" Moxie asked in a muffled voice, pulsing with another layer of worry that Jett would have to answer for his crimes—no matter how warranted his actions had been.

He tipped his chin down to press his lips against her head before answering, "I gave him some encouragement to keep it between us. I don't think—"

Jett stopped when the doorbell rang. Mags raced to the front door and hopped her feet on the windowsill, growling at the newest visitors. Everyone hoped Trevor wasn't stupid enough to be back already. Jett squeezed Moxie's shoulders before joining Mags. He met Frank's gaze for a brief moment before opening the door for two detectives.

"Hi," Jett greeted and snapped his fingers for Mags to take a seat next to him.

"Good evening, sir." The older man dipped his chin. "I'm Detective Bravo, this is my partner, Detective Graham. We're looking for Moxie Hall. Is she here?"

"Can I ask what this is about?" Jett kept his protective tone at bay as best he could.

"Her name was brought up in an investigation we're conducting and we just have a few questions for her. Is she here?"

"She is," Jett confirmed, leaning into the door to hide the rigidity of his back at their request. "What are you investigating?"

"We need to talk to Ms. Hall about that. Do you mind if we come in?"

"Look, Moxie's my girlfriend, so I do mind if you're not going to tell me what kind of investigation this is." Jett's volume didn't elevate, but he wanted to establish a boundary for the men. He wouldn't allow them to come in and bully her with their questions that were undoubtedly about Will.

The detectives exchanged a glance. "You must be Jett Sharpe."

"I am," he verified.

"We'd actually like to talk to both of you."

Moxie made her approach, having stood within earshot for the entire conversation. She didn't want Jett to lose his head—he'd already put up with enough the last few days and certainly the last fifteen minutes.

She noticed he'd placed his right palm on the inside of their door to conceal the open wounds from the detectives, but the other was nearly in plain sight. "Baby, what happened?" she asked, wrapping her arms around his free one, twisting their hands together while hiding his battered knuckles.

"These detectives want to talk to us, but they haven't told me why yet." Jett studied the men standing on the other side of the door.

Bravo asked again, "Can we come in and talk about it? It would really help our investigation."

"Look, why don't you just give us an idea of what this is about so we can decide whether you're coming in, or we're heading down to your station with a lawyer?" Jett explained, his thumb tracking Moxie's hand, slow and steady, reassuring her with each stroke that she just needed to stay calm because he had it handled. "You're not patrolmen, so I have to believe it's more serious than some innocent inquiry. All I'm asking for is a little more information."

Both detectives took a visible sigh, peering at one another before Graham, the older of the two, pulled his phone from the front pocket of his jacket.

"Do you recognize this man?" He held the screen to Jett first.

"Yeah, that'd be my ex-wife's wet noodle baby daddy," he said with a casual, unworried tone.

Graham squared his phone to Moxie and waited for her reply. All she could manage was a nod, initially. "Yes, that's Will." Her voice was nearly inaudible.

"Will Barlow, also known as Billy to friends and family." Graham stuck his phone in his pocket.

"We're neither," Jett informed them.

"Mr. Sharpe, we've been told you're not a big fan of Will," Bravo said.

"If you've heard that then I'm sure you know why," Jett promptly replied. Concealing the bigger reason he hated Will's prior existence, he elaborated for the detectives, "I know I said he's my ex-wife's baby daddy, but to be clear, they got pregnant *during* my marriage. And I know him as Billy, not Will."

"Yes, we spoke to your wife and—"

"*Ex*," Jett quickly and firmly corrected.

"My apologies," Bravo offered. "A missing persons report was filed on his behalf two days ago. He hasn't been seen at work or by any of his close friends or family for over a week."

Moxie couldn't regulate her breathing. She hadn't even done anything to Will, but she knew for a fact Jett had. She feared he'd been caught and they were here to take him away.

Jett could sense Moxie unraveling and didn't want her to answer any questions if she didn't have to, so he provided his thoughts. "I don't see how that has anything to do with us—he's not a friend of ours. If you weren't already informed, I filed for divorce and have done my best to stay away from both him and the ex, though I can't say the same for either of them."

"Can I ask what you mean by that?" Graham furrowed his brows.

"I've made no effort to connect with either of them, meanwhile they've taken it upon themselves to be present at *my* family functions these last several weeks."

Bravo gave his short beard a thoughtful stroke, glancing at Moxie who refused to make eye contact with the detectives. "Mr. Sharpe"—Bravo's gaze never lifted from Moxie—"do you know about your current girlfriend's ties to Mr. Barlow?"

"Mox doesn't have any ties to that asshole." Jett strained to harness his protective edge. "You must've been listening to my piece of shit cousin and his asinine theories. It seemed like he was trying to paint Mox in a bad light now that Hallie's having trouble with her baby daddy again."

"Again?" Bravo asked with a perked brow.

Jett projected surprise but knew exactly what he was doing. "Not even two days after coming home and telling Hallie I was done, she, Trevor, and his wife were all blowing up my phone begging for my help to find out what kinds of shady things Billy was into. They thought, because of my line of work, I'd be able to do some kind of investigation or whatever the hell—as if I cared enough." Jett grimaced in disgusted disbelief, simultaneously trying to calm Moxie's nerves with his steady hand engulfing hers. "In fact, Hallie mentioned being scared, and I heard she's stayed with Trevor and Julia quite a bit these last several weeks. Finding out Mox ran away from a restraining order she clearly needed from an ex—not to mention discovering Billy and Will are the same person—makes me think he *is* some kind of depraved jackass that's tied up in who knows what." Jett leveled his gaze at Bravo.

"Mr. Sharpe, you work on a clandestine team within the military, correct?" Graham asked, getting a glimpse of Jett's injured knuckles when he finally released his leaning grasp on the front door.

Jett gently squeezed Moxie's hand, his thumb continuing to stroke hers as he settled into a new stance with his free hand on his hip. "I do," he confirmed.

Graham pressed the issue, staring at Jett's bruises. "Can I ask what happened to your hand there, Mr. Sharpe?"

Jett lifted his inked hand and spread his fingers, putting the wounds on full display. "Markings of a job well done is all."

"An assigned job from your career? Those look quite fresh," the detective commented.

"Yeah, well, I work a lot." He shrugged, unbothered and glanced down at his injuries before putting his hand on his hip again.

Bravo and Graham exchanged another look.

"We'll need a detailed account of where you've been the last few days, Mr. Sharpe." Graham flipped to a new page in his notebook.

"Let me get this straight…" Jett nearly chuckled, wiping his chin and speaking confidently, "You don't even know if that schmuck wants to be found. For all we know, he skipped out on Hallie, but you're gonna come to *our* house and insinuate we had something to do with what you're *assuming* to be some malicious crime?"

"Just checking off all possible leads is all." Graham shrugged. "Are we gonna have your cooperation with that?"

"So, I'm a *lead*, huh?" Jett shook his head, showcasing an acidic grin. "I'm not at liberty to provide details of my whereabouts as far as work is concerned. I'd suggest you call up your chain of command to figure out why. All I'll say about that is good fucking luck."

"We'll need a local contact, Mr. Sharpe," Bravo insisted. "You must have someone above you we can talk to concerning your whereabouts… Unless you'd like us to assume you don't have an alibi during the time Mr. Barlow disappeared?"

"Detective." Jett took a breath, not typically so arrogant about his job, but in this case he'd make an exception. "What I do is a matter of national security. Even if you had proof of an actual crime and any evidence to suggest I had anything to do with that crime, I wouldn't spend even five seconds in your custody. I'm not—"

"Jett," Frank interrupted the conversation and approached the front door from behind the couple.

Jett took the opportunity to pull Moxie further into the house when he turned, putting his body between her and the detectives who were still on the front porch.

Frank held out his phone. "Cap's got Aidoneus on the line—he wants the department and badge numbers for these two." He gestured to the detectives.

Moxie had no idea what this meant; she'd never heard of Aidoneus. When she looked up at her boyfriend, his lips curled in a tiny smirk.

"They're from County," Jett reported towards the phone. "You fellas wanna share those badge numbers, or should I?"

The second Bravo provided his number, Jett leaned closer to him. "You may wanna watch your phone—it'll be ringing soon."

Jett barely finished his sentence before Graham was fumbling for his buzzing cell. He wasn't on the call long and barely said two words to whoever shouted from the other end before he hung up.

He cleared his throat, glancing at Jett and Frank before his gaze fell on his partner. "We've got what we need here."

Bravo scrutinized him with raised brows. "What about Ms. Hall? We—"

Graham stopped him from saying anything else. After the phone call he'd just received, he knew both Jett *and* Moxie were off limits. He quickly peeked at Jett before urging his partner to get a headstart to their car. "Mr. Sharpe, thank you for your service to our country." He turned to Frank. "Sir." He quickly dipped his chin and left.

Moxie's head spun, she had no idea what just happened. In one blink of an eye she thought Jett may be taken into custody and in the next second the detectives were voluntarily rushing to their car without further questions.

Jett rubbed Moxie's shoulder and shut the door. He placed a soft kiss on her temple before taking the phone from Frank. "Hey, Cap." There was a short pause. "Yeah, they're gone—Aidoneus upset?" He nodded a few times. "Good. I appreciate it, bro. Yep, see you tomorrow."

Moxie gaped at Jett's confident demeanor. He handed back Frank's phone before giving her his full attention.

"What just happened? Who's Aidoneus?" Moxie stared up at Jett, disbelief pouring from her eyes and the scrunch on her forehead.

Jett smirked. "Aidoneus is the boss's code name. He doesn't take kindly to his prized Cerberus squad being interrogated; if anything, that's his job."

Frank grinned at the uncertainty lingering on her face. "Mox, there's a lot we'll never be able to share about Cerberus, but one thing's for sure: Aidoneus sees all. No shot in hell he'd let anything happen to Jett, that's his little golden boy."

Jett rolled his eyes and tucked a stray lock of hair behind Moxie's ear, his hand lingering on her cheek to assure her things were more than fine.

She hoped to one day find a balance of comfort with what Jett did for a living. While it offered its fair share of anxiety for his safety and whereabouts, there was also a sense of invincibility in this squad, apparently. At the end of the day, all she really needed to know was that Jett was indeed her soul's other half. He'd been as reliable as the sun rising every day and setting every night, and she'd not only accept him without restriction, but love him with her entire being— every minute of every day.

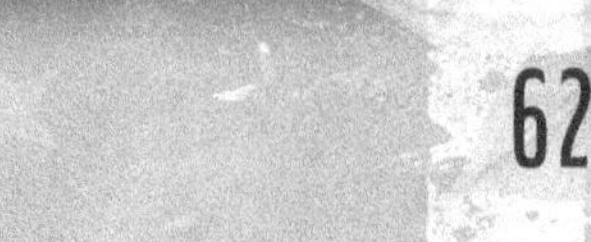

62

A few weeks had passed and life settled into a more relaxed routine. Moxie was much less anxious about being alone when Jett was called to work, and they soaked in every second of their time together because life had never been so good—for either of them.

"Hey, Dollface," Jett called from a few yards away, startling Moxie out of her daze that lingered on the colorful horizon.

A wide grin spread across her face as her boyfriend threw a hoodie over his head during his approach.

"My mom said she's expecting you to hop back into their card game." He pulled the hoodie down to his waist, and took a seat next to her in the grass behind the AirBnB they'd rented, Mags only a couple steps behind him. "What're you doing over here all alone?" He leaned over, placing his lips on her temple. Moxie looked off the cliff's edge onto the roaring Pacific Ocean—another beautiful place Jett insisted on showing her that wasn't too far from home. She caught a lock of wild hair, misplaced by the wind, and tucked it behind her ear before leaning into her strong boyfriend and replying, "Just taking in the view of this beautiful place."

Jett slung his arm around her, smirking. He reached his head towards hers, pressing his lips against the top of her hair this time.

"I'm actually quite grateful to be staring out westward... This means we get to sleep in instead of getting up before the sun to catch it rising."

Jett softly chuckled just behind her ear. "I dunno, Doll, we may've made a mistake inviting family with us. The kids usually wake up at an ungodly hour; no one in that house will be sleeping once they're up."

"Oh, Dr. Brody"—she nestled deeper into him, her head tiling to whisper in his ear—"who said anything about sleeping? I'm just trying to stay in bed longer."

Jett threw his head back, laughing loudly.

"Another reason I put us in the smallest room of the house—it's the farthest away from everyone."

Moxie slid her hand along Jett's jeans, landing on his inner thigh. "Here I was thinking you picked that room to try to pull some Hot Rod moves on me since it shares a wall with the laundry room."

"I'd typically give you anything you want, but you know full well I draw the line at wearing any big-girl panties."

Moxie giggled through her response, "Good thing I don't want you to be in any big-girl panties."

"Mox!" a booming voice shouted from the top deck of the house. "We're starting another round, come back up here so we can all whoop that ass again!" Elliot's grin reached his ears.

Jett flipped him off for her while her cheeks filled with color. They had, in fact, ruthlessly wiped the table with her despite it being her first and only time playing the beloved family game, *Sharpe-E Diem*—their fancy name for Thirty-One. Their game had no special variations, just a silly name they thought was clever, and the family had *zero* mercy for the newbie.

"We're *both* coming up for the next hand," Jett informed him. "So get your final practice round in before the master is up there taking all your money."

Elliot rolled his eyes, both middle fingers raised at Jett but went back into the house where laughter and friendly conversation echoed.

Jett turned to Moxie. "Let's go finish watching the sunset from the beach."

She couldn't agree quickly enough, putting her hand in his and he helped her up. They didn't have to call Mags to follow them as the faithful shepherd was already happily going stride for stride with her parents.

Jett and Moxie sat blissfully and silently in front of a fire Jett had made them at an abandoned pit on the beach. A large piece of weathered driftwood served as his backrest while he held his girl-friend under his arm. The sun had already gone down, but they enjoyed listening to the waves in front of them while watching the stars glittering in the sky. Mags had cozied up near their feet to be closest to the fire, their pretty girl had a long day playing at the beach with her family.

Moxie's dainty hand made a pass across Jett's broad chest. "Jett?"

"Mhmm," he murmured between placing kisses to the top of her head.

"I sure appreciate your efforts taking me to beautiful places." She played with the string from his hoodie before gazing up at him. "But I'm even more in love with this beautiful life you're creating for us."

He brought both of his arms around her, nuzzling his face against her cheek to whisper in her ear, "*We're* creating a beautiful life. I never knew life could be so damn sweet." His hand couldn't help but cup her breast. "What I was doing before you was existing… I'll happily spend the rest of my days showing you how thankful I am for allow-ing me to have your heart, Doll. You make sure I'm not only living, but that I'm completely in love with this life. I'm *so* grateful for you, Moxie Hall." Jett tipped her chin enough for their lips to connect, his tongue soaking in the familiar feeling of her mouth as the waves swept across the shore in the distance.

"Not that I want to get up from this spot, but the water's not going to trap us down here, right?"

"Doll, you know you don't have to worry about anything while you're with me. Like I'd *ever* put you in a dangerous situation," he scoffed, trapping her earlobe between his lips.

Moxie rolled her head onto his shoulder, squeezing the arms he had around her. "I know, I'm just making sure you're also a tide expert with all your other talents."

"My *other* talents, huh?" He reached between her legs, gripping the meat of her inner thighs.

Moxie giggled, one of her hands gently covering his as it wandered along intimate and sensitive territory.

"You, Dr. Brody, have endless talents and I'm so grateful for all of them"—her hips squirmed in response to his fingers that had made their way under her joggers—"especially this one." Her hand squeezed his when he slid a finger through her slick folds. She encouraged him to explore, but turned her head for their lips to connect. While Jett's fingers were magic, she craved more. In one motion, she twisted her body to straddle her boyfriend. Her knees took comfort on the sand while she found a comfortable rhythm grinding on his lap.

"I'm disappointed in your clothing preparations for this evening, Private Sharpe," she seductively scolded with her mouth hovering just over his lips.

Jett threw his head back, belting out a laugh. "Doll, we gotta get you up to speed on titles and ranks—your man hasn't been a damn private for nearly two decades." His strong hands pulled on her cheeks, pressing their pelvises even closer.

She halted the rocking of her hips to back up and work on the button and zipper of his jeans as her lips grazed over his. "Just acting like a damn private then wearing jeans down here instead of something with easier access and less restrictions."

"Are you saying I'm not worth working for?" He smirked.

"Stop." She playfully nudged his cheek with her nose before pecking him. "You know I can get impatient… Plus, I'm just complaining the fabric wasn't letting me feel what I wanted." She successfully opened his jeans and wasted no time tugging on them.

Jett chuckled, helping her remove his pants. "Why do I have to be the one getting sand in *my* ass crack?"

"Like I said, private-status not coming down here better pre-pared," she continued to tease, settling in on a much closer and more pleasurable straddle now that his jeans weren't in the way.

Jett reached for the bottom of his hoodie, quickly removing it to toss closer to the fire. "You're about to get some privates, Doll." He gripped her back and flipped their positions, taking her to the ground and placing her on his hoodie by the fire.

She giggled, tugging on his boxers as he pulled the hoodie into place under her to avoid either of them getting sand in their cracks. He leaned over her for another kiss but Moxie quickly stopped him—she'd never miss an opportunity to expose his chiseled chest.

"Oh, I've gotta take it all off even though I'm the one up here in the open, huh?" He chuckled, but happily fulfilled her unspoken request without hesitation.

"Hey, that was your move, Dr. Brody—and you know the rules about your shirt."

Jett gently held her chin, locking his gaze onto her beautiful blue eyes. The love he felt for her consumed him, the connection unlike anything his mind or heart had ever known. As he looked into her gorgeous face, glowing by the crackling fire, he knew their souls were intertwined in a way that could never be broken.

Telling her 'I love you' wasn't sufficient because what they had was so much deeper than that. Rather than struggle for a way to tell her, he decided to continue showing her. He'd do that tonight and every second of every day for the rest of his existence.

EPILOGUE

It was Mags' twelfth birthday. The pretty girl moved a little slower these days but had seen more love in her lifetime than most people could ever dream of. Jett and Moxie ensured she lived her very best life every single day—she more than deserved it. Not only had Mags been the perfect four-legged constant in their life, but she'd also been the reason they'd met.

They had started a tradition on her fifth birthday—the first one she had with both Jett and Moxie—of celebrating by taking her to all her favorite spots around town and spending the night in the Presidential Suite where it all started. This year was no exception.

Mags trotted into the suite that night, immediately taking a spot up on the couch, not waiting for Jett or Moxie. She still had her beautiful long and luscious locks, but her face had lightened into a perfectly aging sugar mask with more white than tan or black. Each of her paws had also lightened over the years, but she'd never stop being their pretty girl.

"Poor ol' pretty girl, has it been a long day?" Moxie sat next to her, stroking her head as Mags took a large, tired breath.

"It's a tough job managing a full house." Jett smiled, pecking his wife before sitting down to put a hand on Mags' back. "That's why we need a reset from time to time, huh, girl?"

"Like I've been saying"—Moxie affectionately hugged Mags around her neck—"that's your dad's fault. You know Mama was happy with you being an only child. He just *had* to keep begging for babies."

Jett threw his head back. "Oh, so we're lying to our firstborn now, huh?"

"*We* know, right, Mags?" Moxie continued to tease.

Jett had proposed to Moxie before their one year anniversary and they'd been married now for five years. Mags served as the flower girl and obvious star of the show. Their Mags birthday tradition was already so strong at that time that they pushed their honeymoon back a week after the wedding so they could celebrate her birthday first. They hadn't let anything change this tradition, not even the year Moxie felt like she was two hundred and twenty weeks pregnant with their second. They were both fully prepared to leave at some point that night for the hospital. Their sweet little girl had held out two days longer so Mags, fortunately, didn't have to share her birthday.

"Speaking of…" Moxie playfully rolled her eyes and plucked her phone off the coffee table. She answered the FaceTime call from Vera.

Moxie held her phone out for Jett to see as well and they were greeted with their hazel eyed, brunette four-year-old. His face lit up the second he saw his parents.

"Hi!" He waved with a giggle as the phone shook around in his other hand.

"Wy-Wy, what're you doin' baby?" Moxie asked with a bright smile. 'Wy-Wy,' was short for Wyatt John, John being his great-grandfather's name on Jett's side—Papa's name.

"Is that chocolate on your face, bud?!" Jett exaggerated with his eyes wide.

"Yep." Wyatt nodded emphatically and then set the phone down, so all they could see was the ceiling as the little boy continued talking, "Auntie VV gived me some cookies for being a helper."

"Mommy and Daddy are so proud of you for helping," Moxie confirmed. "What did you do?"

"Easty baby pooped in hers pants so I tell'd Auntie VV."

"Oh no!" Moxie chuckled. "Remember we're gonna teach Easty baby how to go on the big-kid potty like you soon, huh?"

Easty baby, short for Eastyn Calla, was their nearly two-year-old daughter. When they'd found out they were expecting a girl, Jett really wanted to give a nod to Mags' flower-inspired name so they landed on Calla for her middle name.

"Yep!"

"Where's Luca?" Jett asked when they saw Wyatt in the frame again. Luca was Vera's son and undoubtedly Wyatt's best friend—they were only four months apart.

"Luca's getting us more cookies."

Jett and Moxie laughed. "Where's Auntie VV?"

"Giving Easty baby a bath."

His parents looked at each other, that likely meant poor Vera had been subjected to a blowout.

"Does Uncle Ray know you fellas are getting into more cookies?" Jett asked.

"He does." Vera's husband, Ray, answered from outside the frame. He picked up the phone and had it facing him briefly before he flipped the camera and showed the two boys who held an Oreo in each hand. "Can't have a proper slumber party without eating junk all night, right boys?"

Both Wyatt and Luca jumped around waving their cookies.

Jett and Moxie laughed watching them bounce on the couch. They couldn't blame Ray for giving in, that's exactly how the boys did sleepovers at their house too.

"We heard Eastyn gave poor V a nice surprise. Sorry about that." Moxie scrunched her face.

Ray turned the phone back to him. "Mox, I need Easty permanently before that potty training thing hits. Your bestie wants to do this again and I don't know if I have the energy." He held his forehead.

Moxie laughed at him and then peered at Jett.

"A little snip-snip will fix that right up, Ray boy," Jett suggested.

"My ass isn't trying to get tamed like that." Ray rolled his eyes.

Jett barked out a laugh. "I guess you're in for a few more then. It's not so bad, and I don't feel like my manhood took a hit."

"I'll vouch for that." Moxie pumped her brows at her husband.

"Get the fuck outta here, you two. We can't all be so perfect." Ray gave a dramatic sigh.

"Is that Mommy and Daddy?" Vera walked behind the chair her husband sat in so she could be in view. She held a towel-wrapped Eastyn in her arms.

"Hi guys!" Vera rocked around and gave Eastyn a couple quick smooches.

Jett would never be able to get over how their daughter was already a little mini-me of Moxie. Her large eyes were the same periwinkle as her mom's and her hair color was nearly identical. Jett and Moxie had managed to create little copy-pastes of themselves.

"Easty baby!" Jett and Moxie sang in unison.

The baby squealed at the sound and pointed to the phone when she looked back at Vera.

"Smelling *much* better with a clean butt now." Vera continued to sway.

"Sorry, V." Moxie showed her teeth.

"It's no sweat." She reached for her husband's shoulder. "I could do this with three or four more little ones in the house."

They all laughed when Ray sighed, holding his head.

"I'm taking the boys to the garage so we can do some man shit. You guys can keep discussing the fantasy of any more kids in this house." Ray handed the phone to Vera.

"V, looks like you've got an uphill battle." Moxie shook her head with a smile, rubbing Mags' face when she rested her head on her lap.

"He'll give in." She shrugged and readjusted herself to sit Eastyn up on her lap and held the phone out in front of them. "I'm not worried, but I refuse to be tagged as a geriatric pregnancy, so his time is and we can read for a bit." She looked into the phone. "You guys take your time tomorrow, you know I love having Auntie's babies over."

"Shit, we'll definitely be sleeping in." Jett wrapped his arms around Moxie who giggled when his mouth connected with her neck.

"Thank you, V." Moxie tried to keep the phone steady. "Goodnight, Easty baby, we love you." She smacked her lips.

"Love you, Easty." Jett waved and blew her a kiss.

The baby was so tired she kept her head on Vera's chest and rubbed her eyes again.

"We'll see you guys tomorrow. Happy Birthday, Nolie Girl!"

Jett and Moxie smiled before hanging up.

"They're definitely having another," Moxie decided after setting down her phone.

"Oh, I know," Jett agreed with a chuckle. "It's cute Ray thinks he wears the pants."

"I warned him early on he'd never be wearing the pants with V as a partner." Moxie laughed. "You know what he said to me?"

Jett slid his hand between his wife's thighs, smiling and awaiting her answer.

"He said, at least he'd be in good company with you."

"And you had to correct him?"

"Dr. Brody, we both know you wear the damn pants around here." Moxie rolled to her side, pushing her leg in between his. "But you're wrapped around my little finger, so you still have a boss."

Jett threw his head back, laughing from his gut. Her suggestive pawing and the placement of her leg on the front of his pants encouraged him to declare bedtime. In one motion, he swept her off the couch, carrying her to the bedroom.

Jett carefully plopped her on the bed, and Mags invited herself up on the mattress next. They welcomed their pretty birthday girl to cuddle; she waited for them to settle before taking her place on top of the pillows near Jett.

"Did you ever think seven years ago that we'd be right here?" Moxie rolled her head on Jett's shoulder as they lay on their backs.

He had two of his three favorite girls on either side of him with Mags snuggling under his right arm and Moxie securely under his left. Jett chuckled while placing a peck on the top of her head. "Definitely would've never guessed *all* this on that first night." He squeezed her. "But I knew shortly after that you and I were gonna have a long and happy life together."

Moxie flipped her body to be on her side, one of her legs comfortably finding a perfect fit between Jett's. She slid her hand across his chest until it landed on Mags where she began softly stroking their senior shepherd.

"Yep." Jett blew out a large breath. "It took you damn long enough to finally let me kiss you, otherwise things would've happened much quicker for us."

"Sorry your balls didn't drop sooner, I would've let you kiss me far before that."

Laughter immediately belted out of Jett and he trailed his hand up and down his wife's back.

"We know who the real MVP is—huh, pretty girl?" Moxie gave Mags her favorite ear scratches. "Mags started the chain of events that gave me everything in life that makes me happy."

"I didn't help?!" Jett chuckled.

"You make me *very* happy, Dr. Brody. And you've given me nearly everything I've ever wanted in life." She kissed her husband's cheek before setting her head on his chest.

"Well, shit." Jett smiled, encouraging her to look at him when he gently hooked her chin. "Nearly everything? What did I miss?"

He'd eliminated the man that brought her nightmares to life, given her a happy home with Mags, a ring, her dream wedding, the ultimate honeymoon, thoughtful anniversaries, a son, a daughter, had plans in place for retirement from the team that took him away for days and weeks on end at times, and above all else he had given her his entire heart. He'd give her the sun, the moon, and all the stars if he could—he didn't know what else she possibly wanted, but he'd make it happen.

Moxie perched her hands on his strong chest, gazing deep into the captivating hazel eyes she'd fallen more in love with everyday since they'd met. They held one another's adoring smiles for a long moment before she disclosed the one thing he hadn't given her yet.

"The only thing I still want is forever with you, Jett."

He pulled her in until their mouths nearly touched. "Doll, you know I'm gonna give you forever. It's a work in progress and I'm thoroughly enjoying the process."

DEAREST LOVELY READER,

Thank you ~~soooo~~ very much for dedicating your precious time to reading my novel. 🐼🤍 I put absolutely everything into each of my stories and my hope is that you love my characters just as much as I do. Okay, maybe not all of them, there's usually someone we can all collectively agree needs to suffer the sensation of stepping on Legos barefoot for the rest of their miserable lives. 😄👏

If you'd like to help me keep writing, there are a few things you can do to help:

Review

I'd LOVE for you to go to your favorite review site and add a review for *Clandestiny*. My books don't get pushed on the larger platforms if I don't have reviews. If you've already put in the time reading, I encourage you to take one final step for me by sharing your thoughts so other readers will pick up my books!!

Share

Share my book with others. That's right: lend it out, purchase another copy for them, give friends/fam the title to swoop on their own—however you want to share it, PLEASE DO!!

Follow

Follow me on the socials. As an eldest millennial, I'm doggy paddling for my life on there. I'd love to have my amazing readers join me to make that experience much more enjoyable. Engagement is key, so don't be shy—reach out!! Following me is also the best way to be the first to know when new content is coming your way. 😊😍

Again, thank you so very much for joining the ranks of my beloved readers, I'm grateful to have you along for this wild journey.

😘🤍 *Love,*

I would love for you to stay connected!!
Here are a few ways:

Baley Noal Official Website

As of November 2024 I officially have my own website!! You can find links for purchasing all of my books, news, and EXCLUSIVE MERCH. Not to mention, this is the site where I'll drop BONUS CONTENT related to my books!!

@ baley.noal

Get real time updates and see what else I create by following me on Insta. I would LOVE to hear from you!! (Seriously, I super love connecting with all of you.) I'm also a huge fan of giveaways, so if nothing else, follow along for a chance at some exclusive freebies. 😊 💕

Spotify

I've created a playlist that is FULL of *Clandestiny* vibes. If you'd like to know what I was listening to, or felt inspired by for a few scenes, check out the playlist.

Amazon Author Page

It's free to follow and you'll be updated when I have new content available.